# *the* SILENT MADONNA

## BOOK TWO *of the* **SANTA LUCIA** SERIES

## MICHELLE DAMIANI

RIALTO
PRESS

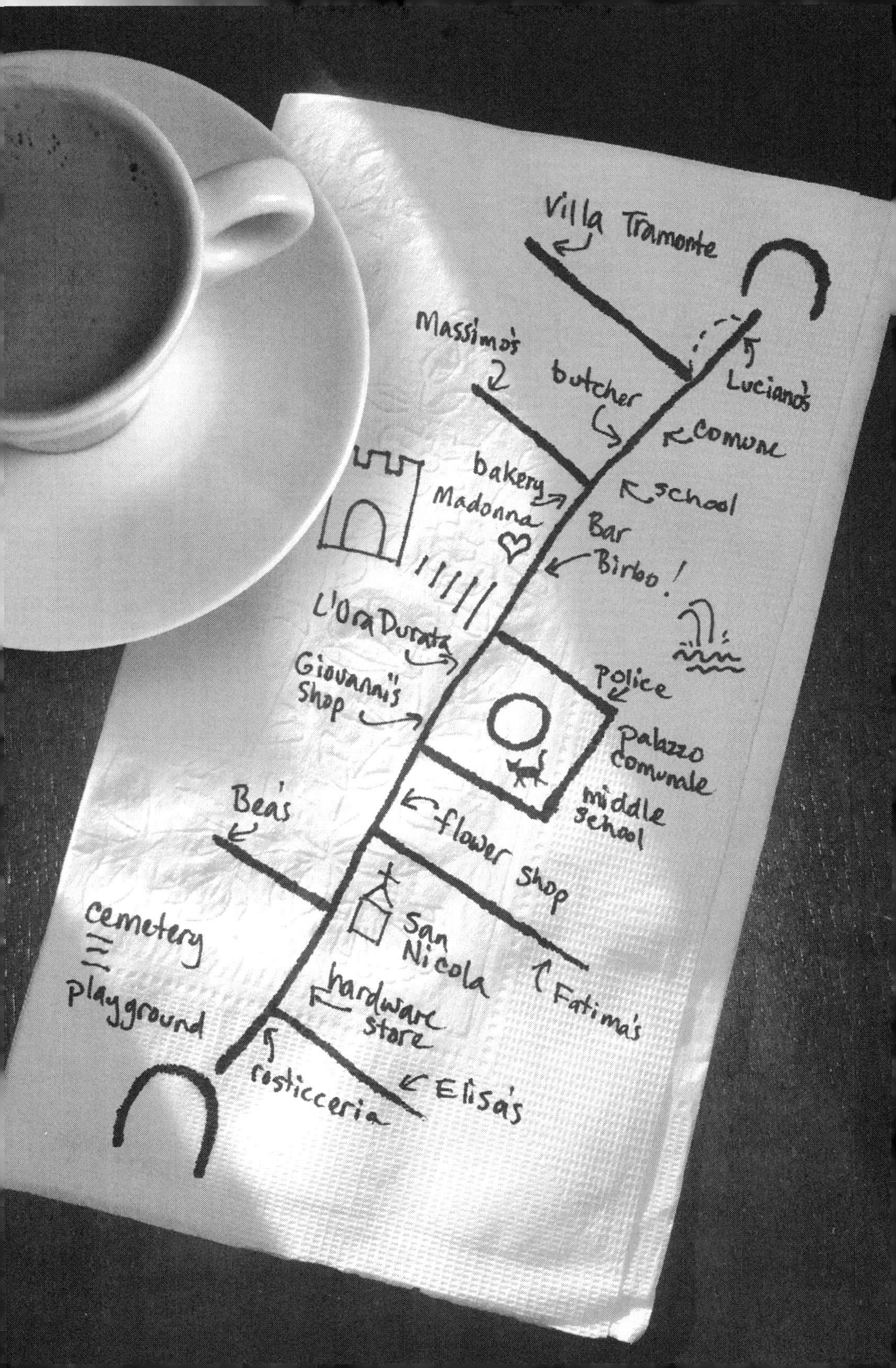
Villa Tramonte
Massimo's
butcher
Luciano's
Comune
bakery
Madonna
school
Bar
Birbo!
L'Ora Durata
Giovanni's
Shop
Police
Palazzo
Comunale
middle
school
Bea's
flower shop
cemetery
San
Nicola
Fatima's
playground
hardware
store
rosticceria
Elisa's

# A NOTE ON THE ITALIAN

Italian words in the text are followed by the English translation or can be understood by context. For interested readers, there is a glossary in the back of this book.

# CAST OF CHARACTERS

## MAIN CHARACTERS

| | |
|---|---|
| Chiara | *The owner of Bar Birbo, she therefore hears all the rumors and secrets.* |
| Edo | *Chiara's nephew who lives with her and helps at Bar Birbo, he recently acknowledged to himself and others that he is gay.* |
| Luciano | *A retired schoolteacher who lost his daughter and wife, which drove him to lose himself.* |
| Massimo | *Father to Margherita, he was once married to Giulia, Luciano's daughter who died. A year later, he married Isotta, Giulia's virtual twin.* |
| Anna | *Massimo's mother.* |
| Elisa | *An 11-year-old girl who struggled in school until Luciano began tutoring her. She is Fatima's best friend.* |
| Fatima | *A 12-year-old immigrant girl from Morocco, injured in an accidental fire during the village festa at the castello. She is Elisa's best friend.* |
| Ava | *The daughter of a florist, she is Santa Lucia's guerrilla gardener and perennially unlucky in love.* |

| | |
|---|---|
| Alessandro | *The owner of the derelict castle, newly arrived to Santa Lucia.* |
| Madison | *His very American wife.* |
| Fabrizio | *A writer from Bologna, he and Chiara recently began a relationship.* |
| Francy | *Fabrizio brings Francy to Santa Lucia.* |

## VILLAGERS

| | |
|---|---|
| Magda | *Moved to Santa Lucia from Germany years ago with her husband who has since disappeared in Thailand.* |
| Bea | *Santa Lucia's source of fresh eggs and fresh gossip.* |
| Patrizia | *Chiara's best friend who helps her husband, Giuseppe, in his butcher shop.* |
| Giuseppe | *Patrizia's husband and the maker of Santa Lucia's famous chicken sausages.* |
| Sauro | *Santa Lucia's baker.* |
| Giovanni | *The joke-telling owner of the little shop on the piazza.* |
| Fabio | *Ava's brother and her opposite In almost every way. He accused both the gay tourists and Santa Lucia's immigrants for starting the fire.* |
| Salvia | *Ava's mother.* |
| Concetta | *Elisa's mother.* |
| Arturo | *Older villager who is sure his French wife is cheating on him.* |
| Rosetta | *The school principal.* |
| Paola | *The owner of the fruit and vegetable market.* |
| Marcello | *The town cop, his mother is desperate for him to get married and give her a grandchild.* |

## THE END OF FALL

*S*torm clouds faded against the Umbrian sky. Light began to ripple in waves, illuminating the town of Santa Lucia in a patchwork of glow and shadow. The heaviness that had pressed upon the hilltop village eased, as the air's murkiness evaporated.

A vitality infused the breeze winding through town, like children chasing each other, laughing, around a glittering olive grove. As the clouds parted further, a dazzle of light tumbled down, shining directly on Santa Lucia's Madonna, tucked serenely in her niche. The ancient marble statue absorbed the light before redoubling it and sending it back into the village. Shadows hid around corners as the Madonna's brilliance radiated into the street and down the alleys of Santa Lucia.

The flash caught Chiara's eye through the windows flanking Bar Birbo's entrance. She watched the still street for a moment before unlocking both the glass and wooden door, to allow the drifting morning air into her cafe. She breathed in, tugging her sweater more tightly around her chest. After two weeks, the smoke had finally gone. Really gone, not the loss of awareness that comes from living with a smell for so many days that it takes on the same familiarity as Bar Birbo's waxed wooden door. That door had been shut tight against the townspeople yesterday, as it was Monday, Bar Birbo's *giorno di chiusura*. Chiara made sure the door was latched into its open position now, ready to welcome the townspeople back into the *espresso*-scented fold.

Chiara inhaled again, deeply this time. Yes, the gritty smell had dissipated. Last night's downpour, in all probability, did the trick. That's what the villagers had been prophesying since the fire—one good storm would put it right. All the lingering odor needed was a rinse of rain. Chiara could practically smell green blades poking up between the charred trees of the olive orchards that surrounded the *castello*. Too bad, she thought, that neither the storm nor the collective manpower of the town could put the *castello* and groves to rights. When Chiara looped through the castle yard during her walk with Patrizia yesterday, it looked much the same. Like a ghoulish mimicry of its former humble grandeur.

She moved toward the castle stairs and stopped at the Madonna, trailing her fingers against the base of the statue. She closed her eyes and breathed, more than said, a prayer for Fatima.

Opening her eyes, Chiara watched a figure walking toward her, and she paused to greet whatever neighbor it might be.

Luciano.

Poor man.

Luciano approached Chiara and raised a hand in greeting. She smiled and held the interior glass door open for him. "*Caffè*, Luciano?"

"*Sì, grazie.* This morning fog weighs heavy on my bones."

Chiara ducked her head and grinned. Stepping up and around the counter to grind the beans, she said, "Pastries aren't here yet, but I have a *cornetto* from yesterday I can give you."

Luciano sighed. "Yes, thank you, Chiara. That would be much appreciated."

The buzz of the grinder and the scent of coffee filled the bar. Chiara tamped the *espresso* grounds into the basket before slipping it into her La Pavoni. "And Fatima?" She ventured.

"The same."

Chiara nodded, staring at the drops of *caffè* squeezing out of the machine. As she turned to hand over the cup and the pastry on a plate, she greeted Arturo, now pushing open the glass door. "*Buongiorno,* Arturo . . . *Bentornato,* welcome back. *Caffè*?"

"*Sí, grazie.*" Arturo nodded at Luciano, but Luciano was blowing into his diminutive cup and didn't notice.

Chiara turned back to the grinder and called over her shoulder, "How was France?"

Arturo pushed his overlarge glasses up onto his nose and said, "Fine, it was fine. Esme's parents had all the relatives to work the vines, so not too much strain this year."

Chiara nodded, setting Arturo's *caffè* in front of him before walking around the counter to collect the box of pastries from the driver in the three-wheeled Ape.

Arturo said, "I can't believe I missed all the action. I *knew* we shouldn't have left the morning of the festival. I *told* Esme, but she insisted that her parents needed the help." Arturo grumbled, "Why they couldn't wait a few days, I can't say. And not one plate of pasta in two weeks."

He stirred sugar into his *caffè* and went on looking from Luciano to Chiara who unpacked the delivery box, setting the pastries on doilies in the display case. "So you two were there? At the fire?"

They shook their heads. Chiara said, "Edo was, though."

As if on cue, Edoardo opened the door that led to their upstairs apartment. He smiled and said, "*Buongiorno a tutti.*" He slid open a drawer to whisk out an apron, winding it trimly around his hips.

Chiara noted, "You're up early. I thought you wouldn't be on until the morning rush."

Edo nodded. "I FaceTimed with Trevor before he had to go to work this morning, and since I was up . . ." He shot a glance at Luciano. Had word of his boyfriend found its way to his former teacher?

Luciano gazed at the wall lined with bottles of liquor. "Trevor? Oh, yes, that British man that helped out at the fire. Aren't we all glad he was here?" He smiled knowingly at Edo.

Edo's laugh rang out into the bar that was already warming up with the day.

"How nice to be amused so early in the morning," Fabrizio said as he walked into Bar Birbo, a newspaper tucked under his elbow. He leaned over the counter and kissed Chiara's cheek. "*Buongiorno, amore mio.*"

Luciano and Edo winked at each other over their cups and Arturo grinned. Clearly he'd already heard that Chiara had started dating Fabrizio. This good gossip made up for the rather boring discovery that Fabrizio worked as a writer in Bologna, rather than as the covert operator or government plant his mysterious behavior had suggested.

Arturo waited until Edo had started sipping his own *espresso* before prodding, "Edo, you were there?"

Edo answered, "The fire? I was."

Arturo said, "Oh, that's right!" His face registered sudden awareness, and he quickly changed the subject. Leaning across the counter, he asked Chiara, "Is it true about Stella? She really had an affair with Vale?"

Chiara nodded, wiping up spilt sugar from the counter. Arturo laughed, "Dante must have been furious! Mr. Mayor waltzing through town so important while his wife sleeps with the town handyman."

Seeing Chiara's discomfort with the conversation—she and Stella had been childhood friends after all—Fabrizio turned to Luciano. Shaking out his newspaper he asked, "Any news on Fatima?"

Luciano shook his head. "No. Each of us thinks we see movement, but it's too easy to doubt ourselves. Our eyes see what they want to see."

Fabrizio cocked his head and smiled at Chiara. "Isn't that the truth." He flattened his paper and said, "For years I worked the city beat for *Corriere di Bologna*. Smoke inhalation is dangerous, but people do recover."

"That hope is what sustains me."

Chiara and Edo, unbeknown to each other, whispered twin and fleeting prayers to the Madonna to intercede and keep Luciano from drinking again when hope flagged.

Arturo shifted his weight impatiently. He turned to check for new arrivals who might have more news—would anybody tell him about Massimo and Isotta? He'd even tolerate that bossy German woman, Magda. But only Carosello the one-eyed dog, trotted down the street in his ever-lasting quest for morsels. Arturo sighed and tried again. "I heard that the family that owns the *castello* is coming back . . . What a surprise they are in for."

Chiara straightened the towel over the rack and said, "Not the whole family, I don't think. Just the son? Or the son's family?" Chiara thought for a moment and went on, "Anyway, they come in the next day or two. Or so Dante says."

Shaking his head, Arturo clucked. "I walked around the *castello* this morning. *Uffa!* Our mayor is going to get an earful."

"To be fair, for all he knew, all the people with claim to the *castello* were dead and gone. How could he know a distant heir lived in New York?"

Smiling, Arturo said, "I sure don't envy Dante."

Edo leaned against the counter and sipped his *espresso*. "I don't imagine any of us do."

Giuseppe the butcher opened the glass door to allow his wife, Patrizia, to enter. The couple greeted the room at large as Chiara and Edo moved around each other in a choreographed *espresso*-making dance. Patrizia placed her hand on Luciano's arm. "Anything?"

Luciano shook his head.

Patrizia thought for a moment. "I'm sorry. I've been lighting candles for her every day. Little Elisa, too . . . she must be so frantic. Her best friend in the hospital and her father suddenly gone."

Luciano started to answer but waited as Patrizia turned to accept her *cappuccino* from Chiara. "She's coping as well as can be expected."

Patrizia tapped a pack of sugar into her *caffè*. "Since he left, I've been hearing awful rumors about Carlo. Did you know he—" she lowered her voice to avoid catching Arturo's attention. The man was a horrible gossip.

"He...*hit* Elisa's mother? I found out yesterday from Paola at the *fruttiven-dolo*. How terribly, terribly sad. Normally a father leaving would concern me, but do you think it might actually make Elisa's life easier? Because *that* would be a blessing."

Luciano, who was still struggling to make sense of the discovery that Carlo and Concetta adopted Elisa from infancy, offered Patrizia a weak smile before standing to pay for his *caffè*. As he reached into his pocket he said, "Perhaps. I would be glad of any blessing for the child."

Luciano dropped a euro into the scuffed copper plate, and then turned to the door, right as Magda entered. She stopped short at the sight of Luciano and barked, "Well? Is she awake?"

Luciano shook his head and exited into the warming morning light of Santa Lucia.

Luciano entered his house and called, "Isotta?"

From the hallway, the young woman appeared. "*Ciao*, Luciano. I'm almost ready."

Luciano said, "Are you quite certain about leaving? I confess I like your company. Not to mention your *ragú* is far superior to the jarred kind."

Isotta smiled before ducking back into the bedroom she'd been using for the past weeks. "Nice as that sounds, I'm tired of living in dread of seeing Massimo or his mother." She added, "I left plenty of *ragú* for you in the freezer."

Luciano loitered outside her room, hands in his pockets. "Have you told your parents? About—"

"I tried." Isotta shook her head. "I can't."

Luciano cast her a curious expression.

She said, "It's embarrassing. I thought I had gotten over being the least remarkable of five sisters—"

"*Cara...*"

"It's true! I finally did something my parents could be proud of, landed myself a catch of a husband. And then it turns out that Massimo only married me because I look like—"

Luciano stiffened, and Isotta rushed on. "Oh, Luciano. I'm so sorry. I didn't mean to bring up your daughter."

He said, "It is quite all right. I've gotten used to the fact that you look so much like her. But you aren't, you know... Giulia."

Isotta moved a sweater from one hand to the other. "I hate that my minor tragedy comes on the back of your major one."

"Please don't worry yourself. I have to learn to talk about it without drinking to blot it out. Carry on."

Isotta studied the old man, his flyaway white hair framing his face like the morning fog that still wreathed the distant hills. She said, "How could I explain it to them over the phone? I'll wait until I get to Florence."

"Elisa is going to miss you."

"I'll miss her, too. Watching her draw has been a tonic. What a rare gift."

Luciano nodded.

"And I'll miss you, too, Luciano. You know that?"

Luciano nodded again.

"I wanted to wait until Fatima woke up, but... I can't go any longer not talking to my parents. In their last call, I could hear their suspicion."

"You need your parents' support. It's selfish of me to want to keep you here."

"Well, I don't know how much support I'll get from them. They thought I won the lottery when I married Massimo. I'm not sure I can convince them it was right to leave."

"Do you want to take the wedding photo? Of Massimo and Giulia?"

Isotta shuddered and thought irrelevantly of a child skipping over her grave. "No. Thank you, though."

Luciano nodded again.

Isotta clicked shut her suitcase and heaved it off the bed. "Are you sure you can spare the time to take me to the train station on your way to the hospital?"

"Yes, of course. It would be my honor."

Isotta blinked back tears. How she would miss this old man's chivalry.

As Luciano went in search of his car keys, Isotta placed a hand on her belly. If he dropped her off in Girona in the next twenty minutes, she'd have time to wave him off, and then race to the pharmacy without him knowing. The suspense was killing her.

Through the airplane window, Alessandro Bardi watched the morning sun shine on the undulating water of the Mediterranean. His breath caught, as it always did when he prepared for touchdown in Rome. He craned his head to peer to the edges of his limited vision, impatient for the first view of the palm trees lining the water and then the increasing cluster of humanity that led to the eternal city.

Beside him, Madison yawned and pulled off the face mask she'd brought with her, rejecting the one offered in the first class cabin. A whiff of cucumber drifted with the movement. She stretched before pressing the button that transformed her bed back to a chair. Glancing at Alessandro she said, "You're awake!"

"For hours."

"I told you to take some of my Ambien. I slept like a baby."

Alessandro grinned. "Snored like one, too."

"I did not!" Madison's face looked like she'd caught sight of herself in a fun house mirror. "Did I? Oh, God, I must look a sight, too. Don't look at me! Let me go do my hair and face."

Alessandro put his hand on her leg to stay her. "You look perfect as ever and you know it. Wait a second—the next turn we make I think you'll be able to see the Coliseum."

But Madison had already grabbed her overnight bag and pranced to the bathroom, ignoring the "Fasten Seatbelt" lighted placard, as well as the admonishment from the flight attendant. "*Miss!*"

Madison called over her shoulder. "Emergency! Won't take a moment!"

In the sudden quiet, Alessandro noticed the familiar tickle against his ribcage.

In less than a half hour, he'd be stepping onto Italian soil. The thought moved something indefinable into place.

Different this time, though. His previous visits had included trips to elaborate Venetian palaces and trendy Roman apartments and elegant lake villas, but he had never imagined this moment. When he would be reclaiming the home of his ancestors. He checked his phone for an email from the firm he'd hired. Of course there was nothing, even with the free wifi. Italians were just waking up.

Madison sat back down in a plume of mint and raspberry. As she buckled her seatbelt, ignoring the glares from the flight crew, she chuckled, "You won't have heard from them already."

"I know, I know."

Madison leaned back and closed her eyes. "I can't wait to see the photos. What do you think the castle is like?"

Ale sighed. "I can't imagine."

"I bet it has lots of turrets. Like the one at Disneyland."

Shaking his head, Ale said, "I already told you, it can't be like that. It was built as a fortress—"

Madison dismissed his words with a wave of her hand. "You don't know. Not until we get the photos."

"I know enough to know *that*."

Madison opened her eyes and smiled. "Whatever. It's a castle! Imagine the parties we'll have—"

Grinning, Ale said, "I know. It'll be such a scene. We'll have good wine, and food, and we'll for sure put in a top-of-the-line sound system. I hope we can get it in shape soon. The agency said with the fire…"

Opening her bag to find her tube of lip gloss, Madison groaned. "Oh, Ale. It's fine. Stop worrying. It's a *castle*."

"Yes, but what if it's in terrible shape? No one has lived there for generations."

"That's what construction crews are for, darling. And cleaning ladies. An army of them."

After a bumpy landing that had them both swearing at the pilots, they exited swiftly from the plane and joined the line at passport control. Ale gazed longingly at the shorter EU line, but Madison tugged his hand. "Don't you dare!" Grumbling, Ale pulled out his US passport. Why did he even bother to keep his Italian citizenship if he was never allowed to use it?

In baggage claim, they waited and watched the same suitcases circle around and around. And around. Madison complained, "A-*le*! How long does this take?"

Ale said, "Everything takes longer in Italy. You might as well get used to it."

"Ugh. It's stupid. Why *should* it take so long, just putting suitcases on a belt."

He said, "Your suitcase was pretty heavy."

Madison rolled her eyes.

After a few more minutes, Ale checked his watch for the tenth time and grumbled, "Okay, this is ridiculous! There's only that one taped duffel bag going around." He peered around and located a help desk. He stalked over to it, Madison prancing behind him, fluffing her hair. With eager eyes she watched as Alessandro laid into the man at the counter. Ale was gesticulating at the belt and the clock and using motions and tones he never used in New York. She couldn't follow the words, but hearing him speak in Italian always widened her smile.

Finally, the bored man at the counter looked at Ale's ticket and pointed at a carousel at the other end of baggage claim.

Madison pulled his sleeve. "What's he saying?"

Ale scowled. "It's over at that carousel."

"We were at the wrong one the whole time?"

"Doubtful. They must have changed it."

"The nerve! And he doesn't even seem sorry!"

Ale shook his head. He tried not to notice that the new carousel was surrounded by people hauling suitcases off the belt. While there was no one at the carousel with the taped duffel.

A buzzing distracted him. He yanked his phone out of his pocket and moaned, "Oh, no."

"What? What is it?"

"Oh, no!" Ale flicked the screen. "The agent's photos. The castle. It's in ruins. Ruins! A total money pit! We'll never be able to fix it up in time for summer!"

Madison grabbed the phone from Ale's hand and peered at a photo, using her fingers to zoom in. "It's kind of grainy and dark. Maybe it's not so bad?"

Ale stared at the screen. "Maybe. The message does say he had to take the photo in the rain. But still...look!" He pointed at a burned down arbor.

Madison sighed. "And no turrets."

"No. There's a round tower-type room on this edge, I guess."

"Maybe there's a part of it he didn't photograph! Maybe he was showing you the worst parts so that he can charge extra for hiring us an architect?"

Ale shrugged, defeated. "Maybe. I guess we'll see in a few hours."

They found their luggage and loaded it onto a trolley before walking outside to their waiting limousine. The driver held up a sign that read "Bardi." Ale nodded and muttered, "Alessandro Bardi."

The driver tipped his hat. "Welcome to Italy!"

Ale left his luggage on the curb and stepped into the climate-controlled air of the limo.

At Bar Birbo, the morning rush was over. Giovanni had told the last of his accumulated jokes before returning to his shop on the *piazza*, and Magda had complained about an article in the newspaper before going in search of the mayor. Chiara breathed a sigh of relief. Reaching for the broom, she heard Edo drop onto the stool.

"Tired?" she asked.

"Exhausted," he answered.

Chiara nodded. "Yes, me too."

"Well now, I thought you were sleeping much better now. *You* know." Edo winked.

Chiara smiled. "Don't get cheeky, Edo." She focused on nudging the sugar packets out from under the bar and into her waiting dustpan. She grinned to herself, remembering Edo's capering eyes when he found Fabrizio making breakfast in Chiara's bathrobe yesterday morning. Edo's teasing and Fabrizio's sly comebacks made clear to Chiara how much she'd missed during all those years of loneliness. Yes, she had known she felt alone, but she had only intuited the kaleidoscope of giddy and contented moments that love delivered.

"Actually, Edo, there's something I want to tell you."

"What's that?"

Chiara considered before saying, "I'm thinking of getting a divorce."

She braced herself.

Edo grinned, his lean face lightening. "It's about time."

"You don't think it's wrong? Your parents get so angry...I haven't brought it up in years, for fear of their speeches about the sacrament of marriage."

"Come now, Zia, you can hardly believe I'd take some moral high ground. Look at me." He spread his arms wide, his brow furrowed in concentration and his handsome cheek twitching in his attempt not to laugh.

"Okay, you've made your point."

Chiara took out a fluffy white rag to buff the counter before asking, "Have you told them?"

"Nah, waiting for the village gossip train to beat me there."

"Edo..."

"*Lo so, lo so*...I know. You don't have to say it. I'll tell them."

"When?"

"When the time is right."

"So about when Carosello grows back his missing eye?"

"Oh, that reminds me, I saw him the other day pawing through our trash. We really need better lids."

"Nice try, Edo."

"Okay, okay. But it's hard!" Chiara smiled at her nephew's sudden petulance.

"Of course it is. But that doesn't mean it's not worth doing."

The bar was quiet as Chiara cleaned the counter and ran the rag underneath the warm water to clean the milk-foaming wand, and Edo sat lost in thought.

Finally he sighed. "Will they be furious? Will they cry?"

"Who can say? If you want, I can tell them about the divorce first."

"That might work," Edo grinned. "What's prompting this? You never even talk about your husband."

"Well, as he's in jail for child solicitation, it's hardly a topic for the *aperitivo* hour."

Edo said, "Chiara..."

"It's okay. I know I sound bitter. It's a holdover. But now is time to cut this marital noose. I want to be with Fabrizio with no reservations."

She imagined Fabrizio's face when she told him her decision, his slow smile. She couldn't wait.

❧

Anna whispered a thanks and goodbye and hurriedly hung up the phone.

She listened—the water in the bathroom squealed off. Massimo would be toweling himself dry, slipping into his expensive suit (maybe the one that brought out the smolder in his eyes—he hadn't worn that one for too long) to head to the bank. Lately he'd had to hug the walls as he made his way to the car, but today, today he would be able to walk with his customary authoritative gait. And Anna would be the one to make that easier for him. It was a mother's job after all, to make things easier for her child. Anna was glad to do it.

She flitted from the stovetop to the counter to the refrigerator and back, preparing *caffè* and slicing cake. Thank God her sources had been accurate last night. How happy Massimo would be to celebrate with a slice of her good prune cake. His favorite! Anna clucked to herself, grinning as she neatly poured hot milk into the small pitcher.

Massimo's footsteps approached the kitchen. Anna ran her fingers through her hair, then smoothed it, tucking the ends to curl becomingly at her jawline.

Massimo slumped down at the table, unaware of his mother's birdlike movements as she slid a piece of cake in front of him and poured the dark and slightly acrid *caffè* into the white cup with the blue stripe that he had used every morning for years.

Anna smoothed her skirt and alternatively bit her top and bottom lip. She sat down, then leapt up for sugar, and then sat down again. Wringing her hands as Massimo mutely stirred his *caffè*, she finally blurted out, "She's gone!"

Massimo idly stirred his *caffè*. "What's that?"

"Isotta. She's gone. Now things can get back to normal!"

Massimo stared at his mother's left temple. She reached up to pat her hair, making sure all the strands were in place.

He shook his head. "You don't know what you're talking about."

Anna scowled. "Don't talk to me that way. I know exactly what I'm talking about. I just got off the phone with Esme, and you know she lives between Luciano's house and the parking lot. She saw them leave, and Isotta had her suitcase."

"So?"

"What do you mean, 'so'?"

"So I'm supposed to be happy about this?"

Anna scowled. "It's over. We can go back to normal." She repeated. Was Massimo half asleep? Why did she have to repeat herself and explain this to him like he was a child?

Leaning back in his chair, Massimo examined the crack in the ceiling as if he'd never noticed it before. When in reality it had been there half his life. Or maybe more.

"Massimo!"

Massimo sighed and pushed away from the table. "I need to get Margherita up so I can say goodbye before I go."

"You didn't even eat your cake!"

"I'm not hungry."

Anna watched her son leave the kitchen and wondered where she went wrong.

But no, it wasn't her. It was that vixen, Isotta. Massimo hadn't even loved her, but now look, she must have cast a spell on him. He wasn't *right* anymore.

She heard Massimo and Margherita's voices murmuring in the next room. Margherita's soprano tones lifted querulously, "Mamma? Mamma!"

Anna stood up and started slamming the dishes into the sink, muttering, "She's not your mother, damn child. She was never your mother."

She should have known it was a mistake to bring that witch into her house. The meek ones may appear innocent, but they could wreak the most havoc. Like Giulia.

Well, mistakes could be fixed.

Like Giulia.

Isotta watched Luciano's pale blue Fiat recede down the chest-nut-lined road and turn left at the roundabout.

She exhaled. For a few moments, it had seemed that Luciano planned to stay with her until her train left, but luckily he couldn't find a parking spot. Isotta convinced him she was going to walk directly to the train, so a goodbye in the car was exactly as good as one two minutes later beside the train.

Even with her nervous energy, it had been impossible to not be moved by the tears in the old man's eyes. She wondered if they were for saying goodbye to her or saying goodbye to a final reminder of his daughter.

Isotta shook her head angrily. She had to stop assuming that her only value was in her resemblance to Giulia. Not only was it not healthy, but she hated to think that Massimo had gotten so thoroughly underneath her skin.

She sighed and walked into the center of Girona. There must be a *farmacia* nearby. Train stations and *farmacie* went together like bread and Nutella—there! The green cross glowed and undulated, calling her closer. She watched the light ripple across the sign and let it lull her into a trance state. Anything to avoid the battering "what if?" thoughts. She'd already walked that road to no avail. Her monthly cycle was hardly regular, but it had never been this late. Then again, she'd been under more stress than she had ever been before. If she was pregnant, not just tense and carrying a lingering stomach bug or stress-induced nervous stomach—*no*. Stop. No good came of that thinking. She knew that already. She couldn't be pregnant, she simply couldn't. No husband, her family could hardly be expected to be supportive . . .

Isotta allowed herself to be pulled forward. She moved through the store as if through water, revolving around other customers, swooping up the first pregnancy test she saw (they were all the same, weren't they?)

floating to the counter, plunking down a €20,00 note and walking out, not even waiting for change. Uncharacteristic for a woman who constantly did math in her head and was far too aware of how little money she had in her bank account. At a time when she might need quite a bit. And yet she couldn't wait for the teenage boy with the pierced nose and the curious stare to make change.

Box in hand, she headed for the train station.

Bathroom, she needed a bathroom.

The faces in the station blurred, only the blue icon clear, a beacon calling her into the land of female bathroom needs.

Isotta rushed toward a stall and locked herself in. She had ten minutes until her train left. Was that enough time? She ripped open the package and tugged out the directions. Yes, barely enough. If she hurried. Her eyes skimmed the instructions. Nodding, she lay them on the floor.

Two minutes later, Isotta huddled against the door of the stall, clothes back in place, instructions tossed into the waste bin on the wall, one hand gripping the slippery plastic stick, the other clasped against her mouth.

She watched, waiting.

Of all the ways she might have imagined this day. This was not it.

She watched. Waiting.

"Ale! A-*le, wait!*"

Alessandro paused his stride to allow his wife to prance down the cobblestones on her teetering heels. She whined, "Why don't they fix these old streets with some concrete or something? The roads are the worst!"

As if in punctuation, her pinprick heel wedged in the space between the ancient stones and Madison's arms pinwheeled. Alessandro grabbed hold of her hand. "I told you not to wear those. They are completely impractical."

"But we're visiting your castle!" Madison pouted. "I wanted to look nice."

Alessandro studied his wife's shoes for a brief moment. True enough, the shoes set the right tone. A shade of coral only found in designer shoes, plus they elevated his taller-than-average wife into an arresting blond pin-up. She looked perfect. "You saw the photos. It's a wreck. You'll likely show it up."

"Aww, Ale! So sweet!" Madison rubbed her lips together and said, "I wish I could see our friends' faces when I post selfies of us in front of our castle! Sookie will be so jealous. All she has is that God-awful heirloom jewelry collection." She stopped to rummage through her bag, grumbling, "Did I bring my stick? You hurried me out of that hotel so fast."

"Again, the castle is not in a photogenic state."

"Oh, Ale. Such a Gloomy Gus. I'm sure we can find some part of it that works as a backdrop." Madison located her slim telescoping phone holder and slipped it into an outer pocket of her purse for easier retrieval.

They walked down Via Romana, Alessandro studiously ignoring the faces peering down around curtains. He tried not to telegraph the presence to Madison of what were likely the town busybodies. If she thought she had an audience, she would ratchet up her voice, when he was trying to remain inconspicuous. At least for the present.

They stopped so Alessandro could study a hand-drawn map. "I think it's up here a little ways. There should be some stairs. On the right, I think?" He turned the map upside down and squinted to read the writing from his conversation with his grandparents. It was difficult—they themselves had never been here—and related what they had heard from their own parents.

Madison pointed an expertly painted nail. "Ale! There's stairs, leading up right there! With that tuxedo cat! Oh, that's darling, where's my phone?"

Before she could locate her phone in her large and glossy designer bag, a scruffy dog trotted down the stairs, startling the cat who fled to the *piazza*. Madison clutched Alessandro's arm. "Gross! Look at that dog! His fur is all matted! Ew, is that trash on his tail?"

Alessandro cocked his head at the beast and decided not to point out what was probably a missing eye. "I think he's dashing." Carosello looked up, as if in recognition of a kindred spirit. He panted for a moment and then jogged away, following the cat.

Madison groaned, "You and your strays. Anyway, let's go up the stairs. That has to be it, right? What's that sign say?" She gestured at a blue sign with an arrow that pointed to the top of the stairs.

Alessandro read aloud, "*Il Castello.*"

"What's that mean?"

Alessandro sighed. "Castle. It means the castle."

Madison hugged his arm. "I'm so glad your parents taught you Italian."

"Little kid Italian, the rest is from University—"

"Okay, let's go! I can't wait!" She tugged his arm, but as he turned to follow her, his vision snagged on the figure that had been behind his head the whole time, tucked into the wall.

"Wait."

"Wait? Why wait? It has to be up the steps, you said so."

"I want to see this."

Alessandro gingerly stepped toward the Madonna perched in an ethereal blue niche. "These old Italian towns have Madonnas secreted away all over the place. I've never seen one like this." Alessandro raised his hand toward the Madonna, whose own hand was lofted in benediction. Mary's smile beckoned him closer. Her eyes radiated a direct warmth. Could she see into his soul? "What is this—marble? Usually they are painted and—"

"A-*le*! Stop looking at that stupid statue. You said yourself these towns have a kabillion of them. And we are about to claim your birthright!"

"It's not exactly a 'birthright'"

Madison moaned, "Whatever! I can't believe you aren't racing up the steps! What's gotten into you?"

Alessandro sagged. "I don't know. I guess I'm a little scared."

"Scared? That's weird."

Alessandro ran his hand across his stubbled cheek. "I know. I should be excited. But it feels so big. I don't want to mess it up."

"Mess it up? It's already messed up, you said so yourself."

"No, that's not what I mean. But I don't really know what I mean."

"Never mind. Let's go."

Madison squealed and grabbed his hand, pulling him up the stairs.

Within moments they stood in the castle yard.

Fabrizio leaned across the counter, his chin in his hand. Chiara felt his eyes on her as she unloaded the dishwasher.

"What?" She laughed.

"Oh, nothing. Admiring the view."

Chiara snapped her towel at him. "You're terrible."

Fabrizio waggled his eyebrows.

Checking to make sure no customers approached, Chiara strolled to Fabrizio and dropped her head level with his. Her gaze drifted from his eyes to his mouth. He tilted his face to kiss her, lips softening. They pulled their faces apart and took a beat before opening their eyes. He grinned. "You know, our relationship isn't a secret anymore. We don't have to be clandestine."

She ran her finger over his lower lip. "I know."

He leaned back and boasted, "In fact, now that everyone knows I have your stamp of approval, they're asking if they can be characters in my book."

Picking up a glass to buff off the water spots, Chiara asked, "What do you say?"

His eyes shone as he said, "I promise them worthy roles for all."

"That must go over well."

"Indeed."

Setting the glass on the shelf, Chiara asked, "You writing today?"

Fabrizio nodded. "Yes. The rest of the morning. Then I told Dante I would stop by."

"Dante? Why?"

Fabrizio shrugged. "When he was in here the other night, we were talking politics and he said he had an old *Avanti* newspaper article written by Mussolini."

"Really? I didn't know that."

"Maybe you never talked to him about fascism?" She smiled and Fabrizio said, "Mostly I think he's glad to talk to someone who doesn't care that his wife left him for a handyman. How about you? When do you finish work today?"

Chiara looked at the clock behind her. "Soon. I'm going to the hospital before noon."

"Still no news?"

"No." Chiara watched a mother and child race up the hill. Late for school? No, the child was too small. She turned back to Fabrizio. "It's funny, I never really knew Fatima, beyond seeing her skip down the street with Elisa. But I've gotten to know her family. I like to bring them *caffè*. Hospital coffee," she said, seriously, "is not to be tolerated."

Fabrizio touched her hand. "Dinner tonight? I'll cook."

Chiara bit her lip in thought. "I can't. I'm back on this evening. Edo has a Skype date."

"A late dinner, then. Have you had Giuseppe's chicken sausages? They are tremendous." Fabrizio's grin was infectious.

Chiara smiled back. "Once or twice."

A buzzing splintered the warm lull of the bar. Fabrizio pulled his phone out of his pocket and turned his back. Chiara reached for another glass to dry and tried not to count how many times this had happened this last day or two.

After a minute of furious pecking at his phone, Fabrizio turned back. Chiara forced a smile and said, "*Tutto bene?*"

Sliding his phone back into his pocket, Fabrizio said, "Yes. Everything is fine."

Chiara nodded and reached into the under-counter refrigerator to pull out a green bottle of mineral water. As she poured the popping water into a tall glass, she chided herself. People got texts, they didn't have to announce their contents. This is what came from having last dated in the pre-cell-phone era.

The door flew open and Magda stalked in. Flinging down her newspaper, she said, "Unbelievable! I just tried to talk to Dante about how to deal with the *castello* owner, and he refused to listen to me!" Magda flipped through the paper and pointed. "Look! Right here! It says that Alessandro Bardi is arriving from the United States this week. Maybe even today. Does Dante have international experience? No he does not!"

Fabrizio raised his eyebrows in mock horror while Chiara tried not to laugh. Magda waved the paper. "Are you listening to me?"

Chiara pulled her face into a caricature of seriousness. "Yes, of course, Magda. Go on."

"I ask you . . . who has more experience with cross-cultural diplomacy— Dante who has rarely left Umbria, or me who graduated from a top-shelf school in Germany? Not to mention that because of my vacation rentals, I am well versed on cross-cultural problem solving."

Chiara's lips twitched as she remembered Magda laughing at her American guests' request for ice. Not behind their backs, she had actually brought them to the bar to hoot at their ridiculousness. In Italian, so the guests had shifted uncomfortably, unsure of the joke. Then again, that was years ago, or more. Ever since the fire when Magda had revealed to Chiara that her parents had been Nazi sympathizers who had belittled Magda as a child, she had been far less hostile. As if some of the air had leaked out of her combative balloon.

Chiara realized Magda was still talking and tuned back into her words like her radio warming up on a frigid morning. "*Then* he had the nerve to say I should mind my small affairs of hostessing. Does he think that's all I do? Greet visitors with a basket of bread?" Magda mimed a simpering smile as she obsequiously held out her arms, laden with imaginary pastries.

Smiling despite herself, Chiara reminded Magda, "Dante has a lot on his mind with Stella gone."

Magda harrumphed and made a derisive comment about cuckolds as Chiara went on, "And he feels responsible for the fire. You should have sympathy for that."

Magda's eyes narrowed. "What are you saying? That I'm responsible? Because—"

Chiara flung out a hand. "You misunderstand me. He feels responsible, like you feel responsible, but in reality no one is responsible. It was an accident. Yes, it was your idea to use the *castello* for the *festa*, but Dante didn't have to agree, nor did anyone else. It was a good idea, it made sense, no one could have predicted the wind would blow those embers to the vines in the arbor. But it's a weight when you blame yourself."

Magda grumbled in reluctant agreement.

Fabrizio leaned across the counter to kiss Chiara's cheek. "I'll see you this evening, *cara*."

The afternoon sunlight slid fast away as the autumnal chill draped over Santa Lucia.

No longer could Luciano and Elisa work outside, even cloaked in jackets and the blankets they swaddled around themselves to ward away the press of cold. Elisa propped her chin on her hands and gazed around Luciano's meagerly lit living room. She could tell he had made an attempt to scour away his years of devastation, but the house still smelled funny. Like greasy ashes.

She gazed up at the light fixture, wishing for two more bulbs. Even one would do. The numbers on her page liked to dance when the lights went dim, and it was all she could do to fix them in place with her intermittent concentration.

"I know. I need new bulbs." Luciano walked in, carrying a tray.

Elisa flushed at being caught. "What? Oh!" Elisa made a rare attempt at laughter. At least, it was rare since Fatima was hospitalized. The sound that should be joyful was as wistful as those sightings of Fatima's fingers fluttering across the sheets and her eyes moved behind their fragile lids. "I was thinking about this math problem."

"Elisa. You are many wonderful things, but a wonderful liar you are not."

Elisa's arms dropped from reaching for her mug of tea, and she sat rigidly. Lip trembling, she asked, "What do you mean?"

Luciano regarded Elisa curiously before plunking the tea in front of her. "Well, clearly you were thinking I need a new lightbulb. Or more probably, two."

Elisa hung her head.

Luciano pushed the mug closer to her. "You must forgive my poor attempts at humor, Elisa. I seem to be out of practice."

Nodding, Elisa said, "Thanks for the tea."

Luciano hesitated and then asked, "How are things at home?"

"Good."

"Is that right?"

"Yeah, I mean, I guess so. I mean . . . what do you mean?" Elisa narrowed her eyes and gazed up at her *maestro*.

"*Allora*, I imagine having your father leave changes your household. Perhaps in some good ways, and some less good ones."

"He wasn't my father."

Luciano mused at the word choice. "Wasn't?"

"I mean, he's not ever been."

"I understand that. Nor your mother your mother in the biological sense of the word. But nonetheless, they have served as you parents."

Elisa snorted.

Luciano grew serious. "Indifferent parents perhaps, but parents. They have been all you have. It must be a challenge to have him gone."

"No. He was awful."

"Awful?"

"*Sì.* Awful."

Luciano stirred his tea. Bar Birbo had been full of stories lately, of Carlo hitting Concetta. Had he hit Elisa as well? The thought stifled Luciano's breath. "Well, then. So your home is better now."

"Definitely."

"And your mother . . ."

"I don't know who she is, I told you."

Luciano offered an apologetic smile. "Yes, I know. And I'm sure the mystery is uncomfortable for you."

"Do *you* know who she is?"

"I'm afraid I don't."

Elisa took a hesitant sip of her tea. "They said she lives in Santa Lucia. They don't know about my father, but my mother lives right here."

"Or she used to."

"That's true. Maybe she moved away." Elisa propped her head back in her hands and stared at a tattered cobweb waving in the draft that pressed through the windows.

Luciano ventured. "Do you want to know?"

Luciano wondered if she'd heard him. But then she answered softly, "If she's nice I want to know who it is. If she'd like me."

"Elisa . . ."

"When are you going to see Fatima?"

"Tomorrow afternoon."

"Can I come?"

"Of course." Luciano paused. "So how is the math sheet?"

Elisa pulled it closer to her but instead of asking about the problems she whispered, "Do you think she'll ever get better?" Elisa's mind was filled with the words of her fight with Fatima.

Luciano watched Elisa's face contort with shadows before answering, simply, "I wish I knew."

Alessandro cheered, "It's better than I thought!" as Madison groaned, "It's worse than I thought."

The castle rose up into the clearing blue sky. The light that settled around it was heavy, liquid, and imbued with a cobalt sheen that made Alessandro wonder if he'd ever properly looked at a sky before. Yes, there were scorch marks all over the castle, and the olive trees closest to the castle perimeter were burned into shards. And though the debris had been stacked and piled, there was still enough to make the area feel like a mix between a rubbish heap and a desolate wasteland.

Yet, there was something here. A heartbeat, a shrouded vibrancy. Alessandro shook his head; he was not usually given to such irrelevant musings. Very unlike the finance pro he knew himself to be. Maybe it was being back in Italy. He always loosened and seemed to fit in his clothes differently once surrounded by the cadence of his first language and the stately umbrella pines, the air tinged with the smell of grilling meat and baking almonds.

He'd tried importing that Italian feeling to his SoHo apartment, even getting a bonsai-sized olive tree for his windowsill. But a particularly busy month of working sixty-hour weeks and partying in his downtime meant he'd failed to water it. Still, he hadn't been able to throw it away. Luckily, Madison had had no qualms about tossing out the desiccated tree an hour before their friends arrived to admire their remodeled kitchen. At the rising cooking scents wafting up from Santa Lucia, Alessandro suddenly realized that they'd only cooked in that kitchen a handful of times since that night.

Alessandro dropped Madison's hand and moved to a window in the castle wall. The glass had long since gone, so he stuck his head in the room. His eyes adjusted to the darkness, and he spied a large wooden table piled with metal chargers or plates of some kind. He noticed a sliver of light carving the floor, and realized it came from a doorway around the corner. He must have missed it, as he felt pulled into the center of the castle yard by a magnetic tug.

He walked around to the door, hoping against hope that it would be unlocked.

The door opened with a modest shove, and Alessandro hesitated for only a moment before stepping across the threshold. Madison frowned and followed her husband into the gloom. Alessandro cursed himself for not bringing his flashlight. Of course the castle would be stone and therefore impenetrable to ambient light, and of course there wouldn't be electricity. He stepped carefully to the center of the room and ran his fingers across the table and yes, a pile of oxidized silver plateware and cutlery. How had this not been stolen?

When he had found out that the castle had been used for a town festival and there had been a fire, he assumed that the town must have been helping itself to his inheritance for generations. But even the charred log in the fireplace looked to have been untouched for a hundred years. There was a pile of brocade heaped on the floor, and though this did look mussed, the fact that it remained at all was startling. It must have been worth a fortune. And that tapestry on the wall! He wouldn't touch it for fear it would disintegrate, but he allowed his hand to hover over it, the errant fibers tickling his palm. Had the town really preserved the state of the castle since his ancestors abandoned it for a flat on the Grand Canal?

Madison's whine startled him out of his reverie. "Ale...A-*le*! Let's get out of here. It's creepy."

Alessandro nodded and took her hand to guide her out the door.

There would be plenty of time to explore. When he had a flashlight.

They stepped outside, and Ale flung his hand over his eyes at the momentary flare of brightness as his wife yelped and rummaged through her bag for her Gucci sunglasses.

Still blinking, he peered around the edge of the castle. A breezeway connected the main part of the castle to what was probably a kitchen. He could see the charred and splintered remains of an arbor that must have once stretched between them. A series of rooms stood open and facing a small courtyard. Alessandro squinted against the sunblindness that had yet to lessen and let his vision search the darkness as he walked toward the open rooms.

Something white moved, an apparition.

Suddenly the apparition turned and almost crashed into him.

Alessandro leapt backward with a shout and Madison, who was still searching for her sunglasses, screamed at the sound of her husband's uncharacteristic yell.

It was a woman, dressed in a white smock, holding a pallet of small rosemary plants. "*Mi dispiace! Mi dispiace!*"

Alessandro rubbed his eyes. Yes, the woman was still there. His mind was playing tricks on him. She continued apologizing. Alessandro held out a hand to forestall her. He said, "It's all right, really. I was just startled. My name is Alessandro Bardi." He gestured to the castle, unsure of how to say, "This is mine" without sounding more pretentious than he'd like. Could a person name-drop castle ownership? It suddenly occurred to him that that's exactly what he had been doing back in New York the past two weeks.

Ava's eyes widened and her mouth fell open. *This* was the castle owner? This man with the genial features and soft eyes and an academic—almost Florentine—sounding Italian? She caught her breath. "I apologize, I heard you were arriving soon, but I thought I would have time to plant this rosemary. It was burned..." She pointed to the edge of the castle yard as if in explanation.

Madison tugged her husband's arm. "Ale? What's she saying? Who is she?"

Ale just shook his head, not taking his eyes off the woman. "Why are you planting the rosemary?"

"I told you, it burned..."

"Yes, yes, I see that, but why are you replacing it?"

The woman looked confused at the question. Instead she said, "I'm so sorry."

Ale held out his hand. "I'm Alessandro. Ale." Did he already say that?

Ava regarded his hand quizzically for a moment before slipping her own within his. "Ava, *piacere.*" She shivered as if a warm breeze wound through the icy tendrils of an early spring day. Alessandro's eyes widened and he released her hand. Stammering he turned to introduce his wife. Ava nodded and shook her hand. "*Piacere.*"

Ava turned back to Alessandro. "I'm sorry you have to see the castle for the first time in this state. We did try to clean it up."

"Yes, I can tell."

"There's a lot of work to do, still. Obviously. But once the walls are washed and the trees replanted..."

Alessandro turned his head to examine the groves. "The roots of the trees look like they are coming right out of the earth. They seem ancient."

Ava hung her head. "They were. They are. It's a tremendous loss. We talked to olive tree experts to see if we could each donate an ancient tree from our plots to replant here, but we learned that the odds of those trees taking once uprooted was lower than the odds of the trees themselves regenerating."

"Olive trees can come back?"

Ava shrugged. "It is possible."

Madison glared at Ava. "Ale, what's she saying?"

Alessandro ignored her, his eyes never leaving Ava's soft features and animated eyes. Were those freckles across the bridge of her nose? He'd never seen an Italian woman with freckles. "Can I buy you a *caffè?*"

Ava's eyes shot toward Madison.

Alessandro stumbled over his words. "My wife and I would love to buy you a *caffè*, and you can tell us more about the work that has been done and the work still to do. We are out of our element."

Ava chewed on her lower lip briefly before nodding.

"Elisa! How was school?"

Elisa dropped her backpack by the door. With her husband gone, Concetta no longer snarled at a stray backpack, or even papers cluttering the table. "Fine."

"Keeping those grades up?"

Elisa went to the refrigerator and peered inside, the artificial light reflecting off the bare shelves. "You didn't go grocery shopping?"

"No." Her mother broke into tittering laughter. "I thought I'd do some gardening."

"Gardening?"

"Yes, I planted. Out there." Concetta gestured vaguely toward the steep brambles that could be considered a yard, but was more often attributable to the town's common property, as a trail cut through it that went all the way to the bottom of the hill.

Elisa closed her eyes and turned away from the window.

"You've been doing a lot of gardening."

Concetta laughed girlishly again. "Yes, well. With your father gone, and your brothers moving to Spoleto to be closer to school and their new jobs, I have so much time." She thought for a moment and then whispered, "Your father never allowed me to have a garden. Not even a little one. He said it wasted time." She smiled broadly again. "Do you want to see it? The weather is getting cold, so there's not much I could plant, but Ava brought some rosemary bushes."

"Ava?"

"You know Ava? The florist's daughter." Concetta turned away and busied herself opening and shutting the broom cupboard before sweeping up the dirt she'd tracked in the house.

"Why would Ava give you rosemary?"

Concetta sighed. "She had some extra from the castle, and she heard me talking about wanting to get some plants in the ground."

Elisa nodded and tried to tamp down a sudden sense of alarm. She didn't like the idea of her mother talking to people in her sudden free time.

Concetta straightened. "Do you want to see the garden or not?"

"Maybe later. I need to get lunch and start on homework."

"Ah, going to study with Luciano, eh?" She tried to sweeten her tone, but she couldn't keep out the edge of acidity that bored holes in her words.

"No, I did that earlier. While you were gardening." She gave her mother a meaningful glance.

"Okay, Elisa, I get your point. I'll shop tomorrow, okay? Just because your father is gone doesn't mean you can get sassy."

"Sorry, Mamma. I'm hungry."

Concetta stepped into the living room and tugged her purse into her lap. Her fingers sifted through the contents as she shook the bag, listening for the telltale sound of coins slipping against each other. She raised her fist out of her bag, and then opened her palm to count the coins. "90 ... 95 ... a euro! Why don't you take it to the *rosticceria* and get a slice of pizza before they close?"

Elisa didn't look convinced. "Are you sure? Won't you need that money to go to the store this afternoon?"

"No, it's okay, I found some bills in your father's wallet." Concetta paled.

"He left his wallet?"

"Well," she stammered, "You remember what a hurry he was in when he left."

"He's not coming back for it?" Elisa did not want to see him. What if he said more mean things? Elisa tried not to think of it. It made her feel like that time she got lost in the department store because Concetta assumed she was right behind her, but in fact she'd been so terrified by the escalator that she'd ducked away. It had been a long time before a worker found her.

Concetta's face stiffened into an expression of grim determination. "No, he's definitely not coming back for it. He's not coming back at all."

It was, of course, what Elisa wanted to hear. Then why did her belly fill with dread?

The three-hour train ride and two-hour delay in Perugia did nothing to diminish Isotta's shock.

Yes, part of her had expected that blue cross in the stick window. And yet.

It felt like a memory of a TV program, rather than her own life. A faded daguerreotype.

Right now, as she and her suitcase walked the familiar streets toward Santa Maria Novella, there was a miniature *human* growing within her body.

Pregnant.

She repeated the word over and over again until it lost its meaning. Preg-*nant*.

The fact that Massimo had bestowed his share of this baby in her while probably imagining his dead wife? Immaterial. Utterly besides the point. This baby was all hers. The thought of Massimo or his mother or her parents claiming any part of this little person's existence filled her with an indignation completely foreign to her. Her grief and despair had condensed within her, transforming into this spark of a human. She wondered how long it would be until the baby had fingernails. She wondered how long the baby had been inside her. She wanted to lie down and wonder and wonder.

But first she had to cross the threshold into her parents' house and tell them she had left her marriage. Oh, this was going to be rough. Very, very rough.

She wished she'd been able to prepare them over the phone, but she also knew that that would have only offered her the illusion of girding them. She would have to face Nero's flames sooner or later. Maybe it was actually better to tell them now, with this secret tucked within her.

Before she was ready, she arrived before the wagon-sized gate that marked the entrance to her family's apartment complex. Steadying her breath, she wrangled her keys out of her shoulder bag and began flipping through them to locate the main entrance key. Isotta jumped as the ring tumbled out of her hand, jangling to the ground.

Sliding the key into the door, Isotta slipped inside and closed the door behind her, effectively trapping her in darkness. Her hand slid along the door, waiting to brush against the light switch. The cold switch plate shocked her fingers briefly before she pressed the button to illuminate the stairwell.

Isotta drew in a deep breath and hitched her suitcase against her side before heading up the steps that curved to the right, up to her family's apartment door. She touched it lightly before trying the handle.

It caught momentarily before releasing.

So someone was home.

She could hear water running in the kitchen. Her mother, undoubtedly beginning dinner preparation. Isotta closed her eyes and wished for the presence of one of her sisters, belatedly realizing that her sisters would be at work. After months out of the workforce, wedged into the fabric of Santa Lucia, she'd forgotten to consider that. Her hopes of a buffer dissipated into the stale air of the room. Did her childhood home always smell like couch cushions gone slick with age? Was it always so close? She couldn't catch her breath and had to order her lungs to behave.

"Hello?" Her voice wavered. This was not how she wanted to begin. She cleared her throat and tried again. "Hello!"

Isotta's mother strode out of the kitchen, drying her hands on her apron. "Isotta? What are you doing here?" Her brow furrowed, an echo of her frown.

Isotta dropped her purse onto the couch.

Caterina raised herself on tiptoes to peer into the shadows behind Isotta. "Is Massimo here?" she asked, absent-mindedly smoothing her flyaway hair.

Biting her lip, Isotta steadied her breath.

"No. I left him."

Her mother's mouth gulped like a landed trout.

"What? Isotta . . . how can . . . *what?*"

"I left him."

Caterina's eyes narrowed as she found her natural ire. "How can you be so stupid?"

Isotta sank onto the couch. "Mamma. Please."

"Seriously, Isotta, what would possess you? You must be ill. Go back. I'm sure he will forgive you if you tell him you were in a fever—"

Isotta swatted away her mother's hand as it reached for her forehead. "I'm not sick. He is."

"Massimo is sick? And you leave him?" Caterina shook her head. "How did I raise such a heartless bitch?"

As her mother strode into the kitchen to attend to an overboiling pot, Isotta mumbled, "You would know a thing or two about that."

Caterina yelled, "What did you say?"

Isotta's lips tightened as she straightened and called back, "Nothing."

The sound of banging pots echoed from the kitchen.

Well, this went about as well as expected.

~

Ava led Ale and Madison down the castle steps, but catching sight of Magda leaving Bar Birbo, Ava flung out her arm to stop their progress. Alessandro stepped beside her and looked at her curiously. She held her finger to her lips as she waited for the last of Magda's footsteps to die away.

She said, "I apologize. I thought it better to wait a moment."

Alessandro chuckled. "Okay. And where are we going?"

Ava pointed straight ahead. "Right there, Bar Birbo."

Madison whined, "Ale, what's she saying?"

Alessandro shot a of look of apology at Ava, though his face also registered relief that the words themselves would, hopefully, be lost. "She's saying this bar up here is where we can get coffee."

He turned back to Ava, and gestured to the Madonna above her shoulder. "That's beautiful."

Ava turned, surprised. "Is it? I suppose so."

Alessandro looked back at the Madonna, his hand lifted again, a mirror of Mary's own. "Yes," he breathed. "It's beautiful."

Ava stopped and regarded the Madonna. "She's so much a part of our daily routine, I guess I haven't noticed." She pointed at the hem of Mary's gown. "See how it's worn away here? That's where we touch her feet for luck." Alessandro pulled back a touch and considered Ava, his brow slightly furrowed. "Really?"

"Yes . . . my mother used to lift me to touch the Madonna on the way to church, many years ago."

"May I?"

Ava nodded, and tried to bite down a smile that threatened to break the somberness of the moment.

Alessandro murmured to himself as his fingertips brushed across the marble hem of her gown.

Then he grinned at Ava. "Now I'm lucky?"

Ava glanced at Madison. "Well, maybe you have to be a resident for it to work."

"I do own a house here. A *castello*, in point of fact."

"True. But maybe you have to actually *live* here." She stopped herself from asking if he planned on moving to Santa Lucia. She liked the thought of his slight foreignness brightening her street side conversations. His wife, though . . .

Ava stepped across the road and pushed the door of Bar Birbo open with a sigh masked by the groaning of the hinges.

Chiara turned and smiled at the group as Ava said, "*Ciao*, Chiara. I was just at the *castello* and practically ran into Alessandro Bardi, the owner. I gave him quite a scare. He may require *espresso*."

Chiara enunciated her Italian slowly, "Welcome to Santa Lucia, Signor Bardi."

Alessandro grinned. "Alessandro, please. Ale. Thank you. I'm looking forward to learning about your charming town."

Chiara said, "You speak Italian!"

"Yes, some from my parents, but mostly through university. A fact you didn't notice because of my flawless local accent."

Ava, Chiara, and Alessandro hooted in laughter as Madison tugged her husband's arm. "What's going on? What is everyone laughing about? It's not nice to exclude me!"

Alessandro put his arm around her and said, "And this is my wife, Madison."

Chiara greeted her, "*Piacere.*"

Madison frowned. "Doesn't anyone speak English?"

Alessandro stopped laughing and quickly scanned the assembled faces. To his relief, they beamed back quizzically. He patted her arm. "It's fine, honey. I'm getting the lay of the land. Do you want a coffee?"

She brightened. "Yes! A caffè mocha with nonfat milk. And whip."

Alessandro regarded her uncomfortably. She went on, "What? I'm on vacation! And I didn't have breakfast. I'm allowed a few extra calories. You had that chocolate pastry thing this morning at the airport, and you know Derek would force you to fast tomorrow if I told him."

Scanning Ava and Chiara's faces again for recognition, he saw mostly bemusement on Chiara's expression and flicker of something like sympathy in Ava's. Did she understand more than she let on? Just in case, Alessandro whispered to his wife, "They don't have that here."

"What do you mean?"

"That's not a real drink."

"Sure it is, I get it all the time."

"No, I mean it's not a drink you can get in Italy."

Madison guffawed. "You can be so stupid sometimes. It has an *Italian name*."

"But it's a bastardization of—"

Madison sighed dramatically. "You just don't want me gaining weight, and didn't even notice I ordered it with *skim* milk—"

"Of course I'm not thinking that! In fact, it's unlikely they have skim milk either—"

Swiveling her head, Madison looked for the photo menu with the drink she ordered every Tuesday and Thursday after hot yoga (though admittedly without the whipped cream).

As Ava stared at her hands clasped on the bar, Chiara followed Madison's gaze, trying to see what the American was looking for. Not spotting anything, Chiara asked Alessandro, "Is there something wrong?"

Alessandro shook his head, trying to figure out how to smooth out all these sudden conversational wrinkles.

Huffing, Madison said, "Sweet Jesus. No menu? Fine." She leaned across the bar.

Chiara took an instinctive step backward before stopping herself. "*Sì?*"

Madison said, "I . . . want . . . a.. caffè mocha."

Chiara turned open mouthed to Alessandro who ducked his head and tried to blend in with the posters behind him for a festival recently passed.

Chiara ventured, "*Un caffè?*"

Madison smiled broadly as if praising a puppy. "Yes! I mean *sì!*" She turned to wink at Alessandro. "A caffè *mocha*. With *skim milk*." If the woman didn't understand that part, it wasn't so big of a deal. She'd tried and the weight loss gods could hardly punish her.

Chiara tried again. "*Un caffè.*"

Madison turned to Ale and rolled her eyes at this woman's dullness.

Alessandro put his arm around his wife. "Sweetheart, a mocha is not a drink they have here. Maybe they do in some parts of Italy, and that's where Starbucks got the name." Not true, but if he allowed her to save face, maybe she would be mollified.

"But they don't have it here?"

"No."

Madison pouted.

Alessandro comforted her. "I can order you a *cappuccino* and we can put cocoa powder on it and that will be close. And even better, really, because the coffee in Italy is so delicious. Much more delicious than Starbucks."

"Really?"

"Promise."

Anna stormed out of the *alimentari* with her sack empty of the pasta and apricot juice she had planned to purchase.

Not one of her neighbors exhibited the slightest sympathy for her situation. She had tried telling them about how Isotta used witchcraft to entangle Massimo. How else would such an ordinary-looking nobody have the power to break the heart of a man like her son?

Even Magda ignored her, studying the ingredients on a package of sugar-flecked cookies. Chiara at the bar hadn't cared either! Or Edo!

Patrizia either, though she had a daughter, so she couldn't understand the bond between a mother and a son, which was far, far stronger than the bonds of marriage. Her husband's malice had strengthened that mother-son relationship, since they found comfort only with each other. How could anyone understand? They couldn't, that's what.

Anna shook her head as she battered through the sudden icy wind. If the people of Santa Lucia were going to look at her like she was the villain just because her conniving daughter-in-law fled, well then she would take her business elsewhere. Lifting her chin as she passed Giuseppe's butcher shop, she hurried down the twist of alleys to the town's lower parking lot.

A sound, like the tug of a guitar string stopped her short.

What was that?

A long-haired white cat slunk around the corner toward her.

Did the cat make that noise? Yowling for food, perhaps?

The cat sat on his haunches and regarded her haughtily.

She had never liked cats.

Zipping her jacket up higher and adjusting the hood around her head more securely, Anna took a step forward.

That twanging sound again.

Anna shot a look at the cat, who contemplated the turbulent grey sky.

He must have heard it, too? But he seemed nonplussed.

This was ridiculous. She couldn't let a sound stop her from getting on with her grocery shopping. If she hurried, she'd be home from Girona with exactly enough time to make Massimo lasagna with little meatballs. The dish had been his favorite since a childhood hiking trip in Abruzzo. The meal never failed to please her son. She imagined how he would push back from the table after third helpings, and groan with happy discomfort. Then he'd take her hand, as tenderly as he used to before—

BAM!

A sharp stab to her temple and a flurry of rustling blackness.

Staggering backward, Anna saw a small black bird roll through the air to land at the cat's feet.

The cat leaned down to sniff the bird. Lifting a tentative paw, the cat nudged the little creature.

Anna raised her hand to her temple. There was a small hole in the hood of her jacket, and an ache where the bird hit, but no blood. How lucky she'd had her hood pulled over her head.

Still holding her temple, she bent over to look at the bird. Was it dead? What was wrong with it? Divebombing people was hardly typical bird behavior. Could birds get rabies? The bird stirred, and the cat recoiled before hissing and turning tail to run down the alley. *That* was definitely not typical cat behavior. The bird shuddered and hopped onto its narrow feet before shaking its head (did birds normally do *that*?). It cocked its beak to gaze beadily at Anna whose hand moved from her temple to her mouth in suspense. The bird hopped one, two, three times toward Anna who backed away. With a sense of drama birds were certainly incapable of, the animal stretched out its wings pointedly for a few moments, then took flight.

Anna trembled. What could it all mean?

"*Buongiorno!*" Ava called from outside.

Drat. That nosy woman, back again.

Elisa slid her backpack off her shoulders and dropped it onto the chair. "Where's my mother?"

Ava brushed off her knees and came inside. "She went to the store for more soil."

"And you . . . stayed here?"

Ava shrugged. "The plants need to go in the ground before it gets too cold." Ava gestured behind her. "It would be better if we evened out the mound, but your mom seems to like it there."

Elisa's eyes shot to the far side of the yard. "That's right. She does."

Ava shrugged again. "It's your space, I'm just here to help." She washed her hands in the sink and called out, "You hungry? I brought some *biscotti*."

Despite herself, Elisa sat down and accepted the cookies.

Ava sat across from her. "So, Elisa! How old are you now?"

Her mouth full of cookies, Elisa mumbled, "Eleven."

In a stagey expression of surprise, Ava answered, "Eleven! I can hardly believe it. Feels like just yesterday your mamma and papà were pushing you on the baby swing at the playground."

Elisa's hand paused midway to her mouth. Had that actually ever happened? She couldn't remember her dad ever going to the park with her or even her brothers.

Ava said, "Your father works at the Albini factory, is that right? They make washing machines?"

Elisa nodded, not really listening. She had one memory of her father surrounded by green, but that must have been from one of her brothers' soccer games.

Ava seemed not to notice Elisa's vacant expression. She leaned forward and broke off a bit of *biscotto*, popping it in her mouth. "He's worked there for awhile?"

Elisa's gaze refocused. "He left. So I don't know where he's working."

Ava nodded sympathetically. "Ah, yes. He left. Terrible shock, I'm sure. But before he left—"

"Okay, I need to do homework. Thanks for the cookies." Elisa went to her room to unload her schoolbooks onto her bed. Her hands stilled at a rustling from the stoop. Hoping Ava hadn't yet heard anything, Elisa darted to the front door. Before opening it, Elisa peeked outside to the back and saw Ava kneeling in the dirt, her back to the house. Elisa breathed a sigh of relief and quietly opened the front door. Her mother stood on the landing, typing on her phone with a slight smile, bags of soil piled beside her.

"Mamma?" Elisa whispered.

Concetta was so absorbed, she didn't notice Elisa.

"Mamma!"

"What? What is it?" Concetta scowled. "You almost made me drop my phone."

Concetta leaned to pick up a bag of soil, but Elisa stood in front of her. "Mamma, you have to stop letting Ava come over."

"What do you mean?"

"She's so nosy! All those questions! It's weird."

"I like the company. Nobody knows what to say to me since your father left." Concetta shrugged. "It's nice to work in the yard together. Ava says that gardening is like going to a spa. So relaxing." Concetta giggled, and stretched out her fingers, dirt wedged under each of her nails. "Not a clean spa, obviously."

Elisa said, "Well don't relax so much that you share with her all our . . . stories. She wouldn't understand."

Concetta's face grew grim but her voice was relentlessly cheerful. "I don't know what you can mean, Elisa."

"She's *weird*. I *told* you."

"I don't think you are used to people being nice to you."

This was both so impulsively accurate, and at the same time, lacking in insight that Elisa grew confused. To her daughter's stunned silence, Concetta went on, "She's a damn sight more normal than that old man you hang out with."

"Luciano is my friend."

"Ava can be your friend, too."

Elisa shook her head. "No way. She's too weird. I remember once I was walking with Isotta and she watched me all the way down the road."

Concetta said, "She was probably watching Isotta. I mean, if Anna is to be believed, that woman has the mark of the devil upon her."

"She's nice!"

"She's gone, so it hardly matters."

Massimo clicked off the phone and strode out of his bedroom.

He almost ran into his mother, standing outside his room. "Was that Isotta?"

"Yes. Well, no. She didn't answer."

"Massimo . . ."

Massimo gritted his teeth and walked past her, into the kitchen. Was there a bit of leftover *torta* from dinner? Massimo ran his hands over his firm stomach and debated cutting another slice.

Hearing his mother's footsteps following him, his hand finished its arc and grasped the cake slicer.

"Masssimo . . . You can't do this."

"Have a slice of *torta*?"

Anna said, "Massimo. You need to let her go."

Massimo slumped onto a kitchen chair.

Anna went on, "She left. She's not coming back. You need to get over it."

"Like I needed to get over Giulia?" Massimo began shoveling the cake into his mouth.

Anna's sharp intake of breath rang through the still kitchen. "I don't know what you mean—"

"This whole thing was your idea! You are the one who said that the best way to get over Giulia's death was to find a woman who could occupy the same place in my heart."

"I didn't mean Isotta."

Massimo scowled at his cake.

Anna went on, "She's not good for us."

"Us?"

"Us. You. Me. Margherita."

"Oh, yes, because Margherita really despised having Isotta here. What with all the cuddling and playing and reading together. That sure stressed her out."

"There's no call for that tone."

Chastened, Massimo started pressing his fork against the cake, making criss-cross patterns as the *torta* was squeezed against the plate. "I'm sorry, Mamma. I know you're right that it's easier without her, but I love her and I want to bring her back."

"Oh, darling...can't you see? She *can't* come back here. Look at the wedge she's forced between us. We never used to fight like this. She's a tempest, blowing in, blowing out. Just let her go." Anna smoothed her hair for a moment and took a deep breath before saying, "I've been getting signs."

Massimo said, "Signs? What kind of signs?"

"You know how I get feelings about things. I can hear Giulia calling, from beyond the grave. She doesn't want you to replace her. She's angry. She's going to stir up trouble."

Massimo shook his head. "I'm going to bring her home and she'll forgive me, you...both of us. Things will go back to normal, only better. You'll see."

Isotta looked up at the knock on the door. "Yes?"

Isabella stepped around the door. "All right if I come in?"

Isotta laid aside the book she was reading. "It's your room."

"Ours."

Isotta snapped, "Only now that I've returned home with my tail between my legs."

"Oh, Isotta."

Isotta crossed her legs and tried to loosen the waistband of her jeans without raising suspicion. She sighed. "I'm sorry. I'm tired. It's been a tough reentry."

Isabella sat down on the end of the bed.

Isotta blurted out, "I had to leave him. I had to."

Isabella nodded. "You don't have to talk about it. I know that if you left Massimo, he must be a monster."

The words came out before Isotta could stop them. "You have no idea."

The sisters realized their mother stood in the doorway. Caterina smirked. "Well, this I have to hear."

Isabella glared at her mother. "Mamma, please—"

Isotta stayed her with a hand on her arm. "It's fine. I have to tell sometime. Might as well be now."

Caterina entered the room, arms crossed in front of her. "Let's have it."

Isotta closed her eyes before slowly saying, "I found out that Massimo, he . . . he used me."

At Isabella's sharp intake of breath, Isotta opened her eyes. "I mean . . . he married me because I look like his wife. The one that died."

Isabella looked confused. "People have types, Isotta. You know that. I myself only date guys with beards, and—"

"No. You don't understand."

Isotta shot a look at her mother bristling as she stood by the bed. Reaching for her purse, Isotta said, "Maybe it's better if I show you. Luciano—that's Giulia's father, I stayed with him in Santa Lucia before I came back to Florence—"

Isabella shook her head. "Wait, who? Now I'm confused."

Isotta said, "Okay, let me try again. Luciano, the father of Massimo's wife, wanted to give me this picture. I didn't accept it, because it felt strange, but at the last minute I took a photo of it."

She held her phone to Isabella who gasped. Caterina snatched the phone away and frowned at the screen.

Isabella whispered, "That's not you?"

Isotta said, "No."

Isabella said, "That's Massimo, and, and . . . Giulia?"

Nodding, Isotta said, "On their wedding day." Her face rigid, she watched her mother.

Shrugging, Caterina tossed the phone on the bed. "You wanted a bicycle. Now you've got to ride it."

Isabella gasped, "Mamma!" She clasped Isotta's clammy hand in her own warm one.

Glaring at Caterina, Isotta said, "It doesn't matter."

And she suddenly found that it didn't.

Ava walked out of her father's flower shop and collided with Alessandro, walking with his head up to better examine the liquidity of the sky.

Small pots leapt from her arms to scatter across the cobblestones, fragile stems bent at uncomfortable angles. Ava yelped at the destruction of her baby rosemary and lavender plants strewn across the ground and yelped again to realize the person she'd crashed into was Ale.

He grinned. "*Dobbiamo smettere di incontrarci in questo modo.*"

Ava frowned in confusion.

Ale's eyes searched hers. " 'We have to stop meeting like this?' No? Doesn't translate?"

Ava shook her head before crouching down to scoop dirt back into the little plastic pots. Ale kneeled on the street beside Ava and likewise began brushing the silky earth. Lowering his voice, he said, "Sorry, just trying to be funny, I guess. It's peculiar though—isn't it—that both times we've met have been in this dramatic fashion."

Tucking a lock of wavy chocolate-colored hair that had escaped from her thick ponytail, Ava nodded.

Ale went on, "I'm glad I ran into you." He cleared his throat. "I want to thank you. For your work. Fresh plantings do cheer up the space. Are those for the *castello*, too?" He gestured to the plants in Ava's shallow cardboard box.

Ava stammered, "No. There's a family down the way, the mom mentioned needing some plants in her yard. I'd like to give flowers, but it's the wrong time of year. Do you need more—"

"Oh, no, no. I wasn't hinting. You've already done so much." Ale stood.

Ava stared at the last of the loose bits of earth. Deciding there wasn't enough left to salvage, she rose. Alessandro nudged the pot he'd been filling into the box, his finger brushing against her hands as she nestled the plants more securely. Their eyes met with a jolt, like a latch fitting into place. The edges of Ava's brain droned warnings, but she couldn't break the eye contact. Shouldn't it be uncomfortable? Awkward? She had always been awkward around men.

Ava's mother's voice called from the stairs leading to their apartment above the shop. "Ava! Can you stop by the hardware store and tell your brother—"

Her voice broke off as her daughter flushed pink and stared at her feet. Finally, Ava's mother prodded, "Ava? Who is your friend?"

Ava said, "Oh! Mamma, this is Alessandro Bardi. He owns the *castello*. Alessandro, this is my mother, Savia."

Alessandro stumbled between sticking out his hand and leaning in to press his cheek against the older woman's. Instead he nodded in what he hoped was a friendly enough way to cancel out his possible rudeness. "*Piacere.*" Ava ducked her head.

Savia's expression clouded briefly before it cleared. "Owner of the *castello*, eh? You must have been furious!"

Alessandro grinned. "A bit, yes. But at the same time, I discovered I owned a *castello*, so that was an upside."

Savia's laugh was more of a grunt. "You live in New York City?"

"Yes."

Smiling broadly, Savia asked, "Good job?"

Ale's eyebrows leapt up. "Yes. Finance."

Nodding, Savia pronounced, "That's good to see. So many young people don't believe in the power of solid employment. Certainly in Italy, but I imagine in the United States, too. My son, Fabio, has a good job, not as good as you, maybe, but steady. At the hardware store." She gestured down the road. "Ava here has yet to land a real job."

Ava grumbled, "Mamma..."

Savia smiled indulgently. "Well, she's a big help to my husband and whatnot. Besides, she's sweet, and pretty, and chaste. Everyone loves her at church. Don't they darling?"

"Mamma!"

"What? I want our new friend—Alessandro is it?"

"Ale, yes."

Savia's grin broadened. "Ale, eh? We're at nicknames so soon. Well, I want Ale to get to know us. He must only be here for a little bit?"

Ale answered the question Ava had been longing to ask herself. "A few months at least. Probably much longer."

"Is that right! Even though you have a good job?" Savia frowned as if Ale had tried to swindle her.

"Yes, I got a leave of absence. This will take time to sort. Soon though, I'll have to start working at the Rome office and come here sporadically on weekends to check on progress."

"Your boss is okay with this?"

"My boss is my father-in-law." Ale winced a hair at the word and covered it up with a broad smile. "He's looking forward to Italian vacations, so he's all for my staying to make sure it's perfect."

"Father-in-law?" Savia scowled. "You're married."

Ava busied herself brushing flecks of dirt off the plants in her box.

Nodding, Alessandro said, "Yes. I am." He chanced a glance at Ava, but she studiously avoided his gaze.

Savia stared at Ale, frowning. "Then what's the use of—"

Ava piped up, "Well, then, I'm glad you've all met. Alessandro—"

"Ale, please."

"Ale, I hope you enjoy the rest of the day. Looks like rain later. I need to get these babies to their new home. Mamma, I'll be back for lunch." She pressed her cheek against her mother's and attempted to walk steadily down the road.

Dante winced at the sound of footsteps behind him.

Lowering his hat brim over his eyes, he bolted down a narrow alley, panting at the unaccustomed exercise.

He wasn't scared to run into the *castello* owner, of course. Why would he be? He'd caught sight of the Americans already. Indeed they'd be hard to miss with the Amazon-like woman towering around greeting everybody loudly in her leaden accent, like she was an American soldier doling out chocolate after the Second World War. And the man, Alessandro, striding beside her.

Americans.

He vastly preferred the Australians. He liked them even better than the British, who swanned around, impossible to please, yet acting like they were entitled to everything because their currency was stronger. No, Australians were grateful for everything and didn't feel the need to toss their money and politics around.

He wished the *castello* owner was Australian.

But even so, he wasn't ducking them *exactly*.

True, he wasn't looking forward to meeting the American and having to pretend a level of apology he didn't feel. It wasn't *his* fault the *castello* got burned, after all. Everybody agreed. Simple bad luck, really.

"Dante!"

The mayor looked up, his hand reaching involuntarily to his mouth.

The woman bustled up to him. "Why do I always feel like I'm chasing you?"

"Oh, *buongiorno*, Magda."

"Where's the fire?"

"Fire? There's a fire?" Dante straighten and lifted his nose to sniff the chilly air.

"Sorry, just an expression." Magda snickered.

Did she startle him on purpose? The woman was inscrutable. And so, so tiresome.

He glared at her.

Magda's face grew serious. "I wanted to talk to you about L'Ora Dorata. It looks like Luigi is going to sell it. The restaurant wasn't doing well even before the fire. I always told him he should serve some of the special cherry jam from over the mountain, but he never listened to me. And see? Now, he has to sell the *trattoria*. The only restaurant in Santa Lucia!"

Dante didn't bother masking his eye roll. "Seriously, Magda? You think the restaurant went under because he didn't serve your favorite jam? You don't think it's perhaps because of the fire damage? That wooden roof was completely destroyed, as were the interior beams."

Magda scowled. "I know that. I'm not an idiot. I'm pointing out that it wasn't making money. Luigi tried too hard to appeal to vacationing Romans. Why would Romans come to Santa Lucia for *cacio e pepe* when they can get better at home?"

"Well, he used the local pecorino, which has a more pronounced grassy flavor—"

Magda waved her hand in front of her face as if being accosted by a pernicious moth. "Yes, yes, I know all about your precious pecorino. You'd think Germans have no taste buds, the way you talk."

Dante paused to consider. This was true, he did think Germans had no taste buds. This seemed a fair assessment, given their propensity to ask for beer with their grilled lamb. Plus, they wanted their potatoes on the *same plate* as their meat. Dante shook his head.

Magda leaned forward to get Dante's attention. "*Anyway*, as I was saying. Dante?"

Sighing, Dante said, "Yes. The restaurant."

Magda straightened. "Well! I hear a chef from Modena wants to buy it. But that's a mistake. Since obviously my guests will be the primary customers, my opinion matters, as you know. But you went flying down the street." Forehead wrinkled in thought, Magda went on, "Why the rush?"

"Ah, well, no rush, I thought... I mean, I need to—"

The wrinkles in Magda's forehead deepened. Dante wondered if perhaps she could lodge euros in there. Suddenly Magda smiled broadly. Her face relaxed and she began laughing.

It was Dante's turn to scowl. "What do you find so amusing?"

Magda continued laughing.

Was this another strange German quirk?

Magda gasped out, "You... are... running... from... *Alessandro Bardi*!"

Dante recoiled. "What? I most certainly am not."

"You most certainly are." Magda steadied her breath. "I know you haven't met with him yet, and here you are bolting at footsteps. You are avoiding him! Like a child escaping a spanking."

"That is preposterous. I'm a grown man, Magda. And the mayor, might I remind you. Compose yourself."

Shaking her head, Magda continued to chuckle. "Things have not been smooth for you for some time."

Was this an oblique reference to his wife running off with the town handyman? The German was just uncouth enough to hint at the thing that everyone else was sensible enough to avoid discussing. In his presence, anyway. He felt relatively sure that Bar Birbo was ringing with gossip.

He had taken to making his own *caffè*.

It had nothing to do with Alessandro Bardi hanging around the bar like it was the scene of one of those American movies with people lingering over their coffee, having, what was it? Oh, yes—*brunch*.

Magda went on, speaking insistently now. "The fire *wasn't* your fault, Dante. It wasn't. So push that out of your mind. Shove it away. Tell Alessandro that abandoned property must be managed by the town, and a town can do what it sees fit. It was an eyesore and a danger besides."

Dante realized this was good advice. Why had no one else said this? It was true, the *castello* was in ruins even before the fire. The way the upper turret crumbled and the roof tiles lay askew like a demented smile. "You think that will work?"

"Of course! It might not be true, but he's not Italian. What will he know? Tell him that's how it's done and it's too bad about the fire, but accidents happen."

Nodding in thought, Dante said, "That could work..."

"*Come no!*" Magda repeated. A smile tugged her lip up again. "But do stop running. You can't outrun your problems. Everybody knows that."

In nearby Girona, Madison peered at her husband over the top of her restaurant menu. "Can you even believe it?"

"Believe what?"

"That we're here."

Alessandro smiled and leaned back in his chair. "I can't, actually."

Madison put her menu down. "You have a castle, Ale. A *castle*. Sure, it needs a lot of work. Like, a lot. But still. It hardly feels real."

Putting his menu besides his wife's, Alessandro warmed. "I know! Before we got here, I thought owning a castle would be lavishly exciting, like House Hunters International but way, way cooler. But now, I keep thinking about how my ancestors *walked* there. In that falling down castle, people lived and thought and dreamed and maybe even schemed, and they wore clothes like the Medici... my *relations*. These are my *roots*."

Madison rolled her eyes, but Ale didn't notice. His monologue continued. "Like... those olive trees all around the castle? The unburned ones,

I suppose . . . they produced olive oil that my great-great grandparents driz-zled on their meat. *That same oil.* I've never thought about it before. I can't wait to buy a bottle. We should bring some back for—"

"You lost me." Madison said. "Who cares what it was like before? Or who lived there or whatever? We'll fix it up and have parties and our friends can fly over, and those villagers who don't even know what a mocha is won't believe their eyes at all the American style. Plus, they'll love our dollars." Her voice dropped to a whisper. "The town is so *poor.*"

Alessandro reached for his menu.

Widening her eyes, Madison asked, "What?"

"Nothing. Do you know what you want?"

"No. I can't read this menu. Order me something with chicken."

"You don't want the pasta with *porcini* mushrooms like we had last night?"

Madison pulled a face. "So many carbs!"

Sighing, Alessandro scanned the menu. Meanwhile, Madison stood. "I'm going to the ladies. See if *this* place has low-cal ranch, would you?" She walked away, with the stride of someone used to having men, and some-times women, watch her backside sway.

Alessandro closed his eyes and concentrated on controlling his annoy-ance. Madison was fun and dynamic, with an energy that drew people to her. It's why he fell for her in the first place. It wasn't her fault that here, on Italian soil, she, well . . . she fell flat.

He flagged the waiter and ordered himself grilled lamb and Madison braised rooster—hoping she'd assume it was regular chicken—as well as a carafe of house wine. The waiter walked away before Alessandro realized that he should have ordered a bottle of wine so Madison could text her father a photo. Ale sighed. Maybe he'd tell her that he ordered a carafe on purpose, a kind of "guess the wine" game. It was the kind of detail that her father would find charming. Steve would slap him on the back and guffaw about his son-in-law turning Madison into an Italian wine snob. His eyes, though, would shine with pride.

Ale's jaw tightened. He did not want to think about Madison's father right now. For the past few years he had felt a niggling worry that working for Steve had been a huge mistake. He'd successfully pushed the concerns away—after all, the work funded what was generally regarded as a fabulous lifestyle. Only now, sitting in the shadow of a mountain where his castle perched, did he give space to his thoughts. Was it fabulous, really, his life? It was exciting, sure, but the past few days he'd been surprised by the patina of emptiness that tinged his flashing memories of New York. At this table now, alone, surrounded by people speaking his first language, and tucking into dishes that smelled like his *nonna's*, he realized the impossibility of his situation.

One of those postcard memories sailed across his mind—the image of his father-in-law punching his arm and saying, "Hey, *paesano*, looks like you'll be working late tonight to finish this, but that will allow you to keep my daughter in luxury. Win win, eh?" Steve snorted and walked away.

Waiting for Madison to emerge from the bathroom, Alessandro wondered if the two wins belonged to Steve and Madison. Working until the cabs slowed their course through the Manhattan streets hardly seemed like winning.

At least right now it didn't. Not when there was a *castello* to explore and people to meet.

He wondered if he'd see Ava tomorrow.

Icy drizzle coated the streets of Florence. Isotta peered out the window, evaluating the cold. Nodding to herself, she decided to borrow Ilaria's sweater, still draped over the couch.

"Where are you going?" Her mother demanded from her chair in front of the TV.

"Out."

Caterina grumbled, "Acting like she's single, parading herself around."

"I can hear you."

"Good."

Caterina watched Isotta rustle through the closet, rifling through hats until she pulled out her favorite, the one with the small moth hole below the felted blue bow. Caterina's voice followed her daughter into the closet. "I suppose you don't care that all the neighbors are talking about you?"

"Not really, no."

"So you get pleasure out of bringing shame on this family."

Isotta stopped and thought for a moment. "I do actually. Now that you mention it."

Caterina almost shouted, "What are you saying! Are you delirious now?" She began muttering to herself, "Though that would explain a lot. She's having an attack of crazy. Zio Leo had one. Maybe that's her problem."

Isotta steadied herself in front of the mirror, cocking the hat over her eye. "I have no idea what you're talking about."

Caterina leaned forward. "And your father always called you the smart one. Pssh!" She settled back in her chair.

Isotta's hands drifted from the brim of her hat. Had he called her that? Her mother had always been so critical of her, she never really thought that her father might feel differently. She suddenly remembered the way he patted her on the shoulder after her mother ridiculed her newest haircut or outfit for the day. She had assumed both of them resented her being born the fifth of five girls, especially after all the miscarriages. But her father . . . maybe to him she had never been a disappointment. It was true he had been the only member of the family to show up when she'd been honored with a scholastic award in high school. At the time, she hadn't paid attention, her head too full of her mother's words about how reading never attracted a man. But *he* had *been* there.

Looking back in the mirror, she reminded herself not to let her mother upset her. Her blood pressure needed to be nice and easy at her appointment. She focused on deep breaths in and out, like the websites said. Of course, the ultimate stress reducer would be moving out of this house, but she had yet to figure out how to make that work financially.

Reaching for the remote, Caterina jeered at her daughter. "I guess you think with all those smarts you are too good to keep his bed warm?'

Isotta shook her head and smiled sadly. "*Senza peli sulla lingua.* Your opinions still roll straight from your brain out your mouth without the benefit of thought."

"You can't talk to me that way!"

Isotta pulled her purse up over her shoulder and checked to make sure she had her wallet. "I believe I just did. Okay, Mamma, I'll see you later. I'm off to prance around the marketplace. I'll keep an eye out for your friends. Give them a big wink for you."

Isotta flew out the door and closed it behind her. Leaning against the ancient wood that muted her mother's howls of indignation, she caught her breath.

What in the world had gotten into her?

She didn't know, but she liked it.

Eventually of course, she would have to tell her family about the pregnancy. But right now, she enjoyed keeping the secret, just her and the baby. Nobody noticed that she wasn't drinking wine with dinner or that she declined the family lunch staple of *lampredotto*, tripe sandwiches.

She would closely guard the secret a little longer. At least until she made sure that the baby was okay. Her dreams had been alarming lately, filled with images of babies made of Florentine leather or twisted olive leaves. Babies made of vapor that congealed into a cackling miniature Giulia tearing at her womb. She knew that the dreams meant nothing, but she wanted to make sure.

Patrizia shook her head. "So Stella really did come back? And I was one of the ones who doubted she would."

Chiara took out a new carton of milk and poured it into the metal pitcher. She set the pitcher under the steamer for a few moments, letting the air bubbles ring through the milk. After the milk foamed, she tapped the pitcher on the counter and tipped froth into each of two waiting cups of *espresso*. She set one *cappuccino* in front of Patrizia and the other in front of herself, in a gesture borne of years of the two of them sharing a *caffè* together when both bar and butcher shop were empty.

Patrizia offered her a sugar, but Chiara refused. Her stomach was nervous lately.

Chiara sipped her *cappuccino* before saying, "It was stressful. I was glad to see her, but the whole time, I kept waiting for Dante to burst in."

Patrizia stirred her *cappuccino* thoughtfully and ventured, "Dante doesn't seem in a bursting mood lately."

Brushing her chestnut bangs off her forehead, Chiara said, "I noticed the same. Looks like the wind has been knocked out of that man. Yesterday Magda started arguing with him about something, what was it? Oh! New benches in the *piazza*. You know how normally Dante wouldn't let anyone tell him anything? This time he nodded and said Magda was probably right."

Patrizia said, "Oh, no. Magda must have gotten such a swollen head."

"She looked more shocked than smug, to be honest." Chiara put down her *cappuccino*. "And Fabrizio said when he went to Dante's, his sink was leaking."

Patrizia frowned. "I don't—"

Chiara shook her head with a smile. "I didn't get it either. But Fabrizio believes that Dante won't even call a handyman."

"Even though Vale—"

"Even though Vale left. Fabrizio tightened what needed to be tightened. But he said he felt so bad for Dante."

A short silence followed, until Patrizia said, "But Dante didn't come in when Stella was here?"

Chiara said, "No. Everyone else seemed to find an excuse to get a *caffè* that day. Even Fabio, and you know he hasn't been in here since before the fire."

Patrizia straightened her shoulders and huffed, "As well he shouldn't! After what he said about Edo!"

Chiara said, "I'm glad I wasn't there for that. Accusing both gay people and immigrants in one fell swoop for a fire started by the wind."

"It was awful. I never would have thought it of him."

Chiara cocked her head to the side, her spoon in her mouth like a lollipop. "Really?"

"He's said things like that before?"

"Not exactly. He's perfectly nice to his customers, but . . . I don't know how to explain it. It seems like it's important for him to be right all the time."

Dropping her chin on her hand, Patrizia mused, "I see that. And remember that time when he was sure someone had broken into his shop? He was so angry, yelling, blaming everyone." Patrizia started to giggle.

Chiara followed suit, and soon the two of them were laughing so hard the rest of the story came out in bits . . .

"And it turned out—"

"He'd left the door unlocked!"

Patrizia held her side. "And Carosello had gotten in—"

"And had a party with the trash bag!"

The two women broke into peals of laughter.

Chiara wiped her eyes, still giggling. "Anyway, Fabio came in with Ava, pretended everything was fine, frowned at Stella for awhile, muttered things I tried not to hear, and then left."

"Ava? Oh, right. I always forget he's her brother."

"I suspect Ava would like to forget that herself. When they were here, he made this offhand remark about how he needed a drink to tolerate being seen with his horse-faced sister."

"What? *Ava*? But she's lovely and he . . . well . . ."

"Yes, you would think the acne scars would have faded by now."

"What did Ava say?"

"What could she say? She got red. Rosetta tried to chide him like he was still in school, but he said how sad it was when people can't take jokes."

"Oh. You know, I have heard him say that before."

"When everyone knows that jokes are funny, and what he says—"

"Not at all funny." Patrizia took a sip of her *cappuccino*. "And Stella? What happened with her?"

"People greeted her, but it was uncomfortable."

Patrizia sipped her *cappuccino*. "I wish I'd been here. I wanted to see her."

"No, you don't. She refused to acknowledge what happened. Acted like her moving in with her daughter's family was a big favor for them."

Patrizia said, "I remember looking up to her when we were girls in school."

Chiara shrugged, turning to put her cup in the sink.

Patrizia said, "Could you forgive her?"

Chiara thought about it. "What's there to forgive? She didn't cheat on me. She needed love and wasn't getting it from Dante. Who am I to judge? It's more that she won't let me *in* anymore. Obviously, she was prickly about the affair when it was happening, but there's no longer anything to protect."

"Except herself."

"Ah, true." Chiara smiled at Patrizia, and then looked up as Giovanni, who owned the *alimentari* on the *piazza*, entered.

Chiara smiled. "*Ciao*, Giovanni, *come va*? You're not open yet?"

Giovanni put his coat on the rack and shivered. "Papà is opening today. I need to pick up supplies. *Caffè, per favore*."

Chiara nodded, and one by one more townspeople came in from the cold, stamping their feet and hanging their coats until the coatrack resembled a black and grey tree with technicolor blooms of pink and purple. Patrizia stayed long past the point that the *cappuccino* bubbles clinging to the sides of her cup stiffened and collapsed. Giovanni had some particularly good jokes today, and she was his most rapt audience.

Laughter rebounded off Bar Birbo's walls, along with conversations about the fire, about the new road to the coast, about the rumors of the *castello* renovation.

Until the door burst open, sending a blast of alpine air into the bar. Conversation stopped, as all heads turned. Luciano stood in the open door, his hair in disarray and his eyes wild.

Chiara was not the only one whose heart squeezed and plummeted in the sudden fear for Luciano's sobriety.

But then he smiled. A triumphant, deliberate smile. Clasping his hands in front of his chest he breathed, "She's awake."

A boom of cheering followed him out of the bar, as he hurried down the street to tell Elisa.

Alessandro stepped into his car with a smile. How nice to have time alone. When Madison had asked to stay in Girona for a massage and facial at the hotel spa rather than joining him in Santa Lucia, he had struggled to tamp down his enthusiasm. Instead, he had nodded and said that a self-care day sounded like far more fun than another fruitless trip, as he again tried to locate the mayor.

Despite Santa Lucia's tiny size, somehow he kept missing the man every time he stepped into the *palazzo comunale*. He got the distinct impression that the mayor was avoiding him. Last time, when the secretary had stared at her desk while informing Ale that the mayor had been called for an emergency, Ale felt sure he saw a bit of sports coat sticking out from the closet. And really, how many emergencies could one town have? Particularly a town closed to traffic?

He knew he should be annoyed for being blown off, but he didn't have it in him. Madison, though, practically stamped her foot at being stood up. In New York, he felt the same way if he was made to wait even two minutes for an Uber, or a call to the super didn't produce a repairman within the hour. Didn't they know that every minute he waited meant a loss of time he could be using to make money or network?

But now he found the whole situation comical. Besides, as much as he'd once relished the image of going head-to-head with the mayor of this backwater town, now it just felt like a bother. What he really wanted was for the mayor to tell him the history of the *castello*, and for someone to walk with him through the groves and point out the oldest olive trees. He wanted to ponder and dream with someone, to consider the history of place and people.

Alessandro shook his head as he started the engine of his sleek rental car. He wasn't thinking clearly. Probably still digesting last night's meal. He'd gone to a *trattoria* alone because Madison had insisted on staying in and watching "Sex and the City" with a room service turkey burger, no bun. It had been the first time Ale had realized the advantages of staying at a hotel geared toward American clientele. Madison's shining eyes when he arrived home, full and happy from his meal of gnocchi made from local red potatoes with a truffled cheese sauce, told him she, too, had been satisfied with her evening. She had been tender with him in a way she hadn't since they arrived in Italy. Maybe this transition rattled her more than he knew.

She would get used it. Give her a completed castle and she would be right as rain, no doubt. Besides, it was too pretty a day to worry.

The drive to his ancestral home pleased him. He liked to imagine it felt more familiar than a town should after walking its lanes for a week or so. There was a sense of tug, a thread of connection, that hooked around his sternum, pulling him up the hill and into the parking lot. The crisp sound of the car door closing rang into the still air.

He'd been in quiet places before, of course, but this quiet was different. It wasn't the absence of sound. Rather, the air hung expectantly.

Ale smiled to himself. If he wasn't careful, he'd turn into a poet like his friend Chase, peppered his twitter feed with haikus. It had been amusing at first, but had grown dull and predictable, and everyone was tired of pretending to be awed by Chase's ability to count syllables. Chase himself swore that without his discovery of his poetic soul, he never would have met his wife, Kendra. Kendra, who so embraced the artist persona that she regularly appeared at restaurant openings in cocktail attire studded with paint flecks. As if she couldn't leave their Chelsea loft without adding a few final touches to her painting. Which also made Chase and Kendra routinely late. This would be forgivable in some couples, but their apologies rang as opportunities to brag about how Chase had been on the phone with Japanese investors and Kendra had been dancing with the muse.

What was wrong with him? He loved his friends, why was he suddenly annoyed with them from thousands of miles away? They had been nothing but supportive of him and Madison leaving their social scene for months to repair and renovate the castle. Kendra had even offered to give them any one of the small paintings that hadn't sold at her last co-op showing. Madison's mouth had drawn into a rapturous "o", which even at the time Ale had found amusing since at Kendra's previous exhibit, Madison had had a few too many lemongrass daiquiris and loudly whispered to Ale that all Kendra's paintings looked like clown explosions.

Now that he was here, it was abundantly clear that no painting of Kendra's belonged on the stone walls of the castle. He'd figure out a way to refuse. Or, worse case scenario, he'd hang it when his friends came to visit, as they planned for the summer holidays.

There was no way, of course, that the *castello* would be party-location ready by that point. He realized that now. But he hoped that a productive conversation with the town's governing body would grease the wheels to get the permits needed and architects hired to get the ball rolling.

If only he could find the mayor.

"*Buongiorno, Marcè!*" Chiara called as Marcello entered the bar. "*Auguri!*"

Marcello beamed and stepped to the counter. "*Grazie*, Chiara. *Cappuccino, per favore*. You are so good with birthdays."

Chiara only smiled. No use telling the young man that his birth forced his mother to miss Chiara's wedding. Each year, Chiara tried to avoid the sinking memory of her marriage by honoring the good that came that day. Namely, Marcello. Drawn upright now, with his shoulders back, neat and handsome in his police officer's uniform.

As Chiara waited for the last of the *espresso* drops to fall into the cup, she spoke to Marcello over her shoulder. "I saw your mother the other day. She's looking well."

Marcello sighed and leaned on the bar. "Oh, yes. She's full of energy. Hard to remember now that she was in the hospital for the *festa*."

The shrill sound of foaming milk prevented Chiara from responding, but as she poured the milk into the *espresso* she said, "You don't sound pleased."

Sighing again, Marcello said, "Well, I'm obviously happy she's recovering and feeling good. I want her to be well. Obviously," Marcello repeated inanely.

"But?" Chiara prompted.

Exasperated, Marcello sputtered, "But she won't get off my back! All the time it's 'When will I have a grandchild?' and 'Oh, my heart has a cramp, I'll probably die without holding a grandchild in my arms.' I mean, really! Now I get why my sister had to move so far away!"

Chiara frowned. "Grandchild? Do you have a *fidanzata*?"

"No! I mean, I date once in a while, but I haven't had a steady girl-friend for a couple of years. It's hard when my mother keeps sizing up my dates' hips."

Chiara threw her head back, laughing. "You're joking."

A smile playing over his face, Marcello said, "Maybe a little bit." He drew out a sugar packet and shook it. "But all her badgering makes me feel like I'm supposed to be on the hunt for a wife. I'm young. Can't I have a good time?"

Chiara nodded and took out a towel to begin buffing the bar. "She wants to see you happy."

Frowning, Marcello thought for a moment and said, "No, she wants to see herself happy, like it's my job to give that to her."

Remembering how Laura used to wipe Marcello's nose before it ran, Chiara asked, "How is your sister? I didn't see her when she was here."

"She didn't stay long. Just enough to help out when mamma got out of the hospital. But you were right, when you said mamma treats my sister differently. Mamma wasn't home a day before she ignored all the work Alicia did to look after her and instead went to pieces with gratitude when I brought home a newspaper."

"*Uffa*. Hard on Alicia."

Marcello blew on a spoonful of *cappuccino* before answering, "It was. It is." He sipped for a moment and added, "Alicia and I talked about it, though. That was good. I'm not angry with her anymore."

"But you are angry with your mother."

Marcello put down his spoon. "I guess so."

Chiara folded the towel and watched through Bar Birbo's window as Alessandro and Madison started walking down from the *castello*. She need to wrap up the conversation before it was interrupted. "I hope you forgive your mother. You know, I wouldn't even have this bar if it wasn't for my parents being overinvolved. So, sometimes it's a blessing."

"Your parents gave it to you? This whole place?" Marcello looked around as if seeing Bar Birbo of the first time.

"Pretty much. They wanted to give it to me outright, but they had helped us buy our apartment, so I convinced them that there's a law that at least a thousand euros needs to change hands for a property to transfer. It was stupid, I think they only believed me because they needed that little bit of money. They moved into our house, and we moved here."

"I didn't know you had a house in Santa Lucia."

Chiara shrugged. "I let the church use it after my parents passed. Anyway," Chiara's words sped up as Alessandro and Madison reached for the door handle. "I know it's hard that your mamma is so demanding. But it comes from loving you so much."

Marcello looked over his shoulder as the door opened. "I know." He reached into his pocket.

Chiara reminded Marcello softly, "Hey, birthday *cappuccino* on me. Like always."

"Thank you, Chiara." Marcello straightened and smiled. "Like always."

Phone ringing in her pocket, Isotta desperately searched for an empty alley to duck into. Too many tourists. Finally! There by the garbage cans, and without the charming stone streets and arresting building facades that compelled tourists like homing beacons.

She clicked on her phone on what must have been the final ring.

"*Pronto?*"

"Isotta?"

"Yes."

"It's Massimo."

"I know."

"Then why did you say '*pronto*'?"

"Force of habit."

"Oh."

Isotta looked up as a group of people passed the alley. They kept walking, and she retreated farther toward the overflowing trash bins. Was there a strike? Why did she have so much time to ponder this stupid question? Did Massimo hang up? Why was he so quiet?

"Massimo?"

"Yes. I'm sorry, I've called so many times and you never pick up, I forgot what I wanted to say."

Isotta gritted her teeth. "Suits me. Goodbye."

"Wait! Hold on! Just give me a second."

Isotta sighed. "I don't know what you could possibly have to say."

"I miss you."

"Seriously? You're leading with that?"

"I do! It's true—"

"We both know who you miss is Giulia."

"No."

"No?"

"No. I loved Giulia. I did. But she's gone."

"I'm glad you finally get that at least."

"I don't know what I was thinking. It's like I was trapped on a cloudy mountain, and couldn't see my way off. I know what it must seem like to you, Isotta, but you need to listen to me."

"I do? I *need* to listen to you?"

"No...yes. Oh, Madonna, I'm back on that mountain. Yes, you don't owe me anything, Isotta, you don't. I just mean...please. Please. Hear me out. Five minutes."

Isotta scanned the empty alley. A stray cat, with fur silkier and sides rounder than any stray had a right to be, slunk around the side of the garbage bin. It glared at Isotta. She switched hands holding the phone, and the cat started at the sudden gesture. It realized she wasn't threatening, and it began to nose around the base of the can. Isotta sighed. "Okay. Five minutes. But you can't order me around." She hated how her voice whined at the end.

"Okay, yes. I know it seems like I used you. To fill a hole. And maybe it's true that my intentions weren't . . . honorable. When we met. But you remember the heat between us, Isotta."

She did. Unfortunately. It would be easier to forget.

"This isn't an insult, so don't take it as one, but you haven't been with anyone else, so you don't know. That charge between us? That passion? That's not usual. That means something. Or at least it did to me."

Before she could stop herself, Isotta said, "To me, too."

Massimo drew in a shaking breath. "Oh, God. You have no idea how glad it makes me to hear you say that. I miss you, Isotta. I miss how you feel against me. I miss the scent of your neck."

Isotta ran her hand over her forehead. "Okay, so you miss sex, Massimo. I get it."

Massimo whistled. "That's not what I mean, Isotta. Since when were you so brash?"

Isotta placed a knowing hand over her belly. "Hanging up now."

"No! I'm not saying it's bad. I like this fire in you. I mean it, I'm smiling right now. I knew you had it in you, I always saw it in your eyes."

Did he? Was that possible?

"Isotta, that's what I mean. It's *you* I miss. I miss how you'd curl up with your books and your bare feet. I miss your laugh. I miss hearing you talk about the animals you would see on your walks." Isotta glanced at the cat who had found a bit of what looked like intestine and was holding it down with a paw while it yanked at it with its teeth. The intestine ripped, sending the cat somersaulting. It immediately sat up and began grooming itself like nothing had happened.

Massimo whispered now, "I do miss sex with you, Isotta. It was like nothing else I've ever—well, it was incredible. But I miss it because of our connection. I miss *you*. I'll never stop being sorry for what I did to you. For what I put you through. It was wrong."

Isotta closed her eyes and focused on breathing. "How do I know this is not just pretty words?"

"Come home. Come home, and I'll show you."

Chiara turned the key in the lock with a sigh of relief. She turned against the door, closed now to Santa Lucia, and leaned against it.

It had been a long day.

Fabrizio's clandestine texting had increased. He spent more and more time turned away from her, typing. When he turned back, a gulf lay between them. All day, her thoughts bounced like summer hail on the terra-cotta rooftops, unable to land on any explanation. She couldn't help but wonder if perhaps her telling him about seeking a divorce had something to do with it. He certainly hadn't responded with the slow smile she had expected. In fact, he had changed the subject, telling her about his conversation with Alessandro Bardi about Italian food in New York. The whole situation left her off-kilter, an unusual state for Chiara. And an exhausting one.

There had been that one moment tonight when Fabrizio had leaned across the counter and touched her elbow to get her attention before saying, "Listen, Chiara, there's something—"

But right then Fabio walked in. Ever since the fire, Fabio's mere presence chilled a room. Nobody could forget the accusations he'd made about the fire. Tonight Fabio was pleasant enough at first, cracking jokes that weren't particularly funny but at least weren't downright insulting. But when people didn't laugh loudly enough, he had grumbled. And then complained about how mistreated he was. That everyone was against him because he'd stated the truth about how immigrants led to jacked up criminal activity.

When Magda had bristled and pointed out that his words were weapons, he'd grumbled that of course "Germans would silence the opposition."

The bar had gone quiet. Seeing the discomfort on Edo's face, Chiara had almost asked Fabio to leave. But just then, he'd thrown down his *cornetto*-crumb-strewn napkin and declared that the immigrants were responsible for this divide in their town, and he for one had had enough of it. He'd stalked out the bar, leaving only the sound of heartbeats in his wake.

Immediately afterwards, Fabrizio left, saying he had a phone call with his editor. He'd walked out without a kiss, or even a stroke of her hand.

Maybe he was stressed about work. That's what he kept saying, after all. But why did that ring hollow?

Edo sank into a chair.

Chiara said, "Hungry, Edo? I don't think you took a dinner break."

"No. I mean, I didn't take a break, but I'm not hungry."

Chiara nodded.

"I haven't told my parents yet. If that's what you're wondering."

"It's not."

"I'm going to tell them this weekend. Sunday."

"Okay." Chiara noticed the sharp lurch of her belly and wondered if it was in empathy with Edo's upcoming difficult conversation, or for herself, as she would undoubtedly get an earful about what happened to her brother's son while on her watch. "Will you tell them about Trevor?"

Edo leaned forward and pressed his hands against his eyes. "I don't think there's much to tell."

Chiara dragged a chair to sit beside Edo and placed a hand on his shoulder. "Edo?"

"It was silly, right, Zia? I mean, he lives in England, which might as well be the other end of the world."

Chiara said, "Did something happen?"

Edo said, "Maybe."

Chiara said nothing.

Edo went on, "We never said we were exclusive. My God, we were only together a few days, we didn't even—" Edo shot a look at his aunt, who looked at her hands now clasped in her lap. He coughed. "We didn't even get to know each other very well. Trying to build a relationship on the back of a three-day interlude was probably a mistake."

Chiara listened, blankly watching as Carosello trotted down Via Romana on one of his endless errands.

Edo said, "I guess I've been ghosted."

This got her attention. "What do you mean?"

Edo offered a wry smile. "Ghosted? You know. He faded out. Stopped calling and texting."

"Maybe he's working hard—"

"His social media feed would suggest otherwise."

Chiara said, "I'm sorry."

Edo stood up. "Not your fault."

"I didn't mean—"

"No, I know. But it's okay. After all, now I'll be available for all those studly guys that pilgrimage through Santa Lucia."

Chiara couldn't avoid the bitterness in her nephew's words. "It'll get better."

Edo examined his hands splayed out on the counter. "But will it? That seems a poor bet."

Chiara's eyes drifted to the Madonna in her niche across the road. She offered up a prayer, a hope, that her beautiful nephew would find love. She allowed Mary's loving eyes to cut through the cluttering doubts. She had to believe the improbable was possible.

"Luciano? It's Isotta."

"Isotta!"

Isotta smiled at the warmth in his voice. Suddenly, she no longer felt alone on an island. She pictured Luciano standing beside his telephone table, surrounded by the clutter of things he could never get rid of, with his cat making figure eights around his legs.

Nothing would change.

Isotta hadn't realized it until this moment, but she'd been harboring fear that Luciano would start drinking again and neglect his bills. His clear voice (and the fact that the phone line still worked) relieved an unseen weight. She counted on the safety of being able to call him. Especially now, when she finally wanted to share the news of her healthy pregnancy. After all the care he had taken of her, he would be happy to hear that a new life had been created from all the mess and chaos. Of everybody, he would be the one person to get that.

"Isotta?"

"I'm here, sorry. Just got distracted." It seemed to be happening more and more. She needed to look up if this was a side effect of pregnancy.

"How are you, *cara*?"

"I'm okay. I've been better. But I'm okay. You?"

A sigh from the other end of the phone line.

"*Cara*, to be honest. I'm not well."

Her heartbeat seemed to stall in her chest. All in a breath she asked, "What is it? What's wrong?"

"Oh, I don't want to worry you. I have no doubt that it's nothing untoward. Only a lingering tiredness."

Was he drinking?

"I'm not drinking."

"I wasn't—"

"Yes, you were. Of course you were. And you were right to wonder. But I haven't had anything to drink since before the fire. I can't. Knowing Fatima—"

"How is she?"

"I have yet to see her myself. The family wants to keep her environment as calm and predictable as possible. No visitors."

"I'm sorry. I know how hard it must be for you not to see her."

"It is. Undoubtedly. But a certain amount of possessiveness over her waking hours is to be expected. They thought they lost their child." Luciano sighed.

"Are you sleeping okay? Or maybe you are getting the flu."

Isotta could practically hear Luciano shaking his head. "Ever the worrier, *cara*. No need to concern yourself. I'm more than seventy years old. My life force is weakening. It's to be expected."

A clutch of fear squeezed Isotta's ribcage. "Don't talk like that."

Luciano chuckled softly and then his voice got more distant before resuming its regular volume. "I'm not going anywhere, *cara*. So"—Luciano redirected the conversation—"have you talked to Massimo?"

"A little."

"*Allora*, he is an altered creature. He appears diminished within his elegant suits. Anna, on the other hand, crows like a rooster at first light."

"About what?"

"Who knows? She is celebrating some triumph with a great deal of self-congratulatory preening."

"Probably that she has Massimo all to herself again. She never liked me."

"It wasn't you, *cara*. I'm afraid no woman will ever be good enough for her son."

Isotta hesitated. "And Margherita? Have you seen her?"

A pause. "Yes."

"How is she?"

Luciano thought for a moment. "When I saw her she was throwing a tantrum about leaving the park, so not at her best."

"A tantrum? Like with yelling? Screaming?" Isotta frowned. "That's not like her." Isotta's hand fluttered to her belly. She'd always felt a kinship with her stepdaughter, and now it occurred to her she had an actual biological cord to connect her to the child.

Luciano said, "It's the age, *cara*. It's not atypical. She's also talking in earnest now, it seems."

Isotta couldn't listen to anymore. Instead she said, "Are you taking care of yourself? Eating well?"

"Yes, I'm going to the store almost every day, and Patrizia brings me a few odds and ends from the butcher shop."

"How is she?"

"Very well. Yesterday I didn't have much energy for a visit, so the two of us watched a very amusing television program. I can't remember the name of it. I'll have to ask her. I'd like to see it again."

Luciano watching TV?

"And Degas?"

"Oh, as feckless as ever. Aren't you? Aren't you, Degas?" Luciano's voice drifted from the phone, and Isotta smiled to hear the cat meowing in response.

"Okay, well, I hope you feel better."

"Thank *you*, *cara*. I'm sure I will."

"Maybe when you can see Fatima."

"This is what I am thinking as well."

Isotta had a fleeting thought—should she tell him?

No, the man had enough to deal with. And she couldn't be sure that the news wouldn't be too much.

"Okay, *ciao*, Luciano. *Alla prossima volta*."

"*Ciao, ciao, ciao*."

The phone clicked off.

"*Buongiorno*, Chiara, Edo," said Fabrizio as he entered the bar.

Edo nodded before ducking his head to glance at Chiara. She was so quiet lately. Edo sighed and prepped Fabrizio's *caffè* as Chiara leaned over the bar to accept the kiss that Fabrizio dropped onto her cheek. With lowered lashes she asked if he wanted anything to eat.

"No, I thank you. Just the *caffè*. *Grazie*, Edo," He nodded at Edo before taking his *caffè* to the table and extracting his paper from under his arm and setting it beside his phone on the table. Chiara hesitated, lingering at the end of the counter. Edo bumped her hip with his own to prompt her to sit with Fabrizio, but Bea entered the bar, with a boisterous "*buongiorno!*" Bea nodded at Fabrizio, and he responded by lifting his cup and nodding debonairly.

Dragging a stool over to her favorite spot at the bar, Bea heaved her considerable girth onto the seat before brushing the iron-colored hair out of her eyes. "The usual, Chiara." She sighed dramatically. "I have eggs for you. Not many, what with the cold and the smoke. And Carosello sniffing around, scaring my hens."

Chiara set the *caffè* in front of her.

Bea raised her voice to catch Fabrizio's attention. "There should be enough to make your pistachio yogurt cake."

On cue, Fabrizio looked up from his paper with a grin. "An inspired notion! Chiara, you heard Bea. After my *caffè*, I'll pick up pistachios. I believe we used the last of them."

Bea said, "Fabrizio, you have to get that recipe for me. I've asked for it and Chiara gives me *a* recipe, but it can't be the proper one. Mine never comes out half so good."

Fabrizio beamed at Chiara. "She doesn't use one. She tosses ingredients in a bowl while she sings. That must be the magic."

Bea laughed. "Must be. I'm usually too busy scolding a grandchild away from the oven or a cat off the table to sing."

Chiara tried to soak up Fabrizio's words, but it was hard to lean into their warmth when lately his rushes of affection were so often followed by chilly patches.

Edo said, "Hey, Bea, did you hear the *castello* owner came back?"

Bea said, "Yes! What's he like?"

Chiara propped her chin on her hand and thought. "A nice man. Speaks Italian, but like out of a book. I thought he'd be angry with us for the festival and the fire. The way he talked about it, I think he was at first, but now he doesn't seem to mind. Which is very generous." She hesitated.

Bea poked Chiara's arm. "*Ma dai*, spill it! What else?"

Chiara bit her lip and said, "Well, his wife is . . ."

"Italian?"

"God, no!"

Bea's smile widened until she cackled. "Say no more, Chiara, say no more."

She swiveled off her stool and reached into the pocket of her coat for a handful of change, dropping it one coin at a time into the scuffed copper dish. "Well, I'll see you later—"

Patrizia opened the door, but before she had greeted her neighbors, her attention caught and she stepped back, staring down the street. Her hand went to her chest and then she lunged forward and yanked the door open. "Luciano! In the *piazza*! Something's wrong!" She raced down the street. Bea tripped in her haste to follow Patrizia, so Edo beat her to the door, pulling it wide for Bea to exit before they bolted down Via Romana.

Chiara paled. "Luciano," she whispered. Drinking again? Causing a scene? She couldn't catch her breath.

Fabrizio bolted up and knocked on the bar to get her attention. "Chiara! It's okay! I'll help. Stay put, it will be okay," he repeated before sprinting out the door.

In the still air of the bar, Chiara felt more than heard the subtle buzzing of a phone.

Fabrizio's phone.

Dare she?

Now, when she should be murmuring prayers?

The phone buzzed again.

Before she could talk herself out of it, Chiara stepped out from behind the bar, and in two strides was at the little round table. She flipped the phone over. The message was from "Francy" followed by a heart. Francy? Instantly, Chiara summoned an image of a thin woman with long and lustrous hair, high cheekbones, and full lips. The message read, "When are you coming home? The house is so empty and I'm tired of making my own coffee." It was followed by a praying hands emoji and a smiling emoji and finally a sparkle of hearts.

Chiara flipped the phone to its resting position. She stumbled back to the bar and thrust her hands into the sink, running the cold water over her fingers without noticing. The door opened and she turned.

Fabrizio and Edo walked in, deep in conversation, which stalled when they saw Chiara, white faced. Fabrizio rushed to her. "It's okay! It's okay, Chiara! He just stumbled and fell. I think he hadn't eaten this morning. Patrizia is getting him a *panino*."

Chiara looked up at Edo, her eyes willing him to answer her unspoken question.

Edo nodded and said. "He's not drunk, doesn't seem to have been drinking. He was totally himself, just embarrassed. Hurt his hand breaking his fall, but he's really okay."

Chiara removed her hand from Fabrizio's and ducked her head against her nephew's shoulder.

"*Buongiorno*, Edo."

"*Buongiorno*, Ava!" Edo smiled as Ava entered Bar Birbo. "*Tutto bene?*"

Ava thought. Was everything okay? She supposed so. Nothing was wrong. Nothing was different. Nothing was changing. "*Sì*. Fine. How are you? How is Trevor?" Ava smiled knowingly.

Edo's lower lip, the one she once fantasized running her finger over, turned down. "That's over."

"Oh, I'm sorry. I didn't know. I didn't—"

"It's okay. It's not like a real relationship or anything." Edo paused and tried for a brighter tone. "*Caffè?*"

Ava nodded. "I suppose. Still. It was nice to see you happy." It was true. Her crush on Edo had evaporated like Santa Lucia's morning mist, leaving only a sense of deep affection. She wondered now how she had been so ignorant about Edo. Of course he was gay. Shaking her head she comforted herself, her religious upbringing hardly left room for exposure to alternative lifestyles, and Edo was so handsome, so charming, so decent.

Edo settled the *espresso* in front of Ava.

Nodding in thanks, she asked, "An apricot *cornetto* too, please?"

"Of course."

The bar was quiet as he opened the display case and used the ancient silver tongs to pull out the pastry. He placed it on a saucer and set it in front of Ava, who put her chin on her hand and gazed into the corner of the bar. She asked, "Where's Chiara?"

"Not feeling well."

Ava nodded distractedly.

It struck Edo how lost Ava seemed. Then again, wasn't she always that way?

Pulling a dishcloth from the drawer, Edo began buffing the glasses. "So what do you think about the *castello* owners?"

"Ale?"

"Yes, and his wife. What's her name?"

"Madison."

"Right, Madison. Not Italian." Edo smiled, easily.

"No, definitely not. You've met them?"

"Once or twice. They aren't what I expected."

"Me either."

Ava thought about Ale. His flash of humor, his ability to switch from Italian to English. His deep chest and deep set eyes. Feeling a blush creep up her cheeks, she quickly rewound her hair in its customary messy bun and asked, "So, Marcello is dating Antonella now?"

"Marcè the police officer?"

"Yes. And Antonella . . . Bea's granddaughter. You know her, she works at the *rosticceria*. She's the one who broke up with my brother and then he spread all those rumors about her about her cheating her way through high school because she's dumb as rocks—" Ava paled. "Edo . . . that reminds me . . . I've been meaning to say . . ."

"What is it?" Edo put down his towel and looked intently at Ava.

"My brother—"

"Fabio?"

Ava's lip tugged down. "The one and only."

"It's okay, Ava, really. You don't have to—"

"Please," she covered Edo's hand with her own. "I know you don't blame me for him. You never would. But I have to say it."

Edo cocked his head to the side before nodding for her to go on.

"I can't make excuses for him. Yes, we both got the same earful about 'morality' growing up. But the way he thinks—"

"It's okay, Ava."

"It's not." Her eyes blurred with tears.

Edo shrugged and said, "He said what everyone else is thinking."

"Not everyone!" Ava said hotly.

"You're right. Not everyone."

Ava said, "I'm sorry. I'm sure even one person feels like everyone." She rubbed her eyes before dropping her hands to gaze directly at Edo. "I get lumped in with him so often."

Edo said, "I've never heard that. Fabio has always been . . ."

"Obnoxious? Arrogant? Loud-mouthed?"

"Quite a sonnet you have going there."

"I know. It was hard to be his younger sister. I guess I haven't recovered."

Edo leaned on the counter. "Why do you think he's that way?"

"I don't know." Ava thought for a moment. "It's like, sometimes a plant won't grow and when I pull it up, the roots don't look right. He reminds me of those plants. Even as a boy he had an awful temper. Blaming me when he lost things, blaming me when he found them. Then yelling when I cried. My parents didn't know what to do. They mostly tried to keep me quiet and out of his way, to keep the peace. My very presence seemed to grate on him. Still does."

"Hmmm. Maybe because your parents adore you?"

Ava bit her lip. "I wouldn't say my mother adores me. Though I know she's relieved I'm not like Fabio. Not that she would ever say that out loud. If she did, the rest of the family wouldn't believe it, you know how Fabio can turn on the charm." Ava sighed. "If my mother has any commentary on me, it's that I need to be a better Catholic."

"I'm sure that's not true."

Ava widened her eyes at Edo before going on lightly, "I like to think no one could live up to Mamma's religious expectations. But anyway, it's true Papà and I are close. Maybe Fabio resents that. I don't know. He's so hard to connect to, it's hard to believe that he even cares about people at all."

Edo shrugged. "Everyone needs love, right?"

"I suppose." Ava tucked the fallen wisps of hair back behind her ears. "No, I don't think Fabio ever felt threatened by me. That can't be it. Growing up, he was always going on and on about how much better he was than me. At everything, even things he never cared about. I seem to remember him calling me a loser from time to time." Ava tried to smile like the wounds had faded, but Edo watched how her smile didn't move to her eyes.

He remembered aloud, "His favorite insult, then. I heard it plenty when we were in school."

Ava shook her head. "He was years older than either of us, it's so strange that he'd bother."

Edo nodded in agreement.

The two of them sat in companionable silence. The bells rang out from San Nicola, one following the other. A generous intoning, resonating up the streets and into the groves.

When the last bell rang, Ava said, "Anyway. I wanted to say—I'm sorry my brother is such an ass."

Edo smiled, his eyes warming. "There's nothing to forgive."

Isotta's phone chimed Massimo's ringtone. She apologized to her family gathered around the dinner table and turned her phone off before dropping it onto her lap.

Caterina wheedled, "Is that Massimo, darling?"

Since shaming hadn't worked to induce Isotta to return to her husband, Caterina had resorted to overtures resembling support. Or would have if they weren't underscored with angry side eyes and muttering insults. Isotta wondered if Caterina even noticed that her kind words were laced with the bitterness of medicine inadvertently chewed rather than swallowed.

Isotta nodded.

Caterina sighed dramatically. "I wonder how *poverina* Margherita is doing."

When would Isotta's heart stop wringing at the thought of the little girl?

Isotta shook her head. She knew she should block Massimo's number, prevent him from prying his way into her heart. For reasons she didn't want to investigate, she had yet to take that step.

Caterina sighed more explosively. "So sad when children must bear the sins of their parents."

This got Isotta's attention. Whose sins, exactly, was her mother referring to? Massimo's for deluding her into marriage, her own for leaving him, or Giulia's for getting herself dead in a scant few feet of calm water?

Isabella turned to Ilaria. "Hey, sister, how's that dashing boyfriend of yours?"

Ilaria's eyebrows furrowed. "My boyfriend?" Her face slackened in sudden understanding. "Oh! You mean that guy who keeps pretending to run into me at the bar?"

Isabella cut her eyes toward Isotta before nodding with meaning.

Ilaria said, "He tried to talk to me about American wrestling yesterday. It reminded me of middle school. Remember, Papà? How you used to teach me about those ridiculous wrestlers so I could talk to cute boys?"

Caterina's voice rose above her daughters' desperate attempt to close conversational ranks around their sister.

"You can't stay here forever, you know."

Silence.

"We married you off. Your place is with your husband. You aren't our responsibility to house and feed. You certainly won't get a new husband with all that weight you're gaining. Your face is positively fat, Isotta."

"Mamma!" Several of Isotta's sisters shouted.

Even her husband gave her a reproaching look. "*Basta*. That's enough."

Caterina said, "*Ma, dai!* Come on! You know she can't stay here, bringing shame on us. She has to go back. Might as well do it soon, before Margherita forgets her and her face becomes so wide Massimo won't take her back."

Isabella whispered, "But Mamma, you know what happened . . ."

Caterina waved away her daughter's words. "Oh, *sí sí*. Isotta hoodwinked a grieving man because she resembles his dead wife. Poor Isotta, who won the lottery and now complains that her ticket was paid for by somebody else."

Isabella said, "Mamma, look at her hair! Look what he made her *do*!"

Isotta lifted a hand to her hair. When would the dark dye wash out so she felt like herself again? Would she ever feel like herself again? Did she even want to?"

She did not.

Isotta said, "It's okay, Isabella. She won't see it. But I'll be out of here soon enough."

Caterina leaned forward, her large bosom pushing at the meatballs on her plate. "You're going back to him!"

"No."

"Then what…"

Isotta said, "I'm applying for jobs. I'll get an apartment. I can take care of myself."

Caterina smirked, "Oh, you can, can you?"

Isotta fought to keep her anger from exploding. "Stop telling me I can't do things! I can do things!"

Caterina rolled her eyes. "Yes, so mature. And when can Isabella look forward to not sharing a room with her married sister?"

Before she could stop herself, Isotta shouted, "Before the baby is born, okay? I promise!"

The sudden silence carved the air into sharp corners.

And Isotta realized she'd revealed the one thing she'd been hoping to keep from her mother a little longer.

The cold rain jabbed the streets of Santa Lucia. Chiara's window rattled as a strident gale muscled against the panes. Chiara moaned and turned over, shoving her softened pillow. Where had all the feathers gone? Burrowing deeper under the faded quilt, she squeezed her eyes tightly.

Soft rapping at her door, and Edo called, "Chiara? Sorry to disturb you, but can I come in?"

With a sigh, Chiara swung her feet around to the floor and pulled her robe around her thin nightgown. "Okay, sure. Come in."

The door swung slightly, and Edo nudged his face into the opening.

Chiara said, "What is it?"

"Fabrizio wants to see you."

"I told you—"

"Yes, and I told him what you said. That you're sick and resting. But he doesn't believe me." A pause, and Edo continued, "I don't believe me either. What's going on?"

"I don't want to talk about it."

"And that's a valid reason when I don't want to talk?" Edo grinned.

"Stop it."

"I'm sorry, Chiara. But you don't have to be alone all by yourself."

"You can't fix this." Chiara dropped her head into her hands as tears skated down her cheeks.

Edo sat beside his aunt. "Hey. It's okay."

Chiara leaned against her nephew's narrow chest and breathed in the smell of the bar, which had always been the smell of life itself to her.

She pushed away, shaking her head. "It's not okay."

Edo clasped her hand.

Chiara inhaled a juddering breath. She whispered, "I saw his phone. Fabrizio's. I know I shouldn't have looked, but I did. He's so hot and cold lately, so when you were all with Luciano, I... I found that he's..."

"Seeing someone else?"

"How did you—"

Edo said, "I didn't. I guessed."

"It's that obvious?"

"No, I mean, you've been off, I figured there must be some sort of trouble in paradise."

Chiara nodded, smoothing her robe over her knees. Smoothing the pile in the same direction.

"Chiara?"

"Hmm?"

"Did you tell him you know?"

Chiara said, "No."

"But—"

"I can't, Edo. I just can't."

"I think you need to."

"What good would that do?"

Edo shrugged and stood up. "I don't know. I'm hardly an expert, but it seems better to finish the loop than to continue unraveling."

Chiara thought for a moment, pushing the robe's pile in the other direction. "I guess you're right. He's downstairs?"

"Yes."

"Okay. Give me a few minutes to change and wash up. Then send him up?"

"Sure." Edo squeezed his aunt's hand. "Anything else I can do?"

"No." Chiara stood, reaching for the dove grey sweater she wore yesterday.

"Listen... I'll close up and go to my sister's tonight."

"Okay. Thank you."

Edo turned and reached for the door when Chiara said, "Wait! Does your sister know? That you're—"

"Yes. I told her on the phone yesterday."

"Oh, Edo, how did it go?"

"Seriously, Chiara, stop worrying about other people. Focus on yourself for a minute."

"I'll do that later. This is important... how did it go?"

"Fine, Chiara, it was fine. Great, actually. She was really supportive. Not even that surprised. She wants to help me talk to my parents. Now, don't worry, that will be fine. And I'll see you tomorrow. *Ti voglio tanto bene.*"

"I love you, too... thank you, Edo. I'm so glad you're here."

"Me too."

Edo closed the door behind him.

After a deep breath, Chiara hustled around the room, throwing on jeans, picking clothes off the floor, then heading to the bathroom to wash her face.

She sat on her bed, poised and ready, listening to Fabrizio's tread on the stairs. In a moment, he appeared in the doorway, rotating the brim of his hat through his hands. His eyes met hers. "Are you feeling okay?"

"No."

Fabrizio nodded. "Can I come in?"

Chiara nodded and gestured to the wingback chair in the corner of the room. Gingerly, Fabrizio stepped to the chair and sat on the edge of the cushion. Turning his hat in his hands again he said, "Chiara, I know you won't be surprised to learn I've had something on my mind. I am sure you resent that I haven't been forthright, particularly when I promised you I would be. The truth is—"

"I know."

Fabrizio looked up. "What?"

"I know."

"But how—"

"I saw your phone. I know that's snooping, and I suppose I should be sorry, but I'm not." Chiara lifted her chin, her eyes glinting in the weak lamplight.

Fabrizio ran his hand down his mouth a few times. "And I suppose I should be angry. But I'm not."

Chiara's eyes narrowed. Was he teasing her?

He smiled wanly and offered, "I've hardly behaved like a trustworthy person. Of course you doubted me. If it's any consolation, I tried to tell you. But it was always easier to avoid it, I suppose."

Chiara said, "So now you're headed back to Bologna."

"Yes."

"And all this was, what?" Chiara looked around the room, to where Fabrizio's books tumbled on her dresser beside a pile of his pajamas. "A way to pass the time? A little game to enliven the boring act in the play? Will I read about the seduction of a love-starved barista in your next mystery?"

"No...What are you saying?" Fabrizio leaned forward, his eyes narrowed. "Chiara, how can you say that? How can you *think* that?"

Chiara's laugh was a sharp retort.

Fabrizio lightly touched Chiara's knee. "I'm serious, Chiara. How can you think that? You mean the world to me."

"Oh, that's rich." She pushed away his hand.

"Look, I'm sorry I didn't tell you about my home situation, and that was wrong, but I'm telling you now. I don't see how that impacts our relationship."

"Really? You sure about that?"

"Yes, of course."

"You don't think your lady friend might disagree?"

"Lady friend?"

Chiara said, "Wife, girlfriend, lover, whatever."

"What?" Fabrizio's mouth gaped open.

Chiara rolled her eyes. "Oh God, Fabrizio, why are you acting like this? Like you're stupid or I'm stupid? I said I saw your phone! I know all about it."

"It?"

"Oh, Madonna, Fabrizio! *Yes!* The jig is up! It's over! You can go home to Francy, and I'll be just fine. Don't you worry about me." Chiara wished her voice didn't quaver at the pronouncement.

"But Francy. Chiara...Francy is Francesco. My son."

Chiara poured Luciano his *espresso*. "And how is our little patient?"

Luciano's smile wavered an instant. "Fine! I hear she's fine."

"You hear? What do you mean? You're at the hospital so much it's making you pale."

"She's not yet ready for visitors beyond her family. I suppose until I see her awake with my own eyes, I'll doubt what I hear."

"You haven't seen her?"

"Not since she woke up."

Chiara frowned. How could Luciano not be allowed to see Fatima? He so clearly served in stead of the grandparents the child left behind in Morocco. In fact, the whole family relied on him, the way he helped them adjust to life and language in Santa Lucia.

Luciano said, "I can surmise your thoughts. But her parents would not keep me from her. It's Fatima herself who is not ready."

Chiara turned away so her scowl didn't trouble Luciano. Odder, still.

From behind her, Luciano sighed. "I did see her through the window in the door. But as she remained sleeping, it didn't alter that nightmare image of her in a coma."

Chiara said, "Is there lasting damage?"

Luciano put down his cup and rested his hands on the bar. "Surprisingly enough, that appears unlikely. The family asked me to speak with the doctor and translate." He chuckled. "Well, not translate precisely, since I don't speak Arabic. But to simplify the doctor's impatient Italian. Anyway, the doctor believes that Fatima may have sporadic physical complaints for awhile. But all the tests they've done show that her brain was miraculously unscathed." Luciano stared at his *espresso*. "I wish I could see her."

Chiara clasped his hand in both of hers. "You will. Soon. I'm sure of it."

"Thank you, Chiara." He sighed. "And once I do, I can take Elisa, which will be a huge relief for the child."

Smiling, Chiara said, "Of course! I know how worried she must have been. To have her friend again—that will be wonderful."

"Yes, that's true. But she's also a child, and you know how children feel responsible for things outside their control. She's been so tense, so worried that she's somehow to blame."

"Blame?"

Luciano shook his head. "That's how children are. They believe they can prevent awful situations by mere wishing. When life goes awry, they failed."

Chiara deferred to Luciano's wisdom here, having never raised children herself. She seemed to always get them as teenagers.

As if reading her mind, Luciano said, "How is Edo?"

Chiara answered, "He's coming back from his sister's this morning. He was low for awhile after the break-up—"

"Ah, I didn't know about that."

"Well, you've been occupied."

"True."

"Anyway, it was hard at first. Trevor turns out to be a bit of a scoundrel."

Luciano gazed into the distance, trying to remember. "I didn't register that."

Shrugging, Chiara said, "Well, we barely saw him, right? The two of them had only a few days together before they tried to make a go of it long distance. Which worked . . . until it didn't."

Luciano said, "I'm very sorry. I confess I derived more than a little joy in seeing Edo happy."

"*Anch'io*. Me too."

"It is interesting . . . he's nearing twenty-five, *davvero*? It's not often I see someone as mature as he is falling in love for the first time."

Chiara smiled weakly. "It's different. Now, for him. The world doesn't shine approval on Edo the way it did for us when we were young."

Luciano nodded in thought before reaching for Chiara's hand. "Edo will be okay."

She bit her lip, knowing the pain of being alone. "I hope so."

~

"So the person you thought was his lover was actually his son?" Edo's brow furrowed in his attempt to keep up.

Chiara covered her face with her hands. "Yes! So embarrassing."

"His son."

"Yes! I just assumed Francy was a woman. I don't know why, I did know a boy named Francy years ago, in middle school I think. But mostly, it's a woman's name, isn't it?"

"I didn't even know Fabrizio had a son."

"I didn't either."

"You didn't? Why didn't he tell you?"

"*Allora*, from what he told me last night, I gather that his first marriage didn't end well."

"He's been married before?"

"Oh, Edo, neither Fabrizio or I are fledglings in the nest. I was married, why shouldn't he have been?"

"Oh, okay. So you knew he'd been married."

"No."

Edo frowned at the drizzle hazing Via Romana.

Chiara went on, "It was a complicated divorce. He didn't tell me for the same reasons I didn't tell him about my first marriage. It brought up too much."

"You didn't tell him about—"

"No, I didn't. I mean, I have now, but not until right before the fire."

Chiara hated the look of doubt on her nephew's face. She was tempted to tell him the story that Fabrizio had told her. About how Fabrizio's wife had grown depressed and withdrawn after Francy started nursery school. Fabrizio had sympathized with her, alone and bored while he was traveling through Italy and abroad. He tried to help her, forwarding her job or volunteer ideas, sending her loving messages during the day so she'd know he was thinking of her, bringing back regional treats for her to incorporate into the cooking that became more and more elaborate. This deference and care lasted until Francy was ten, when Fabrizio had come home early to surprise his wife and found her in a compromising and frankly disgusting position with their hirsute neighbor. The neighbor had raced out of the house, pulling clothes over the private parts which Fabrizio in his shock had not been able to take his eyes off. They were hairier even than he would have imagined, if he'd ever spared a moment to consider his neighbor's pubic hair. The man boasted a thicket, a veritable bramble. A bramble his wife had twisted her fingers through as she moaned in ways she'd never moaned with him.

Fabrizio had lingered long enough at this part of the story that Chiara's heart ached. The trauma of the betrayal obviously still stung. Fabrizio then explained that after the neighbor left, he'd marshaled his inner resources. He needed to know more, so he stayed stoic, distant. His comfortable journalistic posture. Fortunately or unfortunately, his preternatural calm convinced his wife that he knew more than he did and, in her anxiety, the whole story burst out. The string of affairs. Not a string, actually. More of a knotted rope. Turns out, Fabrizio's wife had slept with almost every man in the building, some multiple times. That woolly neighbor had been riding his wife for the fifth time, a kind of record. She had slept with almost everyone at his work, which explained the looks of sympathy he constantly got whenever he was at the office. She had slept with the fathers of Francy's friends. Married, not married, widowed, it didn't matter. She slept with them all.

She admitted she had a problem. She blamed her rigid Catholic upbringing which punished her nascent sexuality. She blamed him for not being as wild in the bedroom as she had seen men in the porn videos she'd taken to watching. She promised she had gotten all that out of her system. That she would now enjoy plain-pasta lovemaking as a demonstration of real love. She would never stray from her marital bed again.

Fabrizio hadn't known what to think. For Francy's sake, he didn't want to end the marriage. But he also couldn't wrap his mind around the image of his wife offering herself to every Gianni, Franco, and Alfredo. It would have made more sense if she had told him that she'd taken to visiting the moon in his absence. How could the woman he married, that he had frankly thought of as a bit aloof in bed, how could she be a wanton sex-crazed housewife?

He wrestled with what to do for a week, until the decision was made for him because he broke into his wife's computer and found that she was in the process of planning an afternoon tryst with Francy's teacher, a man she met at the post office, as well as coordinating a lunch-time meeting with Fabrizio's own cousin.

It was the drop that overflowed the pot. He ended it, and she went insane.

Sobbing, banging her head against the wall, slapping herself, punching her chest until she knocked herself into a heap on the floor, scrambling through the kitchen drawers for a knife to stab herself and cut off the offending parts of her body. Fabrizio had dropped Francy off at his mother's and deposited his wife at the hospital.

She'd emerged a year later, a pale and fragile version of herself.

In the meantime, Fabrizio had secured a divorce.

Anytime he felt slightly guilty for leaving her, he looked his wife up on Facebook. She had rebounded, her feed full of images of her with different men, showing off what must have been expensive breast implants.

Meanwhile, he'd raised Francy essentially on his own for years, until she stabilized enough to care for her teenage son.

Fabrizio knew that she'd filled Francy's head with lies about where she'd been and Fabrizio's role in the divorce. Yes, she had been a terrible wife, but Fabrizio didn't want to turn his son against her. He figured his son didn't need to carry the grief. So to Francy's questions, he'd always said that people sometimes grow apart. He maintained this story even when

Francy began casting suspicious glances at his father.

Fabrizio took it in stride, trusting that it would all eventually work out. He tolerated his son's overprotectiveness of his mother and somewhat derisive attitude toward himself.

Chiara couldn't begin to tell Edo all this. Not her story to tell, and anyway, with Francy between gigs, Fabrizio had invited him to Santa Lucia. She hoped the two men got along. Particularly since Fabrizio had mentioned that Francy was gay. He was only a little older than Edo, and if he was anything like his father—smart, thoughtful, considerate, disarming— well, stranger things had happened.

As Ava pressed the seedling into the earth, she noticed a shadow rising behind her.

With a gasp she turned around. "Oh! Oh, *ciao*, Alessandro."

"Ale, please. I'm sorry I startled you."

Ava turned back, brushing the dirt she'd scattered more firmly against the stem, securing the seedling. "That's okay, I was in a zone. Your shadow—"

"Yes." Ale crouched beside her, watching Ava's sure hands shake another seedling out of its plastic pot and into her hand. "What are you doing?"

"Planting."

"I can see that. But what are you planting?"

Ava sat back and considered her morning's work. She gestured to the far end of the playground. "*Allora*, I put some ground cover over there, where the kids play soccer so much the grass wore away. If the cover takes root and spreads before spring, it may withstand those rough feet." Ale chuckled. Ava pointed to the other end of the playground. "And in that bare spot, I put in some grasses. They don't look like much now, but eventually they'll make the playground more attractive, separate it visually from the graveyard."

"That's a graveyard?"

"Beyond that wall, yes."

"Ah. And here? What are you planting?"

Ava cocked her head to the side and patted the earth. "Bay leaf bushes. To add interest and also because the cooks in Santa Lucia keep breaking off pieces of the one by the parking lot. It's struggling."

To Alessandro's silence, Ava went on, "This is the wrong time to plant, of course. But it's a pretty day and the season has been mild so far. Though the old timers tell me that means we're in for a *brutto* January. Hopefully the plants will survive the transplant."

"If they don't?"

Ava considered. "They're all grown from cuttings, and I'm running out of room in the flower shop. So I haven't lost much. It's worth a try."

Standing, Ale said, "Well, you have quite an eye. The *castello*, the playground. The town is lucky to have you as a landscaper."

Brushing off her knees, Ava stood. With a laugh she said, "Oh, I'm not the landscaper. Santa Lucia hasn't had a landscaper in years. I just have time on my hands, so . . ."

Ale surveyed the playground. "You do all this without getting paid?"

Shrugging, Ava answered, "It makes Santa Lucia pretty. And I enjoy it."

"You do, don't you?"

"Oh, yes!" Ava's cheeks flushed. "I love it. My father is a florist, so I grew up around cut flowers, but this is so much better. Making things grow, nurturing them so they bloom, clipping what needs clipping to bring more energy into the core of the plant. It's fascinating. And when I have a big space like this, it's like, it's like, making a painting with real growing colors."

Ale regarded her levelly.

She ducked her head and said, "That sounds stupid."

"No. It doesn't."

Ava darted a look up at his face. Was he teasing her? But no, he looked serious.

Their eyes locked. As Ava felt her knees weaken at the moment's intensity, Ale broke his gaze to the rolling green hills feathered with mist. He mused softly, "You must despise me."

"What! No!" Was she too loud?

Ale said, "Sure. I mean, with my coming back, you lost your project at the *castello*."

Ava said, "I have this, and some yards..."

Ale shifted his weight. His arm was just a few inches from hers. Ava imagined she could feel his body heat even through his thick sweater. He regarded her seriously. "Nonetheless. I don't want our return to change things. For you."

Ava trembled at the kindness in Ale's eyes, the warmth and interest.

Brightening, he said, "I can't believe I didn't think of this before! I'll hire you as the *castello*'s landscaper!"

"What! Oh, no, I couldn't."

"I know it would be a lot of work, I wouldn't be asking you to volunteer. I'd pay you."

"That's not—"

"I haven't liked any of the landscapers my contractor suggested. All froth. They want something regal, and they want it to look good now, no patience for later. But you live here, you've always lived here . . . Haven't you?"

Ava nodded, suddenly ashamed of her limited life.

"So you appreciate this *castello*. In your bones, even. You know what I know—this wasn't a *castello* for displaying wealth. It was for protection, for the village, for the church. And when I hear you talk about the plants—you *get* it. I don't want the landscaping to serve as a decorative frame for the *castello*, I want the landscaping rooted. I want it to work with the *castello* not *for* the *castello*."

Ava tried to laugh it off. "Alessandro—"

"Ale."

"Ale. I'm not a professional. You can't ask me."

"But I *am* asking you. I don't care that you aren't a professional. Look at this—" He gestured widely at the playground. "You have vision, you have a real taste. Plus," he finished lamely. "You like plants so much."

"I do like plants."

Ale asked, "Why, Ava?"

Ava, caught off guard, answered without thinking. "Because they are easy to love. You plant them and you nurture them and they almost always grow."

"So plants are love."

Ava frowned. Is that what she said? She responded slowly, "I suppose so. Though it sounds ridiculous when I hear it out loud."

"Well, I want love at the *castello*. What do you picture there? If you could do anything?"

Ava clasped her hands to her chest. "Anything? Oh, I'd put in old, historic varieties of heath. And flowering vines against the wall. I'd put in apple trees, because I saw old renderings of the *castello* that showed apple trees that must have died from disease long ago."

"Apple trees? I didn't think of those as native."

"They aren't. I wondered if someone brought them down from Asia by way of Venice during the crusades. All I know for sure is that they must have been here. You've seen the tapestries in the room with the walk-in fireplace. They have images of cider pressing."

"Huh. I hadn't even noticed that. When the tapestries come back from the restorers, I'll have to look at them more closely. So heath and apple trees. Go on."

"And grapevines. I feel like those must have been there. I'd want to research a little, bring those back. A kitchen garden, of course, with herbs and vegetables. And right now there's no perimeter between the castle yard and the olive trees. I think that's right for the east end of the *castello*, where the kitchen was, but not for the rest. I would want some variegation to blend with the silver of the olive leaves, to create a textured boundary."

Ale stared at her. "You have to take this job."

Ava shook her head. "I can't."

"You can. I trust you to do this."

"It won't be perfect."

Ale considered with a smile. "Who needs perfection?"

The bell over the door of Bar Birbo jangled.

Chiara leaned into the ground coffee beans she was pressing into her La Pavoni before turning.

"*Ciao*, Chiara! What do you make of this news about the *castello*?"

"*Ciao*, Bea. What do you mean?"

Bea settled herself on a stool, gesturing for Chiara to make her her usual *caffè*. "Well! The owner met with Dante. Oh! That reminds me. Magda said she heard that Dante told Stella she's never welcome in Santa Lucia again. What is he, God? If she wants to come back, she's welcome at my table. I want to hear about that handyman . . . I always thought there was more to those hands than his ability to fix a shingle."

"So . . . about Dante?"

"I'm getting there, I'm getting there. So, Alessandro. He met with Dante and they agreed that Alessandro wouldn't pursue legal action in exchange for having all permits for the renovation of the *castello* greased by the mayor."

Chiara slid the cup onto its saucer. "Dante agreed to that?"

"What choice did he have? He needs to keep the disaster out of the papers. If everyone found out about it, and then found out how our lord mayor had been cuckolded by his wife . . . well! That would be a story, wouldn't it? *Scandoloso!*"

Chiara said, "Still. Dante has always been such a stickler for following rules. It's been part of his campaign against corruption, trying to pull Santa Lucia out of Italy's dark days."

Bea waved this away like a pesky mosquito. "Oh, words are easy, but when your reputation is on the line . . . who would do differently?"

Chiara said, "Also . . . so strange that Alessandro would make that deal. I thought he was Americanized."

Bea nodded and took a noisy sip. "I know! My guess is he's been talking to someone local, and found out how to use the fire to his advantage."

Chiara stiffened as the bar's opening door alerted her to new entrants.

Seeing Chiara's plastered smile, Bea narrowed her eyes and whipped around toward the door.

Fabrizio entered the bar with a young man, who looked to be in his late twenties. Handsome, in a haughty way, with well-shaped eyebrows and an expensive haircut framing a pale face with blurs of rosy color under his high cheekbones.

"*Buongiorno*, Chiara. *Buongiorno*, Signora Bea," Fabrizio nodded in greeting. His posture was tight, both nervous and proud.

Chiara walked around the bar to greet the boy. Fabrizio beamed as he held out his arm to welcome her into a triangle of the three of them. "Chiara, this is Francy. Francy, Chiara."

They smiled their "*piacere*"s, Chiara moving to kiss Francy's cheeks until stalled by his hand thrust out into the space between them. She flushed and shook his hand, her smile faltering.

"*Caffè*? Do you want *caffè*? Or something to eat? Fabrizio? A *cornetto con marmellata*?"

Fabrizio beamed and turned to his son. "Chiara procures the best *cornetti* in Umbria."

Francy smiled indulgently and said, "A daunting challenge, I imagine." To his father's crestfallen expression, he added, "From what you tell me, Chiara is a talented woman." Fabrizio smiled again and, threaded his arm through his son's, guiding him to the bar.

Bea scowled and scooted backward, allowing the men room. She took an infinitesimal sip of her *caffè* and examined the range of alcoholic options she never ordered, given she only drank a bit of beer with dinner.

Chiara smoothed her hair, trying not to notice Francy following her motion with his eyes.

Fabrizio leaned forward, an invitation for Chiara to press her cheek against his, but she had turned to wash her hands and so missed the gesture.

Fabrizio chuckled uncomfortably and loudly announced, "I'll have my usual, Chiara, a *caffè lungo*, if it's no trouble. Francy? *Cappuccino?*"

"Yes, thank you."

Chiara nodded and placed the cups under the La Pavoni.

As Chiara bustled about and Bea pretended to admire the bottle labels, Fabrizio pointed out the recently framed photographs of the *castello* on the walls, telling Francy about how Chiara had found them in a box in the storeroom after the fire. Just then, the door to the upstairs apartment opened, and Edo stepped into the bar.

Chiara threw him a grateful smile before frothing the milk for Francy's *cappuccino*.

"Edo!" Fabrizio shouted, over the whistling of the frother. "I'm glad you're here. I want you to meet my son." Chiara had completed whipping up the milk mid-sentence, and so the words "my son" hung in the air, like a ball, suspended mid-catch. Fabrizio grinned crookedly before pushing his son toward the bar to greet Edo.

"*Piacere,*" nodded Edo, looking curiously into Francy's eyes. He was not what Edo had expected.

"*Piacere,*" answered Francy, appraising Edo. He was exactly what Francy had expected.

Luciano knocked softly on the hospital door.

Fatima's parents looked up with wide smiles of welcome, waving Luciano and Elisa, who trailed behind him, into the room. Fatima's face remained stoney. Luciano wondered if she had just woken up.

After whispering to her daughter, Salma drew away from the bed. Fatima grabbed her mother's hand, anchoring Salma to her side. Luciano hung back, suddenly unsure as he watched Fatima whisper furiously to Salma. Elisa slid her hand into Luciano's.

Salma spoke in clipped tones with the shadow of a frown. Straightening, she stayed beside Fatima, but insistently waved Luciano and Elisa into the room. Fatima's father looked from his wife to Fatima to the new arrivals. He shrugged and dropped into a chair by the door, offering his place beside his daughter to Luciano and Elisa.

They faltered a little before moving to Fatima's bedside.

Fatima stared at her bedsheets, stretched taut across her lap, briefly peeking up at Elisa. At that brief bit of eye contact, Elisa burst into tears. Grabbing Fatima's hand, she sobbed, "I'm sorry, Fatima! I'm so sorry! I know I messed up, I knew it when it happened. I didn't know how to fix it and I got so confused. And then you were here and I was so scared and I'm so, so sorry!"

Fatima's eyes filled with tears. She leaned back against the pillow. "It's fine."

Elisa started to go on, but stopped when Luciano pressed her hand. She startled and looked up at him. Nodding as if in silent assent, she said, "I'm sorry. I wanted you to know I'm sorry."

Fatima said, "It shouldn't matter, should it? It's done. How are things at school?"

Elisa stuttered, "School?"

Fatima nodded.

Frowning Elisa asked, "But Fatima . . ."

Fatima said, "I'm going to be so behind on my homework. I told Mamma to get it. I could at least be doing something useful, but she says

I need my rest."

Elisa sagged against Luciano.

Luciano rested a hand on the railing of the bed. "How are you feeling, dear heart?"

Fatima frowned. "Fine. Or I will be when I can go home. It smells weird here." She peered up at Luciano's face. "Your face doesn't show it."

"Show it? What do you mean, *cara*?"

Elisa looked up at her *maestro*. He looked the same as ever.

Fatima closed her eyes and leaned back. "Bruises. Cuts. From the fight."

Luciano's voice dropped. "Fight."

Fatima nodded. "I may be small, but I'm not blind. I saw you. Drunk, fighting with Massimo. Even though you told us, promised us you wouldn't drink anymore."

Luciano said, "But I wasn't—I mean, Massimo hit me but I—"

Fatima leaned back against the pillows. "It shouldn't matter. Who cares, right?"

Frowning, Elisa tugged Luciano's hand. "What is she talking about? What's wrong with Fatima?"

Luciano's gaze didn't waver from Fatima's face.

For a brief moment, Fatima's eyes flashed before she murmured, "I'm tired." She pleaded with her mother, "Mamma, now?"

Fatima's mother nodded and bustled around, thanking Luciano and Elisa for coming, and assuring them that Fatima would love to visit with them once she returned home.

Luciano thanked her for allowing them to see Fatima, but somehow, he didn't think he'd seen Fatima at all.

"What's good here, Chiara?" asked Fabrizio, flipping open his menu.

"Here? I have no idea."

Francy slid his menu to the side. "You have no idea? Didn't you rec-ommend this *trattoria*?"

"Yes, I asked Magda what restaurants her guests like in Girona, but I never go out to eat myself."

"You don't?" Was it her imagination, or did Francy actually sneer? Maybe he caught wind of the odors from the bathroom. Their table sat in a most inauspicious location.

"We sometimes went to L'Ora Dorata before it closed." She shrugged.

Fabrizio clapped his son on the shoulder. "Francy can't identify, I'm afraid. He and his friends dine out quite a bit."

Francy responded with a tight smile. "Yes, well. It is Bologna. Our range of options is staggering."

Fabrizio went on with a sideways smile. "One day, Edo you must visit us in Bologna. Francy has some friends around your age. They can intro-duce you to our golden city. The university, the music, the arcaded walk-ways..."

Francy studied the menu.

Edo looked from Francy to Chiara. What was going on? Why did this suddenly feel like a double date?

Edo said, "My parents come here a lot. They serve typical Umbrian specialties. I'm sure the *tagliatelle* is quite good, especially with *porcini*, after the recent rain. And of course the *gnocchi al Sagrantino*."

Francy looked over his menu. "Sagrantino?"

"It's a wine from the Montefalco area, across the valley," Edo gestured, suddenly not sure which direction Montefalco lay. He'd never actually been there.

Francy looked back down at his menu. "Yes, I'm quite aware of what Sagrantino is. I'm just not sure why anyone would compose a sauce from it."

Fabrizio shifted uncomfortably and avoided Chiara's eye contact. He said, "Francy is a bit of a wine enthusiast. He arranges a marvelous wine dinner every year to benefit the local farmers who—"

Francy said, "I'm sure no one is interested in that."

Fabrizio cast a quizzical glance at his son. He opened his mouth, but then closed it again.

The waiter appeared, as if a gift from God. "*Pronti?*"

Fabrizio said, "Chiara, do you know what you'll have?"

Chiara scanned the menu. "I'll have the *tagliatelle* with *cinghiale*. That's *bianco*? Or *rosso*?"

Chiara wasn't sure why she bothered asking if pasta came with red or white sauce. She didn't really care.

The waiter scribbled with his pen on the corner of his notepad, spurring the ink. "*Bianco*."

"White sauce! Yes, I'll have that. Edo?"

Edo cut his eyes to Francy before announcing, "I'll have the *gnocchi*."

The waiter said aloud as he wrote, "*Tagliatelle al ragu, gnocchi, e poi?*" He turned to the other two.

Fabrizio closed his menu, saying, "I'll have the *tagliatelle*, also."

"Okay, *e voi?*"

Francy's eyes lingered on the Umbrians across the table as he ran his tongue over his bottom lip. "I'll take the *carbonara*."

The waiter hesitated. Fabrizio leaned toward his son. "That's not Umbrian, Francy, you may be happier if you order a local—"

"The *carbonara*." Francy grinned and then asked the table at large with a hint of a smirk, "And I suppose a bottle of Sagrantino?"

Chiara shrugged and Edo looked away. Fabrizio nodded faintly, "Yes, a bottle of Sagrantino, *per favore*."

"*Subito*," the waiter slid the menus together, scooped them up and strode to the kitchen.

Fabrizio cleared his throat. "So, Edo! How is your protege doing?"

"My protege?"

"The Moroccan immigrant you're tutoring."

"Oh, he's fine. He got a job. At the supermarket here in Girona."

"A job! Well, isn't that marvelous. Did you hear that, Francy?"

Francy smiled coldly. "I'm right here, of course I did. Who is this person, Edoardo?"

"A young man who moved to Santa Lucia from Morocco a few months ago. My old teacher set it up. We get together a few times a week so I can teach him Italian."

"I see. And you have special training, I take it?"

"Well, Luciano says that the work only requires a willingness to make a fool of myself, and at that I am quite proficient."

Fabrizio and Chiara laughed hard enough that the diners at the next table turned to look at them. Francy stared blankly ahead.

Into the ensuing silence, the waiter appeared with a bottle of wine. He pried off the cork and then stood ready to pour. Edo and Chiara both insisted Francy taste the wine. He pushed his glass forward, and Edo and Chiara avoided eye contact as Francy swirled the wine and held it to the light before plunging his entire nose into the glass. His lip curled downward before he took a sip, coughed, sighed, and said, "It's fine."

The waiter filled the other glasses before bustling back into the kitchen.

Francy seemed more interested in swirling his wine than drinking it as he turned to Edo.

Chiara said, "So, Francy. Your father said you had a tour in Asia."

Francy leaned back and sniffed. "Yes."

Chiara nodded. "That's wonderful. I've always wanted to see new places. Traveling is expensive, though."

Francy said, "That's a solvable problem though, isn't it?"

Fabrizio put a hand on his son's arm. Fabrizio sat back and studied the oil painting across the room, of wildflowers spreading across a valley.

Edo cleared his throat and said, "I'll be right back. Need to freshen up." He stepped to the back of the restaurant, glad to enter the fumes rather than deal with the tension at the table. What was Francy's problem?

Edo took his time, blousing his shirt just so and putting his individual locks of his hair in place. After he brushed his eyebrows with his fingers, he stepped out of the bathroom. He spotted Chiara at the other end of the restaurant, chattering with people who looked familiar. No doubt former bar patrons. Chiara knew people wherever she went.

His own name caught his attention. Edo hung behind the partition, listening as Fabrizio and Francy whispered furiously.

Fabrizio said, "I've never seen you so determinedly displeased. Why are you behaving in this stupid manner?"

Francy said, "Maybe I'm devolving to fit my surroundings."

"Francy, whatever can you mean? I've never been surrounded by such easy joy and charm in my life."

Francy said nothing.

Fabrizio said, "Listen, I get that chatting with our older generation is not your idea of fun, but talk to Edo. He's a wonderful person, Francy. His boyfriend recently broke up with him, so I know he's single."

Francy said, "I have no interest in puffing the feathers of a guy slighted by other men."

"Just because he's single doesn't mean—come on, Francy. He's funny and sweet, and you know he's attractive."

Edo tensed, waiting for Francy's response. He told himself he didn't care, Francy was obviously a pretentious twat. But he leaned in to listen harder.

Francy said, "He may be good looking by Santa Lucia standards, but he's not handsome enough to tempt me." A pause before Francy hissed, "Seriously, Papà . . . I don't know why you had to find a partner *here* of all places."

Edo could listen to no more. He strode across the restaurant to stand beside his aunt. She looked up at him with laughing eyes and he hugged her fiercely before turning to introduce himself to her friends.

"It was awful. A literal *incubo*," reported Chiara over her shoulder as she poured milk into Patrizia's *cappuccino*.

Patrizia settled onto the stool. "A nightmare? Oh, Chiara, not that bad, surely?"

"It was, yes. Since when am I prone to exaggeration?"

"Well ... that's true." Patrizia reached for a sugar packet. "What made it so awful? Fabrizio is so wonderful and you are so in love, I figured the rest would unfold like a dream."

Chiara snorted as she placed Patrizia's *cappuccino* in front of her and began pulling one for herself. "Where do I start? Francy clearly thinks he's too good for this town. He's like the Italian version of what's her name? Alessandro's wife?"

"Madison?"

"Madison. Yes, that's right. I can't ever remember." Chiara turned down the music and stirred her *cappuccino*. "He's like that, but clever."

"Clever?"

"Yes, with his big words. And it's like that makes him more dangerous."

"What do you mean?"

"Oh, it's hard to explain, but it's like he gets all these digs in, he is subtly gibing, but never crosses the line, so Fabrizio remains blissfully unaware."

"*Uffa.*"

"There's more." Chiara sipped her *cappuccino*. "Fabrizio seemed to think it was a double date."

"What!"

Chiara shrugged.

"Chiara ... no. Really?"

"*Davvero.* I kid you not."

"But Edo didn't ... I mean ... Did he?"

Chiara laughed. "Quite the opposite. Edo wouldn't give me details, but he overheard Francy complain to Fabrizio about Edo. Not handsome enough for him, or something ridiculous."

"*Edo?* Edo is *gorgeous!* Does the boy from Bologna have *eyes?*" Patrizia protested indignantly.

Chiara grinned. "That's true. But in fairness, both you and I are a touch biased."

Patrizia grumbled and clinked her spoon onto her saucer.

Chiara went on, "Edo didn't like him anyway. How could he, with Francy looking down on him for everything."

"Oh, Chiara. I take it back. It *was* a nightmare."

"Seriously awful. The entire meal was civilized small talk about nothing anyone cared about. I can't remember a time I had less to say."

Patrizia spooned a bit of milk froth into her mouth, closing her eyes. She ventured, "Does this change anything for you? About Fabrizio?"

"No. I mean, I wish his son was as wonderful as he is, but if that's the price for dating Fabrizio, I'll take it. In fact—" Chiara studied the street to confirm that no one was in danger of entering the bar.

"In fact? What is it?"

"I finally connected with Riccardo. About handling my divorce. He's coming tomorrow."

"A divorce!"

"You disapprove after all?"

Patrizia considered. "No, just surprised. You've stayed married this whole time he's been in jail."

"I don't want this marriage as any part of my life with Fabrizio." Chiara sipped the last of her *cappuccino.* "Anyway, his jail time is up in the next few years, maybe less, I can't remember, . . . and what was I going to do? Welcome him back here with open arms?"

"No, you couldn't do that. I guess I always thought his release was so far off it hardly mattered."

"I did too. But not anymore."

106

Riccardo tapped the bottom of his papers on his desk. "Are you sure about this, Chiara?"

Chiara said, "Yes, absolutely. Why, shouldn't I be?"

Riccardo shrugged. "It can be expensive to get divorced. I want to make sure it's worth it for you."

Chiara's gaze drifted outside the bar. Unfortunate, that her closed day fell on an unseasonably warm afternoon. Tourists milled Via Romana, perhaps spillover from Cascia's Saffron Festival. Couples and families walked down the cobblestone streets, enjoying the soft air. Some drifted up the stairs to the *castello*, only to turn around again when they met the barrier. A chain hung across the top of the steps and sanders, jackhammers, and drills announced "off-limits."

Chiara didn't miss the *castello*'s ready availability, but she realized she might come spring, when the warmer weather pulled villagers to congregate in the castle yard at sunset.

But now at least, it didn't bother her overmuch, this closing of the *castello*. Perhaps because she had a divorce on her mind. She said, "What do I spend my money on? My car is ancient, and I never take vacations." She laughed aloud, the ringing tones rebounding off the walls of the bar. "This! This divorce will be the greatest vacation ever!" Continuing to chuckle to herself she murmured, "Freedom from that human waste. No tropical paradise could be better."

Riccardo watched her, a look of confusion drifting over his face, before clearing. "Ah, I see what you mean. Though one cannot underestimate the charms of Majorca. We went last summer—*bella*."

Chiara said, "Maybe in a few years. After I restore my coffers. How much do you think this will cost?"

Riccardo's fingers flicked through his papers, eyes scanning. "It depends. It might not be expensive at all, if he just signs the papers. The costs go up the more he fights it."

Chiara said, "Well, that's okay then. Why would he fight it?"

Riccardo looked up and smiled. "Perhaps he will be less eager to let go of the marriage? He does have more to lose."

"Oh, Riccardo. Ever the charmer. No wonder the girls in school were so in love with you."

"But not you."

"Well, as we know, only the truly exceptional could catch my eye," Chiara said lightly.

Riccardo frowned. "Don't be hard on yourself, Chiara. We all looked up to him. Handsome, athletic, smart—"

"Into prostitutes..."

"*Uffa.*"

"I know."

The air was tender with unspoken thoughts. Chiara said, "Anyway...you were saying about the cost."

"Ah yes. The more he fights, the more expensive it will be."

Chiara swung her legs and mused, "For him, too, I expect."

"Yes."

Chiara said, "Well, he has no money, so he can't fight it."

Riccardo frowned. "We can't count on that, Chiara. Stranger things have happened. Inheritance, gifts—"

Chiara waved this away. "His family won't talk to him. They had to leave Santa Lucia in shame. I doubt they'll forgive him enough to help him fight a divorce."

"Maybe," Riccardo hedged. He said, "Look it's my job to look out for pitfalls. To keep you safe."

"I know, and I'm grateful. But I think it will be fine." She hopped off her stool. "Thanks for taking the time to come by."

Riccardo stood as well. "Oh, it's no problem. It's nice to come back, and I can't tell you how pleased Pina will be when I come home with a kilo of Giuseppe's chicken sausages."

Chiara's laughter rang through the bar. "You can't tell me you have yet to find a good butcher?"

"Not like Giuseppe." Riccardo said. "The man is the god of pork. And even chicken."

"Even without a decent butcher, you and Pina still enjoying living in Spoleto?"

"We're just outside, and yes. The farm is a lot of work, but we hired some boys to help out. From Santa Lucia, actually, Pina's distant nephews or cousins or whatever. You know Guido and Matteo? Carlo's boys?"

Chiara furrowed her brow in concentration. "I don't think—"

"Oh, you must. Carlo left in some sort of scandal I think. Wife kicked him out. She's the one somehow related to Pina. I just heard bits of the story through the grapevine. They have another child, but she's not biologically his? Or maybe not hers either? Elisa! That's her name!"

"Oh, yes! Elisa! I do know the family. How are the young men adjusting?"

"Quite well. We have them set up in the barn apartment. They're great boys, hard working. Busy, of course, with school and soccer. They often talk about Elisa. Worried about her, I think. Here with just her mother."

Chiara blinked as she put all this information together. "I think she's okay. She's under Luciano's wing."

"Luciano! He's not still drinking?"

"No. Thank the Madonna."

Riccardo nodded and crossed himself. "Thank the Madonna."

"It's unbelievable, Chiara! I offered them my expertise and poof! Instead they hire some overpriced designer from Rome. Rome!" Magda shook her head as she stirred her cooling *caffè*. She had yet to take a sip. "You've seen my apartments. You know how special they are. Elegant enough for my American guests, and in keeping with the Umbrian style. This *castello* will be an abomination, Chiara. Mark my words."

Chiara nodded noncommittally. She expected Fabrizio any minute. Hopefully not with his son. Francy's direct stare seemed to bore through Chiara. His predisposition to hate everyone and everything rattled her until she lost the thread of Fabrizio's words and even her own thoughts.

Magda said, "I bet they're doing it up all marble and gold. What Americans think of when they imagine a *castello*. I saw that all the time in Germany. Americans expecting castles out of their Disney movies—all alabaster and doves flying about." Magda waved her arms over her head. "It's like they don't know that castles were built before the baroque period."

Baroque period? What was Magda talking about? Chiara blinked her eyes and tried to focus.

"Short and squat. That's how most *castelli* are. After all, their original purpose was as a fortress, not a status symbol. Stupid, grasping Americans don't get that. These don't either. Mark my words, Chiara," Was Magda repeating herself? "That dear *castello* will be shrink-wrapped in gold."

Chiara didn't know if this was entirely fair. Alessandro didn't seem a man intent on flaunting his wealth. She'd seen him talking to the old women in the *alimentari*, and walking through the groves with his hands thrust deep in his pockets. Plus, he'd abandoned his designer wear for simpler clothing. His wife, however . . . well, but that couldn't be helped. And anyway, given the argument she'd overheard between the two of them when Ale hired Ava for the landscaping, it seemed Ale played the cards.

The door opened. Fabrizio grinned at Chiara and Magda while shuttling Francy into the bar. "*Buongiorno, buongiorno!* Another nice day. Is it always sunny so late in the year?"

Chiara smiled and shook her head while Magda snorted. "Ha! Absolutely not. Foggy and cold almost every day, that's the usual."

Fabrizio took his place at the bar beside Magda, "Ah, well. We must be lucky, I suppose. I know I am." He reached across to float a kiss onto Chiara's cheek.

Did Francy flinch? Chiara tried to breathe in Fabrizio's scent and ground herself. She was probably imagining things. Fabrizio did make her feel like a girl with a star crush. No wonder she was getting paranoid. Forcing a smile she asked, "*Caffè?*"

"Please!" answered Fabrizio. "*Cappuccino per te*, Francy?"

Francy nodded.

Fabrizio turned back to Chiara. "Two then, I'll have that instead of my *normale*." He moved to the end of the counter to chat more easily with Chiara, leaving Francy and Magda. Eyes brightening, Fabrizio said, "Francy's lyrics are going well, it must be this Santa Lucia air ... he's agreed to an outing in the next few days. I considered the sea, but I suppose we can't count on the weather to be as nice as here?"

Magda broke in. "Oh, you don't want to go to Le Marche now. It's positively miserable. Cold and empty. Grey, too. You're better off staying inland."

Fabrizio looked to Chiara for confirmation. She nodded as she bustled about grinding the beans. "She's right. It's *brutto* in winter. Lovely in spring, though. And summer with all the sunflowers." She looked up as the door opened. "*Ciao*, Bea."

Bea lumbered to the stool between Magda and Francy and pulled it out to better accommodate her bulk. She settled herself with a groan. "*Ciao*, Chiara. *Ciao a tutti*," she said, nodding to the rest of the bar. "Do you have any *cornetti con marmellata?*"

Chiara placed a *cappuccino* in front of Fabrizio and then Francy before turning to the display case. "*Allora*, yes, *frutti di bosco* and *albicoccca*."

"I'll take the apricot."

Chiara nodded and slid the pastry onto a plate. "Any *caffè?*"

"Maybe later."

Francy took his *cappuccino* to the vestibule between the bar and the outdoor seating, examining the faded prints lining the walls. Chiara watched him, and wished she'd repainted. She knew the walls weren't exactly pristine; she'd noticed some cracking last time she'd served the tourists who liked to sit there in the winter. It allowed a view of the falls without the biting wind and errant spray.

Magda said, "Norcia would be a good day trip. Or Spoleto."

Bea pulled Magda's arm. "What are we talking about?"

Magda answered, "Fabrizio and Francy want to head out of town and have asked for my expertise. I plan everyone's touristic trips, you know."

But Chiara and Fabrizio had their heads ducked together, whispering and giggling. Magda grumbled. "Well, I guess Chiara can suggest something."

Bea clucked, gesturing to the couple. "That developed fast."

Magda smirked and whispered, "I suspect it was going on long before any of us got wind of it."

Bea tore a piece off her *cornetto* and popped it in her mouth. "Hmmm. Maybe. I never understood love at first sight." She guffawed. "I wasn't convinced I loved my husband until after we had our third child and he brought me a melted mozzarella and prosciutto sandwich."

Magda's smile was tight. She pointed with her chin toward Fabrizio. "Well, he's not bad looking and he's in the money, so what's not to fall in love with?"

Bea's hand stalled in its arc toward her mouth. "He's rich?"

"As a lord."

"How do you know?"

Magda shrugged and took a sip of her *caffè*. "I looked him up after they started dating. After what happened with her last husband…"

Nodding, Bea took a napkin to clean a dab of jam glistening on the bar. "Good for Chiara."

"Good for all of us, I say. He'll bring his rich friends, they'll come spend money, maybe one will even buy that rubbish pile of a restaurant."

Neither of them noticed Francy listening from the doorway.

❧

Elisa paused in the street at the sight of her mother and Ava, deep in conversation. She crept closer and slid into the alley closest to the women conferencing with heads ducked close together. A more unlikely duo Elisa would be hard pressed to imagine. Her mother's mismatched floral tunic at odds with her zebra print leggings, neither top nor bottom flattering her weighty figure. Then Ava, trim and neat, even in her gardening clothes. Rather than sullying her image, the dirt on her knees and the cuffs of her shirt almost looked dabbed on for character.

Elisa leaned as far out of the alley as she could reasonably risk, and strained her ears. The crows overhead called to each other, breaking the fragile silence, and Elisa glared up at them. Wasn't it too dark for crows to be out?

A murmur, that's all she could make out. She closed her eyes to focus on her hearing, but couldn't pick out any words.

Her name! She heard her name. Then her father's. Was her mother telling Ava about the fight before her dad left?

The two straightened, peering up the street, clearly expecting her to return from Luciano's.

Sigh.

She hadn't learned a thing.

Elisa tipped her head up to catch the waning light. Maybe if she called her brothers, they could convince their mother to get back to the privacy she'd always relied on. So far, they had only laughed when Elisa complained, reminding her that their mother had never had a friend before. This was what women did. Like Elisa herself and Fatima.

"But mamma and Ava are so different!"

Just like her and Fatima.

Elisa peered around the corner and once both women were facing the other direction, she popped out of the alley and strolled toward them like she was returning home in a casual way.

"Elisa!" Ava called gaily, walking toward her for a moment before realizing that Concetta stood unmoved. She covered her confusion with running her hands through her wavy hair, pulling it into a knot at the base of her slender neck.

Elisa nodded. "*Ciao.*" She gave Ava what she hoped was an accusatory glare. Elisa didn't realize that given the trembling vulnerability of her person, she could at most manage appearing worried.

Ava stumbled. "It's good to see you! Your mamma and I are talking about spring planting. Your yard is going to be a heaven!"

"It's just a yard."

"Well, yes, of course," Ava laughed uncomfortably. "But you don't know how lucky you are. Most people in Santa Lucia don't have a yard at all."

Elisa said, "I never thought of it. I always think of the outside of our house as part of the town. So brambley."

Concetta's phone buzzed and she took it out and smiled at what she saw.

Elisa said, "Okay, I'm going to watch some TV."

Concetta turned to Ava and said, "Thanks for coming by. It was a big help."

Ava shot a glance at Elisa who stepped away, into the dimness of the house. "Anytime."

Ale darted a look over his shoulder at the sound at the door. No, it was just the wind.

He returned to stirring his *espresso* and listening to Chiara. She was delightful, with charming anecdotes about Santa Lucia. He'd been so disappointed to arrive the other day only to discover the bar closed. The town itself seemed to breathe more openly when Bar Birbo's waxed wooden door hung open.

Chiara laughed as Bea continued her story about Sauro the baker's experiments with gluten-free bread. Bea held her side and said, "He . . . he said he got the recipe . . . from the computer!"

Chiara's laughter pealed through the bar. "The computer!"

Bea slapped the counter. "Yes! Some tourist from Rome or Milan or wherever had asked about gluten-free bread, and Sauro . . . oh you should have seen his face. Well, I didn't see it either, but Arturo was there and told me about it." Bea pulled an open-mouth expression. "The tourist told him about celiac disease and how all good bakeries now have gluten-free choices and how Italy is actually leading the world with gluten-free foods."

Chiara shook her head. "I don't think I've heard the word gluten that many times in my whole life."

Bea guffawed while Ale watched the two of them like a ball bouncing back and forth. "I know! But Sauro, he couldn't stand to hear that Italy is tops for something that he isn't doing. So he ordered the flour."

"Oh, no. It's too funny . . ."

"And he made his bread with it . . ."

"I can't stand it!"

"And it spread out all over the oven like tar! Took him an hour to scrape it up!"

The women shrieked with laughter while Ale chuckled with them. He didn't know any of the players, though he had stopped into the bakery just the other day and gotten a cream-filled *cornetto* that was far better than he expected, given the stamp size of Santa Lucia. The baker clearly knew what he was doing. Or he did, by the standards of a generation ago. Perhaps he was faring less well in this new gluten-phobic world.

Gesturing with his spoon, Ale commiserated. "I feel for him. I tried to make gluten-free bread when Madison went on a diet a few years ago."

Chiara's eyes flashed with humor as she asked, "Get all over your oven?"

"Well, I put it in a loaf pan. But—"

Bea leaned toward him. "What happened?"

"I lost a loaf pan to the experiment."

Their laughter rang through the bar. Ale wasn't sure why. He'd told the story of Madison's gluten-free escapades a dozen times at cocktail parties to polite tittering at most. But now the whole thing seemed uproariously funny. Maybe his friends had felt borderline uncomfortable at his using his kitchen for cooking. He knew Madison hadn't wanted any part of it and had been horrified when he'd suggested trying bread baking, the science of it intriguing him. Also, he barely admitted to himself at the time, he had a kind of longing to dig his hands into dough. Back then, he figured he didn't get enough Play-Doh as a child. Now he wondered.

He almost didn't hear the door opening. But once he did, his head swiveled around and he stood straighter.

No, it was the mayor.

Dante didn't look any happier to see Ale. In fact, it looked as if he might back out of the bar. Instead, he picked his way forward, gesturing to Chiara, tucking her towel back into her apron.

"White?" she asked Dante, who nodded.

With a sound like a plucked bass string, Chiara uncorked the bottle and poured a glass for Dante.

"So, Alessandro," Dante began, with artificial cheeriness. "How goes the renovations?"

"Well, we hit a snag, Signor Sindaco, which I'd like you to smooth over."

Dante winced and shot a glance over his shoulder, perhaps measuring the number of steps to return to the street.

Ale chuckled. "*Sto scherzando*. I'm joking. As you promised, everyone is working quickly and the permits went through without a hitch. Record time, I'd say. Especially for Italy."

Dante drew a full breath. Thank God. All his years as a captain of people and governance paid off. He had called in every favor in his secret book, but it was worth it to keep the last few months from hitting the press. No doubt headlines of the mayor who fudged the paperwork to allow a festival on private—if seemingly abandoned—grounds would have only preceded the tabloid headlines of the once formidable mayor who had his wife stolen from under him by Vale the handyman.

With an admirable show of bravado he said, "It always helps to know the right people. I'm fortunate in that regard." He sipped his wine and then added with a stiff heartiness, "I am delighted the renovations are progressing. How nice it will be for Santa Lucia to have the *castello* occupied again."

Alessandro studied the mayor. He couldn't be for real. There was no way that his moving into what had once felt like public space could be anything other than resented. The truth of this often bothered him. How could it not goad the mayor?

His discussions with Madison about how to keep their proprietorship of the castle from negatively impacting the town had led nowhere. She could barely acknowledge that Santa Lucia had any sort of claim on the castle that had been part of the town's everyday existence for generations. In fact, she didn't even bother trying to pronounce Santa Lucia correctly, and he had stopped reminding her that Lucia sounded like loo-*chee*-ah.

Ale peered at the assembled faces. They averted their eyes. So they must see the mayor's words as false, too. Maybe the mayor wanted to avoid ruffling Ale's feathers. Ale sighed. He wished he could rejoin Chiara's conversation with Bea, which had moved on to the disappearance of what sounded like some bad character on the edge of town.

But Dante continued, "I'm confident you are doing everything in the very best style. As it should be! Bring it back to its former glory, eh?" He swallowed another sip of his wine and barreled on. "Yes, I believe once the *castello* is rejuvenated, it will be just the thing for you and your wife. You'll be very happy here in Santa Lucia."

The flat tone didn't convince Ale, who scraped the last of the sugar into his mouth. He considered for a moment and then said, "You know we won't be living here full time."

Dante's mouth fell open for an instant before he drew himself up.

"You're not?"

"No, we'll still live in New York. We'll use the *castello* for vacations."

"Ah. So the house will for the most part be—"

"Empty. Yes."

Ale could see the euros and cents flashing across Dante's mind as he calculated the cost of a renovation that would only be enjoyed once or twice a year. Maybe not even that. Madison tired of places easily. Ale's mind flicked to that house they bought in Martha's Vineyard with the lawn that tumbled down to the sea. Madison spent more time furnishing the house than she did vacationing in it. After two trips to the completed house, Madison had declared that the Vineyard was over. The ink on the sale papers hardly dried before she started scrolling through real estate listings in the Rocky Mountains. Just when she was sprinkling cocktail party conversation with mention of ski getaways in Wyoming, they'd gotten word about the castle.

Even though they had been in Italy barely a month, Madison already seemed to be growing bored. He hoped the trip to Rome to select fabrics and surfaces would re-energize her. And maybe if he could get her through the phase of waning novelty, she'd find herself feeling at home and content.

Dante mulled. "Empty. I see."

Ale roused his smile from the place it had gotten lost in his dwelling on matters of hearth and home. "When we're not here, our family will be checking in, making sure all is running smoothly. My family doesn't travel, but Madison's parents are excited to stay."

He wondered what the town would make of his mother-in-law. Madison wouldn't ever admit it, but something was seriously wacky about her mother. Annual plastic surgery had turned her face into an emoji, and though nobody talked about it, it was impossible not to notice that she had a serious problem of stealing rolls of toilet paper from every public restroom she visited. And she visited many. Ale wondered if she had a kidney condition on top of her other quirks.

Despite himself, he was growing fond of this town, and he winced at the thought of inflicting his domineering father-in-law and cipher of a mother-in-law on Santa Lucia. But it couldn't be helped. He only hoped that the castle's charms would fail to prove adequate to overcome the terrible provinciality of the region, so their stays would be far fewer than they were currently promising. Though last time he heard Madison on the phone with her mother, the two had been planning Christmas themes at the castle for the next five years. He'd thought about mentioning that King Arthur was English, not Italian, but realized it didn't matter. All he'd get for his wasted breath would be an eye roll.

"Your wife's family. How . . . how lovely."

Ale wondered if he and the mayor were watching the same film on the screen of their imagination—the father-in-law swanning into the butcher shop demanding to be served first and making cracks about intestines for sale, his mother-in-law scurrying behind him, seeking out another bathroom while shoving the loose sheet from the roll in her purse back out of view. Madison prattling alongside them, pointing out the sights for which she had no context and no real interest. He sighed. Sometimes he wondered how he wound up here.

Little did he know that Dante was wondering the same thing.

The door opened and both of their heads turned, but it was Edo, unwrapping his scarf to join Chiara behind the bar.

There was a definite chill in the air. The breeze prickled as if it had plucked ice shards off the surrounding olive leaves to abrade any skin unlucky enough to be left exposed. Edo stopped and retied his scarf.

"Delay much?" He asked himself.

"Maybe," he conceded.

But it wouldn't help matters if he got sick too. He wasn't convinced that a neck open to drafts led to respiratory infections, but at the same time, the notion was so ground into him, he felt, rather than knew, that it *could* be true. And after the spate of warm days, these drafts might well compromise his immune system. Or so Bea said, anyway, explaining to the bar clientele this morning why Chiara's cold was so debilitating.

Tucking the scarf into his down jacket, and pulling the edge over his chin, he began crossing Santa Lucia. Every step felt like walking toward the gallows, but wasn't that a touch too dramatic, even for him? Delivering Umbrian folk music CD's to Fabrizio wasn't worth all that. He wanted to help Chiara, he reminded himself. Poor Chiara! She looked miserable. Unfortunate, as she had just filed the paperwork for a divorce. He was sure she wanted to celebrate, rather than sleeping through lunch. For the second day in a row.

Edo's steps faltered outside the entrance to San Nicola, Santa Lucia's lone church. He wondered what his parents would say about Chiara's divorce. Really, was it more immoral to divorce a pedophile or remain married? The answer was pretty clear to him, but his parents would probably sneer that he was hardly in a position to assign morality.

Then again, his parents had surprised him when he told them he was gay. They didn't welcome the news, of course. But they quietly nodded before changing the topic. Really, it was the best he could ask for. Since he wasn't dating anymore thanks to Trevor's sudden disappearance, Edo's sexual orientation wasn't likely to come up in conversation. Maybe that breakup was a blessing after all. To give his parents time to get used to their son's . . . situation.

Anyway, his parents would have to adapt. Their son was gay, and Chiara would soon be a divorcee.

She must be serious about Fabrizio. Edo understood that, Fabrizio was a good guy—amiable once he dropped the authorial remove. He was fun, he didn't take himself too seriously, he was thoughtful, and he liked people.

A great match for Chiara. If only it didn't make Edo wonder about the future. Chiara hadn't mentioned it and he didn't want to bring it up, but would Chiara move to Bologna? He couldn't see Fabrizio living in Santa Lucia, as much as the older man spoke lovingly of the town.

He arrived. Edo sighed and raised his hand to knock on the door.

It opened, and Edo's heart fell to see not Fabrizio, but his son.

"*Ciao*, Francy."

"*Buongiorno*, Edoardo." Francy backed up to allow Edo passage into the house.

"I don't need to come in." Edo lofted the plastic bag of CD's up like an offering.

"My father's not here, but he'll be back shortly. Allow me to pour you some *caffè*," Francy insisted.

Edo wondered how rude it would be to refuse.

Francy said, "I know he wanted to say hello and thank you."

"Yes, okay then. *Caffè* would be good, thanks." Edo offered up a silent prayer that Fabrizio returned quickly.

Francy closed the door behind Edo and walked up the stairs to what Edo supposed must be the kitchen. The smell of coffee reeled him forward.

Francy pulled a seat out at the table and gestured for his visitor to sit. Edo gritted his teeth, how was he supposed to make conversation with this man?

He began, "So . . . Spoleto today?"

Francy nodded as he bustled in front of the stove, pulling out cups and saucers. He poured the *caffè*, and brought it to the table along with the milk and sugar and a plate of prune-filled cookies from the *forno*. Fabrizo must have picked them up. Edo couldn't imagine Francy pulling back the bead curtain to enter Santa Lucia's tiny bakery with its rotating arrangement of rustic offerings like shatteringly-crisp sheets of fried dough for Carnevale or wine-must scented bread during the harvest.

Edo said, "Have you been before? To Spoleto?"

Francy folded his body into the seat opposite Edo. "No. I planned to attend the Two Worlds Festival a few years ago, but something came up at work."

Edo blew into his *caffè*, hoping it wasn't awful. Extraordinary fussiness about coffee topped the list of occupational hazards of his job. "I didn't think musicians had emergencies."

Francy responded with a small grin. "Not many, nowadays, since I perform solo, but back then I worked for a booking company."

Edo took a hesitant sip of his *caffè* and blurted out, "This is wonderful!"

To the sound of the distant opening door, Francy said, "I have a friend bring it from Trieste when he travels there for work."

Fabrizio appeared in the kitchen with a plastic bag of bottled water. The smile that stretched over his face at the sight of the two men at the table practically bowled him backward. "Edo! How is Chiara?"

"Much the same, I'm afraid. She's sorry she couldn't bring these." Edo gestured to the CD's on the table.

"I would have collected them."

"I know. She knows. It's okay, I have to stop by Giovanni's anyway." Edo didn't add that Chiara had teared up at the notion that Fabrizio might insist on seeing her. She had looked up at Edo with such horror, her hair untidy around her head like a baby chicken, her nose bright red and her lips cracked from trying to pull a full breath, he had offered to bring the CD's she had promised Fabrizio for his road trip.

Francy muttered, "If your car had bluetooth like every other car..."

Fabrizio ignored him. Edo, whose own car with an old-school tape deck currently sat in a shop after the accident that prompted him to get sober, was happy to follow suit.

Edo asked Fabrizio, "Francy was telling me he's never visited Spoleto...same for you?"

Fabrizio got down a cup and poured himself *caffè* as he answered, "Once, years ago. It's been on my list since I arrived in Santa Lucia. But I find once I'm happy somewhere, it's hard to leave."

Perhaps out of hopes that Fabrizio's words telegraphed his reluctance to remove Chiara to Bologna, Edo grinned and said, "That is exactly what I would have expected from what I know of you!"

Fabrizio joined the young men at the table, and said, "I didn't know you made a habit out of studying character."

A knock at the door interrupted Edo's response. Which was lucky, as he didn't have one. It had never occurred to him that one could study character. Fabrizio leapt up. "That will be Savia, the seamstress. She patched the hole in my jacket and said she'd be bringing it by. Just in time. I worried I'd have to double up on my suit coats what with this cold tang in the air."

Tang in the air? Edo had never met people like these two. He felt his own lack of education press in on him. He looked at his hands, resting in his lap, and clenched them. School had not been his strong suit. He never found it important or relevant. Then again, he'd never been with people who talked like this.

Edo sipped his *caffè* and tried not to notice Francy staring at him. Was there something on his face? Was he drinking his *caffè* wrong? He ground his jaw together and added an extra spoonful of sugar that he didn't want, hoping to annoy Francy.

Fabrizio returned to the table with Savia. Edo greeted her and asked about Ava. Savia said that Ava was off with Alessandro and his wife in Girona looking at stone options for the *castello*. Edo wondered how an eye toward garden design translated to interior decorating, but he shrugged it off.

Savia gazed at Francy in an appraising way. Edo recognized that look. Like a fox debating how many bites it would take to gobble a rabbit. His exiting the closet meant that Savia no longer aimed that expression at him, thank the Madonna.

Testing the weight of the moka, Fabrizio decided to make a new pot.

Savia reached for the plate of cookies. "Oh, these are my favorites."

While the water heated, Fabrizio sat back at the table. "So, Edo. You seem to have figured me out already. I admit I'm disappointed that I'm so easily read."

Edo shrugged. "That's not necessarily a bad thing. It's not like complicated people are the ideal." He couldn't help but glance at Francy.

Francy said, "Santa Lucia must be a poor location for you to practice your craft."

Savia's mouth worked like a landed fish. She huffed, "A poor location! Santa Lucia is a wonderful town! Full of wonderful people!"

Quiet reigned.

Edo leaned imperceptibly toward Savia. "Francy means there are fewer people in Santa Lucia than a place like Bologna. Fewer subjects for people watching."

"Fewer interesting people, he means. Personally, I don't think cities offer anything better than Santa Lucia. Besides places to waste your money. But he seems to think Santa Lucia is nothing at all!"

Savia stood, brushing the crumbs off of her chest. "Well! I have some small-town things to do that I'm sure wouldn't be of interest to *him*," she pointed at Francy. With that she flounced out of the room.

Fabrizio leapt up after her. "My coat!"

Francy frowned. "I didn't mean . . . that's not at all what I meant. I've upset her."

Edo said, "It's okay. She'll forget it all later when Giovanni tells her his latest joke." Hoping to steer the conversation into friendlier waters, he said, "But to your point, Francy, you know small towns actually do offer plenty of opportunities for character observation. Because people themselves change constantly. I would think you'd know that, being a songwriter and all."

Francy took a sip of *caffè*, looking up into Edo's eyes that were creasing in the corners from his spreading grin. Edo helped himself to a cookie and said, "Then again, I don't know your music. Perhaps you sing about under-appreciated pizza toppings."

It took a moment, but then Francy's eyes flashed with understanding and he sputtered, spilling his *caffè*.

Edo readied his excuses so he could get out of this increasingly odd situation.

Dinners at Isotta's house were predictably boisterous affairs. With five young women and two parents and usually a complement of boyfriends, Isotta often had to squeeze her eyes shut just to hear herself think.

The new silence felt oppressive. Disarming, even.

Ever since the week before when Isotta had dropped the bomb that she was carrying a child, the house was muted. Isotta tried to hope that the silence portended thoughtfulness and a detour into gentleness. This was likely foolish longing. More probably, it was the crackling inhale before a monstrous storm.

A rapping at the door startled the family. Except Caterina who smiled slowly. "Why don't you get it, Isotta?"

"Me? Why? It's probably Ilaria's boyfriend. Wasn't he coming over?" Isotta looked at her sister, who concentrated on spinning her pasta on her fork.

Caterina's face drew into a pinched expression. "Do as I say."

Isotta shrugged, stood up and walked through the living room to open the door.

Massimo.

Staggering backward, Isotta lost her breath. Reaching quickly, Massimo steadied her.

"Get off me!" She yelped.

"Isotta, what's wrong?" Massimo said.

""What's *wrong*?" You show up and ask '*what's wrong*'?"

"But your mother said—"

"My mother? My mother called you?"

To Massimo's look of astonished innocence, Isotta called out, "Mamma! *Mamma!*"

The family had been peeking around the corner, and Caterina now stepped forward. "Yes, darling?" She smiled placidly.

"What is Massimo doing here?" The ice in Isotta's voice chilled her vocal cords into a strangled whisper.

"Why, I invited him of course." She offered Massimo a winning smile and a wink.

Massimo narrowed his eyes and leaned forward to whisper to Isotta, "I apologize, Isotta. Your mother told me you wanted to see me, that you had news—"

"News! *Si!*" Caterina licked her lips. "Isn't it time you tell him your news, Isotta?"

Isotta shook her head furiously, her face hot.

Caterina clucked. "*Comunque,* I can tell him for you of course. I figured you'd want to tell him yourself, but—"

"No! I . . . I'll do it. Come on, Massimo, let's go for a walk."

Caterina clucked again. She never made that noise; it was getting annoying. "Oh, I don't think so, Isotta. You've already proven that you are too headstrong and sneaky by half. Apparently this whole bookish prude thing was a ruse all those years. You'll tell him here." She turned to Massimo and simpered, "That way we can all celebrate together."

Isotta took a breath and pressed her clammy hand to her flushed cheeks. Her heart beat so furiously she felt in danger of it beating a hole through her ribcage. This couldn't be happening. She looked around at the rest of her family. Her eyes met Isabella's and she pleaded wordlessly. Isabella nodded as if in agreement and said, "Mamma, let them go."

Caterina said, "Don't interfere, Isa. You know as well as I do that her leaving Massimo ruins us all. Who will marry my daughters once Isotta gives birth to a bastard?"

The room drew in a collective breath.

Massimo's mouth gaped and he swept up Isotta's hand. "Are you . . . are you pregnant?"

Caterina laughed gaily. "*Oopla!* Looks like I spoiled the surprise!"

Isotta sank onto the edge of the couch and dropped her head into her hand.

Massimo sank beside her, his arm around her shaking shoulders. "For how long?"

Isotta shook her head angrily.

Massimo gentled his voice further. "Isotta? How long have you been with child?"

Her eyes filled with tears that she indignantly brushed away.

Caterina said, "Three months. Though apparently she's only known for a month or two." Caterina jabbed her husband in the side. "And she's so good with numbers, huh? Look how far that got her. You see now?" Isotta's father slumped in his chair and stared out the window. His inability to protect his daughter was cleaving the meat from his bones.

Massimo touched Isotta's hand and softly said, "Can this be true?"

Isotta nodded and covered her face with her hands.

Massimo sighed.

Caterina clapped her hands together. "Well, you better start packing if you're going to get back to Santa Lucia tonight."

Isotta stared at her mother. "Wha . . . what?"

Caterina shrugged. "Massimo will want to take his pregnant wife home. Won't you, Massimo?"

Massimo blinked at his mother-in-law as if seeing her for the first time.

Caterina went on, "In fact, if you *don't* go, Massimo could sue to bring you back. You abandoned him. After forming a relationship with his child and getting yourself pregnant. Isn't that right, Massimo?"

Massimo stood. "While that may be true, I'd rather Isotta come home because she wants to, so I'd thank you to back off."

It was Caterina's turn to look slapped. Isotta's father's gaze ripped from the window and he assessed his only son-in-law. Caterina gasped, "How...how...dare..."

Massimo drew upon his authoritative posture and boomed, "You must have heard me. This is my wife and you will not speak to her this way. It's insulting. To me, to her, to the child she's carrying. Come on, Isotta."

Isotta faced her husband, astonished. Holding out his hand, he said in soft tones that carried throughout the room, "I know you think my home is as bad as this one. But I'm offering you a chance for something different. I'm willing to change. I doubt that can be said for this household." Massimo looked around at the assembled faces. Caterina's mouth shrank into a line as her husband stared at his hands, smiling.

Isotta nodded and slipped her hand in Massimo's.

## WINTER

*C*hiara's virus decided it best not to annoy her for too long.

A few days later saw her chirping and laughing and pouring the mayor another glass of wine, with no more than the merest suggestion of a cold to trouble her. Dante reached for the bowl of peanuts, popping them in his mouth, seemingly without tasting them. "I don't like the sound of it, Chiara. Having the *castello* standing empty much of the time?"

"You complained for years about the eyesore of a derelict *castello*. Won't you be glad to see it restored?"

Dante sighed. "Did I? Maybe. That feels like another lifetime."

Chiara had never seen him so vague.

Dante chewed thoughtfully and said, "I suppose I wanted the *castello* rehabilitated, and hated that we didn't have jurisdiction over it. But at least people could wander up the stairs and take in the view from the castle grounds."

Walking in, Magda overheard Dante. She shook her head. "It's a catastrophe."

Chiara said, "Magda—"

"It is! This town is built around that *castello*, and now it'll be like we are serfs for foreigners."

Chiara thought it best not to mention that Magda herself was a foreigner.

Dante drew himself up, with a suggestion of his former commanding manner. "Nothing to be done. It's their *castello*." His posture suggested confidence, but his eyes were anxious, ready for Magda's certain criticisms.

She scowled and said, "I know. It's a tragic end to what was already a tragic episode. Now Santa Lucia has no *castello* and no *trattoria*."

Chiara poured herself a glass of water and said, "Still no interest in L'Ora Dorata?"

Dante shook his head. "None."

Chiara sipped her water. "Alessandro seems a reasonable man. Maybe he'd be willing to open up the grounds when they aren't here—"

Dante and Magda's snorts mirrored of each other. They gave each other sidelong looks before Magda said, "You're an optimist, Chiara. I'll say that for you." She and Dante continued to chuckle as the bell over the door signaled another arrival.

Chiara smiled tentatively, prompting Magda and Dante to turn around and see who had arrived. When they saw Fabrizio and Francy, they both turned back to the bar, exchanging scowls as Dante sipped his wine, and Magda debated aloud having one as well.

"*Buonasera*," Chiara greeted the newcomers.

Fabrizio and his son approached the bar.

"Wine?" she suggested.

"*Caffè*," answered Fabrizio. "You're looking well!" He added with pleasure.

"Yes, much improved."

Francy narrowed his eyes. "It doesn't look like you were sick at all."

Chiara forced an awkward laugh. "The state of my handkerchiefs suggests otherwise."

Francy pressed his lips together, saying nothing.

Fumbling, Chiara set the filter basket to catch the ground beans. Magda and Dante exchanged more glances.

Setting the basket into the La Pavoni, Chiara turned back to the men.

"Your trip to Spoleto? You had a good time?"

Fabrizio said, "Yes! What a lively town. We've been remarking on that the whole walk here. Right, Francy?"

Chiara looked toward Francy, who was investigating the faded food offerings in the case.

Fabrizio laughed. "Well, we were. The Roman amphitheater is stunning."

The bell over the door announced Edo's arrival. He stamped his feet and reported, "Wow, if I didn't know better, I'd predict snow."

Everyone nodded and turned back, Francy taking an extra beat, staring at Edo so long, Edo wondered if his nose had snotted. He nonchalantly rubbed his hands over his face, but it seemed okay.

Magda said, "We have Roman ruins right here in Santa Lucia, you know."

Fabrizio startled. "No! Where?"

Chiara held out her hands to forestall his anticipation. "It's not much, only a bit of wall or maybe the start of an aqueduct to move Santa Lucia's water to someplace in the valley. There aren't enough ruins for anyone to try to figure out, but enough to make us wonder."

Fabrizio stirred his *caffè*. "How strange that I haven't noticed."

Magda gestured for a glass of wine as Chiara said, "Unless you're spending a lot of time in the graveyard, you'd miss it. It's one of the walls."

Edo moved behind the counter and washed his hands. "She's underselling it. The lettering is surprisingly intact. It's not a large example, but it's a clean one."

Fabrizio said, "Francy venerates anything ancient Roman. He has since he was a child."

Edo shrugged. "He should see it then. There's enough daylight now, if you hurry."

Fabrizio suggested, "Maybe Francy, you'd like to go with Edo? See the ruins? It's a bit chilly for me."

Edo turned suddenly. "Oh! I wasn't suggesting a walk together."

Francy blurted, "I'd be delighted for the company. If you can get away for a beat."

Edo shot a look at Chiara, who turned her head. "That sounds fun, for sure. But I have some things I have to take care of. Upstairs. So. I'll see you all later."

Francy's eyes lingered on the closed door far after everyone else had started discussing the best Umbrian examples of Roman architecture.

The rolling suitcase bumped across the threshold. Shivering, Isotta stopped in the entrance. Massimo put his arm around her. "Cold?" he asked.

She shook her head, allowing herself to be pulled deeper into the house she thought she'd never see again. She must be mad. How in the world did she allow this to happen? "Where's your mother?"

"I told you, she's with Margherita at her sister's house. We didn't know you'd be returning, of course. Otherwise I know she would have been eager to welcome you home."

Isotta shivered again.

No.

She couldn't do this. She couldn't walk back into the viper den. Anna would not be pleased to see her, and the fact that Massimo even said that made her queasy. Did he actually believe his words?

She started rolling the suitcase out the front door back into the alley.

"Isotta! What—"

"No. No way. I can't do this."

"Isotta. We had a deal." Massimo said, evenly.

"No. No deal. I can't live here with you again. I must have been delirious after living with my parents. I'd forgotten. I'd forgotten what it's like here. I can't be me here. I can't be anything."

"Isotta!" Massimo pitched his voice low and held Isotta by the elbows, looking at her with concern. "I remember how pregnancy hormones—"

"Oh my God! Massimo, this isn't about what hormones are running through my body—it's about the hell you put me through for months and the fact that your mother—God, there's something *wrong* with her. Can't you feel it?"

Massimo bit back his usual defensive response at any assumed slight on his mother. Instead he said, "It was a lot. I get that. But now we can be honest with each other. It will be so much better."

Isotta broke away and began walking down the alley. "Well, we can be honest from different houses. I'm not setting foot in that place again."

"Where do you think you're going! You're hysterical!"

Isotta shook her head. "Actually, I feel quite rational all of a sudden. I'm going to Luciano's."

"You can't stay with that man!"

Isotta turned. "Is that right? And why is that?"

"He's a drunken maniac!"

Isotta shrugged. "We've all sinned. He's moved on. Why can't you. Seriously, Massimo . . . why the grudge?"

"He . . . he . . . he . . ."

"That's what I thought."

"I remember my mother told me some stories after Giulia died."

"How dare you! How dare you bring his daughter's death into it."

"She was my wife!"

"And his daughter! If he blundered, isn't that understandable? Massimo, why can't you get it through your presumedly intelligent brain? Maybe he did or said something in his grief. In yours, you married his daughter's twin!"

"Isotta—"

"No! I won't have you talk about him like that. He lost everything, and even so, he managed to see me when nobody else could. If you love me, if you really love me like you say you do, then that alone should secure your compassion for him. Without him, who knows where I'd be right now?"

Massimo clenched his jaw and stared at Carosello, who barely gave him a glance as he jogged on to the *piazza*.

Isotta drew in a steadying breath and started walking again.

Massimo's voice stopped her short. "Okay."

"Okay?"

"Yes. Okay. I don't know what to make of Luciano. I haven't since Giulia's death. But you're right. I can't think of anything specific he has done to offend me besides be in your corner when I couldn't or wouldn't. You should stay with him."

Isotta had an impulse to look around for hidden cameras.

Massimo said, "And if he's not there, or he can't take you in, I'll get you a room at Magda's. It's low-season. I'm sure she has availability."

Isotta knew that if she stayed at Magda's it would mean questions and suppositions and gossiping. Luciano's too, but at least that had been the status quo before she'd left. Massimo must be serious about changing if he agreed to deal with that.

She nodded. "Okay. Let's go."

Grey clouds filled the sky above Santa Lucia. Thickening, then stretching, they created dappled shadows along Via Romana. Edo paused his sweeping to watch fog follow drizzle. Before condensing into a hazy rain again. The Madonna's outstretched hand radiated a pearlescent glow against the oscillating darkness.

Edo's gaze caught on a figure approaching the door. Francy. He stood outside the lit bar for a moment before pushing the door open. Edo turned to grit his teeth, shoving the broom in a corner. He turned back with a smile. "What can I get you?'

Francy said, "A Campari and soda, *per favore*."

Edo nodded and began assembling the drink. The feel of Francy's eyes on him made him uncomfortable and to fill the silence he said, "Fabrizio says your songwriting is going well."

"It is."

Was Francy going to say anything else? It didn't appear so. Edo tried again. "He said you got a recording contract. That must have been exciting."

Francy nodded.

Edo placed the drink in front of Francy. Reaching into the bins of chips and nuts, he said, "You know, for a musician you're on the humble side."

This caught Francy's attention. "Humble?"

"Sure. I have high school friends trying to break into the industry, and it seems like they talk about nothing but their music and their parties and their followers. I'd describe you as downright restrained."

Francy took a sip of his drink and tentatively said, "I lack the gift of effortlessly talking with strangers. Without an instrument in front of me, I confess I am out of my depth. You though . . . you can improvise a conversation with anyone."

Edo set the bowls of salty snacks in front of Francy. "Interesting." He considered for a moment and then added, "My fingers don't strum a guitar as well as I would like. But I always supposed that was my own fault because I wouldn't take the trouble to practice."

A grin spread across Francy's face. "You are quite right."

The door opened and Arturo bustled in. "*Un caffè*, Edo."

Edo nodded, turning to grind the coffee. Arturo's fingers tapped the bar. He looked over at Francy and offered a perfunctory hello before leaning toward Edo. "So what do you think of our Alessandro Bardi?"

Edo set the *espresso* in front of Arturo and said, "Ale?" He shrugged. "I like him. Why?"

Arturo licked his lips. "That wife of his. Charming, charming . . ."

Edo smiled wanly and said, "He came in here often before they left for Rome. A well-mannered guy. Lots to say." Edo shot a look at Francy. Francy was stirring his drink and missed the barb.

Arturo dumped a packet of sugar into his *espresso* and said, "We won't recognize the *castello* when the Americans finish with it."

Edo wiped down the back of the bar as Arturo continued offering tid-bits of gossip. Eventually, Arturo shared all his news and left.

Francy drained the last of his drink and said, "Thank you, that was well made. I should leave as well. I need to get to the store before it closes. Without restaurants, I'm forced to cook. Or perhaps my father will, as I have a song I'd like to finish."

Edo didn't think he had ever heard Francy say so much in one go. He wrung out the washcloth and said, "The butcher shop across the street sells fresh pasta and gnocchi if you want something easy."

Francy smiled to himself as he took out his wallet. "Do you think I should get a bottle of Sagrantino to make a sauce for the gnocchi?"

Edo ran the washcloth under warm water again, wringing it out a final time before draping it across the faucet.

Francy dropped a handful of euros on the tarnished copper plate and repeated, "Should I get a bottle of Sagrantino to make—"

"Oh, I heard you. I was thinking of how to answer. You want me, I'm sure, to say, 'Yes' and maybe even offer a recipe so that you can have the pleasure of despising my taste. But I enjoy sabotaging contempt—small town life offers so few opportunities to tease people that way. So I've made up my mind to tell you that I prefer a *tartufata* sauce. And now despise me if you dare."

"Indeed, I do not dare." Francy said with an admiring smile.

His unexpected archness left Edo without words.

Her house shone bright against the winter rain. Elisa hoped this meant her mother stood at the stove, stirring something tasty. She walked in and grinned at the sweet and yeasty scent. Elisa took off her coat, shaking out the icy droplets. She jumped as Ava's voice called from the kitchen. "*Buonasera*, Elisa! How was school?"

Off guard, Elisa yelled, "What are you *doing* here?"

Ava appeared in the doorway, wiping her hands on a towel. "Your mother...she asked me to come."

"Then where is she?"

Ava said, "She had a message or something she needed to respond to. She's in her room I think."

Elisa shook her head and grumbled, walking toward her room.

Ava called, "Do you want a snack? I made—"

"No! I don't want a snack! I don't want to talk! I want to be left alone!"

Ava turned her head away and blinked.

Elisa's hands tightened into balls at her sides and she snapped, "It's freezing. You can't be gardening. Why do you need to be here?"

Ava bit her lip.

This gesture of vulnerability enraged Elisa. "Why can't you just go?"

Ava whispered, "Elisa, I want to help. I know it's hard with your father gone and—"

"You don't know anything! You think you know things but you don't! You hang around here like you don't even have a life! You are so *weird*!"

Ava turned around and walked to the kitchen, collecting her jacket and purse.

Returning to the living room she said, "I...I was only trying...I didn't mean..."

Elisa glowered.

Ava said, "It's not a good time. I'll go. You can tell your mother that...you can tell her goodbye."

She hurried out the door.

Elisa watched her leave and said to herself. "She's so stupid. Look she didn't even put her coat on."

A sniffing sound alerted Edo. Was Chiara sick again?

He knocked on her door. "Chiara? You need anything?"

A soft moan was his response.

"Chiara! Can I come in?"

He heard a faint squeak of "*sì*" and threw open the door.

Chiara was sitting on her bed, dressed for work, with a letter crumpled in her hands.

Edo sat beside her. "Zia? What is it?"

Chiara angrily rubbed her eyes free of tears. "Fabrizio left."

"Left? What do you mean?"

"He left. For Bologna."

"I thought he was taking Francy back next week."

Chiara nodded.

Edo ventured, "So he went early?"

Chiara nodded and hiccuped.

"Chiara—"

"I don't think he's coming back."

"What? What do you mean?"

"The last time I saw him, he was so distant. Asking me all kinds of questions about my parents and my husband. Then made up a stupid excuse and left."

"Maybe he didn't make up an excuse? Maybe he really did have to go?"

Chiara coughed a kind of laugh. "Nobody has to suddenly polish their shoes."

Edo grew still, "He said that?"

Chiara nodded. "And then this was waiting on the door this morning." She held out the note.

Edo gingerly took it. "You want me to read it?"

Chiara said, "You might as well."

*Chiara—*

*My father asked me to write to you as he is busy with packing after his extended stay. We're returning to Bologna this morning. I have a gig opportunity that he wants to attend. Papa asked me to apologize for him.*

*Sincerely,*

*Francy*

"See?" Chiara wailed.

Edo turned the paper over to examine the blank back side. "Well, it *is* a bit strange."

"Something happened, Edo. Fabrizio is a writer. He would never trust someone else to author his own message. And he would never allow one so cold. Unless he decided—"

"Hey, hey, hey. It's okay. Anyone who has seen you and Fabrizio know you are golden together. Maybe he was stressed about getting Francy back in time. Or something. I can't believe that anything could happen that would make him leave you voluntarily."

"I . . . I . . . think it's something about the divorce. Maybe he thought it was too much pressure. His first marriage was so soured. It wasn't meant to pressure him, I didn't feel right being shackled to another man. I wasn't suggesting we get married after knowing each other for only a few months!"

"Of course you weren't."

"Or maybe he heard something about me?"

"Who would say anything about you?"

"There are people."

"Pssh."

A pause.

"Edo—"

"I know, Zia, I know. But you are going to have to trust that this is a misunderstanding and he'll be back before Christmas. Can you call him? Email?

"I don't have his email address. I have his phone number."

"Then call him. Or text him!"

"I can't! If he's feeling pressured by me, the last thing I want to do is hound him when he's trying to get space."

"Okay, maybe not today. But you'll call him? I mean, if he doesn't call you."

Chiara nodded, considering. "If he doesn't call me. Maybe."

The sound of knocking rang through Luciano's house.

Isotta rushed into the kitchen, where Luciano was reheating yesterday's *farro* and sausage soup. "I'll get the door."

Luciano, focused on stirring the soup, didn't answer.

Isotta paused before saying, "You might want to add some red pepper flakes. I left them out because the spice doesn't agree with me, but I think you'd like it better."

Luciano began rummaging through the cabinet next to the stove.

Isotta used her hip to nudge Luciano out of the way so she could reach behind the pepper and oregano and pluck out the red pepper flakes.

With a furrowed brow, Luciano said, "I would have found it."

Isotta said, "You okay?"

Luciano concentrated on selecting a bare pinch of red pepper flakes to sprinkle over the bubbling soup. His nod was more a suggestion of a nod. "Yes. Only . . . I'm worried about you, Isotta."

Isotta patted his shoulder. "If this doesn't work, it doesn't work. It's worth it to me to try."

Luciano shook his head. "After what he did."

"Yes. Even so." Isotta's hand moved over her stomach.

Lifting the spoon to his mouth, Luciano tipped in a bit of soup without really tasting it. He nodded anyway, and turned toward Isotta. "I believe in your competence, I know you can handle yourself. But to be quite honest, I hate the thought of him hurting you again."

"It's dinner. How bad can it be?"

Luciano looked up at Isotta without answering.

She said, "I wish I could reassure you that I won't get hurt, but all I can do is tell you that I don't feel made of glass. That must have meaning. All my life, I have been vulnerable or powerless or something. I'm not anymore. It's like you said, maybe having such bad things happen to me and still come out the other side has actually helped me in a strange way."

Nodding, Luciano said, "Massimo is waiting." He considered. "Peculiar that he didn't knock again. Perhaps he left."

Isotta said, "No, that's him showing me how patient he can be."

"How are you so sure?"

She lightly kissed his weathered cheek. "I just am."

Walking to the front door to fetch her coat off the rack, she called over her shoulder, "Now, don't make this stranger than it needs to be. Come say hello."

Luciano's lower lip turned out. "I don't want to."

Isotta walked to the kitchen with her coat on and drew Luciano away from the stove, still holding his wooden spoon. She murmured, "He's done wrong by you. He's done wrong by your daughter. But it's not like you to hold a grudge, if he's willing to change."

"You don't know. Maybe it's *exactly* like me."

A fleeting expression of bemusement crossed Isotta's face. "No, it's not. This man is your ticket to your granddaughter. Now, make nice."

This caught Luciano off guard, and he allowed himself to be led to the door. Isotta threw it open to reveal Massimo, shifting his weight from one foot to another. He thrust out a bouquet of flowers and said, "*Buonasera*, Isotta. I was beginning to think—"

"I needed to get my coat. I'm ready."

"You look nice." He smiled at her winsomely. She wished her stomach would stop backflipping at the sight of that full-lipped smile.

"Thank you. And here is Luciano." Isotta practically pushed the man forward.

"Ah. Luciano. I didn't see you there. *Buonasera.*"

"*Buonasera,*" Luciano said, begrudgingly.

"I . . . ah.. I appreciate you taking in my wife. If . . . ah . . . if I can contribute financially . . ."

Luciano stared at Massimo, doubt shadowing his face.

Isotta sighed. "Well, off we go! Don't wait up, Luciano. You need your sleep."

Luciano muttered something indistinguishable and closed the door behind the couple.

Massimo shook his head at the solid door. "He hates me."

Isotta began walking toward the parking lot at the upper end of town, where Massimo always parked his car. "Can you blame him?"

"What do you mean?"

Isotta stopped and regarded Massimo. "You'll just need to try. To like him, I mean. Luciano's heart is soft. He can't resist anyone who is open to him."

Massimo hesitatingly took Isotta's hand. When she squeezed it, he tentatively stroked her cheek. Isotta's breath caught. Slowly, Massimo lowered his face, tenderly pressing his lips against hers. The kiss deepened, and Isotta's mind darted uncomfortably, at war with her body that wanted nothing more than to melt into Massimo's strong embrace. She pushed away. "No!"

Massimo drew back, bringing his hand to his mouth. "Isotta?"

"No. I won't turn that page again."

"What . . . what do you mean?"

"If we want to see if we can make this work, I . . . we . . . can't be ruled by our bodies."

Massimo hazarded a faint grin. "Why not? If I remember, that can be quite wonderful."

Isotta said, "Too wonderful."

"Is there such a thing?"

Isotta nodded. "Yes. When it's blinding. Don't you see, Massimo? Our marriage was based on heat and lies. If we want to build something real, we have to start with neither."

Massimo thought about it. "That will be hard."

"Yes. I know."

"Well, I suppose you make the rules now."

"Massimo—"

"I know that sounds bitter. I was looking forward to—"

"I know—"

"And I didn't know that you didn't want—"

"I *do*. Want. It's only—"

"Look, we're finishing each other's sentences. That must count for something." He sighed as he rustled through his pocket. Extracting his car keys he pushed the unlock button with more force than usual. Lightly he broached, "So while we're making plans. Where does Margherita fit in?"

Isotta said, "I'm dying to see her. But I don't want to be in her life if you and I have no chance. It feels cruel. To her. And maybe to me, too."

He said nothing as he opened Isotta's door and settled her in. As he sat behind the wheel he asked, "You feel okay?"

She nodded, biting her lip.

Massimo flicked the ignition until the car was purring and he backed out of his spot, then rolled forward, down the hill toward Girona.

He said, "I understand your hesitation. After everything that happened, you can't trust me. But I want you to know, I'm going to do anything I can to prove to you that I'm a changed man."

Isotta glanced over at Massimo. Was this charming talk designed to seduce her away from her conviction that they remain chaste? But no. He didn't squeeze her knee or suggestively grin at her. Instead he watched the road, his face still and serious.

The clock bells hurried Elisa's steps and she sprinted up the school stairs, her backpack flapping against her tailbone. Settling into her seat, she swiveled her head in its habitual orbit, looking, as she always did, for Fatima's return.

Elisa almost fell off her seat when her eyes snagged on that familiar head of dark spiraling hair. Fatima was back! Elisa wanted to wrap her arms around her friend. She would have to wait though, until the teacher released them for break.

Instead, she watched Fatima. Even though Fatima had been absent from school for a month, her hand was still the first in the air while Elisa was still parsing out the teacher's question.

Elisa chewed her lip.

Actually, it was a *little* surprising. Fatima always knew the answer, but rarely raised her hand more than once a class. But now, every question released Fatima's arm like a slingshot. And the teacher called on her, every time.

Other students, who had been leaning toward Fatima and pulling her sleeve to welcome her back, gradually began slumping back in their chairs and grumbling.

Fatima herself seemed not to notice. She demonstrated a math problem on the board and then turned, beaming at the class. Only Elisa grinned back, so grateful to see her friend upright and triumphant. The rest of the class suddenly found their pens fascinating. Fatima accepted her teachers pat on the back, then strode to her seat.

Elisa frowned. Something about this felt wrong to her. Then again, Elisa was used to being wrong. Her mind wandered...

A rise in the noise around her alerted her to the end of class. With the others, she fetched her snack from her backpack and looked for her friend. Fatima was close behind her, and the girls smiled shyly at the sudden return of old patterns. Impulsively, Elisa said, "I'm so glad you're back!" She didn't add how nice it would be to not sit alone at snack-time anymore. Especially since the colder weather meant staying indoors.

Fatima nodded. "Me too. Mamma would have kept me at home another week at least, but I begged and begged. Home is so quiet."

Fatima and Elisa found their usual place in the classroom away from the girls twirling the radio-knob and the boys secretly playing soccer under the desks with an empty water bottle.

Elisa unwrapped her piece of bread folded around a slice of *prosciutto*. Smiling, Fatima nodded toward Elisa, "You have snack now."

Elisa chewed thoughtfully. "Yes. Sometimes."

Fatima looked like she was about to ask another question, but instead she focused on taking out her piece of focaccia.

Elisa ventured, "Fatima . . . about what happened before the fire . . . the coin . . ."

"I don't want to talk about it."

"But I want to explain. To apologize . . . at the hospital—"

"Stop! It doesn't matter!"

Elisa's eyes welled with tears. "But it did matter and then you were gone and it was scary."

Fatima pressed her hand against the side of her head. "It's so noisy in here. I want class to start."

"Ava? *Ava!*" Edo was practically nose to nose with his friend before she noticed him.

"Oh! Sorry. What is it?"

"What do you mean 'what is it?' You asked *me* if Chiara had heard from Fabrizio and I was answering you."

"Oh. Has she?"

Edo said, "She got a postcard. Pretty vague. Cryptic even. We thought maybe he was writing in code in case the mail got intercepted."

Ava looked confused. "Why—"

"Ava. It's a joke. Of course not. But you know, he was always so mysterious."

Ava sipped her *cappuccino*, lost in thought.

Edo said, "I've been thinking. You know how I told you how Francy acted way too good for everyone? I think he convinced Fabrizio that Chiara wasn't good enough."

Thinking for a moment, Ava replied, "Well, that fits with what my mother said. When she had that coffee with you and them, she came home so mad."

Edo said, "In fact, maybe Francy told Fabrizio something awful about Chiara."

"What could he possibly say?"

"It wouldn't have to be anything true."

"You mean he'd lie?"

"I wouldn't put it past him."

"Edo . . . really? I know the man spurned your good looks, but that doesn't make him some sort of cartoon villain."

Edo mugged, "It might just."

Ava chuckled and took another sip of her *cappuccino*.

Slowly, Edo said, "Hey. I have an idea. Maybe you should go to Bologna and check it out."

"What?"

"You know, go on some pretense. Like you need seeds or plants or whatever. Look up Fabrizio and act all breezy. Get an idea of the situation."

Ava shook her head. "That's crazy."

"Why crazy? Don't you want to know?"

Ava put down her cup. "I think your loyalty to Chiara is blinding you a little, Edo."

Muttering under his breath, Edo turned around to buff the La Pavoni.

Ava hesitated and then said, "I can't go to Bologna anyway. I'm going to Rome for a week or two. Maybe more, depending on how it goes."

Edo's hands stalled as his head jerked toward Ava. "You are? Why? When?"

Ava licked her lips with studied casualness. "I need to meet with some vendors. For my dad's shop, but also for the . . . for the *castello*." Ava stammered.

"Ah, the *castello*."

"Look, I have to put orders in soon if we want the plants to arrive in time for spring. And I need to research what vendors can get. Alessandro," she blushed, "is thinking he wants to put in historic species of plants, the kind that once grew around the *castello*."

"He does, does he?"

Ava held out her hand. "Stop."

"I would Ava, *ma, dai*. Come on. It's too easy."

Ava strengthened her voice. "I won't pretend I don't know what you are referring to. But you're wrong. Alessandro is married. Why would you assume I'd be interested in a married man?"

Edo thought about pointing out that her last crush was on him, so she hardly focused her emotional energy on available men. Instead he said, "I may be gay, my dear, but that doesn't mean I don't have radar for the straights."

"You know you shouldn't speak to your elders like that, Edo."

"You've got like two years on me, tops." Edo went back to buffing. "Anyway, he's smitten with you. Alessandro."

"He is?"

Edo nodded.

"How can you—"

Edo tapped the middle of his forehead with his pinky. "The radar. Remember?"

"Be serious, Edo."

Edo sighed and turned back, resting his arms on the counter. "Because his eyes follow you wherever you go. Like the Mona Lisa or something. Because whenever you speak, it's like nobody else is speaking. When he's in the bar, any time the door opens, he goes breathless like he's about to hear his name called for an award." He straightened. "Frankly, I'd give anything for a man to look at me the way Alessandro looks at you."

Ava stared at her hands now gripping the cup.

Edo went on softly, "It is a shame that he's married."

Biting her lip, Ava nodded.

Edo reached out and touched her hand, lightly. "But somehow I see it working for you."

Ava rubbed her eyes. "You do? How?"

"*Boh,*" Edo shrugged, his vision caught by the sight of Paola walking with Elisa to the *fruttivendolo*. Paola handed Elisa one of Edo's favorite green and thin-skinned mandarin oranges. He made a mental note to stop by and get a kilo later. Turning back to his friend, he said, "Ale doesn't seem well matched, I guess is the truth of it."

Ava sighed. "But she's so blond. And . . . and . . . so busty." Ava blushed faintly.

Edo said, "Well, I can't speak to that. I've never been partial to those particular charms."

"You know what I mean."

"I do. But I also know that good looks might attract, but they can't hold people together."

Ava drummed her fingertips on the bar. "It's wrong to wish for a couple to break up. Right? Like the Madonna would not approve."

"To be honest, I wouldn't call her marriage all that solid."

To Ava's shocked face, Edo went on, "I know what you mean. But happy marriages don't end in divorce. And really, does Alessandro seem happy with her? Isn't it right to wish for his happiness?"

Ava said, "I don't know if I'm the right judge."

Edo paused, considering. "You're probably right, there."

"But you really think it won't last? Between Ale and Madison?"

"I do."

"You sound so sure. How can you be so sure?"

"That radar, darling. I told you."

Across the *alimentari*, Luciano spotted Fatima's mother.

"*Buongiorno*, Salma," he greeted, walking toward her.

Salma looked up from the rack of packaged snack cakes. "Oh, *buongiorno*, Luciano. Can you help me? I don't know who of these is good."

Luciano smiled a little at Salma's way with Italian. It's what he loved about working with immigrants. It forced him to consider the vagaries of his language.

He shrugged. "I think they are all good."

Salma nodded. "Maybe I get one of all."

Luciano said, "That's a lot of sweets."

Grinning, Salma said, "For Fatima. She loves sweets and is eating so many! So many good people bring her things to eat." She thanked Luciano, and brought her basket, which Luciano realized was full of the kind of food Salma never purchased—Kinder bars and paprika-flavored Pringles. Clearly she could deny her daughter nothing right now. Luciano understood that. When Giulia had been hurt, he'd always filled her lap with her favorite *caramelle*.

Luciano raised his hand in farewell as Salma stepped into the gathering evening, bag held against her chest like a trophy.

As he paid for his packet of linguini and a ball of mozzarella, Luciano thought about Fatima. How long had she been eating like this? Because in truth, he thought she was looking rather thinner than usual. Maybe it was because she was growing, she certainly seemed taller than before the fire. Then again, it was more likely that she'd done her growing before the fire and he'd missed it. It was hard to spot growth when it was happening.

Lifting his bag off the counter, he laughed at Giovanni's new joke, said goodnight, and began the walk home, still thinking of Fatima. He'd heard from Elisa that Fatima was back at school, and kept expecting her to show up on his doorstep. But his threshold remained empty, save for his cat, Degas. And Carosello, who sometimes sat on Luciano's mat as if Luciano had forgotten to take him inside with the mail.

Luciano passed Bar Birbo, lit against the evening. There was a crowd at the bar, but Edo waved at his old teacher over the heads of the customers. Such a good boy.

Continuing down the road, Luciano considered that Fatima's energy was doubtless low. Maybe she needed to return home immediately after school. That would make sense. Plus, she must have a great deal of catch up work. She was clever, but she'd missed so much school. He decided to stop by, maybe some time next week, and ask if she needed any help with her school work.

Isotta picked up the phone on the first ring, plucking it out of her purse and holding it to her ear as she hurried down Via Romana. "*Pronto.*"

"*Ciao*, Isotta. It's me." The voice hesitated. "Massimo."

Isotta smiled. "Yes, I know."

"Oh. Well, I wanted to make sure you didn't change your mind. I know you were nervous about it, so . . ."

"I'm almost there. I got sick this morning, so it took longer to get out the door."

"Sick? Are you okay? The baby . . ."

"Baby's fine, which is why I got sick. Or at least that's what the doctor tells me. I thought it would be done by now. Second trimester and all."

"Is that bad? Did you check?"

"It's fine. The doctor said it might happen. While also letting me know that my morning sickness has been better than it is for most women, so I should, apparently, be thanking the Madonna."

The statue of Mary caught Isotta's eye, looking down from her heavenly blue niche. It felt like divine intervention to come upon her exactly as she mentioned Mary. She assured Massimo that she was almost there, hung up, and stood before the statue. She had touched the statue once or twice before. Of course she had. After all this time of watching locals run their fingers over the hem of her skirts, how could she not? But she had never before felt called, pulled, like this.

She listened to her heartbeat slow, yet grow louder in her ears. That blue of the niche was intoxicating, similar to the shade above Santa Lucia. Isotta suddenly realized that she hadn't noticed Santa Lucia's undulating light in quite some time. It had become backdrop—like the salmon-hued *comune* and the waxed wooden door of Bar Birbo.

Isotta tentatively reached a hand forward, pausing in midair before plunging her fingers through what felt like a magnetic energy field to touch the marble at the base of Mary's robes. The day was cool, and Isotta expected the marble to be freezing, but perhaps because of its protected position, it was almost warm.

Instantly, it seemed like an egg cracked on Isotta's head, sending spirals of warm liquidity through her body. Her bones relaxed and her fingers slipped away from the niche to fall back to her side.

Bar Birbo's door opened, and Bea, the lady with the chickens, came out. She initially looked confused by Isotta's standing transfixed but then she smiled in recognition. Bea stepped beside Isotta and said softly, so as not to break the spell, "Isn't she beautiful?"

"Yes," Isotta breathed.

"This isn't your first time touching her?"

"No."

"But it's different this time."

"Yes."

"*Allora*. Mary knows when we have need of her."

Isotta didn't turn her head.

Bea went on, "Now you'll have good luck."

This brought Isotta back to herself, and she startled. "Oh, I'll need it!" Without thinking she added, "I'm meeting Massimo and Margherita at the park."

Isotta had always thought of Bea as a bit brash and loud. In fact, she often avoided her, unsure of what Bea might say. But the older woman's eyes softened as she pulled Isotta in for a kiss on each cheek. "Then off you go, child."

Isotta nodded and hurried down the road, turning into the playground to see Massimo putting Margherita in the swing. He looked up at the movement, and grinned at Isotta.

Isotta faltered. She wasn't sure if she wanted Margherita to recognize her after the months of absence, or if she wanted to start from the beginning with the little girl. She understood her role now, in a way she hadn't before. Wouldn't it be better to have a fresh start? Maybe this was why she'd delayed seeing Margherita. She had told Massimo she wanted to feel more stable with him to avoid another transition for the little girl, but maybe what she really wanted was to make sure Margherita attached to her for her. Not because she resembled Margherita's mother.

Shyly, she walked toward the swing. Massimo tightened his daughter's firmly affixed scarf and mittens. His eyes didn't know where to land, and Isotta could tell he was muttering nonsense. She took heart in his own insecurity and stepped forward. Kneeling beside the swing, Isotta murmured, "*Ciao*, Margherita."

Margherita scooted backward in surprise and appraised Isotta with suspicion. Isotta could see the wheels turning in the child's head, trying to process her memories with the woman standing before her. Isotta realized she probably looked different than the last time she saw Margherita. Her hair was back to its original blond (well, almost original, she had resorted to a bottle to help it along), and her face had filled out with the pregnancy, along with her breasts and hips and belly that were, thankfully, hidden under her puffy down coat.

The little girl reached out a mittened hand and patted Isotta's hair before running it down Isotta's cheek. Her face brightened into a wide smile. "Mamotta!"

Isotta laughed in return but looked up at Massimo for understanding. He looked sheepish as he answered the unasked question, "I wasn't sure if you would feel comfortable with Margherita calling you Mamma again, given . . . so I kept telling her we were meeting Isotta. She must have mixed them."

Isotta stood and, with her arms open, wordlessly asked Margherita if she could lift her from the swing. Margherita held out her hands and pumped her legs, bouncing to get into Isotta's arms. "Mamotta!"

Massimo said, "We can get her to call you something else."

Isotta curled the little girl against her chest and breathed in her scent of drying honeycomb. "I like it."

The little girl smacked a kiss on Isotta's cheek before wiggling to get down. Once her feet planted, she began toddling around Isotta's legs in a circle, making plane noises. Then she burst away to run around the playground, her arms stretched out from her sides.

Isotta looked up at Massimo and laughed. She found his eyes trained on her. He moved closer, resting his hand on her shoulder in a gesture that seemed convivial until he pulled her close. She stopped moving, almost stopped breathing, at the brush of his lips against her ear. He stroked her hair back from her neck and kissed her in the spot he knew made her quiver.

She pulled away and said, "No. We talked about this."

With a wounded expression, he said, "Not even a kiss hello?"

Isotta tried to smile. "How many people do you kiss hello like that?"

Massimo grumbled, "Nobody else is irresistible."

In a matter-of-fact tone that she failed to feel, Isotta said, "You'll have to try harder. Anyway, even if this was the time, it is certainly not the place."

"Okay, okay." He paused and added. "I love the hair by the way. It reminds me of when I fell for you."

Isotta smiled, pleased. As Margherita sailed into her arms again, Isotta noticed a threadbare quicksilver hugging the wall. Squinting into the shadow of the closed *rosticceria* she called, "Elisa!"

Elisa stopped as if she'd run into an invisible post. She turned around. "Me?"

Isotta laughed. "Yes, you. How many other Elisas are here?" She mimed craning her neck looking for a hidden windfall of Elisas.

Elisa giggled into her hand.

Isotta said, "You haven't been to Luciano's." Turning to Massimo, she added for his benefit, and maybe also to land a point, "Luciano tutors Elisa in math. He's also encouraged her in her art, which is quite extraordinary."

Elisa's blush heightened the rosiness she already carried with the cold. "Oh, no. It's not."

Isotta insisted. "It is. Anyway, we haven't seen you. Luciano has a stack of paper and nobody to use it."

Elisa scribed a half circle in the dirt with her toe. "I didn't want to bother you."

"Come over. I'll make tea. Come anytime."

Elisa nodded.

Squeezing the little girl in her arms, Isotta said, "Now we were about to play on the slide. Right, Margherita?" Margherita yelped and squirmed to get down. Over her pealing, "Slide! Slide! Fast, Mamotta! Sooooooo fast!" Isotta asked Elisa, "Do you want to play, too?"

Following Margherita's running form with her eyes, Elisa said, "Okay."

Isotta took Elisa's hand and led her to the slide. "Oh, good! I'm so glad. I'm a little too topply to climb ladders nowadays. I'm grateful for the help."

Isotta noticed the starveling look in Elisa's cheeks suffused with a quick glow of pleasure.

At the knock at the door, Fatima's family stopped talking. Who could it be?

Fatima's brother leapt up and offered to check. The deep murmuring at the door suggested a man, but not until Luciano entered the room did anyone guess their visitor. They were unused to guests, even now, almost two years after their move to Santa Lucia.

Fatima scrambled backward against the couch, where she had been reading a book that wouldn't be assigned until after Christmas vacation. The book dropped to the floor, and Fatima kicked it in her haste to draw her legs up to her chest.

Fatima's brother announced, "Luciano says he'd like to help you with your homework, Fatima. To catch up."

Salma dropped a bookmark into her novel and said, "This is nice!"

Luciano smiled and greeted each member of Fatima's family. At one point or another, he had tutored each of them. His face fell at the sight of Fatima's open-mouthed expression, but he put down his bundle of books on the table. "*Buonasera*, Fatima. I thought you might be behind in your studies."

"I'm not."

"You're not?"

Fatima shook her head. The rest of the family watched the interchange with bemusement. Their Fatima was *always* ahead. Not even a *coma* slowed her down.

Her brother offered, "As soon as the hospital let her, Fatima started working. It only took her a few days to catch up on the weeks she'd missed." His mouth twitched in pride.

Luciano attempted a smile. "I see. I should have known, perhaps." Turning to Fatima and sitting on the chair closest to her, he added, "I do hope you haven't been working too hard. You need to take care of yourself."

Fatima glared at her knees and grumbled, "I know that."

Luciano studied Fatima for a moment. "Fatima, if there's something—"

"I can take care of myself." Fatima rose. "As a matter of fact, my stomach hurts, so I'll go to bed. Good night. It was good of you to stop by."

Luciano said, "If you ever want to come after school with Elisa, we've been—"

"Mamma needs me here. Goodnight." She scuttled down a shadowed hallway.

A heavy silence descended over the room.

Fatima's brother said, "Mamma, you shouldn't keep her home if—"

Salma broke in, "I do not."

More silence.

Her mother said, "Fatima is more tired than she is saying. Her head and stomach often pain her, and I think she's most comfortable here. But if she needs help . . ."

Luciano rose. "She won't. She's correct. She's perfectly capable."

A chill rain settled over Santa Lucia, turning the cobblestones to onyx.

Anna called Massimo to the dinner table. As she plunked a dish of pasta scattered with local pecorino cheese on the table, she sneered, "And how was your 'date'?"

Massimo said, "Why do you have to say it like that?"

"Massimo. Seriously. A grown man should not be dating his wife."

Massimo dug the tongs into the bowl to pull out a heaping serving of pasta.

"Massimo? Right? Don't you think that's a teensy bit strange? And then the other day you had to meet her at the park with Margherita? If she valued her mothering job, she'd be living here, under my roof. Not dating my son like some strumpet looking for action."

Straightening his napkin on his lap, Massimo sighed before saying. "Mamma. You have to be patient. After what we did . . ."

"We? What on earth can you mean? I've always been nothing but kind to that woman." Anna clutched her chest, face aghast, before she reached for the tongs to serve herself. "More cheese, my treasure?"

Massimo looked around, alarmed. "Margherita isn't here, Mamma. We tucked her in an hour ago."

"I know that! What, am I senile, now?" Anna scowled, and then shoved a forkful of pasta into her mouth. She muttered, "Can a mother not call her child a nickname anymore? Is that not 'allowed'? Are there new rules Isotta is writing? Should I get a copy of the handbook?"

Putting down his fork, Massimo said, "What are you talking about?"

Anna chewed fiercely before answering, "You know damn well what I'm talking about. Ever since Isotta came back, it's been nothing but, 'Isotta thinks this,' and 'Isotta needs that.'"

"She's my wife!"

"She doesn't act like it! Living with that waste of a man. Like you don't even matter!"

Jaw clenching, Massimo said, "I appreciate your indignation on my behalf. But I understand what Isotta says. She wants to build something real—"

Anna said, "Something real doesn't mean you need to be her errand boy. Her servant."

"I went to the pharmacy for her *one* time! You seem to forget she's carrying my child." Massimo stood up.

"Sit down. You haven't finished your dinner." Massimo didn't move, and Anna said, "I apologize, Massimo, for my strong words. It pains me when you don't get what you want, and I know you want her here. As your mother, I'm on your side. Always."

Massimo sat back down and picked up his fork.

All morning, Elisa hunched over her paper, taking quick glances out the window. She almost couldn't believe it when the clouds thinned and scattered, leaving a warm blue. Finally! Weather wouldn't prevent her from playing with Fatima this afternoon. After Fatima being sick for so long, and then the early evenings and cold rain, Elisa felt like she had been given a birthday present.

Elisa knocked on Fatima's door. "*Ciao!*"

"*Ciao, Elisa,*" Fatima greeted her friend.

Elisa couldn't stop grinning. "Park today? I'm so glad it stopped raining!"

Fatima allowed herself to be tugged toward the playground. "Okay, but not the swings."

Elisa stood still, unsure of what to do next. They *always* went on the swings.

She asked, "Do you want to visit Luciano, maybe?"

"No!"

The word rang throughout the still park and over the valley.

Elisa recoiled and covered her ears.

Fatima's voice carried an unmistakable hard edge. "Luciano's house is boring. I want to do something fun."

Elisa looked at her feet, then around the park.

Fatima said, "I have a great idea!"

"Yay! What is it?"

"The *castello*! Let's go there!"

Elisa's stomach dropped. "The *castello*?"

Fatima grinned, but the grin only bent her cheeks. "Sure! There are lots of rooms to explore. You know we usually play castle times anyway. It will be perfect!"

"But we *never* played up there."

"So? I've poked around a few times. There are some cool secret things I could show you."

"I...I...I don't think we're allowed." To Fatima's frown, Elisa said, "And there are people up there."

"I've watched. They aren't there all the time, and anyway there are storage rooms they never go in." Fatima's gaze was already pinned up the hill.

Elisa rubbed her hands together. "I told my mamma that I'd be here if she needed me."

Fatima glared at Elisa. "She never needed you before."

"Things are different now."

Fatima snapped, "Oh, of course. I'd forgotten."

Elisa hung her head and said nothing.

Fatima sighed. "Okay, let's stay here."

"Really?"

"Yes, it's fine. I can sit on the swing and you can swing."

"Okay!"

"And you can tell me all about what Carosello has been doing."

Elisa giggled. "Did I tell you what happened at the hardware store?" She settled on the swing and pumped her legs lightly.

"No, what?"

"Fabio left the door open, and Carosello went in and ate all the garbage. Then he got sick and left that everywhere."

"Ew!"

"Throw up *and* poop."

"*Eeeeew!*"

"It was so gross. It still smelled bad the next week when I went in for mamma's new hand shovel."

"Fabio must have been so mad."

"Oh, he was. But he thought it was someone, like a burglar or something. He was yelling about it for a long time before someone realized that nobody had broken in and only the garbage was taken."

Fatima shook her head. "Carosello is so gross."

"I know, and he's so cute."

"He can't be gross and cute at the same time, Elisa."

Elisa's eyes widened. "Can't he be?"

Fatima shook her head and looked out over the valley. "No. He can just be one."

"Oh. Well, he's gross then."

Fatima nodded. "He is. Somebody should give him a bath."

Elisa and Fatima looked at each other before shrieking in unison, "*Eeeeeewwwww!*"

Chiara watched as the men strung lights across Via Romana. She knew bigger towns boasted more impressive Christmas garlands, but she loved the simple strands crisscrossing the street, falls of lights hanging in front of the church and school.

Her breath made little bursts of steam in the cold air. After admiring the work for a few moments, she turned back into the warmth of Bar Birbo. Approaching the counter, she counted the bottles of *prosecco*. The bar was sure to be full of townspeople the next few days, raising a glass together. She wanted to be prepared.

To own the truth, she *needed* to be prepared.

Preparations kept her busy, and kept her thoughts from sinking. The bar had never been so clean, so well stocked. Even the upstairs was ready, several boxes of Edo's favorite *panettone* ready to bring to family celebrations. Edo had finally persuaded her to join his parents and siblings for Christmas. She'd been reluctant, but the kindness in her brother's telephoned invitation had convinced her. Edo must have told his father about Fabrizio leaving, and he undoubtedly felt sorry for her. Even so, Chiara looked forward to the holiday. Her relationship with her brother had been strained since his marriage and consequent conviction that Chiara gypped him out of his inheritance. But her relationships with his children, Edo's siblings, were wonderful. All of them worked at Bar Birbo at some time or another, and through them she was often reminded of the fun she once had with her brother.

The opening door cut off her thoughts. "*Buongiorno*, Magda."

Magda grumbled.

"Something on your mind?'

"Yes, as a matter of fact. I had renters scheduled for the whole Christmas week, but this morning—they left! The banging and clanging from the *castello* drove them away!"

"Ah, yes. It has been noisy."

"It has!" At the sound of the door opening, she turned. "*Buongiorno*, Isotta."

Isotta hesitated for a moment before crossing the threshold to hang up her coat. She hadn't been in Bar Birbo much since she'd returned from Florence. She wasn't sure if they knew about—

"You're pregnant!" Magda announced.

Isotta looked down. Luciano must have been either weary or lying when he said the pregnancy wasn't noticeable. "Yes, I am." She wasn't sure . . . should she sound happy? They had to know the circumstances, about Giulia, about her sham marriage. She decided to opt for truth. "It was a surprise to me, too."

"*Auguri!*" Chiara smiled with real warmth.

Patrizia stepped into the bar, shivering, and asked, "Who are we congratulating? Did everyone see the lights?"

Chiara nodded, but before she could say anything, Magda pointed at Isotta. "That one's pregnant."

Patrizia clasped her hands to her chest. "Oh, how marvelous! A new baby! Chiara, I'm buying Isotta here whatever she wants!"

Isotta blinked back tears at this sudden kindness. "Oh, you are so lovely . . . I came for hot milk."

Patrizia said, "Two milks! I'll have one as well. Are you feeling sick? Tired? I was both with my daughter."

Isotta answered, "I'm feeling better now. A bit more energy."

"Do you know if you are having a boy or a girl?"

"No, I—"

The door flew open and Bea strode in. "Whew! *Fa un freddo cane!* It's a cold dog out there!" She unwound her scarf and unbuttoned her jacket. "You need to turn the heat up in here, Chiara." She looked over at Isotta and nodded. "Looks like you are having a baby."

Isotta smiled and accepted the frothed milk Chiara handed her. "Yes, I am."

"A boy, I'd wager."

Patrizia shook her head. "But look how she's carrying! All forward, like a soccer ball. I was the same. I bet it's a girl."

Bea said, "Listen, I've had more than my share of babies. That one's a boy."

The two women argued, Magda huffing once in a while about old wives' tales and that she should order a scan. Isotta hadn't realized that this was exactly what she needed.

~

Elisa watched Fatima slink down the castle stairs before throwing herself on a *piazza* bench. Like she'd been there all morning. Elisa approached her, hoping Fatima wouldn't ask to play at the *castello* again. Last week Fatima had convinced her that nobody worked at the *castello* on Sundays, so it was a perfect day to explore. Still, the whole time Fatima led her across the castle yard, Elisa had expected someone to yell, "*Hey*! What are you doing! Get out of there!"

When Fatima showed her the secreted trap door, opening into a dank darkness, with stairs that led lower and lower, Elisa had only nodded warily. And then flinched when Fatima pressed a flashlight into her hand. Fatima had cajoled her to step down into the cavern bellow the *castello*, which proved too much for Elisa. She fled. Elisa didn't want to tell her friend that it was too creepy. Why did Fatima like it? Especially as it was right around the building from where she had fallen into a coma.

"*Ciao*, Fatima."

"*Ciao*, Elisa. How about the park?"

"*Okay*!"

Fatima leapt up and the two girls walked toward the playground.

Elisa's steps slowed at the *fruttivendolo*. She called Fatima back. Hesitating, she said, "I have a little money. Do you want to get something here? Sometimes she even gives me something free."

Fatima looked from Elisa through the window to the rotund woman sitting on a stool behind the counter. "Paola?"

"Yes."

Fatima watched Paola pointing at the crate of cabbage as she chatted with a customer. It looked like the principal.

Fatima tugged Elisa's sleeve. "I don't want to see the principal. She'll ask me about my schoolwork and how is my breathing and it's boring."

Elisa bit her lip and cast another look into the shop before agreeing with a nod and springing off after Fatima. Once at the playground, they stalled. The park was full of teenage boys. Elisa's eyes raked the space, looking for Stefano, the boy she'd once paid for doctoring her report cards.

She spotted him. Stefano. Mean and gross Stefano. "I don't want to play after all." Seeing him reminded her of that moment, before the fire, when Fatima had realized that Elisa had stolen from her to pay Stefano. That feeling of a mouse scurrying in her chest intensified, and Elisa's breath turned jagged.

Fatima noticed where Elisa's gaze snagged. Her own vision lingered on Stefano. She licked her bottom lip. "Are you sure? It could be fun."

"No!"

Fatima pulled her gaze away. "Okay. Let's go for a walk instead. We can pick flowers for bouquets."

Elisa looked quizzically at her friend. "Bouquets?"

Fatima stammered, "Well, when I was . . . sick . . . people brought so many flowers. It cheered the house up. I thought it could be fun, but if you don't—"

"Where would we go?"

Fatima pointed to the steps framed by tall walls at the other end of the playground. "We can go through there into the groves."

"But Fatima—"

"What? What is it?"

"That's the cemetery."

Fatima followed Elisa's outstretched finger, pointing to steps of blocked stone.

Elisa went on, "That's too creepy."

Fatima reached for her hand. "It's okay. We don't have to stay there. We'll walk through it and then we'll be in the groves." Fatima pointed. "See? It's only a minute in the graveyard."

Elisa allowed herself to be pulled up the stairs. The sound of the boys laughing spurred her footfalls.

Fatima slowed down once she reached the graveyard. Elisa tugged her forward. "Come on!"

"Relax, Elisa. Nothing is going to bite you."

Elisa chewed her lip. "You said . . ."

"I know, but it's not a big deal, and look! It's cool. Do you have relatives buried here?"

"I think so."

"Wow. Are they in the wall? Or a little house? Or in the ground?"

The silence lengthened. "Let's go, Fatima."

"Oh, come on! It's like a little town. We can play shop with these little fences and houses. I guess I assumed this would be like a Moroccan cemetery, with white rocks on the ground. Look at all those flowers and leftover Christmas things. I wonder who brings them."

"Let's go!" Elisa was practically yelling.

Fatima stopped hopping from the gravel to the paths overgrown with grasses. Picking her way back she muttered, "Okay, okay. I just wanted to have a little fun."

"It's not fun. It's not."

"Okay! I get it. The ghosts spook you."

Elisa glowered.

Fatima said, "Whatever. Look there's the path to the groves. Let's go."

Nodding, Elisa followed Fatima through the headstones.

Luciano looked over his shoulder. "Are you quite certain Massimo approves?"

Isotta patted his arm. "Yes, I'm sure."

"And Anna?"

Isotta gritted her teeth. "I'm not concerning myself with what she thinks. Sometimes I think I'd rather live with my mother than Massimo's. Mine might be awful, but at least she's an open book. Anna is sweetness on the outside, but acid on the inside."

Luciano's feet slowed.

Isotta threaded her arm through his. "It's okay. Massimo agreed."

"I still don't understand why this sudden turnaround."

Isotta shrugged. "I lit a candle. Plus, it's hardly sudden, Massimo has changed. I know you've noticed."

From the corner of his eye, Luciano spotted a little girl, a smudge like his memory of Giulia made manifest. The face peered at him from the edge of an alley before disappearing. He shook his head to clear the creaking memories.

Once in front of Massimo's door, Luciano paled. Behind this door, his daughter had once breathed and loved and wept and conceived two children, one who died with her. Behind this door his granddaughter, the last of his family line, went to sleep at night, curled around her stuffed animals. Behind this door was the man who was the source of his daughter's tears and who violated all her memory by bedding her virtual twin.

"Please." He stayed Isotta's curled fingers, raised to knock.

She dropped her hand, and wound it with her other around Luciano's arm. "I know this is hard."

Luciano nodded, his eyes too wide.

Isotta said, "You miss her."

He nodded again. "Every day."

"Of course you do. *I* feel like I lost something, and I never even knew Giulia."

"Maybe because I'm old and my mind isn't what it once was, but often I can't make myself believe she's really gone. That she's not waiting for me in the *piazza*. For me." Luciano trembled with unshed tears.

"I know."

"My little girl."

"Oh, Luciano. I know. I'm so sorry."

The tears shivered before falling over Luciano's lined face. "Perhaps I should have folded her death into my life by now. But sometimes it hits me in ways I don't expect. Like everything will be fine, and I'll smell sweet alyssum blooming and I'll remember how she used to make me flower necklaces—a strike to my heart." Luciano lifted his hand and settled it over his chest. "All over again. I wonder if this pain I feel is my heart breaking."

"That's not strange, Luciano. It's not. Of course your mind forgets or even wraps itself around reality for awhile, but then something jars you out of it and you are face-to-face with what you lost."

"My wife, too."

"Your wife, too."

"And Margherita."

"But now is your chance, Luciano. You can create a relationship with Margherita now. She's so young, she has so much room to grow with you."

Luciano looked unconvinced. Isotta went on, "One thing I don't understand. Before...before I found out about everything...you would join me and Margherita at the park."

"That was a low-stakes situation, *cara*."

"What do you mean?"

"She didn't know who I was. Neither did you. Massimo failed to pay attention, as is his wont—or, was, I suppose. If I blundered, it would not matter. Besides, there was the promise of wine to numb that particular pain."

"And now?"

"No wine, to begin with. Every feeling I have is mine alone. Of greater importance, now I'm with her as her grandfather. What if she despises me?"

"Impossible."

Luciano frowned.

"No, really, Luciano. Have you met a child that hated you?"

"I'm sure there were some in all those years of teaching."

"Maybe if you gave them a bad grade, or maybe if they refused to be loved. But I can tell you because I know, Margherita is not like that. She will love you. No question."

Luciano closed his eyes. "Then there's this. What if she does? Love me? And that love becomes part of me. What is there to prevent Massimo from taking her away?"

Isotta thought about it. Massimo was untangling his heart, he was more thoughtful and considerate. But who knew if his darker side would rear up again, like a poised cobra.

She conceded, "That could happen. I'd like to say it won't, but what do I know? But Luciano...if you knew you were destined to lose Giulia, would you refuse her a chapter in the story of your life?"

"No. God, no!"

"Exactly. So any piece of a relationship with your granddaughter will be precious. Maybe you can simply enjoy what you have?"

Luciano's eyes cleared as he regarded Isotta. Finally, he nodded. "Okay, but by the Madonna, this is harder without drinking."

Isotta wrapped her arm around his shoulder.

He steeled himself and nodded again. "All right. I am prepared."

Isotta knocked on the door. It opened before Isotta finished knocking and Anna announced, "Ah, Isotta! Luciano! How good of you to take time away from your important books and whatever else you two get up to! Margherita! Massimo! Our guests are here!"

Margherita came running from the kitchen and stopped, suddenly shy.

From the steps that led to his apartment, Massimo appeared. He swooped up his daughter, and she rested her head against his chest. He strode to the door. "Isotta," he said, kissing her cheek chastely. He nodded at Luciano. "Luciano."

Luciano took half a step forward. "Massimo. I hope we can let the past—"

"It's done. Let's focus on Margherita. As Isotta says, the best thing for her is to be as loved as possible."

Anna tittered. "Is that what Isotta says? She is always so clever, isn't she? Must be those Florentine schools."

Isotta struggled not to roll her eyes and said, "A treat to see you as always, Anna. Okay then. We'll be back in an hour." Isotta touched Margherita's forehead with her own as she said to the little girl, "Do you want to go to the park?"

Margherita bolted upright. "Park? And pizza, too? With olives?"

Isotta laughed. "Wow, her language progression is astonishing!"

Anna said, "I'm sure you notice it more seeing her only once in awhile. Say, before you go, can I make you a cup of tea? Warm you up before you head into the cold?"

Isotta shook her head and said, "What a generous offer, but no, we need to start if we want to be back before Margherita's nap time."

Anna turned back into the kitchen, mumbling.

Massimo placed his squirming daughter onto the floor. Isotta addressed the child, "Ready, darling?"

Margherita took Isotta's hand and then furrowed her brow at Luciano. "Man? Man comes for pizza?"

Isotta laughed. "Yes. The man is coming too."

Margherita nodded cheerfully and held out her other hand to Luciano.

The older man's eyes met Massimo's, who nodded.

Luciano took his granddaughter's hand, and the three of them walked out the door.

Chiara slumped against the wall of Bar Birbo, her hand falling to her side. The postcard floated to the ground. She closed her eyes and breathed for a moment before leaning over to retrieve it.

Edo opened the door of the upstairs apartment. "*Ciao*, Chiara!" He stopped when he saw his aunt standing still. "Another postcard?"

"Another postcard."

"What does he say this time?"

Chiara glanced at it before striding to the counter. She ripped the card into pieces and flung them into the trash. "Does it matter? It's like the others. These vague and cold allusions to our time together. Why can't he leave me alone?"

Edo's jaw tightened. "I don't know."

Chiara said, "I wish I knew what happened."

"I know. Me, too. I was sure he would be back by now."

The door pushed open and Bea barreled into the bar. "What a wind today! My chickens are hiding out. Hope you don't need eggs."

Chiara hurriedly brushed the bits of paper off of her apron. "*Cappuccino*, Bea?"

The older woman settled herself on a stool. "*Si, grazie.*" She plucked a blue packet of sugar from the canister and shook it as she waited. "*Uffa.* I feel for Patrizia. Out in this weather."

Chiara smiled imagining her friend traveling to Rieti. "Well, she's on her way to see her daughter for the holiday, car loaded with packets of meat and boxes of pastries, so I expect she's satisfied with her lot. Wind and all."

Bea shook her head. "*Such* a wind. And how is that grandson of hers?"

Edo passed Chiara to straighten the pastries in the case and said, "I saw him last week at the butcher shop. Visiting Patrizia and Giuseppe."

Bea said, "Yes, but how *is* he? Still a handful?'

Chiara nodded, setting Bea's cup in its saucer. "I think he'll be a handful for some time. But he's got a special helper in his classroom now, which makes school better for him. So he's not fighting going anymore. Better all around."

Blowing on her *cappuccino*, Bea said, "Good. That's good. Hey, we should get a special helper for Arturo so he can keep an eye on his wife, eh?" Bea broke into guffaws. "You get it, right? Because he still complains that Esme is cheating on him. Seems like he should get to the bottom of that mystery some time."

At the door's opening, everyone turned.

"*Ciao a tutti!*" Isotta said.

Bea appraised her carefully. "Yes, I still say it's a boy."

Isotta laughed. "You and most of Santa Lucia."

"How are you feeling, child?"

"Fine! Well, even! Weirdly better than ever. In fact, I'm going to make a big *cenone* to celebrate the new year!"

Chiara started her hot milk and asked, "You and Luciano? Or are you having people over?"

"Elisa, too. Her mother has a trip to the coast or something."

Bea nodded and waited.

When Isotta didn't say anymore, Bea asked, "And Massimo?"

Chiara and Edo exchanged looks.

Isotta said, "No, he always celebrates the New Year with their family in Perugia."

"Yes yes, we know *that*. But he didn't invite you?" Bea grumbled. "I swear, someone needs to have a talk with that man. Maybe *he* needs a special helper."

Isotta accepted her cup of milk with both hands. "He asked me to come, but I wanted to be with Luciano. Anyway, I don't know if I'm ready for all of that yet."

Bea slapped her hand on her knee. "Oh I know it! But I won't make you say anymore." She winked and chuckled into her *cappuccino* before adding, "Make sure you get lentils from Giovanni's shop. He has the good local ones, for new year's luck."

Rosetta, the school principal, appeared in a gust of cold air. "Is this the coldest December we've had?"

A burble of agreement and Isotta asked Bea, "What else should I make?"

Rosetta stepped to the bar and said, "*Caffè*, Chiara. What are you making, Isotta?"

Isotta was surprised the principal remembered her from the time they chatted at the bakery. "I don't know yet. Local lentils apparently. I was thinking a risotto, maybe an octopus salad if I can get to the fish market tomorrow. For New Year's dinner."

"Ah," Rosetta said. "Chiara, what did your mom always make? I can't remember now."

Edo bumped Chiara out of the way so he could make the *espresso*, and she turned to Rosetta. "*Pizza fritta*."

Rosetta laughed. "That's right! Fried pizza! I remember we all begged our family to accept your family's *cenone* invitation so we could get some of that! Then again, my sisters and I all had huge crushes on your brother. I think we liked him almost as much as the *pizza fritta*."

Amid the laughter, Isotta said, "I haven't heard of fried pizza, is it local?"

Chiara shook her head. "No, my *nonna* was from Naples. I always assumed she brought the recipe from there." She turned to Edo. "We should make some and bring it to your parents."

Rosetta leaned across the counter for a packet of sugar. "You're going to your brother's for New Year's?"

Chiara nodded.

Rosetta gave a saucy wink. "Tell him I said hello. He'll know what it means."

The bar erupted with laughter and the cold felt far away.

Fatima slipped around the corner like a shadow. Tucking her body below the windows, she slid into the open room. She wasn't sure this sort of caution was necessary. The *castello* owners seemed to have left again. Instead, an army of workmen swarmed the place with their hammers and drills, carting stone and wooden beams. They created so much chaos it was a simple thing to walk right through them without being noticed. That walk across the courtyard, adjusting herself to blend with the castle's rhythm, it was the safest and most comfortable Fatima felt in the course of her day.

She was in.

The room smelled faintly of smoke, and Fatima squeezed her eyes, both hating and needing that smell. Farther away from the open door, the silence and darkness descended like a curtain, and Fatima's hands led her to the back wall. She fumbled a little here.

There!

The panel resisted her initial push but Fatima leaned into it and the panel released, sending up a dank smell from the inner depths of the *castello*. Darting a glance over her shoulder, Fatima lowered herself through the opening, stumbling a little as she dropped onto the top step. She had yet to figure out if there had once been more steps here or if the drop was intentional.

The air vibrated with blackness, prompting Fatima to reach inside her jacket pocket for the flashlight she'd started bringing after the first time she'd stumbled on the passageway. Switching it on, she drew the first full breath since she'd begun climbing the stairs to the *castello*.

Slowly she made her way deeper, avoiding touching the dark walls that wept with what was probably water but had a strong mineral odor. She shook her head and crept further. The passageway opened into a small cave lined with wooden barrels. The weak beam bounced over a jumble of dust-caked bottles heaped in the corner.

Fatima didn't linger here, instead she shuffled forward to stay steady over the uneven dirt floor. She passed through a twisting passageway to burst out into an enormous cavern. Fatima paused. Some days she loved running her hands over the giant stone wheels that she figured must be an ancient olive press, especially given the littering of branches and pits scattered over the floor. Should she stop here?

No, she wanted to reach further into the labyrinth this time. The clawing feeling in her chest exhorted her to push forward, to find the end.

There must be an end, mustn't there?

Dropping packets of food onto her increasing pile next to the well in the corner of the room, she bent down to find a pebble. Her hand closed around a good-sized one, and she dusted it off with her hands before leaning over the edge of the cistern. The rough, cool stones pressed into her waist as she leaned carefully, reaching out her hand. She released the pebble and waited. It whistled like fairies singing before the metallic plink announced the stone hitting water far below. Elisa would have loved the image of fairies singing, but Fatima knew she couldn't tell her friend about it. Elisa could be so immature sometimes. It was annoying.

The stones against Fatima's waist began to give, caving into the well. Fatima felt herself pitching forward and lurched back, stumbling until she landed with a thump on the dirt floor. She panted in fear, as the fall of crumbled rock tumbled inward, clattering like a stone thunderstorm. After a few minutes, her heart rate slowed, and she righted herself and stood again, determined not to be so careless.

She didn't know how old these structures were, but that didn't make them everlasting. She needed to watch her hands, watch her feet. Even her elbows. If something happened to her down here . . . she wondered again if she should have convinced Elisa to come with her, but again determined that she preferred her solitude. Even if she could convince Elisa to climb into the underground cavern, her friend would no doubt fill the empty grottoes and galleries—she was inordinately pleased to have found both of these words in her secret research on underground cities—with chatter and sunshine, when Fatima needed silence and shadows.

This discord laid another brick in the growing wall between them.

Her breath and limbs steady now, Fatima panned the flashlight over the walls, wondering which tunnel to take next. The one to the left lead to a room with stacked openings in the wall suggestive of ovens, with the lower opening to hold fuel and the upper one for cooking. Bread? Pottery? Fatima had yet to discover any remnants that would clue her into the purpose of the room. Nor had she found any passages from the oven room into other spaces. There could be one behind the crumbled pile of stone, but she hadn't yet dared to move the rocks.

The path ahead led to a series of rooms, some with paint still coloring the walls. She liked the big room; it reminded her of a ballroom, though she couldn't believe that was really what it was. There were more rooms after that, some of which she hadn't explored. She could do that today.

Or she could venture into the tunnel on the right. That one tilted up, and she wondered if it led to another trap door in the *castello* above.

The beam of light wavered and flickered for an instant. Fatima smacked it on her hand, wondering if she needed fresh batteries. The light surged and Fatima followed, through the tunnel on the right. She stopped instantly at the sight of a wall of cubbies. It looked like the boxes she'd seen at the *posta* for sorting mail. But that couldn't be right. Her research hadn't yet indicated who had once built these rooms—Etruscans seemed to not reach this far east and anyway could it be *that* old? Even Roman seemed too ancient for rooms this preserved—but she was certain it wasn't built at a time of post offices. She ran her hand over the boxes, looking for clues. All she dragged onto her fingertips was a thick smear of what looked like mud studded with tiny feathers. Fatima wiped her hand on her pants—the stuff was foul smelling. Leaving that mystery for another day, she walked through the next passageway to a room with troughs nestled against the sides of the walls. Some were knocked over, but some remained upright and a steady drip drip drip alerted her to a pipe stuck into the side of the wall dripping water onto the edge of a toppled trough. Fatima regarded the pipe for a moment before reaching to lift the trough back in place. It was heavier than she expected and she slipped on the wet ground, falling backward for the second time.

Instantly water started to seep through her jeans and Fatima leapt up, trying again to maintain her footing. Her arms pinwheeled and her feet skid under her, until she fell again, this time on her knee. Hard.

Whimpering, Fatima gingerly stood up, slowly this time.

Scared now, as she often was at the end of her castle escapades, she gingerly picked her way through the tunnels and back up the stairs, heaving herself out the trapdoor.

The light from her flashlight faltered as she broke into the late afternoon sunshine. Noticing its tentative and fairly non-substantive contribution to the light all around her, Fatima switched it off.

It had been three weeks since Ava arrived in Rome. The time passed quickly, rich with the excitement of flower shows and meeting vendors. She had learned more than she thought possible about historic species of grass and drought-resistant bushes. She had always considered plants as her hobby, like children of chefs who dabbled in cooking. But her only training had been what she learned at her father's shop. In other words, not a lot. The call for flowers in Santa Lucia usually ran to modest arrangements, since the villagers more commonly decorated their celebratory tables with snipped olive branches and rosemary boughs. The shop could not have sustained them financially if not for her mother. Savia's involvement in the church community persuaded parishioners and clergy alike to frequent the flower shop for weddings, funerals, communions, and other events requiring pageantry.

So she had never learned, *really* learned, about gardening and landscaping. True, she researched whatever she planted, the soil requirements and water needs. And she studied every garden she entered for landscaping ideas. But that didn't constitute training.

There may not be a degree at the end of it, but the Rome floral and landscaping world? *That* was training.

Most of the vendors and horticulturalists she'd met eagerly shared their knowledge. Together they pored over catalogues, discussing pH and leaf shapes, debating the optimal levels of variegation. She found the steep learning curve invigorating. And rewarding. After several trips into the field to assist landscape artists, architects started requesting her assistance, seeming to forget her novice rank.

Ava flushed now to think of her rudimentary plans for the *castello*, or the work she'd done for friends and family. It was all so *basic*. Everyone had always thanked her profusely when she slapped out some climbing roses or an edging of ivy, but she wished she could redesign every past landscape project. Starting with the *castello*. Luckily with a project that young, she easily revamped her early plans. Ale's patience seemed infinite.

Ironic, really. From the ashes of the castle fire emerged this flourishing opportunity. She only wished the fire worked such wonders on her love life. With Ale's arrival to Santa Lucia, her romantic prospects downgraded from hollow to harrowing. Her soured heart would wish she had never accepted this project if not for how satisfying she found the work.

Ale didn't even know she was in Rome. All those conversations about landscape design and she never mentioned that they could meet for coffee, as she stood just across the ancient Romans sports arena from his office. Ava convinced herself that her work left no room for a social life. And it was true, learning kept her busy, sometimes from sunup to long past sundown. But she and Ale spoke almost daily, sometimes for hours. Under the guise of brainstorming perennials, but they spent far more time sharing stories of their youth and their upbringing. Ale wanted to know about growing up in an Italian village, and Ava wondered how American culture changed his parents' values.

Their conversations would eventually return to native heath varieties. Invariably by the end of the conversation, Ale congratulated himself for intuiting Ava's capabilities. He told her about the architect's stunned admiration for her burgeoning plans or declared that Ava's novel landscaping solutions surpassed those of designers with bespoke websites. She ended these calls with more and more reluctance.

Today would be different. She would call and tell him. Yes, it was her last day in Rome, but if she said she'd been in town since Thursday, it wouldn't occur to him to wonder why she hadn't mentioned it during their phone call earlier that week. And in fact, she'd look cool as a watermelon, what with being in town for a few days and not contacting him.

Also, frankly, knowing that she had a train to catch in the afternoon would be her safety. They could have lunch, go over plans in person, and then she'd return to her regular life. She couldn't stay longer with her cousin anyway, as her cousin's husband was returning from his business trip to Vienna. Newly married, they didn't want to share their reunion with a houseguest. Ava got it. She would go back to Santa Lucia and throw herself into her work.

Ava paused in the street, her rolling suitcase nudging her leg. She had to call Ale while she had any courage at all. It would be simple. She'd dial, he'd pick up, she'd casually mention she'd been in town but far too occupied to call. That she was on her way to the train station, but had time for lunch and they could go over her ideas for the organic vineyard in person. Easy. Anyway, maybe he would be too busy to meet. Then she'd gaily assure him, "Next time!" while ignoring her heart skidding down to her toes.

Her fingers gripped the phone.

Her blood pounded in her skull.

Stupid! She was so stupid! Not even able to dial!

But wait. Maybe stupidity didn't create the pause in her fingers. Maybe God's will stalled her, compelled her to leave the married man alone. With distance, the heat between them could cool. She'd be able to meet him the next time he visited Santa Lucia without blushing.

Ava opened her heavy purse, looking for the pocket to tuck her phone in.

She would not call.

That was the right thing to do.

To beat back the images of Ale's face, she distracted herself by cat-aloguing her upcoming projects as she walked to the train station. The *castello* of course. Also, Dante had called to say that the *piazza*'s land-scaping needed updating, and he wanted her to submit a proposal. This trip to Rome certainly had elevated her perceived credentials, she couldn't imagine getting this offer before. With spring around the corner, she looked forward to helping Concetta plan a proper garden. Ava nervously tucked her hair behind her ears, thinking of Elisa's angry words. But maybe if she gave the skittish child more space...

The nervous feeling continued, so Ava focused instead on how her fingers itched to dig into the earth. To pull it up and turn it over, releasing the scent of both growth and antiquity. Her heartbeat slowed, her breath deepened. Deep in the restorative daydream, Ava accidentally turned left too early and found herself in an unfamiliar alley.

A sudden movement made her tighten her suitcase to her side.

She spun around and lunged back toward the street, too late.

A man pushed her against the wall, yanking her purse off her arm.

"Don't move!" he whisper-shouted in her ear, a blast of sour breath as he twisted her arm behind her back.

Ava had never felt less like moving in her entire life.

The late afternoon sun shifted behind the clouds, leaving the Santa Lucia sky a murky orange. The color of forgotten longing. Elisa sat hunched over her math problems, nibbling the end of her pen. Isotta puttered in the kitchen, filling three mugs with Luciano's favorite camomile tea, while Luciano rifled through his old records, searching for one that wouldn't break Elisa's concentration. He pulled out a dusty copy of *Turandot*. He hadn't listened to this in years. Usually he confined his musical choices to instrumental melodies while Elisa worked, but he had a sudden craving to listen to "Nessun Dorma." He lay the battered record aside, perhaps later tonight—

"Done!" said Elisa, with squared shoulders and self-satisfied grin.

"Is that quite possible? Already?" Luciano smiled in return, pleased to see Elisa looking so proud of herself.

Elisa nodded. "Yes! And you don't even have to check it, *Maestro*. Because I already did."

"Is that so? Well, isn't that marvelous, Isotta?" Luciano asked, catching Isotta's eyes as she carried in the tea tray.

"It is. But Elisa, I hope this doesn't mean you're leaving. I made tea."

Elisa said, "Oh, I can stay."

Isotta said, "I'm so glad. Because I got you a little something."

"You did! What! Why?" Elisa narrowed her eyes.

Luciano's heart turned over. Despite months of gentle nurturance, Elisa was still suspicious at the slightest demonstration of affection. At first that rattled Isotta, filled her with apprehension that perhaps her gestures were too awkward to be accepted by children, a poor foreboding for her own swelling belly. But over time she came to accept what Luciano insisted—Elisa was not used to love. Her life was barren, a veritable wasteland. No seeds could bloom in such dire conditions. He had hoped that her father's absence would allow Elisa to come into her own, but if anything, she only seemed more withdrawn when she showed up on his doorstep. More often than not, she didn't even knock. Just loitered outside the door with the cat.

Once she was pulled into their circle, she revived, like a plant offered water and sunshine. She laughed with flashing eyes, she joined in their conversation, she helped prepare dinner. But as soon as she tugged on her coat to return home, all that found joy drained away.

Luciano wanted to help, but the solution eluded him. Instinctively, his mind turned toward Fatima, as if she held the key to unlocking Elisa's suffering. But Fatima recovered so slowly. Every time he saw her, she seemed to slink away. Elisa never mentioned her, so Luciano suspected that she also felt Fatima's remove. It was a pinch, a loss, but if Fatima needed to heal quietly in the arms of her family, well, he trusted that instinct.

In any case, he enjoyed the afternoons with Elisa, delighting in Isotta and Elisa's burgeoning relationship. Yes, it still took Elisa a good quarter of an hour before her eyes stopped flying around the room, but once she settled, she seemed to belong to them. Last week she'd even made little pictures of Degas with funny messages and hidden them about the house.

Luciano watched as Isotta managed their little friend's skittishness in her new unruffled manner. Pulling her overloaded purse onto her lap, she answered Elisa, "Yes, I was at the *cartoleria*, and saw drawing pens! The same kind my arty classmates used. They have a very fine tip, I thought of you and your cross-hatching. Thinner lines. Only where is it?" Isotta frowned, and started removing items from her purse with bits of commentary. "This candy wrapper is mine, not Margherita's, if you can believe it. Yesterday, hunger simply overtook me and I couldn't walk one more step without chocolate. It was the most delicious thing I'd ever eaten. Pregnancy is good for that...and what's this—right! The package my sister sent from Florence. Luciano remind me to show you later, it's the pamphlet for the sustainable food expo in Modena we were talking about. Remember? Her company is doing the...Oh! Here it is!" She pulled out a pink paper bag in triumph and handed it to Elisa.

Elisa eagerly reached for the bag. "Thank you! My own pen!" She drew out the pen, packaged in plastic and cardboard, and sighed in wonder.

Isotta smiled and turned to Luciano. "By the way, I saw that American— what's her name? Mackenzie or Madison or something? Begins with an M. Anyway, you know the one I mean."

"Married to Alessandro who owns the *castello*?"

"That's the one. She was in the *cartoleria* buying postcards and I heard her on the phone—"

Luciano said, "Sounds like Santa Lucia is rubbing off on you."

Isotta pretended an annoyance her grin denied. "She didn't trouble to lower her voice! I couldn't help but overhear. She clearly assumed nobody in Santa Lucia speaks English."

Elisa looked up from cajoling her new pen out of its plastic case. "You speak English?"

"Not well. What I learned in school, plus my sisters and I watched too many American TV shows." Isotta hummed the theme song from *Friends*, but stopped when she noticed her friends' faces staring at her blankly.

Elisa nodded absently and turned back to her pen. She held it up close to her face. Was she actually smelling it? The child could be so endearingly odd sometimes. Isotta went on, "Anyway, the American was complaining to someone that the *castello* is haunted! Can you imagine?"

Elisa was too busy taking the cap off the pen and investigating the tip to answer but Luciano cocked his head to the side. "Haunted?"

Isotta laughed and stirred her tea. She took a sip. "It's ready by the way, Elisa. Not too hot."

Elisa made dots across the bottom of her paper. Isotta shrugged and carried a mug to Luciano. She went on, "Yes. Apparently they keep finding boxes and supplies moved, and there are all these inexplicable noises. She said they had come to check on the flooring, but she couldn't wait to get back to Rome. Sounded like they were cutting their trip short."

Elisa stopped drawing.

Luciano sat back in his chair, his hand curled around the mug. "Noises...hmmm."

Isotta said, "You don't think it's haunted, surely?"

"Of course not. But it does make one wonder. There are old stories of a hidden passage-way, built to allow fleeing nobles to escape into the hills. Maybe the wind is echoing in?"

Elisa said, "That's just a story?"

Luciano mused, "It could be true. Nobody has ever located the entrance or outlet, but there are all kinds of mysteries about that *castello*."

Elisa's chin trembled. "Like what?"

Luciano took a tentative sip of his tea. "*Allora—*"

He caught Isotta's eye. She shook her head silently, gesturing to Elisa's pale face. Luciano cleared his throat and said, "Oh, you know. Old places always have a certain mystique. So how is that new pen?"

Ava dropped her purse and clutched her hands over her ears as a siren screamed past the police station. The wind from cars speeding by tossed her skirt, exposing her briefly. Ava choked back a sob. It was too much. She tried to hitch her purse over her shoulder, but the strap kept slipping away. Her eyes blurred as she tried to wrap her fingers around the stubborn strap. Finally, she managed to drag it into place.

She didn't know why she bothered. The purse was empty. Her wallet—gone. Her phone—gone. All she had was the memory of that dark alley, those hands flinging her backward and ripping her purse off her arm. She'd crashed into a pile of boxes and waited there, her hands over her head, waiting for a strike that never came.

Instead she had listened as footsteps raced from the alley. It had been a few minutes before she dared lift her head. Empty. The alley was empty. She had slumped onto the ground, unknowingly sitting in a puddle. Yelping, she had leapt up, shaking out her skirt.

Her suitcase stood where she'd left it, like an impotent bodyguard. Why hadn't the man taken her suitcase, too? Maybe he guessed that it would contain little more than outdated clothes. Or maybe running into the streets of Rome with a pink floral suitcase would draw too much attention.

She stumbled to the end of the alley, dragging her suitcase.

In the shadows she spotted her purse.

Empty.

From there she'd stumbled the two kilometers to the police station.

Without her phone, she'd had to ask for directions, over and over. What a sight she must have been. The makeup she'd applied that morning, hoping that she would finally muster the courage to call Ale, streaked down her face. How stupidly she'd played out that call. How Ale would ask to meet, that he wanted to see the flowers in person. They would walk the aisles of plants, imagining this one or that one climbing the rebuilt arbor or nestling up against the side of the castle wall. He would confess that he was hungry. She would smile and say she was too. They'd walk to lunch, and the crowded streets would mean their hips would bump once in awhile. Then, at lunch, Ale would tell her . . . well, she got stuck there. What could he tell her? There wasn't any conversation that could make her happy.

She'd resembled nothing more than a deranged madwoman for that entire lurching journey to the station, and for what? The police couldn't do anything to help. At some level she must have known that, but needed somebody's support, even uniformed strangers, as she replayed the mugger throwing her into a pile of boxes. How would she ever get that film loop out of her brain? It lodged like wisteria.

But there was no support to be found at the Polizia Municipale. An officer handed her acrid *caffè* while another asked questions in a desultory, bored way. They offered her the use of the phone, which she had declined, unable to think of how that would help her.

Only now, as she stood on the street with no money, no phone, and no train ticket, did it occur to her that she should have used the opportunity to ring home. Her mother would have been hysterical and likely would have taken an unreasonably long time to fetch her because she'd have to stop and light a candle (and she wouldn't speed, even with the thought of her daughter adrift in Rome). But at least she'd have some way back to Santa Lucia.

Ava sat on the edge of her suitcase and stopped attempting to check her tears. She supposed she'd have to go back into the police station. Explain again, ask to use the phone. Maybe she could call Edo. He would know how to order her a ticket online for the next train home.

She needed to move. It was getting dark. But her feet ached from the walk, and her legs lacked strength. Instead she gave in once more to stupid, useless tears.

"Ava?"

She instinctively wiped her nose as her head shot up.

Ale stood a few meters from her.

Her mouth opened in astonishment. Now? Three weeks in Rome, and this was the moment the Madonna saw fit to have their paths cross?

She twisted her head away, squeezing her eyes tightly.

"Ava, what are you doing in Rome? Are you okay?"

Ava shook her head.

"What happened to your clothes? Ava!" Ale realized where he was. "The police! Something happened!" He strode toward her and grasped her hands, forcing her to look at him. Ava opened her mouth, but no sound came out. She gasped, then dropped her forehead on his chest. Ale folded her into his arms and stroked her hair. "It's okay. It's okay now."

Recovering her voice, Ava told Ale she'd been mugged. He nodded against her hair, his jaw tightening as she described the attack. He shot a nasty glance at the police station when she told him about leaving without money or a phone or any help at all.

He tucked Ava tighter against his chest as she ended the recitation, spent. He soothed, "It's going to be okay."

"But Ale, I have no money, no phone. Nothing."

"Don't worry about money. We'll go back to my apartment. You can get cleaned up and we'll go get you a phone tomorrow."

"But Ale, I just said, I don't have—"

"Stop. Let me take care of it. Trust me. Okay? Can you do that?"

Ava dared to look directly into Ale's eyes. She saw no challenge, no resistance, no defense. Only warmth.

She nodded slowly. "Yes. I can do that."

"*Ciao*, Elisa. Do you want to walk in the groves again? It's better than the playground."

Elisa didn't think it was better than the playground, but she didn't want Fatima to think she was dumb. Anyway, the playground without swinging wasn't so fun. And Elisa's mother had been really pleased with the bouquet Elisa brought home from her last walk with Fatima. Though, unfortunately, it had given Concetta all sorts of new ideas for her garden. Thank goodness Ava hadn't been around in a long while. Elisa knew that if her mother got flower ideas with Ava around, the two of them were going to sit around the table whispering while they thumbed through catalogues for the longest time. Acting like plants were some big stupid secret. They were just plants. Big deal.

"Elisa?"

"Oh! Right, yes. I don't want to go to the playground at *all*. Playgrounds are for babies."

Fatima regarded her friend curiously. "*Va bene*. Look, I found a way up through this alley."

Elisa nodded and followed Fatima up the steps. "I'd forgotten about this way. You get to see Bea's chickens, and it's the quickest way up."

"No, the quickest way is at the *castello*—"

Elisa groaned. "Oh, Fatima, you're not still going there?"

"I can do what I want. It's not your business."

"But you're going to get in trouble."

"I won't." Fatima set her lips into a firm line.

"You will!"

Turning away, Fatima said, "Nobody ever sees me."

The girls scrambled up the stairs and within a few moments were deep into the groves. Fatima asked, "Does your family have trees?"

Elisa shook her head. "No."

"That's too bad."

Elisa nodded. Was it too bad? Elisa didn't care, or understand why she should care.

The girls gathered the few flowers available in late winter. Fatima's were of uniform length stems, and she collected firm, upright flowers in whites and creams. Elisa's flowers were a riot of color and many of the blooms were already drooping.

Fatima held the flowers to her chest and announced, "Look! I'm a bride."

Elisa giggled and soon Fatima giggled too, and the girls were doubled over at the idea of getting married. Fatima said, "My dress is all wrong, I suppose. And I don't have anything on my head."

"A veil you mean?"

"Yes, that's what it's called. A veil. Or that other thing that brides wear, that goes around the head, what's the word in Italian?"

"Gold like a crown? But thinner?"

"Yes! What's that called?"

Elisa's face fell. "I don't know."

Fatima rearranged the flowers in her hands as she thought.

Elisa piped up, "Oh! I can make you a crown of flowers. Like we used to, before—like we used to. We can pretend they are Persian roses and you are marrying a prince."

"Is he hot?"

Elisa shrugged, unsure how to answer. "Why not?"

Fatima giggled into her hand. "Okay, let's find some flowers."

They hunted up and down the terracing, until they had an armload of flowers. Then the girls plopped down to weave them together. Fatima looked over Elisa's work. "You're good at that."

"Thanks."

"Are you still doodling?"

"Doodling?"

"Yes."

"Well, I guess. Kind of. Mostly at Luciano's—"

"Here use my flowers, you're better at it than me. You can make the flower crowns, and I can plot the story."

Elisa wriggled in anticipation. Fatima made up the best stories.

Fatima leaned back into the tall grasses. "Okay, so how about if we're both princesses in this tall tower. That olive tree can be the tower. We can climb it." Elisa nodded. She hadn't climbed a tree in a long time. "And then these two brothers come to rescue us. They fall in love with us and want to marry us." Elisa squirmed a little. She didn't like the romantic bits of the stories so much as the adventure bits.

Fatima crossed her hands behind her head and continued musing, "But, on the day of the wedding, I fall out of the tower. You try to save me by grabbing my hair, but my scalp gets pulled right off!"

Elisa's stomach lurched. She wondered if there was still smoke trapped in her friend's head.

"I plunge to my death! My limbs are all broken. But the force of my love is so strong that even though I'm dead and all bent up," Fatima sat upright and held her arms at odd angles. Elisa's hands stopped weaving flower stems. Fatima didn't notice, her eyes were shining as she continued, "I appear before my prince and he sees the love burning in my eyes so he doesn't notice that my face is bashed in. Oh! Maybe my guts can be hanging out! Is there a plant we can use?" Fatima's gaze raked the grasses. She didn't notice Elisa turning wan. "Oh, it doesn't matter, we can figure that part out later. So his love is so pure that he marries me anyway. Maybe we should have babies. Do you want to be my sister or my half-dead zombie baby?"

Elisa looked like she might throw up. She wiped the flowers out of her lap and stood up. "It's late. I have to go now."

Fatima squinted toward the sun. "You do? I thought we had loads of time before—"

"No, I really, really have to go now."

Fatima watched as Elisa sprinted out of the groves.

She tried to make the crown herself, but she couldn't do it alone.

Ale heard water running in the kitchen. Was Ava up this late? Maybe she couldn't sleep. The day's events had to have terrified slumber away. Silently, he extracted himself from the bed, praying Madison remembered to take her Ambien. He padded down the hallway and into the kitchen.

The moonlight illuminated Ava's face, framed by loose tendrils of hair. God, she was so beautiful. He wondered why he'd never before been attracted to heart-shaped faces with deep-set eyes. Especially ones with thick wavy brown hair thrown effortlessly into a careless bun at the nape of the neck. Bewitched by the sight of her standing at the sink, bathed in a pool of blue light, Ale moved closer.

Lost in thought, Ava startled to find Ale beside her. As his fingers touched her upper arm, Ava stifled a yelp of pain.

Concerned, Ale breathed, "What is it?"

"Nothing. My arm—"

Ale cocked his head and lowered his body so his eyes were on level with Ava's shoulder. Examining her arm he whispered, "You're cut."

Ava nodded.

"We need to get that cleaned."

Nodding again, Ava said, "I was. I'm sorry to be doing it here. The bathroom sink—"

Ale answered, "Yes." He knew the guest bathroom sink was diminutive, more decorative than functional, with its shallow square basin to catch the spare drops gasped out by the modern faucet.

Examining her arm, he said, "I didn't know you were hurt."

Ava bit her lip. "I didn't either, until I turned over in bed. So stupid."

"Not stupid. It's been an intense afternoon."

Ava looked at Ale, unsaid words swimming into her eyes. She blinked and her gaze shot downward, to their hands hanging inches from each other. "*Allora,*" she said. "I guess I'm done here. Goodnight."

"Wait."

Ava said, "Wait?"

Ale's slow smile winked in the moonlight. "Wait. We need to get a bandage on that."

"A bandage?"

Ale nodded, opening cabinet doors. "A bandage. I know I saw a first aid kit in one of these cupboards. Ah!" He returned to stand in front of Ava.

Her breath caught. Was he standing entirely too close? Ale caught her hand and led her to the wood-topped island. Authoritatively, he said, "This is a two-person job. Here, let me."

Before Ava realized what was happening, Ale swept her up to perch on the island. To her confused expression, Ale smiled. "Better view. Now, let's see what we have here."

Suddenly, they both stilled. What was that? Madison wondering where the party was? They remained motionless for a dragged out minute, before shaking their heads in unison. Must have been someone upstairs. Ava didn't know how anyone could live with people stacked above and below like anchovies in a barrel. She felt suffocated thinking about it. Or maybe it was Ale's nearness. He was standing so close, she thought she could see his chest hair pressed against his white undershirt. And she definitely noticed how his broad shoulders stretched the soft fabric.

Ale was speaking, "No Neosporin, but this looks to be the same concept, an antibiotic ointment. The last thing you want is an infection."

"The last thing I want," Ava repeated. It occurred to her that this zinging magic she felt, this catch in her ribcage, must be one sided. Ale was married. To a gorgeous, perfect American woman. Asleep in the next room. This mutual attraction was all in her head. He was being nice, trying to help. Only she would interpret simple kindness as romance.

After Ale twisted the lid off the ointment he gazed down into Ava's eyes. "Now, this is going to sting a little."

"It's going to hurt?"

Not taking his eyes off of Ava's, Ale nodded once, then twice. "I'm afraid so. But I'll help."

Despite herself, Ava smiled. "How will you do that?"

Ale grinned back. "You'll see." He paused. "Now, don't hold your breath."

Ava hadn't realized she had. She let it out with a small sigh. Ale said, "If you hold your breath, it tightens your muscles. Hurts more."

Closing her eyes, Ava concentrated on breathing deeply and trying not to imagine Ale watching her chest rise and fall beneath her white cotton nightgown. Which she suddenly realized was a little too short, riding up her legs in what was probably an indecent way.

"You stopped breathing again."

"Sorry!"

"It's okay. Breathe. Here goes."

Brow concentrated with the effort, Ale pressed the ointment onto his fingers. The faded light in the kitchen made it hard to find the gash in Ava's arm.

Ava gasped as the ointment slid against her skin. "Oh!"

"I know, I'm sorry."

Her stomach clenched. "You said you'd help with the stinging."

Capping the tube, Ale set it on the island. "I will, *un attimo*. Just a moment." He wiped his fingers on the towel which he rested beside the tube. "Now, instead of focusing on the pain—"

"It hurts!"

"I know it does. But instead of focusing on it, focus on this." Ale raised his hand and brought it to Ava's wrist, resting on the table. Lightly, so lightly Ava wasn't sure he was touching her skin or moving the air above it, he ran his hand up her arm. Ava tried not to moan as a current of electricity followed Ale's hand, up her arm. She closed her eyes.

Closer than she expected, she heard Ale's whisper, "That's better."

Ava tried to nod, but couldn't as Ale's fingers now moved across her right clavicle, dipping gently at the hollow of her throat, to trip across her left clavicle.

Her eyes flew open as his hand cupped her neck with both hands, a bare butterfly of a touch.

Ale stared into her eyes, unmoving.

Ava gazed up, wordless, breathless.

Biting his bottom lip, Ale's fingers drifted to Ava's chin. Softly, he drew her face up to meet his, lowering himself to her, eyes falling closed.

Ava jerked backward. "No!"

Startled, Ale said, "No?"

Blinking to pull back the tears smarting her eyes, Ava said, "No."

Ale reached out and touched Ava's hand. "You haven't thought about it?"

Pressing her hands against her eyes, Ava whispered, "Yes, of course I have."

"And?"

"And what? It's not possible."

A short silence followed. Ale's voice sliced the darkness. "Why?"

With a snort totally lacking in humor, Ava gestured to the kitchen at large. "Why? Ale, look around. Look where we are. Look who you are. Look who I am."

"I see who you are."

"No. You don't. You can't."

Ale stroked Ava's cheek. "Please, let me in."

A sudden flare of artificial light forced the two back from each other like a burst of reverse magnetic power. Madison's cool voice shot from the doorway. "Well, well. What have we here?"

"Margherita! Slow down, *cara*! Wait for *Nonno*!" Luciano called. His cheery words were undercut as he stopped to lean against a wall. He closed his eyes, shook his head, and hurried onward.

Margherita blessedly stopped in the *piazza*. She looked poised to race off again, but grew distracted by Bea feeding the town cats. The little girl lifted her hand to pet the orange tom and Luciano winced, anticipating his granddaughter smacking her small hand against the cat's thin side. His cat, Degas, had taken to hiding under the couch when Margherita walked in. Just two visits, and the cat had learned to equate toddlers with danger. Images of the tomcat swiping at Margherita and having to return her home with scratches on her tender wrists hurried his steps. He wished he'd put gloves on his granddaughter. The weather was warming and he figured she'd fling them off at the park, but they would provide a layer of insulation—

Her hand came down.

And was caught by Bea. "Here, child! Gentle! *Gentle*, see . . ." The older woman held Margherita's hand, stroking the cat who purred like a three-wheeled Ape. So loudly, in fact, that Luciano could hear the rumble from many meters away. Bea said, "See how he likes that?"

The cat pushed his nose against Margherita's knee, rising up on his haunches for greater leverage. The child's laughter pealed around and between the bells now ringing from San Nicola.

Bea's laughter joined the tones, a hint of baritone.

Luciano now stood beside them. "Thank you, Bea. The child got away from me."

"Children do that. How many times have I walked my grandchildren around, hobbling with gout, and praised the Madonna that there aren't cars in Santa Lucia."

Margherita clamored onto the bench and tried to pull the cat onto her lap. The animal allowed itself to be dragged onto the child's thin legs. It draped like a blanket as Margherita patted softly and sang, "Gentle! *Gentle!*"

Bea smiled. "She's a quick study, your granddaughter."

Luciano's chest lifted. "That she is."

"Giulia was the same."

"Just."

Bea's eyes searched Luciano's face. "*Tutto a posto?*"

"*Si, si.*"

"You look pale."

"A good summer, with trips to the coast, I'll be as *bronzato* as a Roman god."

Bea guffawed. "Okay then. But—"

"The slide awaits, Margherita!" Luciano lifted the cat from Margherita's lap. The child's face contorted in protest, but the thought of the playground was beguiling enough for her to smile and take her grandfather's hand.

Bea shouted as they walked away, "Slowly for your *nonno*, Margherita! Show him how you can walk like a turtle!"

Margherita stood stock still, considering, before she got on her hands and walked bent over.

Brilliant!

Margherita's pace slowed and she sang under her breath. A made-up song it seemed, about frogs and turtles in a pond. Every once in a while she jumped sideways with a yelp.

Luciano didn't know why he hadn't thought to turn slow walking into a game. Yes, Bea had raised many children and a handful of grandchildren, but he had been a teacher! He shook his head. Maybe he needed a *caffè*.

Out of the corner of his eye, he spotted Elisa coming out of the *rosticceria* with a slice of pizza. His head cleared as he called, "Elisa!"

"Maestro!" Elisa waved and then got down on her knees. "What are you doing on your hands, Margherita?"

"I's a turtle frog!"

"A turtle frog! Well, that's exciting!" She stood, addressing Luciano. "Can I give her some of my pizza?"

"Most assuredly. And then I wonder if you might be willing to take her to the slide? I'm afraid our zig-zagging walk has fatigued me."

Elisa tore her pizza in half. "Sure. Do you want pizza, too?"

"No. But I thank you, *cara.*"

Elisa looked like she wanted to say something else, but instead she offered the pizza to Margherita, who curled her hand around it, using her elbow to hitch herself onto the bench. The two girls sat side by side, munching their pizza intently as they swung their feet.

Luciano's smile warmed. He adored these two girls. Seeing them together like blooms on a rose bush, it filled his spirit.

Wiping the crumbs off Margherita's shirt (while forgetting about her own, Luciano noticed with a rush of affection for his absent-minded little friend), Elisa took the young girl's hand and led her to the slide.

From the steps leading to the graveyard, Fatima appeared. She stopped mid-stride. Her eyes flicked to Elisa, who didn't see her as she helped Margherita find footing on the steps. Luciano watched as Fatima's head tipped to the sky.

This was most unusual. Fatima looked totally recovered—her cheeks flushed with exercise, shoving something out of sight, into her pockets. But if she were recovered, wandering around the olive groves as the sweater thrown casually over her shoulder would indicate, why did she still decline their company?

Fatima skirted the playground, eyes glued toward the sky, determinedly not making eye contact.

Luciano remembered now, Elisa alluding to a quarrel between them at the time of the fire. Surely, Fatima wasn't holding a grudge against her old friend? His mind raced, trying to derive a clue to unlock this distance. Could it be—

"Fatima!" The word flew from Elisa, though judging from the way she clapped her hand over her mouth, it was unintentional. And unwelcome.

Fatima pretended to smile. "Oh! Hello. Everyone." Her eyes floated to Margherita. "How nice they let you play with Margherita." He wasn't sure if Fatima was aiming this toward Elisa or himself.

His mind awhirl, he ventured, "We'd love to have you join us if—"

"Thank you but I have to get home. I'm so tired."

Fatima did not look tired.

Luciano felt his breath catch and hold. He couldn't make the air connect with his heart, his insides jangled. Was it hot? He was sweating now—

"Maestro?" Elisa said, "Are you okay?"

He pressed his hand against his chest, backing into the bench to sit."Old age, my child. I am as I should be."

Luciano looked up in time to see concern flash across Fatima's face. She took half a step toward him, her mouth opened into a round O, but then irritation troubled her features. She turned away, grumbling about needing to get home.

Elisa sat beside Luciano, and they waited for the world to click back together.

She couldn't stay any longer. It was too hard to want something to happen with Ale, to give life to stirrings she felt in her breast, and at the same time be terrified of that something happening. She knew what it was to be caught up in drama, and she would be happy to steer clear of it forever.

Which is why she told Ale she was ready to go back to Santa Lucia. With the police report filed and her phone replaced by Ale (who snuck it into her hand with a finger over his lips), it was time to go.

Besides, since that night in the kitchen, Madison had been hovering around her like a sticky film on an ancient carpet. Ava couldn't blame her.

Even though she'd like to. She'd like to criticize everything about Madison—from how long it took her to first straighten and then curl her hair every morning to how much time she spent scrolling lifestyle blogs—but Ava knew better. That contempt only masked her jealousy that Madison got to fall asleep with Ale beside her every night. Though Ava had a dream-like memory of Ale sitting in her room with her as she fought off the nightmare attackers that had begun to haunt her dreams.

Ale had tried to convince her to stay, but with Madison standing at attention beside him, arms crossed in front of her chest, there was no possible response but to thank both of them in her halting English for their help during this difficult time, and she'd see them when they next returned to Santa Lucia. Which she hoped wouldn't be too long? Ava tried not to notice Madison glaring at Ale as he answered that they planned to come for an afternoon sometime in the next few weeks to check on the kitchen installation.

Ava nodded and began scanning the TrenItalia website for a train to take her home.

Madison had insisted on accompanying them to the station, but their kitchen designer called with urgent questions that could not be forestalled. Ale smiled knowingly as he jingled the keys and waved goodbye to his wife. Ava couldn't help noticing that Madison's answers sounded remarkably similar to the ones Ale himself had given earlier in the day, on the balcony, before Madison woke up. In a conversation that ended with him closing the glass door and whispering into the phone. Nodding with a smile before signing off.

In the end, only Ale accompanied Ava to the train station.

Ava wasn't sure how the air between them could crackle so much, when she was so tired. Hard as it was to leave, it would be easier not to live in Ale's orbit.

Their walk was a silent one, both of them staring straight ahead. Not touching, save when Ale put his hand on Ava's back to guide her across the crowded street, car horns blaring in protest.

Ava shook her head. How anyone lived here was beyond her.

Shrugging, Ale said, "It's not for everybody." Ava wondered if she had spoken her thoughts aloud. Ale went on, "I'm not even sure it's for me anymore."

Before she could prepare herself, they were at the station. Ale suggested they pick up something for Ava to eat on the train, as she had barely touched her breakfast. But the thought of food turned her stomach. She shook her head. Ale nodded and they continued to the departures board to find her platform.

A sea of people rose around them, threatening to carry them apart, but Ale pressed against Ava. He looked down and smiled. "I won't let them divide us."

Ava tried to smile, but couldn't. She wanted to find a dark hole somewhere and cry at the unjustness of life. Ale dropped her bags and put his hands on her shoulders. "Hey. It's going to be okay."

Ava shook her head. His words were meant for someone else. Another person, another time.

He leaned closer. "If you could stay . . ."

The words choked Ava as she said, "How? I can't."

Ale nodded. He picked up her bags and led her to the platform. "Five minutes. Do you want to get seated?"

Ava hesitated before nodding.

Softly, Ale said, "So I guess this is goodbye."

Ava looked at the ground for a moment before she gathered her courage. He had been wonderful. She had to put aside her feelings and do this properly.

Straightening her shoulders, she smiled, then leaned up on tiptoe to press her right cheek against his, then her other, and then a lingering pause before she pressed her right cheek against his again. As she pulled away, she realized his eyes were closed. He put his hands on her shoulders and dropped a kiss onto her forehead. "Goodbye, then, beautiful Ava."

Biting the corner of her mouth, Ava backed away. Lightly, to avoid hurting her sore arm, Ale's hands ran from her shoulder to her elbow, to her wrist. Ava picked up the handle of her luggage with one hand, but left the other in Ale's. She walked toward the train, their hands united, their arms stretching the space between them. Finally, their fingers unclasped and she stepped, alone, toward the train.

Ava chanced a look behind her. Ale watched her silently, hands thrust deep in his pockets. The crowd moved around him as he stood still, illuminated from the windows above. A lock of hair fell over his eyes.

His gaze unbroken, his eyes beseeching, Ale whispered, "Ava?"

She couldn't have heard the word from this far away, and yet—her name dropped like a stone in her belly.

Ava couldn't stand it. She couldn't stand it any more. She was tired of walking away.

Her breath became shallow as the force of their eye contact moved through her. In his gaze, Ava felt naked, sunlit, glorious.

She ran the few steps into Ale's arms and he caught her around the waist, bringing his face to hers for the long awaited, luxuriant kiss. And the chaos of the world melted away.

"Look!" Elisa held up her drawing.

Luciano started to rise from his chair and Elisa started. "No, no, Maestro, I'll bring it." She leaped up to drop the paper on Luciano's lap. "Thank you, *cara*. Margherita tired me out."

Isotta, who had been reading on the couch joined the two at Luciano's chair. She breathed, "Oh, Elisa. This is extraordinary. Is that Fatima?"

Elisa blanched. "No. A person I made up."

Isotta said, "Of course, of *course*! I apologize. I thought it looked a little like her, but now I see your drawing is completely different."

Elisa's shoulders unclenched.

With his forefinger, Luciano traced the eyes. "The expression. It's direct and challenging, but vulnerable. I didn't know you draw people, Elisa."

Elisa laughed. "Neither did I. It's my magic pen! I put it on the paper, and it takes off!"

Isotta and Luciano exchanged looks of pleasure.

Elisa held the page up, appraising it. "I know I could make it better. It looks a little like a cartoon."

She stared at the drawing as she carried it to the table. "Hmmm.. Maybe if I..." She got another piece of paper from the stack Luciano always left her and began working.

Isotta said, "Don't forget your tea, okay, Elisa?" Isotta paused to watch Elisa's hand glide swiftly over the paper. Gently, Isotta asked, "Would it break your concentration if I read aloud, Elisa? Luciano and I were talking about Dante's Divine Comedy and I thought we'd take turns reading it. I remember having to study it in school and hating it—"

Luciano sniffed in horror.

"But I've agreed to try again. Maybe my teacher didn't teach it well."

Luciano grumbled, "You grew up in Florence."

Isotta started scanning the books on Luciano's cluttered bookcase. "This is our next project, Luciano. How can you find anything?"

"It's on the top right shelf, middle of the stack, black binding. Well worn, you might not be able to read the title until you see the cover."

Isotta's fingertips tripped over the books. "Exactly where you said it would be!"

Luciano turned on the light beside him. "I would be honored to read. If that's acceptable to you, Elisa?"

Elisa nodded distractedly. She'd just gotten to a tricky part, the slope of the jaw.

Isotta handed Luciano the book and picked up her cup of tea, then settled herself onto the couch. At the sound of the blanket being shaken out and wrapped around her legs, Degas trotted in. The black cat sailed across the rug to land silently on Isotta's lap, where he turned once before dropping delicately into a little circle, purring lightly.

Luciano gave his cat a dirty look. "That is one disloyal feline."

Isotta stroked the cat's back. His fur was glossy and soft, no doubt the result of the mortadella Luciano snuck into his bowl, despite Isotta's protestations against the dangers of cured meats for cat kidneys. Luciano could not resist his little cat's beseeching mews.

The overhead light sifted down on the living room as Luciano flipped the pages. The stone walls glowed, their harsh edges buffed down by the mellow illumination. From the kitchen, Isotta's stew burbled gently, giving off the scent of softening beans, garlic, lamb, and rosemary. Tomorrow there would be the world to face again for all of them. But for now, they were in a haven of their own making.

Luciano began to read. His voice dipped and lifted like music, carrying the words into their hearts. Elisa put down her pen and leaned her head on her hand. Her eyes snapped and danced. She left off trying to understand the old Italian word by word and instead let the meaning fall like grace around her.

"To grace his triumph gathers thence a wreath
Caesar or bard (more shame for human wills)
Deprav'd joy to the Delphic god must spring
From the Pierian foliage, when one breast
Is with such thirst inspir'd. From a small spark
Great flame has risen—"

Elisa's sharp sigh broke across the room like an arrow. Feeling Isotta and Luciano's eyes on her, she blushed and took up her pen. The swoop of its tip across the paper twined with Luciano's words as Degas purred on.

∿

"You headed over to Isotta's?" Anna asked merrily as Massimo clattered his empty cup and pushed back his chair.

Massimo said, "No."

"Don't tell me you two have had a . . . a quarrel of some kind?" Anna asked, her eagerness barely contained. "Just when things were going so well!"

Massimo didn't answer.

"Darling, it's okay. She's not as wonderful as she makes herself out to be. You are much better without her."

"And the child she's carrying?"

"Well. I haven't wanted to mention this before, but I have to just hint that you can't be *sure* the baby is yours, can you?"

"You're saying she slept around?"

Anna sighed. "It happens. Naive, unattractive girls are always susceptible to a man's attentions."

Massimo frowned. "You think she's unattractive?"

"Don't you?"

"No."

Anna said, "Of course that makes sense. She looks like the woman you lost, so—"

"That's not it. At all. When I see her, I don't see Giulia. She's Isotta, herself." Massimo's gaze moved to the distance. "She's beautiful. Like she stepped out of a Perugino painting."

Anna snorted.

To Massimo's glower, she said, "I apologize, darling. Of course I didn't think you were serious. Anyway, didn't you have a fight?"

Massimo said, "No. We haven't. I'm frustrated because I want her back in the house before the baby comes and she won't agree. That's all." He started to stand. "But you and I shouldn't discuss it. I know you mean well . . . maybe too much has happened. You don't like Isotta so how can you be supportive of our reconciliation?"

"What can you mean? I've been nothing but supportive!"

Massimo frowned. "You mean the part where you called her ugly or the part where you called her a whore?"

"I never said that!"

"Fine," Massimo conceded. "She secretly has sexual relations with one or more other men, impregnates herself, and then passes off the child as mine. Better?"

"I didn't say she did that. You're twisting my words! I'm *supporting* you by pointing out possibilities. Sometimes I worry you aren't seeing clearly, my son."

"Are you saying you *do* like her?"

"I *want* to like her, but . . . but . . . she can't hold a candle to Giulia." Anna leaned against the counter in relief. "There. I said it. I'm sorry, I thought she could replace Giulia, but she can't. She'll always be a poor substitute."

Massimo shook his head. "I've been remembering a lot, these past few months. Thinking. I can't think of one time that I saw you and Giulia laughing, talking together, the way I see Isotta and Margherita."

"Margherita is a child!"

"Even Isotta and Luciano."

"Well," Anna sniffed. "I'm not sure that's any recommendation to either of them. But a mother's love, that's so special. Ask Isotta. I'm sure her relationship with her mother is rich." Anna batted her eyelashes. "Right, Massimo?"

Massimo mumbled something about Caterina being a piece of work, and Anna opened her eyes wide. "Goodness, darling! Isotta has a problem with me, she has a problem with her own mother. What are we supposed to think?"

Massimo said, "I . . . I don't . . . The point is, Giulia was always nervous around you."

"I loved the girl, of course, but she *was* nervous. You know that. You can't blame me for Giulia's little foibles."

"She wasn't always nervous."

"Wasn't she? Because it seems like I saw her with you more than once looking miserable."

Massimo's mouth opened, but no sound came out. Finally he whispered, "I made her miserable?"

"Of course not! That's not what I mean! To tell you the truth—and you know I never speak ill of the dead—I think her parents spoiled her. So nothing could please her. She was sour. It wasn't your fault."

"You think so?"

"It wasn't . . . *anybody's* fault. Giulia was never going to be happy. It's sad really. And Massimo, I . . . I fear Isotta is the same way. I see her complaining so much, wanting things just so before she agrees to move back—"

"You said you didn't want her back—"

"It doesn't matter what I said. I only meant that Isotta is so *negative*, I fear she'd move back in and it would be the same thing all over again."

"But it's different now. I'm not keeping a secret. I can be real with her."

"Can you though? Can you be real with anyone but me? Who knows and loves you, with all your moods?"

"Stop it! Stop it, Mamma!" Massimo drew his hands up to his ears. "You always do this! I feel like I know what's in my head, and then I talk to you and everything gets dark and wrong!"

Anna smiled. "You see what I mean?"

Ava woke up in a haze, her limbs tangled with Ale's. In the quiet, she heard his rhythmic breathing. The morning light sifting in from the enormous plate glass window illuminated Ale's sleeping face, a small smile curving his lips. She nestled against him and let herself tumble into the memory of the afternoon before, at the train station, when she almost walked away. She smiled despite herself, enjoying the deliciousness of the memory. She would never forget it.

That kiss as she ran into his arms. The obliteration of all thought, only rushing gratitude at the feel of his arms strong around her and his lips pressed against her own, his mouth opening a touch to fill her with wild, pulsing joy. As their faces separated, and their eyes opened to read the relief in each other's eyes, Ava had become suddenly aware of a smattering of applause.

Blushing furiously she had tucked her head against Ale. His hand held her against his chest, stroking her hair for a moment. Before he had picked up her wayward suitcase and led her here.

Oh, that elevator ride when all she wanted was to run her hands over his taut body. The feel of his arm around her waist enflamed her. Silently, he had led her to the room. Silently, he had opened the door. Silently, he had drawn her in, for sudden shyness stalled her into a pause outside the door.

Then there was no more silence.

Only the roar of longing, released. Ava smiled into the darkness. It had been a night of alternating passion and gentleness as the two of them sank into the bliss of unencumbered embraces and whispers and giggles.

But now with the day, reality crept in. She sat up, the sheet clutched against her breasts. Open-mouthed, she looked over at Ale, who woke with a start. "Hey," he breathed. "You okay?" He reached to tuck a tendril of hair behind her ear.

Ava shook her head fiercely.

Ale sat up and pulled Ava against him. He kissed the crown of her head, kissed her ear. "What is it?"

For a moment, all thought left Ava. Then the panic rushed back in.

She said, "What are we doing?"

She could feel Ale's smile against her temple. "I can tell you that. Or show you, if you'd rather."

"No! No. I . . . What are we *doing*?"

Ale's hand running over her thigh stilled. "Ah, that."

"Yes. *That.*"

A rush of breath escaped Ale as he sank against the pillows. "I don't know, Ava."

"You don't know?"

"Do *you*?"

"No. But it's your marriage we're violating."

"My marriage was violated long ago."

"What? You mean this is a habit? Like a gym routine?"

"No! No. That's not what I mean. I mean . . . it's hard to explain."

"Try."

Ale closed his eyes. He said, "When I married Madison, we were different people. Well, she was the same as she is now, but I'm not anymore. At all. I think I drifted away from her, from who I was, long ago. Only it's taken me ages to realize. I suppose that's what I mean by violating our marriage. She expected me to stay the man she married, and I couldn't."

Ava wanted to know if he still had sex with Madison, but she couldn't bring herself to ask. She supposed she didn't really want to know.

Ale said, "Arriving in Italy forced me to face it . . . I've been going through the motions, but it's not a real life. How can it be, when my wife and I don't want the same things? I feel badly for her, I feel guilty. But, God. What a farce."

Ava placed a hand on his chest. He plucked it with both of his hands and kissed it. She turned toward him. "Then why stay married?"

"Oh, I've been asking myself that every day since the moment I met you. You and your baby rosemary plants."

"No. You're lying."

"I'm not. I'm most certainly not. I guess before, I thought all women were like Madison, and my life with her was like every marriage. But I met you, and I saw what was possible."

Ava bit back a self-deprecating remark about her hair and chest size.

She let him continue as he interlocked their fingers. "So, it was you, mostly. But also being here in general. I felt happy and knew that for a long time I've been confusing success with happiness."

Their entwined hands arrived in Ava's lap. She stared at their fingers, plaited together. His manicured yet strong, hers still seemed to have some earth embedded in her knuckles.

She said, "But Ale, if you know that, if you knew that—why stay?"

He sighed. "Like, I said. It's complicated."

A short silence followed.

He went on, "I work for Madison's father. You know that?"

Ava nodded, confused.

Ale said, "Well, if I split from Madison, I won't have anything." Ale continued, not realizing that he had switched to English to keep pace with his American thoughts. "Except the castle, I suppose. We signed a prenup to protect her, but in retrospect, I guess it protects that. It was lucky I didn't know about the castle ahead of time. Her father would have written the agreement totally differently. Though how I can sustain a house like that without an income, I have no idea."

"Ale?"

"Sorry, Ava, my thoughts wandered. My Italian is better with being here, but some things are hard to talk about not in English. What it comes down to is that if I leave Madison, I lose everything. I guess I can't do that unless I know for sure I'm leaving for something I can keep."

Slowly, Ava thought aloud, "So you need to stay with Madison until you know . . . what?"

Ale stroked her bare shoulder. "I guess until I know if this is real."

Ava stiffened. "You get to decide that?"

Ale grinned. "Well, it's not like I have a lot of experience here, but I think this is something we decide together. You say the word, you say you think this is real, and I'm out of my marriage."

"Just like that?"

"Just like that." Ale allowed his fingers to drift down, tugging at the sheet Ava still had clutched against her chest. "I'm in love with you, Ava."

She succumbed then to his kisses, the feel of his body pressed against hers.

Edo noticed the paper on the bar as soon as he opened the door.

Chiara's pale face belied her stoic posture. "He's not coming back."

"What?"

"Read it."

It was an article about increasing communism in Bologna. The article included photographs of leaders of the local communist movement. Fabrizio's face leapt out, which confused Edo, since Fabrizio had never espoused any communist values. Skimming the article, Edo realized Fabrizio's companion was a party leader. The two looked pretty chummy.

"How did you get this paper?"

"It was sent here."

"It was *sent* here?"

"Yes. Someone wanted me to see it."

"Francy."

"What?"

"Francy! He probably set this whole thing up. I wouldn't be surprised if he set this date up with this, this woman, whoever she is."

"Alicia Renzi."

Edo looked curiously at his aunt, who said, "I read the article."

"Renzi? Related to—"

"Distant, if at all."

Edo frowned, staring at the photograph before continuing. "Anyway, I bet he engineered this whole thing. You are too provincial for his hoity-toity ass, and he didn't want his father being with you."

"Edo, I know he's kind of obnoxious, but he's not soulless."

"He is! Why should he care about your happiness!"

"He shouldn't, but I'm certain he cares about his father's. If I make his father happy, wouldn't he want me to be with Fabrizio, even if I work in a village bar?"

"You give him too much credit."

"He's human."

"You give humans too much credit."

"And you are biased."

"Yes! Biased against jerks who hurt people I care about!"

Chiara patted his cheek. "You're sweet, Edo. But you're young."

Edo scowled. "I hate when people say that. Just because I don't have grey hairs doesn't mean I don't know a thing or two."

"You do know a thing or two."

"Or three."

"Or even three. But what you don't get is this: If Fabrizio loved me, no amount of his son insisting I'm not cultured or traveled or educated enough for him would make him stay away."

Edo chewed his lip. She had a point.

Sighing, Chiara started to unload the dishwasher.

Edo muttered. "I still say that Francy had a hand in this."

Chiara straightened, and then smoothed her apron over her hips. "Maybe. But the point is, it's over." She focused on inhaling. "That's that."

Sunlight poured in, even through the heavy gauze curtains. Ava guessed it was early afternoon. She had at least an hour before Ale returned to work. A wringing sensation gripped the bottom of her heart. She hated that moment when he left her to her hotel room's sterile opulence.

Wriggling against Ale's back, Ava concentrated on soaking up her lover's warmth, his musky scent, in an effort to push away the foreboding that had become a routine part of her day.

She squinted her eyes shut, ordering herself to stay here and not worry about later.

But the creeping sense of doom invaded anyway.

Once Ale left, to return to his wife, she knew what would happen. She would be left to spiral—was she sure this was real? Could she make that decision knowing it would end a marriage? What if this was basic animal attraction and he left Madison and then two months later it was over between *them*?

It certainly felt real. It felt sensational. Not only the physical intimacy, but those afternoons as they lay on the bed, running their hands over each other's bodies in ways less sexual and more to understand each other. In almost every way, they matched, she and Ale. Aside from his weird interest in American crime dramas, but that difference made her smile. Watching him watching the screen, eyes wide, letting out a yelp of protest—well, it was all rather adorable.

She sighed now, feeling Ale stir beside her.

Watching him enter the state between dreaming and waking, she realized the real problem.

She couldn't say with any degree of certainty if what they shared was real, was love, not until she told him the thing she had never told anyone. But she was scared that when she did tell him, he would reject her. She wanted this shining thing between them, at least awhile longer.

No, she couldn't do it. She'd wait. Enjoy what they had. This total delight in each other. It had only been a week, why spoil it?

Yes, her heart twisted every time Ale walked out the door. Even though he always turned back and pleaded with his eyes for her to say the words to end his marriage. But she couldn't think about that. She slid her hand under the sheet and ran it down the length of his body. Before he even opened his eyes, he moaned lightly and turned to her like a sunflower toward the dawn.

～

"Are you sure you're okay?" Massimo asked, as Isotta pulled her jacket snug around her belly.

"I told you, I'm sure!"

"Okay, okay, I'm sorry."

Isotta shook her head. "No, I'm sorry. You didn't deserve that. I ... I'm in a mood, I suppose."

Massimo glowered. "Luciano? Is he not—"

"Luciano is great. He makes me feel like I belong."

"Oh. Well, then."

"Seriously, Massimo, when will you let go of your foolish resentment? He's such a good man."

"That's what you say."

"Massimo."

He sighed. "Okay, I know you're right." Massimo shook his head. "I realize it doesn't make sense. Margherita certainly loves him. Whenever she spends the afternoon with him, she comes home with silly songs she sings all night. He's just part of a time I'd rather not think about."

Isotta stopped walking. Massimo continued until he realized he was alone. Confused, he turned and faced her. Looking down at her he whispered, "What?"

"Don't you see, Massimo? The 'not thinking about it.' That's been your disease."

She held her breath. If Massimo recoiled or ...

He did tense. She saw that. But then his shoulders sagged. "You're right. I know you're right."

Isotta said nothing.

Massimo stroked her cheek and smiled. "Why is it that no one ever said the things to me that you do."

Isotta shrugged. "I expect people have. Maybe even Giulia. But you weren't ready to hear them."

"I'm ready now."

"I know."

"I'm glad."

A beat. "Me too."

A shadow passed over Isotta's face. "It's strange to me that you're glad, though. This can't be comfortable for you."

Massimo grinned. "Oh, it's not." He tugged her hand. "Let's turn back? I want to be there when Margherita wakes up. I was hoping you would join me?"

Isotta smiled and nodded. "Yes, I'd like that." She paused. "But . . . also . . . it's hard. This being part of your lives, but also separate."

"You said you needed this, this distance. You'll barely let me touch you. I would much prefer you back in my home. Our home."

"The thing is, Massimo. It'll never be our home."

A shadow passed over Massimo's face. "You mean because I shared it with Giulia? You said—"

"No. Not Giulia. Your mother."

"My mother?"

Isotta sighed. "You have no idea what I'm talking about."

Massimo's jaw worked. "My mother is . . . my mother is . . . Why are you always so negative?"

Her mouth hung open for a brief moment before she ventured, "Negative? You can't be serious."

"Negative or . . . whatever! You are the one who is so good with words, so hell bent on me forgiving everyone. Why can't you do the same? You know there is a word for people who serve it but can't eat it."

Isotta stiffened. "Is this really the direction you want to be traveling right now?"

"What do you mean?"

"You know what, Massimo? No. I'm not going to explain it to you. If you can't see the underhanded way your mother treats me—"

"You remind her of Giulia!"

"*Cavolo*, Massimo! Your mother can't love anyone who loves you!"

"That's wrong. That is so wrong. You are so naive."

Isotta unclamped her hand from Massimo's and turned back to Luciano's.

Ava flopped onto the armchair.

She wasn't sure what she expected being a kept woman would feel like, but it wasn't at all as sexy as it sounded. Being with Ale was wonderful, of course. Every second with him—even the ones where they watched a movie together or popped out to buy toothpaste—she was constantly taken aback by rushes of joy and affection. But she was spending an awful lot of time alone.

She wondered if she should get a job. Would that make her lie to her parents about finding work in Rome less uncomfortable? As she watched the line of cars snake around the roundabout beneath her window Ava realized she didn't actually feel at all uncomfortable about lying to her parents. Quite the opposite. She wished she had done it sooner.

Her steps into the wide world may be few nowadays, but they were hers and hers alone. Her parents meant well. She knew they did. But they assumed that they knew better than she did. And she allowed it. Or she had, anyway.

Ava wondered, if her parents hadn't pushed her to go to the science and technology high school, what would she have done? Classics, probably. She liked reading and history well enough. But honestly, given a choice, she wouldn't have gone to high school at all. After all, how much did her *scientifico* degree help her now, working with her father in his flower shop and consulting about landscaping?

Soil.

Ava missed soil.

She missed the feel of her hands plunging into it, turning it over, finding flecks of minerals and wriggling insects. She loved settling roots deep within it and saying a prayer of blessing that those roots take hold and find nourishment within the air pockets and nutrients. It was an unending miracle.

Maybe she *should* get a job.

Soil in Rome was scarce, but there must be shops that would allow her to at least be near growing plants. She had contacts now.

Then again, that would require her to work during daylight hours, the hours that were currently given to Ale.

Ava sighed. Their time together had been short today. Only enough time for a late breakfast and a shower together. Leaning her chin on the back of the armchair, Ava closed her eyes and remembered that shower. The smell of the white tea shampoo Ale liked to bring her. The feel of his hands in her hair. The firmness of his broad shoulders under her fingers.

It was too bad he had to return to work so soon. When he'd left, his eyes locked with hers, tugging her heart to exact the promise he was waiting for. That if he left his wife, Ava would be ready to stand by him, to be his, completely. She wanted to, oh how she wanted to. A little longer, she told herself. She would wait a little longer.

Clouds scudded across the jewel-like sky, puffy and ridiculous. Like the illustration in a children's picture book.

Ava turned back to the room, wrapping her robe against her chest. She'd tell him soon. She wanted to enjoy the simplicity of the world they created—this haven, the few restaurants they frequented where Madison wouldn't deign go, the museums and parks they had walked so often they were more background than focal point. It should feel wrong. Ale being married and all. But somehow, Ava only felt a twinge of remorse.

Her phone's vibration cut into the room's quiet.

Ava turned it over and smiled, reading Ale's message: "Wish I could get away. Will try later tonight. I miss you so."

Settling back into her chair, Ava flicked through her phone, checking email (nothing of consequence), What's App messages (many from her parents asking how her cousin was and how long she planned on staying, plus one from Edo with a photo of Carosello, his head wedged in a pasta box), and Instagram. Her finger paused above the screen. She knew she shouldn't. She *knew* she shouldn't. Yet, she couldn't help herself. Before she could remind herself that this seed never bloomed properly, Ava typed in Madison's Instagram handle.

Today's post appeared and the phone clattered out of Ava's hand.

Slowly she regained her breath.

She reached for the phone, recoiled momentarily as if it burned, and then picked it back up.

Maybe she was wrong.

Maybe she didn't see what she thought she saw.

No, there it was.

Ale and Madison, arms around each other, smiling like movie stars. Wait, maybe this was taken long before, maybe Madison posted it as a remembrance of things past. But there was no mention of that. The time-stamp read an hour ago. The caption read:

> **Truly blessed to be at the limited opening of the Bernini exhibit at #borghesegardens. Even more blessed to be here with my best friend and true love. #luckygirly #truestory #lovemylife #bliss**

But . . . still. Maybe this was even a month ago, before Ava was here, before things with Ale got started. Ale, her Ale, would never lie to her about a transatlantic phone meeting he had to prep for, a meeting that would last over the lunch hour when he usually came to her. Her Ale would never look that relaxed and happy in the arms of the woman he said he no longer loved.

A sheen of sweat broke out over Ava's forehead. Quickly she switched to her internet browser. Her fingers slipped, mistyped, went back, mistyped again, until finally she'd entered Borghese Gardens Bernini exhibit.

Today.

Now.

It was happening now.

Ava looked down at her robe, gaping open, her body exposed. He was off looking sophisticated and trendy with his sophisticated and trendy wife, and here she sat like an idiot. Essentially naked. Waiting for him. Like an *idiot*.

Air. She needed air!

Clothes flew around the room as Ava rummaged through her drawers. She reached past the modest outfit she'd first arrived in to the snug and brightly colored dress she'd picked up last week. The dress Ale had begged her to only wear for him because he wouldn't be able to stand the thought of other men ogling her curves under that slinky material.

She pulled the dress over her head and fluffed her hair. From under the bed she extracted the heels that Ale told her made her legs look like a gazelle's. She didn't have the patience to apply the little makeup she had, but she quickly swiped red lipstick across her mouth. Nodding at her appearance, she grabbed her purse and darted out the door.

Once on the sidewalk, she paused. What was she doing? Where could she go?

She didn't know. There was a hole in her heart she was desperate to fill.

The bustle of the roundabout pulled her forward. Shopping? Food? Her phone lay heavy in her purse. Maybe she should call someone, talk about it. Edo, maybe? He wouldn't judge her for sleeping with a married man. But maybe he would with a *happily* married man, as it seemed

Ale was?

Her legs scissored swiftly but when she arrived at the roundabout, she sagged. She didn't want any of this. She wanted to go to sleep, to have all this evaporate. No, she had to push herself farther into the arms of Rome. Rome would cure her. Or at least obliterate all her thoughts.

She drifted down the street, peering into windows, following couples down the sidewalk with her eyes. Why couldn't she ever be a **#luckygirly**?

The siren song of her bed pulled her to turn back. She'd nap, and then she'd figure out what this meant, and what she should do.

Like a video tape slowed to half-speed, Ava made her way back to Senato Hotel Roma. As she approached the door, she saw Ale walking toward the hotel. Did he see her? Well, she'd make *sure* he saw her.

Ava stepped toward the doorman. "*Buonasera*," she smiled, blinking slowly and staring at his mouth.

"*Buonasera, signora!*" The doorman—Norberto, was it? Umberto? Something with *berto*—looked surprised, but not displeased. Ava took another step toward him, her body closer than strictly conventional. She looked up through her lashes, licked her lips, and breathed, "I wonder if you can help me?" She teetered.

The doorman reached out an arm to steady her, his hand brushing against the swell of her chest in the process. Ava leaned a little further into him and looked up into his eyes as she bit her lip suggestively. He gripped her arms a touch before Ava felt her other arm lurched away and pulled by Ale standing beside her. His eyes flashed.

"*Grazie*, Norberto." Norberto! "I've got it from here."

The doorman shrugged and smiled. "No problem, boss." He turned and faced the street again, while Ale half dragged Ava to the elevator.

The ride was silent.

His hand still firmly on her arm, Ale practically shoved Ava into the hotel room. "What the hell are you doing?"

Ava dropped into the chair, letting her dress ride up. She gazed at Ale as his eyes moved to her exposed thighs. She spun away from him to face the window. "I can't imagine what you mean."

A puff of air escaped Ale in frustration. "Come on. You all but ripped off your dress in the street. Is this what you do when I'm working?"

"Is this what you do when *you're* working?"

"What the hell do you mean?"

Ava's voice was ice. "I know where you were today, Ale. Don't bother lying." She turned quickly so she could see him blanch. The words flew from her. "Some routine you gave me. About your marriage being over."

Ale whispered, "Where . . . how . . ."

Ava turned back to the window, tugging her dress lower over her legs. "Madison keeps up quite the social media presence."

"She..she said she was taking a photo for her father. To send her father. I needed to keep up the story—"

"And what about the story you told me?"

Ale sagged into the other chair and dropped his head into his hands. "I knew I shouldn't have lied. I knew it, but I didn't want you to worry."

"Believe me, I'm worried."

Ale reached for Ava's hand, but she spun the chair away and stared at the building across the road. Metal and glass. So hard. Like armor.

"Ava, please . . . listen! I didn't want to go, but Madison has been getting suspicious. And I didn't want to have to tell you where I was going and invite a conversation that would likely be difficult. Our time together is never long enough. I didn't want to ruin it."

"So you lied to me."

"Yes. I'm sorry. I really am. But, Ava. Are you mad that I lied or that I was with Madison?"

"Both!"

He nodded. "Yes, of course. Of course." Taking a breath, Ale continued, "But I'm going to have to keep doing things with Madison until you are ready to be with me. And I don't think you are. Ready, I mean."

Ava huffed. "Well, I'm not *now*."

Ale's seat spun as he flung himself to sit at Ava's feet. She resisted, but he clung to her hand. "Ava, all these complications are because we can't be honest with the world. But once we are, all this will go away. Far away. I promise."

Ava shook her head, but she left her hand in Ale's. Chin on her knee, he let his free hand run up her leg, but she stalled him with her hand.

"Not now."

A tear slid down her cheek.

"Oh, Ava." Ale rose on his knees and pulled her close.

Fatima tried to focus on her teacher's explanation of the Reform Movement, but her thoughts distracted her. Last night she'd realized that there might well be a prison or dungeon underneath the *castello*. She wondered what the remnants would look like. Chains attached to the walls? Cages?

She couldn't wait to get back into the mazes of tunnels. Though she should probably change her flashlight batteries. Last time they were wavering more than usual, and the thought of being trapped under the *castello* with no light terrified her—delightfully terrified her, quite honestly. Her mind fluttered, over and over, to the memories of roaming those darkened rooms, like a moth continuing to beat its way to the kitchen light. Even as the heat seared its wings.

Fatima glanced up at the clock, catching Elisa's eye. Elisa smiled, but that smile wavered like Fatima's flashlight. Fatima felt badly that she had been spending less time with Elisa lately. But Elisa seemed so young now. Sweet, but young. Her whole class seemed young. She couldn't believe she'd ever had a crush on Mario.

Her thoughts turned to Stefano. He was a man, not a boy. She remembered that day on the playground, months ago, when his eyes had lingered over her. He'd told Elisa that Fatima was too dark for him, but she knew that wasn't true. She had felt the way his fingers lingered over her waist before Elisa had shown up. Elisa took everything so seriously. That was part of the problem.

Sweet, of course. She enjoyed their walks, even though she couldn't tell Elisa anything real, or she would completely freak out. Fatima frowned. Elisa was awfully jumpy, nowadays. Worse than before. At first Fatima had assumed Elisa felt guilty about the coin and fire. Elisa kept trying to apologize, but Fatima didn't want to hear about it. Fatima wouldn't allow herself to think about the stupid stolen coin. No, what she needed was to *feel*, to push herself. Further.

Elisa's jumpiness made her jumpy, too. Fatima shrugged to herself. Maybe Elisa hadn't changed at all, and Fatima's tolerance for it had disappeared.

She would have to find a way to brush Elisa off after school. It shouldn't be hard. Elisa was often helping her mother in the yard or racing off to Luciano's. Sometimes it seemed like Elisa avoided being with her as much as she avoided being with Elisa.

With a sigh, Fatima turned her attention to the lecture. Like the volume on the TV being turned up, the teacher's voice filled her awareness. "So who can tell me about how the Protestant Reformation changed Catholicism?"

Fatima's hand shot up.

It took spotting Chiara and Edo standing on the busy Roman sidewalk for Ava to realize that she'd never actually seen either of them outside Santa Lucia. Had she? She thought for a moment. Maybe she and Edo had been on the same middle school *gita* to the Venetian palaces on the Brenta river. That seemed a million years ago.

Seeing them here, now, animatedly discussing the ancient column in front of the restaurant, Ava wanted to weep. They were reminders of what seemed a simpler time. All around the two, Romans wove between the sidewalks and scooters and ancient remnants of a long-vanished civilization with nothing even approaching passing interest. But here stood Chiara and Edo, in their familiar clothes with their familiar expressions, catching sight of her and waving vigorously.

"*Ciao*, Ava! *Ciao, ciao!*" Ava's hesitation vanished. When Edo called her and said he and Chiara were coming to Rome to turn the dreaded meeting with Chiara's lawyer into a grand day out, she had first tried to make excuses. Her new job, she said, she couldn't get away.

"For lunch?" Edo had asked simply.

Ava knew then she couldn't in good conscience avoid seeing them, but she wasn't sure how she'd maintain the fiction that she had a sensible job and a sensible apartment to get sensible experience she could bring to her sensible life in Santa Lucia. She had agreed, of course. With a rush of enthusiasm to dispel the chill she'd heard in Edo's voice when she had tried to decline.

There was no chill now, as the friends ran to embrace each other.

A hand on each of their arms, Ava appraised what seemed like a mirage from another life. "How well you both look! I hope you brought a bottle of Santa Lucia air . . . I seem to have car exhaust overwintering on my skin."

They all laughed, before turning into the restaurant.

Once seated, Edo asked, "How are you enjoying Rome?"

"Oh! It's fine. Loud, noisy, but fine."

"Do you see much of Alessandro?"

Ava's heart stopped as she tried to read Edo's expression. But her friend was laying his napkin across his lap. Stalling, Ava asked, "Alessandro?"

He looked up now, a small smirk jockeying for position on his serious face. "Alessandro. You remember. Your friend from the *castello*."

Chiara nudged her nephew. "Edo. Play nice."

Edo said, "I will if she will. She's holding out on us."

In a small voice, Ava said, "Oh, right. Alessandro. I forgot he was in Rome."

Edo turned to Chiara and whined, "See? Unfair! I want details and instead I get riddles."

Chiara reached across the table. Clasping Ava's hand she said, "Ignore him. His own love life is a shambles, so he thinks he can live vicariously."

Edo huffed. "It's not a shambles. It's completely nonexistent. No love life whatever! But you are right about the living vicariously." He leaned forward conspiratorially. "So tell me all."

Despite herself, Ava laughed. She mimed locking her lips and Edo sat back in his seat, pretending disgust. "You are no fun. I thought for sure we'd get some juicy stories on this trip."

Chiara studied the menu. "There, there, my boy. Obviously we are not all lucky enough to have torrid love affairs away from prying eyes. We must make do. Now, what should we order? Oxtails?" She looked up. "Seems a fitting meal for two sad sacks such as ourselves."

After watching their love bloom for months, Ava didn't understand how Chiara could be so reconciled to Fabrizio's leaving. Was she pretending a cavalier tone she didn't feel? And how much did Chiara and Edo know about Ale? Maybe nothing. But no, Edo was running his finger down the menu and nonchalantly pretending to answer Chiara but saying as an aside to Ava, "You've been spotted, you know. The strings of Santa Lucia are long."

Ava's mouth dropped open.

Chiara swatted Edo. "Edo! That's enough. She doesn't want to talk about it." Turning to Ava she added, "And that's fine, love. I'm sure it's a complicated situation, though, so if you do need any help..."

"I...I don't."

"There! You see Edo? I told you Ava could handle herself. And here you thought we needed to check in on her."

Edo pouted. "I wanted to make sure. Is that so wrong?" He put down his menu. "All kidding aside, Ava. You don't have to tell us anything, but we'd like to know if we should be happy for you or worried about you."

Ava bit her lip and whispered, "Happy for me?"

Edo smiled triumphantly. "Okay!"

Ava said, "I thought you were meeting with the lawyer..."

Chiara and Edo looked at each other and laughed. Chiara said, "Is that what you told her?"

"I had to tell her something."

Chiara turned to Ava. "My lawyer is in Spoleto. And he makes house calls. Edo, I'm afraid, has made up that whole story."

Feeling foolish, Ava said, "Oh."

Chiara said, "Edo! You are awful."

Edo shrugged then turned serious."I am sorry about the ruse, Ava. But we wanted to see you and didn't want you to feel pressured."

"You mean like I do now?"

The three laughed together.

Edo made eye contact with the waiter, and then said to Ava, "Forgive us?"

The waiter held up a finger to indicate he'd be with them momentarily.

Ava thought for a moment before saying, "Only if you buy me lunch."

"Deal!"

"So now tell me all the town news—" Ava's voice cut off as the door to the restaurant opened.

Madison strode in, with more blond Americans in designer heels than Ava had ever seen in one place. How did she meet them all? Was there some Star Spangled Bombshell What's App group?

Chiara and Edo's gaze followed Ava's. Edo murmured, "Oh, *cavolo.*"

Ava began shaking. How in the world had she chosen a restaurant so unhip it was suddenly hip?

Chiara whispered, "Ava, darling, we can leave. It's no problem."

Ava shook her head. Flustered, she stood. "No, we can't leave. Give me a moment."

Tripping over her feet, Ava made her way to the bathroom. She stumbled into a stall and sat on the toilet, putting her head between her legs. Gradually, her breath slowed. She could do this. She could. She'd stroll out breezily as if she was having lunch with her friends, which she had every right to do.

Ava pulled open the stall door to find Madison, washing her hands. Madison smiled at her in the mirror. "Ava. How nice to see you."

Muttering something, she wasn't even sure what, Ava stepped to the sink and reached for the liquid soap.

"Aren't you lucky your flower thing allows you to return to Rome," Madison said, coolly.

What could Ava say now? She supposed some semblance of truth, something about why she was at this particular restaurant without roving into territory where her face would expose the truth that Ava had been naked with this woman's husband a few short hours ago. Getting out the English words took a Herculean effort. "Yes, I came with Chiara and Edo. For the day."

"So back to the scene of the crime, eh?"

"Crime?" Ava's heart stopped.

Madison said, "Your mugging or whatever you call it."

"Oh. Oh, yes."

Madison said, "I hope this restaurant is as good as they say. Have you been here before?"

"No." Could she leave now, stroll right out?

Madison leaned against the counter. "My friends tell me it was written up in *The Guardian* last month. For some dish, a beef cooked in wine? But I'm not even sure if I can have that—"

She whipped her hand to her mouth. "Oh, God! I shouldn't have said anything!" Her hand drifted to her stomach. "It's early days and Ale and I are superstitious. Don't tell anybody?"

Ava shook her head, but Madison had already left the bathroom.

As Elisa and Fatima walked through the groves, Fatima reached for Elisa's hand with a bit of her old impulsive affection. Elisa smiled. Fatima smiled too, though her eyes held back. Not enough for Elisa to notice. The brief burst of connection made Elisa's heart felt like it could take wing. All her secrets, compounded by Fatima's distance, seemed like old nightmares hastened away by daylight. Right now there was the sun warming her face, a gentle breeze sighing around them, and the olive trees leaning in like old friends.

Fatima stopped to investigate an unusual plant, and the girls discovered it wasn't a plant at all, but rather porcupine quills. As long as knitting needles, the quills were the color of burnished wood, tipped in creamy alabaster. With fierce points though; the girls handled the quills carefully.

"Did people ever write with these? Or only feathers?" Elisa wondered.

"Hmmm . . . I don't know. How could you write with them?'

This prompted the girls to sit on the path and experiment with the porcupine quills, scribing shapes in the chalky earth. Elisa wondered aloud if they could be sharpened and filled with ink.

Almost without her noticing, a scene bloomed in front of Elisa. A bell tower, a spiraling sequence of clouds, a field of poppies. Fatima regarded Elisa's work, then looked back at her own, a crude rendering of the olive tree in front of her. "I wish I could draw like you."

Elisa looked up, not realizing she'd fallen into the flow of creation. "Yours is so pretty!"

Fatima shook her head. "It's not. But that's okay. I'll enjoy yours." She leaned back and let the sun's rays settle onto her face, easing the cold and clamped muscles around her eyes.

Elisa went back to the lines in the dirt in front of her. Looking for an exceptionally sharp quill, she began crosshatching the clouds, exaggerating the roiling shape. "Fatima?"

"Hmm?"

"There's something I wanted to tell you."

Fatima opened her eyes. "What's that?"

"So you know how my dad is gone?"

A pause while Fatima considered how much to acknowledge. "Yes."

"Well, before he left, my parents had a fight."

"Okay."

"A big one."

Fatima's breath caught. "Did he hurt you?" She felt her anger rise. Elisa was innocent. The thought of someone hurting her—

Elisa shook her head and focused on the movement of the quill through the sand-like earth. "Not really. But he was mad. So mad, it scared me."

Fatima's hand reached out to Elisa, but she drew it back, not wanting to interrupt the magic Elisa was creating at their feet. Magic that seemed to be emboldening Elisa to say what she'd been unable to say for months and months. Fatima waited, wondering if Elisa would get to the adoption. Should Fatima act surprised? People hated it when she knew more than a 12-year-old should. Fatima had been surprised when she'd heard, of course. She had wanted to talk to Elisa about it, but hadn't known how. It was easier to ignore, to leave it above ground as she turned yet another corner in her castle hideaway.

"It was scary because it was my fault. The fight."

Fatima returned to the present. "Your fault?"

Elisa sucked in her bottom lip. "Yes. My grades. You know—"

"I know."

Elisa nodded. "Anyway, he told me, he told us, well I guess mamma already knew. But he said he wasn't really my father."

Fatima found that she couldn't pretend not to know. She nodded.

Elisa glanced up. "You knew?"

Fatima said, "I'm sorry, I should have said—"

Elisa went on, the quill falling into her lap, leaving a hairline cut on her ankle where her too-short pants rode up her leg. "Of course you knew. You know all the things."

"I don't! But even *my* parents were talking about it. And nobody even talks to them."

Thumbing the blood off her ankle, Elisa said, "You knew the whole time."

"Not the whole time."

"About my mom, too?"

"Yes. I'm sorry. I thought maybe I should say something, but it was hard and—"

"Do you know who my parents are? The ones who I came from?" Elisa asked in a rush of hopeful breath.

"No! Elisa, how would I—"

Elisa waved at Fatima's words. "You know all the things," she repeated vaguely. "I thought maybe you saw all the answers when you were asleep."

"A coma isn't a crystal ball, Elisa," Fatima's words were harsher than she intended.

Elisa's face looked even younger as she pouted. "I know that."

Fatima sighed.

Elisa squinted in thought. With a tentative smile, she said, "I think *I* know who my parents are."

"No way."

"Well, my mother anyway."

"How? Who?"

"You know Paola?"

"Who runs the *fruttivendolo*?"

"Yes."

Fatima frowned. "Her? Why her?"

Elisa shrugged again, "She's nice to me."

"So you think—"

"I'm sure."

"How can you be sure?"

"Because she acts like she knows me and wants me around. She keeps giving me fruit . . . and she told me I look like her daughter."

"Her daughter is old! She's like thirty!"

"So? Why is that important?"

"Elisa! Paola is *way* too old to be your mother!"

"That doesn't make sense!"

Fatima sighed and rolled her eyes.

Elisa bolted to standing. "Stop it! Stop treating me like I'm a baby!"

"Then stop acting like one!"

"I'm not!"

"Oh really? Stealing money from my pocket? Pretending some old fruit seller is your mother just because she gives you a *mandarino*? Hiding out with Luciano even after he was so drunk at the festival that he fought with Massimo and took off, not even noticing—"

Storms raged over Elisa's face. "You are such a jerk."

She whipped around, an olive branch slapping across her face. Elisa held back the tears, as she tried walking away with dignity. Not realizing that drips of blood still spilled from her ankle, leaving a trail behind her.

Isotta grumbled as she swung her legs over the edge of the couch to plant her feet. Luciano peered over the top of his book at her. "Worried about your date tonight?"

Attempting a smile, Isotta said, "I'm more worried about getting off the couch."

Luciano placed his book upside down and rose. "Here, let me help."

Shaking her head, Isotta planted her feet and rose. "No, thank you. I was mostly kidding." She rubbed the bottom of her spinal column. "But, yes, I'm a little dreading seeing Massimo. He *has* changed in some ways, he's more thoughtful and gentler, but as soon as we talk about his mother—"

"He withdraws like a *lumaca*."

"Yes. Though not nearly as tasty as snails." She paused. "Plus. I don't know. Sometimes it feels like we don't have much in common. I get bored when he talks about soccer or TV programs. And last time, before our conversation went south, he was obviously tuning out when I was telling him about how different people in Santa Lucia appear now that I know them. The only person he talks to besides me is his mother, and I don't want to hear about that." Isotta's sigh was leaden with uncertainty.

Luciano said, "I suppose it takes time. To find common ground."

"I guess. But I worry that our only area of compatibility is Margherita. And maybe banking. We both do like economics, I suppose." Isotta opted not to mention that their physical chemistry was another mutual interest. Partly because she wasn't sure that was even true anymore. Rather than inflaming their heat for each other, their sabbatical from physical affection had lead to a kind of sibling coolness. She wasn't sure what to make of it. Maybe it would shift back if Massimo ever got out from under his mother's wing.

"Are you quite certain you want to go with him this afternoon? I can create an excuse for you."

Isotta plucked her light jacket from the rack. It didn't close around her belly anymore but with the arrival of warmer weather, she figured it would be fine to hang open. Finally she answered. "It's okay. If we can't make a marriage work, I'll want to stay in Santa Lucia, so we can both raise the baby and Margherita. He's a good father, and I suppose it's a decent enough arrangement. I'm sure there have been stranger ones. So, it's good that we keep maintaining our relationship . . . whatever that will look like."

Luciano settled himself back in his chair and picked up his book. "I suppose that makes sense. I would wish for more for you. But since I like you here—" He smiled up at her. "You'll be back for dinner?"

"If I'm not, send out the search party." She smiled weakly. And then looked up at a knock on the door. "Okay, I'll see you soon."

"*Buona fortuna, cara.*"

"Thank you, Maestro."

Isotta opened the door and said, "*Ciao*, Massimo." She leaned and kissed him chastely on the cheeks. His tepid response made Isotta wonder if he, too, felt removed from their former sexual chemistry. She figured hers came from wounding. Maybe his was because he was tired of trying to convince her to come back.

"*Ciao*," Massimo held out his arm to guide Isotta up the street. "I thought perhaps we'd walk the trail."

Isotta nodded.

"But only if you feel okay walking. We can go to a place in Girona and sit if you'd rather."

"No, the walk will be good. This baby has been jumping on my bladder lately, maybe the movement will lull it to sleep."

Massimo held out his elbow for Isotta, but she pretended not to notice and shoved her hands into her jacket.

The air above was an effervescent blue, arching freely, unimpeded by even the hint of clouds. Ahead, the olive trees winked and twinkled, the leaves waving, creating a sea of rustling silver.

The former lovers, man and wife, walked in silence, ignoring the curious looks of women leaning out of windows and curtains twitching back into place as they passed. Only when the sound of their footsteps became muffled by the ancient dirt path did Massimo begin to speak. "About last time—you have to know it's complicated."

Silence answered as the two continued walking.

He went on, "That's not how I wanted to begin." He darted a glance at Isotta, whose lips tightened, but she said nothing. "Isotta?"

She stopped, her voice trembling as she said, "I told you. I'm tired of doing the heavy lifting. Since our conversation, I've realized I always do that. I try so hard to carry other people's burdens, all my life. It's not allowing me to examine my own." Isotta's voice deepened in timbre, as she went on, "And that's not on you, that I do that. But it is on you that I'm done. You walk your journey. I can walk my own. I'm not here to convince you of anything."

"But I want to walk with you. That's what I'm here for. Now."

Isotta shrugged.

"Isotta, listen. You're right. I see that. But you must understand—"

"Must I?"

Massimo's impatience threatened to overtake him, but he faced the valley for a moment before turning back. "That's my way of speaking. I don't mean it that way. I can't change all at once."

"The thing is, Massimo. I'm not sure you can change at all."

"I can. I have."

"Maybe not enough."

Massimo plucked Isotta's hands out of her pockets and held her chilly fingers in his own warm hands. She pulled back. "I don't—"

"Please."

Isotta stilled her body and stared into the trees, the branches moving to invisible music.

"Isotta . . . look at me?"

She dragged her eyes to Massimo's. He watched her intently before whispering, "Thank you." He cleared his throat. "Isotta, you were right. Are right."

Still holding the eye contact, Isotta furrowed her eyebrows. Massimo said, "Sometimes I think you are the single beam of light in my cluttered mind."

Isotta shifted her weight. "Massimo, that's awfully... poetic."

His grin caught her off guard, in a way it hadn't in awhile. "I've had some time."

"I thought you were stewing."

"Stewing? Far from it. What happened last time, what I said. I don't know where it came from."

"Massimo."

"Let's walk. Maybe that will be easier."

Isotta wove her hand through his elbow, and he tightened her arm against his side as they began walking. He sighed. "I've been thinking about Giulia's death. My memories of it have been a black ball, hard to separate out my feelings from reality, what happened from what I feared. I wonder if perhaps her death was... was my fault."

Isotta breath caught and she began to withdraw her arm. "No, Isotta, not that way. But the night before she drowned, we... God, this is hard to talk about with you! We made love. Did it cause a miscarriage, right there in the water? The rescuers said there was so much blood. Did I miss the signs that she was in danger? She was so... different right before it happened. Not herself. Maybe if I'd been a better husband. Maybe if I'd tried for her, the way I'm trying now. Maybe she would still be alive."

What could Isotta say? "What do you mean... different?"

Massimo said, "Flirtatious, teasing. An hour before she had been so weak that Mamma had to give her teas and tinctures to get her color back, and then all of sudden, she was... seducing me... right there on the beach."

"And you—"

"I rejected her. Those were our last moments together. I'll never get that back. I'll never make it right."

"Ah."

Massimo turned toward Isotta. "What's that?"

"It explains some things."

Massimo shook his head. "Anyway, I didn't value her, I didn't listen. It gives me a strange feeling."

Isotta smiled fleetingly. "I think that's called regret."

"Regret. Yes, I think I've heard of it." Massimo said wanly. "Anyway. That's all my fault. The way I treated you was my fault. I wish you wouldn't blame my mother. She's misguided sometimes, and I know you're right, she can be . . . overbearing. I get that she's difficult to deal with. But she's looking out for me."

Isotta hesitated before saying, "It's nice to see you taking some responsibility. But Anna is not as innocent as you make her out to be."

Massimo bristled. "Prove it."

"Oh, Massimo. This is where we get stuck. It's one of those things that can't be proven, but if you weren't so tangled it would be clear."

Somehow Ava made her way to Edo and Chiara. Later she would find a bruise blooming on her hip and have a vague memory of a table's edge. Her apologies to the diners, frothing over like over-salted pasta water, stuck in her mind more than the impact. Without knowing how, she'd arrived to her friends. "We have to go. Now."

They made an excuse to the waiter and guided a blank-eyed Ava out of the restaurant.

Out in the brisk air, metallic with the scent of car exhaust and filled with bleating horns and screaming sirens, Ava collapsed against Edo. Quick with his reflexes, he caught her, holding her to his side and murmuring soft words in her ear while his eyes pleaded with Chiara to help.

Chiara said, "Ava, where are you staying?"

Ava shook her head and wept.

"Ava! There will be time for that later. Right now, I need one thing from you. Where are you staying?"

The authority in Chiara's tone fought through the din and fog of Ava's mind. She said, "Senato Hotel Roma."

Chiara caught the words and repeated them to Edo, who whipped out his phone and typed with one hand. He nodded and said, "Down the avenue. Two blocks, maybe three."

Staggering, the three of them moved like a deformed animal down the street.

The doorman almost didn't recognize Ava, but when she lifted her tearstained face, he nodded and escorted them in. He rushed ahead to call the elevator. The doors opened immediately; the elevator must have been in its neutral position. The doorman reached inside and pressed the number 8. As the doors closed, Ava heard him mutter, "I should have known. *Stronzo*."

The sight of the room sobered Ava. She no longer felt lost. Instead, she clung to one diamond-cut thought. She had to get out of there. She had to return to Santa Lucia. Now. Five minutes ago.

Her spine straightened. Without a gram of hesitation, Ava drew the suitcase out of her closet and flung it on the bed. Unzipping it, she barked out a request for Edo to fetch her toiletries from the bathroom.

Chiara stood by the door, wrestling with how to be helpful. She began, "Ava—"

"There's no time, Chiara. Ale is supposed to be here in an hour. Less. I can't—can you take me home?"

"Of course we can, *cara*."

Ava said, "Good. Thank you. You drove? You didn't take the train?"

Edo bustled in, the crook of his arm filled with tubes and bottles. "We drove."

Nodding again, eyes focused on opening her drawer and flinging everything she found into the suitcase. "Can you get the car? Pick me up outside the hotel?"

Chiara agreed, and turned to Edo. "You go. I'll stay and help her."

Ava's words cut through the close air of the hotel room. "No. I'm okay. I'll work faster alone." Why had she never noticed how stale this room was? It pressed thickly against her lungs.

Chiara said, "Absolutely not. Edo can be back here in twenty minutes. We'll meet him out front."

Edo hugged Ava briefly before dashing out the door. Tears sprung to Ava's eyes but she blinked them away. There was no time.

The sound of slamming drawers rang around the two women. Ava and Chiara stuffed the suitcase. Shoes, dresses, books, everything heaped in a jumble. The suitcase resisted closing, so Ava had to put all her weight on it to drag the zipper around. Finally it was done. A final glance around the room, under the bed, in the closet. She stood. She supposed it didn't matter if she left anything behind.

Together, Chiara and Ava left the room, headed for the bank of elevators. Chiara pressed the button and tapped her foot. As a door glided open Ava remembered. "My drawings! All my landscaping notes! I left them in the desk!"

Chiara turned on her heel. "No problem, let's go back. You still have the key?"

"Wait! Yes, I have it, but I have this feeling he's on his way. Here, you take my suitcase down the elevator. I'll grab the plans and run down the stairs."

"Are you sure? Why don't I wait—"

"This is faster, I need to be out of here. I don't want to see him! I can't!" Ava shoved her suitcase at Chiara who nodded once before pressing the button for the lobby.

Ava bolted back to the room and flung open the desk. She shoved her notes into her purse and then whipped around.

Ale stood in the doorway, key in hand. He appraised her curiously, and then closed the door.

His arms hung loose at his sides. "What is this?"

Lifting her chin, Ava declared, "I should think it would be obvious."

Her heart quickened as Ale moved toward her, but before he touched her, he sat on the edge of the bed. "I'm afraid it's not. Want to fill me in?"

This was ludicrous. Ava drew her purse farther up on her shoulder. "I'm going home. You can do the same."

"But . . . why? Did you get bad news from home? If you need me to come with you?" Ale asked.

Ava rolled her eyes. "God, you can be dense. I almost pity Madison. I'm . . . *leaving* . . . this is *over*." Ava exaggerated her words.

Ale flinched.

Ava strode toward the door. Over her shoulder, she said, "Enjoy your hashtag-blessed life."

Hotel doors close slowly, depriving Ava of dramatic punctuation. Instead, she ran to the elevator. Her plan to take the stairs a dim memory from long ago.

Jabbing the button, she groaned, "Come *on*!" If Ale followed her . . .

The doors opened and she stumbled into the elevator, spinning quickly to hit the button for the lobby. As the elevator doors slid unhurriedly into place, Ava slumped against the wall. The cable released, plunging her down, down, down. Tears slipped across Ava's cheeks. She let them fall, distracted by the voices in her head, racing each other like a merry-go-round. *Loser . . . stop your whining . . . you don't even have a life . . . you're so weird . . . horse-faced . . . so stupid . . . loser.* The words blurred through her brain, both too fast and too slow and the garishly wrong hue.

Ava closed her eyes, allowing the darkness to sink into her bones.

An eternity later, the elevator doors slid open. Ava pressed her hands against her forehead and inhaled. Chiara and Edo stopped their pacing and reached for her. She stepped between them and felt an ache for home. For the sweet breezes and arching skies of Santa Lucia.

## SPRING BEGINS

The poppies lacing the Umbrian fields heralded the true arrival of spring.

Standing in Spello's *piazza*, Edo inhaled the green and licorice scent of freshly chopped fennel. He had always meant to come to l'Infiorata and watch Spellani work all night to create flower carpets for the priest to consecrate in the morning. Each year, though, he'd had some reason to not make the trip. But when Ava casually mentioned that her aunt had a house in Spello and invited her for the storied celebration, Edo leapt at the opportunity. He smiled now, watching townspeople cleaning the street, laying down templates, huddling over designs, and pulling petals off of flowers. The infectious buzz lifted his spirits.

Ava did not appear similarly moved. "Oh, Edo, maybe we shouldn't have come. I don't have the energy for a festival. I want to go to bed."

"*Allora,* Ava, you need a break from moping."

Ava blushed, looking affronted. "I'm not moping."

Edo cast Ava a meaningful look as they walked down the lamplit street.

"What?" insisted Ava.

Edo said nothing.

"Edo—"

"*Ma dai*, I know you don't want to talk about it, why invite the conversation? Think of it this way—I need cheering up too, you know. You're helping a friend."

"You need cheering up?"

Edo nodded significantly. "I do. It's been a slow winter. Not one nibble on any of my social media. Dry, dry, dry. It's a sad state of affairs for poor Edo."

Ava poked him in the ribs. "Well, I think Edo's dry spell may be broken. That guy is checking you out."

Edo's head whipped around, as Ava chastised him, "Not so obvious! That guy standing under the arch next to the olive wood shop. The tall, good looking one."

Pretending to search for a misplaced friend, Edo craned his neck nonchalantly.

His eyes locked with Francy.

Sighing he ducked his head. "That's not a bite on the line, my dear, that's a piece of trash."

"What?" Ava shot a look over her shoulder again. "What do you mean? He's dreamy and he's staring right at you."

"That's Francy."

"Francy . . . Fabrizio's son?"

"I forgot you never met him."

Ava laughed. "No, but Mamma had some ripe insults for him." Pausing to see if Francy was still staring at Edo (he was), Ava went on. "Okay, trash. Agreed. Maybe we should migrate." She consulted her map. "It's hard to make this out, but I remember the teams that make the winning designs are all down this hill. Up the hill seems less crowded, though. Let's move to the bar so I can see the map better. Or we can ask those people—"

"Oh, God, Ava. He's coming over."

"He's coming over? Why?"

"Who knows! The man finds fault with everything. My jacket is probably last year's *moda*."

Before Edo could either sneak away or prepare his face for the confrontation, Francy was before him. "*Buonasera*, Edoardo."

Edo lifted his hand in greeting and shot a helpless look at Ava, who shrugged. Francy didn't acknowledge her presence, and she put a foot out to step away. Edo grabbed her hand and pulled her firmly beside himself. "This is my friend, Ava."

Francy nodded curtly. "Francy, *piacere*."

"*Piacere*," she said, shifting her weight uncomfortably.

Francy gazed levelly at Edo. "I didn't know you came to l'Infiorata."

"First time. Ava has an aunt in Spello, so we decided to check it out."

"Ah, and you two are ... together now?"

Edo scowled. "I'm gay, remember?"

Francy's face lightened with the merest suggestion of a smile. "Sometimes things change."

"And sometimes things don't."

Francy's eyebrows raised. "Indeed."

A beat later, Francy continued, "So Edoardo, while you're here, I wonder if you might want to grab a drink."

Ava disentangled herself from Edo's side and pretended a sudden interest in the old women shredding petals off flowers.

Edo watched her go before turning his attention back to Francy. He said nothing.

"Edoardo? I'm asking if you might want to—"

"I heard you. I'm just trying to figure what you are on about."

"About?"

"Yes. You can't really be asking me on a date."

Francy considered the pink stone wall behind Edo's shoulder for a minute before looking back at Edo. "I am."

"After everything."

Francy cocked his head. "Everything?"

"Yes, everything. You spoiled Chiara's chance for happiness. A woman who never thinks of herself, you took the one pleasure she'd allowed herself in years."

Francy muttered, "My father's money is indeed a pleasure for many."

"What?"

"Look, Edoardo. Yes, I took my father away from Santa Lucia. I congratulate myself for it."

"Congratulate yourself!"

"Yes! For him I have been kinder than maybe myself. I don't even know what I'm doing here, asking you out."

"Feel free to walk away. I promise not to collapse into a quivering pool of tears."

"God, Edoardo. What contempt."

"Why shouldn't I be contemptuous? Of a man who got between two happy people? All for selfish vanity."

"Vanity? What can you possibly—"

"Come off it, Francy. You are many things, but you aren't an idiot, so at least have the grace to assume I'm not one either."

"I don't even know what—"

"Your stupid pride! You couldn't have your father allied with an unsophisticated woman from a backwater town."

"Is that what you think?"

"It's what I know."

A child running past forced Edo to back up. Francy pulled him closer, hissing, "You are seriously mistaken."

"Am I? You just admitted to getting between them. Too pleased with yourself to contemplate the grief you caused my aunt."

"What? I'm not a monster—"

"Fooled me. And the newspaper clipping! Incredibly insulting."

"Newspaper clipping?" Francy shook his head. "I have no idea—Listen! Hard as this is to hear, I did what I had to for my father's protection. Women are always after his money. Chiara didn't look to be any different."

"Money? What money?"

"Don't be coy."

"What are you talking about?"

"Oh, come on. You must know my father inherited a fortune. So did I, when it comes to it." Francy cast his eyes downward briefly. "Since then, women have been throwing themselves at him. I've learned there's a type. They talk a good game about how much they admire my father's writing or his personality, but there's no warmth, no real affection."

"Chiara loved him!"

Francy shook his head. "I believe that you want to believe that. But I'm telling you. I'm cautious and I pay attention to things that wouldn't occur to you."

"So now I'm an uneducated hick?"

A slow smile spread across Francy's face. "Far from it. But Edoardo, I watched your aunt. She's cold, distant. Like she doesn't have a heart to lose."

"Cold and distant? Are we talking about the same woman?"

"Yes! She couldn't even make eye contact with me. That's typical of gold diggers."

"So you told your father that Chiara was after his money. That's the reason he left and never came back. I'm floored, *floored*, that he fell for that pile of crap."

"Well, not quite. I told him that Chiara obviously didn't love him."

"*What?*"

"I don't feel good about that part, believe me. My father has great natural modesty and has been burned before. In short, he's insecure. To convince him that he'd deceived himself was not so difficult."

"I can't even believe I'm hearing this."

Francy shrugged. "I did what I had to do. I'm sorry that it wounded someone you love, but I must protect my father. And I trust my eyes. I watched as your aunt fumbled and paled and never *ever* looked like a woman in love."

Edo thought about it, remembering all those times he had seen Chiara and Fabrizio, before and after Francy arrived. He said slowly, "You're wrong.

Before you came … before you came, she lit up when Fabrizio walked in the bar. She … I can't even explain how much she loved him. You should have seen her grief when he didn't tell her about his life … about you. And then, and then—"

"And then?" Francy watched the shifting play of the streetlight across Edo's thoughtful face.

"It's you."

"Me?"

"You. You come to her town full of pride and disdain and suspicion. Nobody has ever treated Chiara like that before. People love her. They love her because she loves them, all of them, even the ones who don't deserve it. Then you arrived and she probably wanted *you* to like her more than anyone, but you treated her the way you treat everybody. Like we're not worthy of licking your Prada shoes."

"That's … that's ridiculous."

"No. It's not. Anyway, I'm sure she doesn't know about your stupid money."

"Even if my father never told her, it's easy enough to Google."

Edo snorted. "She doesn't have a computer. She can barely text."

"Someone told her then. That German woman, I heard her talking about it. She knows, she told Chiara."

Edo thought about it. "No."

"How can you be so sure?"

"Because right before you arrived, Chiara wondered what I thought about asking our friends who have a house in Santa Lucia but live in Ancona if they would be willing to let you and Fabrizio stay in their empty house. She felt badly that Fabrizio's extended stay in Santa Lucia was thanks to her. She didn't want him using up his meager author's salary on rent."

❧

Isotta rested on the couch, a book propped up on her small mountain of a belly. She watched, as Luciano set the table for dinner. His hand clutched his chest and he paled.

"Luciano?"

"*Si*, Isotta. Do you feel well?"

"I'm actually worried about you."

Luciano's eyes were weary as he thought a moment. "I'm quite well. Only a little heartburn."

Isotta pushed herself to sitting. This rock of a belly pressing her down made it hard to avoid feeling like a patient. "Luciano? Is there something bothering you?"

He paused for a moment. "It's Elisa."

"Is she okay? She seemed okay when I took her and Margherita to the park the other day."

He shook his head. "Something feels wrong. There's a shadow behind her eyes."

"That's been there since I've known her."

He shook his head again. "Maybe I see it differently after noticing that tension between her and Fatima. I keep waiting for the old Fatima to slide back into place. An old man's foolish hoping."

"Maybe Elisa has that same hope."

"Perhaps."

Isotta lifted her gaze to the ceiling, a grid of bricks intersected by ancient waxed beams. She studied the worn, blackened patterns on the wood, lost in thought. She asked, "Is Elisa still making art?"

Luciano considered the question. "I assume so. She draws fairly constantly."

"Are you sure? I'm realizing I haven't seen any papers crammed with doodles in a while."

Luciano moved to the desk where he worked on Elisa's assignments. "Hmm... you may be right. She comes over, we do math, she has tea and

tries to make conversation, but her mind is clearly elsewhere. Let's see..."
Rifling through the pages, Luciano flipped them over, searching. "Here
are a few."

"So fewer than before?"

"I believe so, yes."

"Can I see them?"

Luciano brought the loose pages to Isotta, who moved her book to the
side table. She studied the drawings. "Hmmmm...interesting."

"What? What is it?"

Isotta peered at the paper more closely. "I may be reading too much
into it, but these drawings look different. These are...darker."

"They were always dark, the way she cross-hatches—"

"They were, but before, that darkness was always contrasted. The dark
groves looming around a distant opening, the charcoal cats with their
gleaming eyes. This is just...dark. And what's that? Buried in the lines,
here, and here...why, it's on all of them." Isotta quickly flipped through
the papers, her eyes scanning.

"What do you see? What is—"

"This." Isotta said pointing.

"I can't—"

"Here. This one's clearer." Isotta found the paper she was looking for
and handed it to Luciano.

In the midst of the cross-hatching, there was a curved shape.

Luciano wondered aloud, "I don't...wait, is it a chalice?"

Isotta smiled. "I would have said a cup, but yes, that's what I thought
at first too, until the papers were upside down and I saw—look."

Luciano held the paper up to the light. He breathed. "It's a headstone."

Isotta nodded. "What does it mean?"

Luciano put the paper down and reached for another, finding the
shape and turning it this way and that. "I suppose it depends. On all these
papers, over and over, did she hide a chalice or did she hide a headstone?"

It was barely seven in the morning, and already the streets of Spello filled with tourists.

Ava yawned.

Edo asked, "Will the bars be open? They were still open when we went to bed at two, I can't imagine—"

"Oh, yes, they'll be open. And have towers of *ciambelle* that will make the donuts you sell for our festival seem paltry."

Edo snorted. "Okay, then." He said, pointing, "That bar's open." They walked toward the bar, lit against the dissipating fog.

Ava said, "You feeling better about yesterday?"

"Kind of. Actually . . . no. Not really. It was intense, you know? And even though he insists he's cautious, not classist, I can't believe that. He's a jackass, plain and simple."

Ava said, "You sure about that?"

"I'm sure."

"Because when he came over, I thought I noticed—"

"Ava, don't try to matchmake. You'll make a mess of it."

Ava sighed. True, Francy seemed serious, and yes, maybe a little full of himself. But she was raised with a jackass for a brother, and Francy didn't fit that mode. She said, "Well, if luck is on our side, you won't see him today. There will be thousands of people, so the odds—"

Edo stopped walking. "There he is."

"What?"

"There he is." He gestured to Spello's iconic Roman arch with the olive tree growing from the top of the tower. Francy stood alone, head swiveling as if searching the crowd. He startled when he caught sight of Edo, seemingly filled his lungs with air, and then plunged toward them, skirting around the groups of townspeople still laying flowers into intricate images.

"*Ciao*," he said, breathless as he arrived in front of Edo and Ava.

"*Ciao*," they repeated.

"Good day for l'Infiorata. I thought it might rain and ruin the flower carpets, but look!" He pointed up at the sky. "The clouds are already breaking up."

Ava and Edo said nothing.

Ava began inching away, but Edo slammed his hand into hers.

Francy caught the movement and looked up into Edo's eyes. Levelly, he said, "I would like to buy you a *caffè*."

"I'm with Ava."

Francy shook his head in frustration. "I apologize. I'm not being clear. I would like to take you both to *caffè*. Perhaps a pastry to prepare for the day. Ava?" He offered Ava his arm.

Shooting Edo a confused look, she nonetheless tucked her free hand through Francy's elbow. With her other hand she pulled Edo forward and mouthed, "Jackass?"

Edo rolled his eyes. What was Francy playing at?

Ava, in her nervousness, began to prattle. About her girlhood trips to l'Infiorata, about the one time she had come to visit family early enough to help collect flowers in the fields of Colfiorito, about how her family's team had never won, but she enjoyed it, about how she and Edo hadn't worked last night, but on their *giro* through town they had seen several stunning displays and how she couldn't wait to see them finished.

Francy listened and asked, "Did you see the one at the top of the hill? The one with Saint Francis and the wolf?"

"Yes! It wasn't my favorite—the wolf doesn't match my image of the legend—but Edo loved it. Talked about it the whole way back down the hill. Didn't you, Edo?"

"It wasn't the wolf I liked," Edo muttered. "I liked how they used calla lilies to make butterflies."

Francy nodded, pleased. "Indeed, an ingenious touch. As well as the layering of flower petals into a vibrant melody."

Ava shot Edo a triumphant look, reminding him that he had said something almost identical, though far less colorful.

Francy said, "*Eccoci qua*, here we are." He asked Ava as his eyes flitted to Edo, "If this is okay for you?"

Ava looked to Edo, but, getting no response, she turned back to Francy and said, "This is where we were headed."

Francy smiled. Edo was caught off guard by how the expression softened Francy's haughty features. Edo's double-take elevated Francy's grin to a laugh before he said to Ava, "Excellent. This is my favorite bar in the *borgo*. Especially today. Their *cornetti* are a little more crackley on the outside and a little more tender on the inside. Shall we?" He stepped back to allow Edo and Ava to enter the bar before him.

Standing at the bar with their breakfast, Ava asked Francy, "Aren't you here with a group of friends?"

Francy said, "Yes, they're still sleeping. I wanted to catch you, so I woke early. I've arranged to meet up with them in about an hour. I hope I can encourage the two of you—" he glanced at Edo, stirring his *caffè*. Francy cleared his throat. "The two of you to join our party?"

Ava studied Edo, who shrugged and looked away. She said, "We wouldn't be imposing?"

Francy said, "Quite the opposite. In fact, if you don't have plans with your family, I hope you will allow me to invite you to lunch with our party? We've rented a dining room at the old hotel that serves meals only on occasion. There's a remarkable view over the valley. It would be an honor to have you as my guests."

Ava and Edo exchanged glances.

Edo's mind spun. If he expected anything from Francy today it would have been an increase in hostility. Where did this graciousness come from? Was it possible that Francy's entire bristling persona was legitimately based on protecting his father? Was this Francy's way of showing that he didn't bear Edo any ill will after his tempestuous words the night before?

Edo said, "Thank you." He lifted his eyes and found Francy's. Their gaze locked. For a few moments, the rest of the bar fell away as the two men's connection vibrated between them. Francy's smile spread slowly across his face. The spell broke when a toddler bumped into Ava, who lost her balance and crashed into Francy.

Effortlessly, Francy caught Ava and responded to her fervent apologies by saying, "It's no trouble, please don't worry." He put a hand on each of their backs to lead them out of the crowd that steadily filled the bar. Over the increasing din, he said, "This may be a good time to get a closer look at the flower carpets in the *piazza*? Before the crowds make it impossible?"

Ava nodded, but Edo was distracted by his phone buzzing in his pocket. "I apologize, *un attimo*."

Edo squinted at the screen, confused by the unknown number. He blinked and then held the screen closer.

His face fell.

The morning dawned fresh in Santa Lucia. The resonance of the air drew the villagers out of their homes and their gestures of greeting—initially jerky from the long time spent huddling indoors—gently unbound. Their limbs loosened. They gathered in the *piazza*, Bea with a platter of biscotti warm from the oven. She offered cookies to Patrizia and Giuseppe stepping out of their butcher shop, and Magda and Dante deep in argument about mosquitos. Bea waved away the thanks that followed in her wake, like cinnamon-scented hazelnuts.

There was a crispness to the breeze. An iridescent undertone. The townspeople stood taller to breathe it in as it pinked the curves of their cheeks.

Gossip stalled. Instead, conversation turned to hopes. Travels intended, recipes exchanged, new babies on the way. Isotta's, of course, and Patrizia had just learned of her daughter's pregnancy. Her eyes shone as she shared the news with her neighbors who hugged her fiercely.

Laughter rose as Giovanni stepped out of his *alimentari* with a fresh selection of jokes. He stood in a beam of early light, hands perched on his aproned waist, surrounded by a retired stonemason, a baker, and an electrical engineer.

The individual tones evened to a light burble, a wave of sound, rising and falling together.

Movement appeared from down Via Romana, where the road curved toward San Nicola and the playground. Carosello jogged up in the middle of the stone-lined road. It almost didn't look like him, but rather some mythical beast with his head shrouded in shadow. A kind of antler. Or a giant sideways horn, erupting from his ear.

The townspeople pointed, laughing. They remembered his foray into the hardware store, and wondered if this time his trash exploration had yielded an umbrella.

As the dog approached the *piazza*, the voices died away. One by one, then three by three, silence hit like a hammer. Carosello trotted proudly into the *piazza*, head turning from side to side to show off his prize.

From the one-eyed dog's mouth waved a human leg.

"Edo! *Che succede?*" Ava yelped as Francy caught Edo around his shoulders and guided him to a bench.

"I...I...Chiara..."

"Chiara! What happened to Chiara! Is she okay?"

Francy leaned toward Edo, a frown creasing his face.

Edo shook his head and said, "The text. From Magda. She says that Chiara heard from her lawyer."

Edo bit his lip and looked down again at his phone. "Her soon-to-be ex is demanding the bar."

"What?" yelped Ava and Francy in unison.

"Right." Edo rubbed his hands over his forehead.

Francy frowned. "That can't be right. Normally, a couple would split the bar after a divorce."

Ava gasped, "You mean Chiara is going to have to work with that guy?"

Francy shook his head. "More likely it means that he's going to force the sale of the bar right away to liquidate that asset, and then she'll have to give him half the proceeds. Unless she can buy him out. Could she buy him out?"

Edo shook his head. "No. No way. She keeps this close to her chest, but there's a developer, a hotel chain I think? Who comes around once every couple of years and offers to buy the bar. She's never considered it, never would. She knows what that would do to Santa Lucia, but last time I was there when he came. He had papers with the value of the bar, and it's astronomical."

Ava wondered aloud, "It is?"

Edo nodded. "It's a former *palazzo*, and it's way bigger than it looks on the outside. Chiara only uses a few rooms of it. There are also frescos that she's never restored, plus the view of the falls, and there is this medieval balustrade…"

Francy asked, "Would this man know the worth of the bar?"

Edo shook his head. "No. Probably not. But if you are right and he forces a sale, it'll come out."

Ava said, "But if we all helped? I bet people would help—"

"Chiara would never accept. Anyway, the text doesn't say anything about splitting the bar, it says he's taken it. Something must be…I don't know. But either way she's going to lose it. It's the thing—" Edo floundered and dropped his head into his hands. He struggled against the tears, but felt them threatening to overwhelm him.

Francy stood. "I can't imagine how devastating this is for you. Made worse, I'm sure, by having to share this moment with a virtual stranger. I wish I could offer support, but I suspect my absence would be the most welcome assistance right now."

Edo wiped his eyes.

Francy stood. "I suppose this means we shouldn't expect you for lunch?"

Ava and Edo shook their heads. Ava rubbed Edo's shoulder and said, "No, we need to get back to Santa Lucia right away."

Francy asked, "And you do have transportation back? You won't have to wait for a train?"

Edo shook his head again. "No, Ava drove. We can be home in under an hour. But what is to be done? What on earth can be done? She's ruined, *ruined*! Our home..."

Francy reached a hand out, then thought better of it and said, "I'm so, so sorry. My condolences to you and your aunt. Please drive safely."

Ava nodded. As Francy walked away she called out, "Goodbye!"

Francy turned back for a moment before ducking his head to hurry up the hill.

At first Elisa didn't notice the soft whispering. But the more knots of people she passed in the street, the more it began to knock on her consciousness that something was wrong. Her feet slowed as she approached the *alimentari*. Giovanni, the owner, stood outside with one of the ladies who lived in the alley at the top of the hill. Elisa stretched her ears to catch the voices.

"But that's impossible," insisted the lady.

"It's true! I saw it myself."

"You know how Carosello is, always nosing around the trash. Giuseppe probably butchered an animal and—"

"An animal that wears pants? I'm telling you, Signora, it was human.

Besides, Bea asked Giuseppe, he hasn't left any bones out for trash. He leaves the small ones for Carosello, like we all do, but that's it."

Elisa stopped, ashen. She leaned down to tie her shoes, taking her time. Carosello? The dog? With a *human* bone? It couldn't be . . .

The lady wrung her hands, "What does Chiara say? She must have heard about somebody missing or dead?"

Elisa couldn't hear an answer, Giovanni must have shaken his head. Slowly she switched legs to tie her other shoe.

Giovanni's voice now answered, "We can't ask her now. What with the bar—"

What did that mean? What about the bar?

Elisa's thoughts began to chase each other like mice across a waxed kitchen floor.

The lady grunted in acknowledgement. "Yes, of course. But it could have been someone from outside of town, right? One of those hikers or bikers got into some sort of trouble, maybe a heart attack. Died somewhere. You know, that's probably what happened."

Giovanni murmured, "Perhaps . . ."

Elisa straightened.

What the lady said made sense. Carosello ranged all over the place and the terrain around Santa Lucia was rough. Of course it was somebody who died outside of town and the dog stumbled across the dead body. It was gross. It was so gross it made her feel faint, but at least it wasn't—

She had to check. She had to know.

She ran down the street, barely noticing the voices streaming behind her. "Where is she running off to?"

And the answer, "Who knows? She's always late to somewhere."

Elisa slipped on a patch of cobblestone, slick from plants being watered outside the florist shop. Hopefully Ava wouldn't pop her head out, with more of her nosy questions. Now was not the time. She continued running, building speed. Her feet felt winged as she raced past terra cotta pots with *ginestra* beginning to bloom, sending out a perfume of floral honey. As she began to lose her breath, she arrived at her front door. She panted for a moment, not wanting to alarm her mother by her state.

For once her senses were focused, razored.

She turned the knob and opened the door calling, cheerfully, "Mamma?"

The house was dark. No one answered.

"Mamma?" She called, louder this time. Maybe her mother was out back again, gardening or scrolling through her phone. Elisa closed her eyes.

The house had an odd, echoey quality. Like the dust had spun cobwebs, reverberating with the sound of her voice.

"Mamma? Are you home?" Elisa slid her backpack off her shoulder and lay it down by the door. She crept through the house. "Mamma?"

Her mother's bedroom door was slightly ajar. Elisa knocked, thrumming into the eerie silence. Elisa put a hand against the door and took a breath before pushing it open.

What . . . what had happened here?

The room was in disarray, drawers flung open, clothes hanging out, hangers twisted and fallen on the floor. Were they robbed?

Elisa walked to the bureau, where her mother kept her jewelry box.

Gone!

She ran to the living room. The TV was there. But it was old, heavy, like an oven. Maybe nobody would want it. It hardly worked even, though robbers wouldn't know that. She ran into her room. It looked unchanged. But Elisa had the strangest feeling that her mother had recently stood here. Stood here for a moment before hurrying away. Elisa raced to her brothers' room now, her heart jackhammering in her chest. The wall of medals looked disordered, but she couldn't tell if anything was missing.

Elisa ran through the house again, yelling, "Mamma! *Mamma!*"

Where could she be? At the store? But her room . . . did the robbers hurt her? Was she somewhere bleeding? Should she check outside?

Elisa ran into the dim kitchen, pirouetting as her eyes scanned the surfaces, there! On the table, a piece of paper. She snatched it up, breathless.

*"Elisa—*

*I can't do this anymore. I tried. But I couldn't. I'll come back for you if I can.*

*Be a good girl.*

*Love,*

*Mamma"*

Elisa let out a wail of desperation and flung herself through the back door, into the yard.

The sun shone weakly beyond the hills.

But Elisa could see, past the tangle of lengthening shadows, the opened earth of her father's grave.

"I don't know what to say, Edo. I wish you hadn't come home. I told Magda not to text you." Chiara frowned and stared at her clasped hands.

"I'm glad she did. How could I be gone at a time like this?"

Chiara stared after Carosello, jogging by with what looked like a canned tomato label stuck to his shoulder. "That dog needs a bath. I should give him a bath."

"Chiara! You have more to worry about than a flea-bitten dog!"

Chiara's eyes were challenging as she gazed at Edo. "I'm well aware."

Edo reached across the bar to where Chiara sat on the customer side. He clasped her hand. "I'm sorry, I shouldn't have snapped at you. I'm completely lost."

Bitterly, Chiara said, "Glad to have the company."

"Oh, Chiara."

"I don't know what I'm going to do."

"I know. Of course I know. So now, please, tell me. Magda only said that he's getting the bar."

Chiara sighed and then stood to check the closed sign. She lowered the blinds. It wasn't Bar Birbo's closed day. She knew people would be turning the handle, confused about why it wasn't opening. But they'd know soon enough. Those that didn't know already.

She came back to the stool and collapsed onto it. "That's pretty much it. Riccardo got a response to the divorce agreement. It agreed to the divorce, but not to the terms. Instead, he's demanding the bar, because he paid for it."

"Paid for it? What do you mean he paid for it? I thought Nonno and Nonna gave it to you."

"They wanted to, but they had just helped us buy that apartment over by the church, and Papà was sick, so I couldn't let them walk away with nothing. They wouldn't even have the bar's income once we took over. They moved to our apartment, and I told them that in order to complete the transaction, we'd have to give them a thousand euros."

"I'd forgotten about that apartment."

"It's not memorable. It's small, and I don't like going there since my parents both died in it. Even before that, it wasn't exactly full of happy memories."

Edo debated asking what she meant since her husband was only jailed for having sex with teen prostitutes after they had lived and worked at the bar for years, but this wasn't the time. Instead he asked, "And he paid for it? You didn't?"

"We were married Edo, and I didn't have a job besides working at the bar. My parents didn't pay me a salary. It was the family business. Our real income was *his* money." Chiara shivered.

"So because he paid the thousand euros he technically owns the bar and can kick you out?"

Chiara nodded.

Edo's face cleared. "*Aspetta*! Even though he paid for it, shouldn't your name be on the deed or whatever?"

Chiara took a deep breath. "That is the worst part. The part I haven't told you." She closed her eyes and went on, "When we transferred the property, there was so much going on, I didn't pay attention to the papers changing hands. He was my husband, I trusted him to handle it. Such a naive fool." Chiara's eyes filled with tears. "When Riccardo got the response and researched the paperwork, it looks like my signature was forged. The bar is totally in that bastard's name."

Edo yelped, "*What*? You have to prove it's not!"

Chiara went on, "Riccardo isn't optimistic. It's been so long, and with the money being his . . ."

Edo mulled over her words. "What if you bought it from him? We could ask my parents? Mamma's family has plenty of money."

Chiara measured her next words carefully. "I already asked."

"And?"

"They politely declined."

"No! Let me try, or my sister, you know she loves you and she worked here for years, she could convince them—"

"No, Edo. They were quite clear and firm. And as kind as they could be given the situation."

"Still bitter because you got the bar."

"Maybe. I guess they think that even with the bum husband that came along with it, I got the better deal. Or maybe they don't have that kind of money. Or they have better plans for it."

Edo poured himself a glass of water. "I can't believe this is happening."

"Me neither. Can I have a glass, too?"

Edo nodded and took out a bottle of *frizzante* that Chiara preferred. He poured a glass and handed it to her.

"Does Riccardo have an idea of how long this will all take?"

Shaking her head, Chiara said, "No. But soon. According to the paperwork, it's not my bar. I could get kicked out at any moment. Probably when he's released in a week or two? I don't know."

"And you'll have to move."

Nodding now, Chiara said, "As will you."

"Right. Where will you go?"

Biting her lip to stall the tears, she said, "I asked the church, the apartment isn't being used right now, I could have it back without displacing anyone, but how could I live here and not live *here*? How could I walk by the bar everyday and see *him* standing there, laughing and talking with my friends?"

"No way. No way! I don't see it. He wouldn't show his face here. Who would be his customers? Who would want to have coffee made by a pervert?"

"He claims he's rehabilitated. That the bar will set his feet on a godly course."

"Ridiculous."

Chiara shrugged. "Riccardo said it's the exact thing a judge will drink up. Especially an old-school judge who tends to side with men. Riccardo said... he said..."

"Tell me."

Sighing, Chiara tried again. "He said that the whole 'my frigid wife forced me to turn to a life of vicissitude' angle plays well. The crazy part is that you are probably right, and he won't want to stay here and have to face his former friends and neighbors. Chances are he'll sell it. I can't bear to see it."

"So you're not going to fight it?"

The tears sprang free now. "No. I can't. It'll cost me too much in legal fees, and then I won't have a job to pay Riccardo."

"So it's over."

"Yes." Chiara's head sank into her hands. "It's over."

Elisa tossed and turned on the worn couch.

The thoughts plagued her, churning up waves of panic.

It had only been a few days since her mother left, but the panic was still there. What was she going to do? The money in the jar was almost gone, and she couldn't keep conveniently showing up at Luciano's at dinner time. In fact, she got the sense that maybe she should be there less. Luciano and Isotta seemed to be watching their words with her, observing her, prodding her with gentle questions. Elisa suspected that they had grown tired of her.

What was she going to *do*?

Her thoughts ran through the same cycles. Maybe she should tell someone that her mother left. But no, what would happen then? She wouldn't be allowed to live alone, she would be sent somewhere. But she had nowhere to go. Would she be put in an orphanage, like she read about in books?

She wished she could talk to Fatima about it, but that friendship had dried like a dandelion. She didn't understand it, and that confusion cycled with the confusion of what to do now.

Exhausted.

She was exhausted. She wasn't sure how much longer she could do this. Yes, her brothers had offered to come back and take care of her, but she'd already told them that she would be living with Paola, the greengrocer. Looking back, she realized that she had said that because she wished it were true. In any case, her brothers had been grateful to have a reason not to abandon their lives in Spoleto. They were making money now, and promised to send some to her to give to Paola for her care. They seemed sure their mother wasn't coming back. According to gossip they had heard from their mother's old school friends, Concetta had taken up with a midshipman, someone she'd known in high school and had connected with on Facebook. Elisa didn't have the energy to feel surprised.

A knock punctuated the thought. Her mother! Her mother was back!

No, that couldn't be right. Her mother wouldn't knock. It must be someone else. Prickles of danger made the hairs on her arms stand at attention.

No one could know.

Elisa looked around the house as she stood and walked to the door. Dishes scattered, but that wasn't strange for her household. She only knew other people regularly washed dishes after spending so much time with Luciano and Isotta. Elisa opened the door.

Oh, *damn*.

Ava.

"*Ciao*, Elisa."

Elisa scowled.

"Can I come in?"

Elisa didn't know how to refuse her, so she backed up to allow Ava entrance. She realized that she didn't have the lights on. Then she realized that with nobody paying the bills, the lights would soon be permanently off. What was she going to do? She sagged.

"Elisa!" Ava shouted. "Are you okay? Here, let's sit you down and get you some water. Or have you eaten?"

Elisa muttered, "I'm fine. Stop fussing."

Ava breathed a sigh of relief and then looked around the room. "Is your mamma here?"

"No."

"Okay. I just... I thought..." Ava looked at her hands, letting her words trail away.

Elisa took a deep breath and announced as firmly as she could, "She told me to tell you she's done planting. All done. You don't need to come back."

Ava looked up in surprise. Choosing her words, she said, "Elisa, I heard a terrible story. And it made me want... it made me want to make sure you were all okay."

"What story?" Elisa's eyes narrowed.

"*Allora,*" Ava said, "I heard Carosello found something . . . surprising. People are asking a lot of questions."

"This is why you come here. To ask me about the leg."

Ava blanched. "You know. No, Elisa, I don't want to ask you anything. I only want to know if you, or your family . . . if you need anything."

Elisa stared at Ava, as if watching puzzle pieces align.

Ava, uncomfortable with the scrutiny, went on. "I know you don't feel as comfortable with me as you do with . . . other people." Ava's voice hardened a little. "But please believe me, I care about your family."

"Why?" Elisa asked.

Ava said, "Your mamma, she told me things. I know your growing up hasn't been easy. My growing up wasn't easy. I guess I don't want anyone to suffer alone like I did."

This was new information. Elisa wasn't sure whether or not to trust it. She said nothing.

Ava went on, "Look, it's not the same. My parents were fine, not always great, my mom pushed me a lot. But my brother—he picked on me in a lot of the same ways your mamma told me your father picked on you."

"I don't want to talk about that!"

Ava placed her hand on Elisa's arm. "You don't have to. You don't have to say a word, Elisa. I just want you to know I get it. Not all of it, but some of it. When I was growing up, I would have given anything for my brother to disappear. But if he did, if he . . . disappeared . . . I think in some ways it would have been scary."

Elisa's eyes filled with tears.

Ava said softly, "It's not your fault, Elisa. You got caught up in grown-up things, too big for a kid. It's not your fault."

Elisa chin trembled and she began to cry. She leaned forward, and Ava caught her in her arms and soothed, "It's going to be okay. I promise."

"I can't believe it."

"So you heard?"

"What, am I dead? It happened a week ago, of course I heard!"

"And Chiara? Where will she go?"

"She can stay with me!"

"She won't though."

"No, she won't."

"She's too proud. Always has been."

"You mean you could do it? Stay in someone's spare room while your filthy ex-husband stands in your spot?"

"No. I guess not."

"What will she do then?"

"I don't know. I don't think she knows."

"I talked to Edo about it . . ."

"What did he say?"

"Nothing. He doesn't know either. Or he's keeping mum. He's loyal, he might not be telling her plan, even if he knows."

"We deserve to know it too! Bar Birbo is ours as much as hers."

"We'll know, soon enough."

Beat.

"I can't believe it."

"I know. What will Santa Lucia be like?"

"Hey! You all know about Chiara and the bar?"

"Yes!"

"I heard he might not keep it open. He might sell it."

"Sell it! Maybe one of us—"

"No, turns out Chiara has been holding out on us. I heard that there's a hotel chain offering to buy it for ten million euros."

"Ten million euros!"

"That can't be right!"

"That's what I heard."

"For a bar?"

"A *palazzo* with waterfalls, yes."

"Still, that seems like too much. Someone was pulling your leg."

A pause.

"What if that pervert brings his new girlfriend? I won't be served coffee by some ex-prostitute. And that's just the kind he likes you know."

"Haven't you been listening? He's not going to work here. He's going to sell the bar."

"You can't be sure though. He told the prison priest he wanted the work."

"And you believe that?"

"He wants the money... only the money."

"I always knew he was a bad seed. Remember, I told you? I said, 'Mark my words.' Remember?"

"No, I don't remember. Besides, you think everyone is a bad seed. You've probably said that about me."

"I have not."

"Are you *ragazzi* talking about the bar?"

"Yes! Do you think it's going to be sold?"

"I heard he's going to turn it into a brothel."

"No!"

"In Santa Lucia? No way."

"Why not? No one will look for one here. He can do his filthy business out of reach of authorities."

"You are *pazzo*. There's not enough business here."

"You think everyone in Santa Lucia is so God-fearing? There are definitely enough people here for a brothel."

"That doesn't even make sense. Even if that were true, it's not like we don't have police here."

"Police would be the first customers."

"What are you muttering now?"

"Nothing."

"Look, one thing we know for sure. Bar Birbo won't be Bar Birbo anymore. If it's a hotel or a brothel, or even if it's still a bar. It won't be Birbo anymore."

Sigh.

*Sigh.*

"That's true. Poor Chiara."

"What is she going to do?"

"Hey, what about her boyfriend! Maybe he can help."

"Where have you been hiding, with the sheep? Her boyfriend left months ago."

"Oh. That's why I haven't seen him... Don't roll your eyes at me! I've been working!"

"We've all been working. How can you not know her boyfriend left?"

"He's not coming back?"

"I heard her talking to Patrizia once when I walked in. He's sent some postcards, but that's it. She thinks it's done."

"Then it probably is."

"*Sono d'accordo,* I agree. Chiara knows these things."

Fabio hurried out of the hardware store when he saw Ava passing. "Ava!"

Ava regarded her brother with distaste. "What?"

"I want to talk to you. You must know about the dog? And the leg?"

Ava drew in her breath and tried to gaze around casually. "I heard something about that, yes."

"Don't you think it's weird that no one has gone to the police?"

"Police! Do the police know?"

"No, and that makes no sense. I asked everyone who was there, but none of them reported it."

Ava shrugged. "Well, maybe they don't think it's a police matter." She paused. "*You're* not going to report it, are you?'

Fabio glowered. "I tried, but they won't listen to me. Went on and on about third-hand accounts. Those guys are such losers. They can't get over the fact that they were passed over for jobs in better places, so they just parade around—"

In a rush of breath Ava interrupted, "So it will always be a mystery, eh? Ah well, Santa Lucia has plenty of those—"

Fabio grinned. "That's what everybody thinks. Which is why it'll be so fantastic when I give the police the evidence they need to solve this 'mystery.'"

"No, Fabio! You can't!"

"I'll be a hero. People will finally give me the respect I deserve."

"They won't." Ava muttered as she turned away.

"What's that?"

She spun backward. "I said, they won't! You don't get it Fabio! You haven't gotten anything, ever! You know nothing!"

He chuckled. "Oh, I know some things."

Ava's hands and feet grew cold. "What do you mean?"

"You see, I've been investigating."

Ava thought she might be sick. "Investigating?"

"Yes. In people's yards."

"Trespassing, you mean. Spying."

Fabio shook his head. "There's nothing wrong with that. Anyway, I bet you can't guess what I found this afternoon. Or maybe you can. You with all your *smarts*. Remember, Ava? How our parents sent you to that fancy pants American summer camp so you could learn English? While I had to stay and start working at the hardware store? Oh, yes, you showed such *promise*. Such a good, good girl. I knew it was a fake. You're a big *fake*."

Ava couldn't catch her breath. "You are making no sense."

"I'm telling you what I found."

"You aren't telling me anything! You're making the same accusations you've been making since we were kids! 'Everyone is mean to me! Everyone is nice to Ava! I'm done with people treating me bad.' It's *disgusting*, Fabio! Grow *up*!"

Ava turned on her heel.

"Ah, so you don't want to know what I found in your *dear friend*'s yard?"

Ava's breath caught.

Fabio grinned.

Ava said, "What . . . what are you talking about?"

Chuckling, he said, "I thought that might get your attention."

Ava hesitated, unsure of what to say.

Fabio grinned and went on, "Your poor friend Concetta, who was left alone caring for her three children when her husband 'disappeared'. Two boys—I can't remember their names—and little Elisa. Poor, poor Elisa. A friend to immigrants and drunks and whores."

"Fabio. What have you done?"

"You're not listening. It's not what *I've* done this time. It's what *they've* done. Or you've done. Or both—I'm not clear on that part."

"I . . . what . . . you're bluffing."

Fabio shrugged. "You are simple minded. The evidence is there. In that mound behind Concetta's house. A mound covered with your rosemary. Did you think no one would find out?" Fabio *tsked* and shook his head, before wheedling, "Now tell me, did you help with the murdering or just the burying?"

Ava's legs gave out, as Fabio examined his fingernails and murmured, "This is going to *kill* mom and dad."

❧

Closing time.

All day, Chiara had sat with the loss, the suffering. Silently. She refused to speak about it. Steadfastly, she averted her eyes and changed the subject when customers entered, faces pinched with sorrow and worry. It went against her grain, but she simply couldn't step into their discomfort and cleave it with her presence. Chiara could feel the distance she forced between herself and the people who came to console her, a rawness on her skin.

She ignored it all.

She didn't feel their pain. She didn't bristle at their curiosity. She didn't cower at their smugness.

The gulf of despair kept her from caring.

This.

Her bar.

She could only conceive of the edges of such a loss.

As she wiped her soft cloth against the shine of the counter, she wondered, had she ever truly noticed the flecks of crystal in the stone? Had she ever appreciated the feel of the fabric's catch against a scatter of sugar, invisible to the eye, but apparent to the touch? And, once again, *what would she do now*?

All week it had been like this. She'd falter at the spill of sunlight across the floor. At a tabby cat slinking in and making herself at home in the corner chair. At the merry yodel of milk frothing in the gleaming metal pitcher. At the satisfying thump of the pastry case door sliding back into place. At the scent of grinding coffee beans threading throughout the moments of being alone and the moments of being with people.

Had she ever *noticed*?

As Chiara stacked the dishes in the dishwasher, she wondered how much of the tearing feeling in her chest was caused by the impending loss and how much was due to a kind of anger she'd never known. That the man who had violated not only their vows but any sense of decency could be the cause of her loss—it defied logic.

She knew that life wasn't fair, that bad things happened to good people. But she could not wrap her mind around good things happening to bad people in a way that affected so many. She had to wrap her mind around it, to catch up with reality. Plans needed to be wrenched into place. At the bottom of all these thoughts glittered one hard truth.

She had to leave Santa Lucia.

She could not stay and watch someone else run the bar—whether he succeeded or ran it into the ground, she couldn't watch. It would be like watching as someone paraded about town in her skin. Impossible.

Where could she go?

Maybe twenty years ago, she would have felt liberated at the opportunity to discover someplace new, a novel adventure. Now? Her connections meant too much. She'd miss the routines and habits of her life, yes, but it was the people, their effortless ebb and flow, that she couldn't bear to consider leaving behind.

She thought of going to another small town. But she knew she'd always be comparing it to Santa Lucia. She thought of going to a city and felt suffocated at the looming anonymity. Besides, her savings wouldn't be enough to support her in a big city.

Would she have to get another job? Most decidedly, but she would push off that decision as long as possible.

Surfaces clean and dishes safe in the humming dishwasher, Chiara gazed around at the empty table, the long counter, the broom propped in the corner, the sugar packets lined up neatly in their metal container. She walked around the bar, dragging her fingers lightly across the surface. Standing still, she closed her eyes and breathed. Memories rushed into her mind—running into the bar after school, her braids flying, calling for a *cornetto*. Flirtatious conversations with boys as she worked the register and tossed her curled hair over her shoulder. Hands reaching across the counter to join with neighbors in times of heartache and times of joy.

The memories filled her, a dam broken, until she sank onto a stool, and dropped her head onto her folded arms.

The light fixtures above flickered. A warning? A calling?

In the tumult of Chiara's mind, up seemed down. Right seemed wrong. Nothing in her mind or heart behaved. Her eyes caught on the Madonna outside.

The Madonna. Ethereal, glowing.

Chiara stood. She removed her apron and folded it carefully on the bar.

Nodding to herself, she stepped to the door and opened it wide.

"*Un caffè*, Chiara," Anna ordered, striding up to the bar.

Chiara hesitated a beat before nodding and turning to grind the beans.

Normally she made Anna *caffè* without any emotional hitch. But right now, while she lived in dread of Riccardo's call to leave Bar Birbo, Chiara craved the bar's banter and communion. She didn't want to spend even one moment waiting on Anna.

It wasn't so much that she believed even half the gossip she heard about Anna. It was that every time Anna came in the bar, she wanted to run down Isotta, and Chiara couldn't pretend to listen to it. She had grown to like the Florentine woman. She didn't notice any of the airs that Anna accused Isotta of flaunting. Nor did she see Isotta as remotely conniving or devious. Chiara remembered the note Isotta left on the counter yesterday. Simple and heartfelt, Chiara propped it on her kitchen table.

Fortunately, Bar Birbo was filled today. She could serve Anna and then move on.

"*Salve*, Chiara," Anna said before glancing over at Fabio stepping up to the bar. Chiara startled. Oh, no. The pair of them.

Anna said, "Fabio! I haven't seen you for a long while! How are you? How's the shop?"

Part of Chiara wanted to intervene, but spring had brought an unexpected surge of tourists. A large group entered the already crowded bar. Luckily they were Italian, and Chiara easily shepherded them outside to the falls. She assured them that someone would take their order in a moment. As she jogged back into the bar, relief flooded her at the sight of Edo tying his apron around his waist. "*Buongiorno*, Edo." She shot a tentative glance at Fabio before saying, "If you could get the tourists outside, I'll take care of the bar."

Edo followed Chiara's eyes before responding with a small nod. He grabbed his notepad and gazed intently at it as he walked out to the *terrazza*.

Chiara sighed and dropped Anna's *caffè* in front of her. Fabio raised his finger to indicate his order of a *caffè* as well. Within moments the *espresso* was made and delivered, and Chiara was able to move to the other end of the bar where Magda and Dante debated England leaving the EU. Even though they seemed to agree, their voices raised dully over each other. Chiara suddenly realized their argument resembled a play poorly acted. Their hearts were not in it.

She swiped up empty sugar packets and turned to the baker and the butcher who were lamenting together the lack of rain this past winter. Leaning forward she added that the drier winter also meant higher milk prices. Soon, Chiara was cocooned, as separate as she wished from Anna and Fabio's conversation. She wished she could so easily escape the ache in her throat.

Back at the other end of the bar, Fabio poured a packet of sugar into his *espresso* and said, "Crazy about that leg, huh?"

Anna stirred her *caffè*."It is! I heard they found remains of a biker below Santa Lucia. Must have been his."

"You heard that, huh?" He smiled a deliberate smile.

"Is it not true?" Anna leaned forward.

"*Boh*," Fabio shrugged. "If that's what everyone is saying..."

Anna said, "Oh, you know this town. Everyone always so eager to believe anything told in whispers. But I bet *you* know something."

"I might," he said with a leer.

"I should have known! If anyone could solve this mystery, it would be you! Don't keep me in suspense, Fabio!"

Fabio's lips stretched across his teeth. "That leg. What if I told you that I know where it came from? That I know *who* it came from?"

Anna's sharp intake of breath made her stand at attention. "Someone from Santa Lucia? Someone I know?"

Fabio licked his lip. "Maybe."

"Tell me!"

"You know, I think I will. You can help me figure out what to do."

Anna waited, hardly daring to breathe.

Fabio leaned toward her and whispered, "The leg bone is from a whole body."

Anna stayed silent.

"A body buried at Carlo and Concetta's house."

Anna's eyes searched his.

Fabio went on, "Carlo, you know, who disappeared last fall."

Anna nodded. "Yes, that's right. It's just Concetta and her daughter living there now." A thought struck Anna. "That daughter. Who is always with . . . with Isotta."

Fabio nodded. "I bet she's mixed up in it, too."

"Isotta?"

Fabio nodded again and took a sip of *espresso*. "Sure. Carlo disappears, then Isotta flees Santa Lucia. You don't think that's connected?"

Anna nodded eagerly, forgetting that this was also the time that Isotta had found out that Massimo had married her because she was a dead-ringer for his ex-wife.

Fabio went on, "Then Isotta comes back, she becomes so *motherly* to Elisa, and then . . . poof! Elisa's mom disappears!"

Anna gasped. She thought for a moment and said, "I heard Concetta ran off with her high school boyfriend. Living in some port city on the east coast."

Fabio shook his head. "You can't believe everything you hear. I bet her bones are scattered somewhere."

Anna breathed, "Do you have proof?"

Fabio shrugged. "I found remains. And I talked to my dear sister, you know she was helping Concetta with the garden. Ava wouldn't admit it. But what she *didn't* say convinces me I'm right."

Anna leaned back a bit and regarded the younger man. When had he started to make so much sense? She couldn't believe she'd spent years rolling her eyes at his limited world view and quick temper. He saw good and evil in this town as clearly as she did. She grabbed Fabio's hand again. "You have to tell the police."

Fabio nodded. "I agree. My sister tells me that's wrong, that the little girl will be 'traumatized'," he jeered, his fingers making quotes. He went on, "But the town needs to know how things are very, very bad. Everyone will thank me."

"Of course they will! You'll be a hero! Uncovering a conspiracy!"

Fabio nodded. "I think the immigrants are mixed up in it too."

"Probably true. In fact—"

A thwack startled them out of their whispered conference.

Everyone looked around for the source of the cracking blow.

It was Giueseppe the butcher who noticed the bird on the ground outside the windows that framed the door. "A bird! It must have flown right into the glass!" He looked around. "How bizarre. Has that ever happened before?"

Chiara frowned and shook her head.

Giuseppe nodded slowly, peering at the bird who was now twitching and shaking.

The bar watched. There were no sounds but breathing. After a few moments, the bird shook itself upright and then hopped from one side to another. It stretched its wings, staring beadily into the bar. With a flutter of blurring black wings, the bird took flight.

Into the quiet, Giuseppe said, "It's like I was saying, Sauro, the lack of rain means less food for the animals, their behavior changes..."

The noises of the bar picked back up and soon it was all as it had been moments before.

Anna leaned toward Fabio. "So you'll tell the police?"

Fabio drained the sugar from his *espresso*. "Some of them have it in for me. They treat me very unfairly. They may even be in on it."

Anna shook her head. "Something this important, they'll have to listen. Tell the captain what you found, he's back from his vacation at the end of the week. He'll make them investigate whether they want to or not."

Fabio nodded. "That's exactly what I was thinking."

Ava's phone rang as she walked down Via Romana, and she answered it without thinking.

She heard an intake of breath and Ale's voice saying, "Oh, thank God, you picked up."

Ava curled her fist and knocked her forehead with it. Why hadn't she checked the number?

"Please, Ava, listen for one minute. It's not true. I found out what Madison said to you. It's not true!"

Ava said, "For clarity's sake. What's not true?"

Ale said, "She's not pregnant!"

Ava didn't say anything.

"Ava, did I lose you?"

Ava rolled her eyes and said, "I'm here."

"She was lying! I only found out because I heard her bragging to her mother about her conversation with you."

"Maybe she is pregnant and hadn't told you yet."

"No. No way. Madison refuses to deal with getting her period so she's on so much birth control it would take gladiator sperm and a battle ax and a miracle to make that happen."

"Interesting. You didn't mention that she can't be pregnant because you aren't sleeping with her." Ava stopped and studied the chisel marks in the stone.

A long silence ensued. Ava nodded to herself.

Ale's voice wavered on the end of the line. "Yes. I've slept with her. I can't not."

"Mmmmm—okay."

"Ava, please. It's not out of love or even out of lust. Madison is insistent that—"

"I don't need to hear this. Your sex life is none of my concern. I'm sending the bill, by the way, for the plans I drew up for the *castello*. You'll need to get someone else to finish it for you. I'm done."

"But Ava, why? I'm telling you she's not pregnant. We can go back to how we were. Before. Nothing needs to change."

Ava laughed bitterly. "No. I don't think so."

Ale stuttered, "I told you I'd leave her. As soon as you tell me you're ready. It's up to you."

Ava spoke over him. "See right there? That's the root of your problem. You want me to decide for you whether or not to leave your marriage. I don't make this choice. You do. Don't put this on me. It's unfair. To me . . . to the woman you married. I don't know why it took me so long to see it."

"Ava, I—"

"You either love me or you love your current life. You don't get both."

❧

Chiara stepped in the bar.

Had the light always slanted in through the door in just that way?

She gazed across the road to the Madonna. She sent up a prayer of thanks for the role this bar played in her life. Pulling her sweater from the hook, she idly realized it was the same sweater that Fabrizio placed around her on their first walk in the groves. How long ago that seemed. Fabrizio was gone, changed. Soon, this bar would be gone, changed. Then she'd be gone and changed.

She checked the clock. One hour until her lawyer came. She kept the closed sign in place. No one needed to know what was happening, that today was the day she would lose everything. Eventually, of course, she'd have to tell them.

What would happen to the bar? She thought of the townspeople who relied on it as a place to stop, connect, pause. She thought of Magda, if the buyer of the bar turned it into a villa with rooms for rent, it would ruin Magda. Briefly, Chiara entertained a vision of her and Magda, roommates in a seaside flat. Nattering and bickering over who made the coffee and who emptied the trash. She smiled and shook her head.

A knock at the door startled Chiara out of her reverie.

Her lawyer! Early! It must be worse than she thought. Would she at least have time to pack?

She slowly walked to the door, savoring the precious moments when the bar still felt like hers. She twisted the lock and pulled back the door.

Riccardo's eyes were warm and sad.

"Coffee?" she asked. Ever the hostess. Maybe she could work in another bar. Or did she have enough saved up to buy a smaller bar somewhere? Maybe Riccardo would know. She liked his wife, Pina. Maybe she should move to Spoleto.

"Please," answered Riccardo removing his coat and hanging it.

He turned to her.

And smiled.

That smile. It arrested her, arrested her as she was reaching for the grinder.

"What is it?" she breathed.

"It's over."

"It's over! Already!" Her knees buckled under her; Riccardo helped her to a stool and went on, gently, "No, Chiara, I mean, it's over. He's offered terms for you to be able to keep the bar. Terms I'm convinced you will be willing to meet."

"Terms? What terms?" Chiara insisted wildly. "You said before he wouldn't stop until he forced the sale of the bar."

Riccardo pulled up the stool next to Chiara and leaned toward her. "I know. I know that's what I said. He must have had a change of heart or found a moral compass or maybe the Madonna interceded." Both of their eyes flitted to the Madonna in her niche. "All I know is, I got the documents last night."

He opened his satchel and drew out a sheaf of papers. "He says here that he's willing to sign over the whole building to you, if you give him a thousand euros."

Chiara looked up in disbelief. "That doesn't make any sense. He had the upper hand, why would he take so much less?"

Riccardo read the document and said, "He says here that he's not interested in a protracted legal battle. When I called his lawyer to confirm, he told me that your husband is engaged to be married and wants this behind him as quickly as possible. He only wants enough money to get married. A thousand euros is what he fronted for the bar. If you give it to him, he'll sign the building and the business over to you."

"Engaged? What kind of woman does one meet while in jail for having sex with a teenage prostitute?"

Riccardo shrugged. "You'd be surprised." He clicked his satchel closed. "Regardless, I read through the agreement carefully, there are no hidden loopholes. This is it. Sign it, give him a *bonifico* for a thousand euros, and the bar is yours."

Riccardo's arm surrounded Chiara as she began crying in disbelief and sudden joy.

All the while, the Madonna watched, serene in her niche of Byzantine blue.

Ava's head was full. When could she count on space in her brain again? She hoped a day of working in the groves would help. Give her something green to focus on, something that wouldn't betray her, humiliate her, leave her, concern her.

There she went again. Ava shook her head and focused on yanking the dandelion greens from the foot of the olive tree. She listened for the sound of the minuscule roots tearing from the earth and sympathized.

Again!

Clearly not even plants were beguiling enough to distract her from the torment in her head. Now not only did she have memories of Ale to send her thoughts flying, she worried about Elisa. How could Elisa's mother leave her? Leave Elisa *alone*? She had assumed she understood Concetta, thought better of her than this. No, she wasn't a model of virtue, but Ava had related to her wounding, her desire to get her life on track. But now—

"Ava!"

"*Ciao*, Edo."

"*Ciao*. Looks like we had the same idea."

"Glorious afternoons call for being outside. It's the nicest day we've had to work in the groves." She doubted Edo was sent out by *his* demons. Especially since he no longer feared eviction from Bar Birbo. Santa Lucia as a whole seemed swept in a surge of good feeling following Chiara's news.

Edo nodded and continued standing.

Ava prompted gently, "Are you going to work your parcel?"

"Yeah. I was just thinking."

Ava turned her attention to a stubborn patch of dandelion and said, thwacking the earth, "Thinking?"

Edo nodded. "I never thanked you. For accompanying me to Spello. I know you didn't want to go. And then everything fell apart, and you were such a godsend."

"It wasn't just me. Francy was there, too."

Edo said nothing.

Ava began tugging at another dandelion plant. "Do you ever hear from him?"

Edo said, "Francy? No."

"Did you want to?"

Edo hesitated. "No."

Ava sat back on her heels. "That sounds like a yes."

"He's a jerk." Edo paused. "Right?"

Ava said, "If he's a jerk, he's the most chivalrous jerk I've ever met."

Edo smiled.

Ava examined her trowel. "And the most attractive."

"Ava!"

Ava shrugged. "A girl has eyes. It can't be helped." She thought of Ale. The way his hair felt when she ran her fingers through it, the resistance of his chest, the power of his arms when he lifted her up into his embrace. She shook her head.

Edo dragged his toe, inscribing a semicircle in the dirt. "He is attractive, yes."

"Very attractive."

"Okay! Okay, he's a very attractive guy who can sometimes be civilized. Maybe you brought that out in him." Edo grinned, but his dimple flickered as if unsure whether or not to commit to the expression.

"Somehow, I don't think I'm his type."

"I doubt I am either, after the things I said to him."

"Oh, Edo."

"What?"

"We saw him the next day, he was kind and courteous and frankly enchanting."

"Maybe . . . but . . ."

"But . . ." Ava shoved her trowel into the earth. "But . . . what?"

Edo shrugged, frowning. "Even if he somehow forgave me for being an ass the day before, there's no way anything could happen now. Maybe he's not the elitist bastard I thought he was, but who would align himself with a family that runs a bar that almost got swept out from underneath them by a pervert ex-con?"

Ava sighed in exasperation and wiped her gloved hand across her forehead. "You can be so insanely dense sometimes. It's getting aggravating. If you want me to tell you how plain it is that Francy is into you, I can do that, but do us both a favor and stop playing dumb."

"Playing dumb?"

Ava blew a strand of hair off her face. "Oh, come on, Edo. He obviously doesn't have a problem getting his hands dirty for love or he wouldn't have bought the bar."

The silence went unbroken as the words rushed over and over into the space. They faded, leaving a distant songbird warbling in the distance.

Edo slumped to the ground beside her. "What did you just say?"

"Oh Edo, I'm sorry, I'm sorry! It was meant to be a secret! Zio Riccardo will be so angry with me! I promised and promised I wouldn't tell."

"What did you *just say*?"

"Francy. It was Francy. He saved the bar."

Edo's mouth worked in confusion. "But . . . *why*?"

Ava gazed at him, wordless.

Edo slowly said, "You must be mistaken."

"I'm not. When Riccardo heard from Francy, he called me to ask if I thought Francy could be trusted."

Running his hands over his face, Edo asked, "But . . . how much did he pay that sleaze bag?"

Ava said, "I don't know. Riccardo didn't mention that appraisal from the hotel, so I guess Francy paid what everyone, including Chiara's ex, thought the bar was worth. Half a million euros, maybe?"

Edo gasped. He thought for a bit and said, "But . . . why the secrecy?"

Ava shook her head. "I can't say for sure. From the way he conducted the whole transaction, I think he doesn't want anyone thinking they owe him. This was cleaner. Only now I've messed it up." She dropped her chin to her knees.

"It's okay, Ava. I'm glad I know. I won't tell Chiara. Frankly, I think it would confuse her, given the Fabrizio situation."

Ava closed her eyes. "That part hadn't occurred to me." When she opened them again, she watched Edo's face shift with grief. As her friend pressed his hands against his forehead, Ava whispered, "What is it?"

"I blew it. Look at this—he was an actual good guy. Like, an amazing person. And he tried to ask me out, more than once, but I had turned this gorgeous human into an evil caricature. All because my pride was wounded. And even though I behaved like I was this small," Edo held his thumb and forefinger a centimeter apart, "he saved the bar. Why? Why would he do that?"

Ava looked wonderingly at her friend and rubbed his shoulder. "Oh, Edo."

"You ready, Mamma?" Massimo asked, standing by the front door, a hand on the doorknob.

"Almost!"

Massimo's sigh was soft, but not soft enough as Anna called from the bathroom. "*Con calma, tesoro mio*! Patience." She floated out of the bathroom on a wave of perfume. "It's not every day my son invites me to dinner! I want to look nice!" Anna's smile was wide as her eyes sought Massimo's.

"You look pretty, Mamma."

"Good, then," Anna nodded, then brushed lint off her lacy pink dress. She muttered, glancing up at Massimo through lowered lids, "I don't want you to be ashamed to be seen with your old mother."

"Very pretty. Let's go?"

They stepped out into the inky darkness. A soft breeze stole down the alley and swirled around them as Massimo paused to lock the door. He asked, "Margherita okay at your sister's?"

"Oh, yes. They were happy to have her. Especially when I told them about our date!" Anna pushed her arm through Massimo's. Instinctively, he pulled it closer.

The drive to Girona passed quietly. Massimo studiously watched the road curving away ahead of him, while Anna alternated between straightening her dress and adjusting the radio station away from current hits.

Massimo found the last empty spot on the street in front of the restaurant. "Tonight really is our night!" His mother crowed.

Massimo stepped out of the car.

A few moments later found them seated at a table for two, with Massimo snapping for the waiter as Anna read the menu like a bestselling novel. She wiggled in her seat and pointed. "Look! They have pasta with fava beans. You love that."

Massimo said nothing, his attention on the waiter weaving toward them. When Massimo ordered a bottle of Pecorino wine, Anna clucked in pleasure. "Oh, Massimo! You remembered! But we haven't ordered, what if you want meat?"

Shaking his head, he said, "Then I'll order a bottle of red, too. I want you to have your favorite."

Satisfied, Anna leaned back. "Looks like we are in for quite an evening!

Isn't it nice to have this time together?" She batted her eyes. "Just the two of us?"

Massimo said, "It seems like it's always been just the two of us."

Anna rested her hand on her chin. "All our best times, right? Oh, here's the *vino!*"

They sat in silence as the waiter uncorked the wine and poured a small amount in Massimo's glass.

"*Buono,*" pronounced Massimo. After the waiter poured full glasses of the jasmine-scented wine, Massimo cleared his throat. Before he could say anything, Anna leapt in. "Remember all the bottles of Pecorino we polished off during our seaside trips?" Anna laughed gaily. "Oh, those were wonderful times." She took a sip of wine, then shook her head at the power of golden memories.

Leaning toward her, Massimo asked, "Is it to your liking?"

Anna smiled and clutched his hand in both of hers. "It is. It's wonderful. Just like you, darling. Just like us. Aren't we so lucky?"

Anna sat straight and gazed around the restaurant, as if expecting heads to turn and nod in acknowledgement. Visual tour of the restaurant complete, she simpered into her glass of wine.

Massimo began, "There was a reason I wanted to go out tonight."

"Of course, darling. To spend time with me. I'm so glad you've realized how you've neglected your dear old mother."

Massimo shook his head. "I've been talking to Isotta and—"

"Isotta! I thought that was over!"

"Over? Why?"

"You had that fight, and I thought for sure you'd see reason after that. We don't need her, darling. All we need is the two of us."

Massimo paused. "And Margherita."

"What about her?"

"How does she fit in?"

Anna's expression soured, like she accidentally swallowed a mouthful of sediment."She's my granddaughter." Anna lifted her finger to wave over the waiter. The waiter nodded his intention to be right with them after he finished serving another table's *antipasti*. Anna looked back to Massimo. "Don't twist my words, darling. It's not attractive."

"But you—"

Anna sighed as she straightened her napkin. "Of course, I meant the two of us together *for* Margherita. I would never neglect your precious child."

Massimo sat back, his face pale. Blinking in thought, he barely registered the waiter's approach. Anna's ordering of the *tagliatelle* with wild asparagus and baby tomatoes filled his ears like the rush of an ocean, close and crashing.The waiter turned toward Massimo, who signaled that he'd have the same as his mother. They'd order *secondi* later.

Anna smiled as the waiter walked away. More couples and families filled the restaurant. Something sizzled in the kitchen, as waiters set plates in front of eager diners. Anna watched a small boy assiduously attempt to twirl his pasta, prodding the strands with his fingers when his parents weren't looking. She smiled. "Oh, Massimo, remember when you were small? How you'd beg to go asparagus hunting and you'd eat a whole plate of *tagliatelle*?"

Massimo's face cleared. He leaned forward and reached for the bottle. "I do remember that. More wine, Mamma?"

She tittered. "I haven't even gotten my food yet! Are you trying to get me drunk?"

Massimo started to speak and then stopped as the waiter paused and dropped a basket of bread between them. He murmured that he'd bring their *salumi* in a moment. Massimo barely acknowledged him, though he had no memory of ordering *antipasti*.

Instead he softened his voice. "Do you remember how Giulia would bring home those armloads of asparagus? We'd ask her where in the world she found so many, and she wouldn't tell us? Said it was a family secret?"

Anna's face clouded. "Why are we talking about her? That's rude." She took a gulp of wine.

Massimo nodded. Gently he said, "I apologize. I shouldn't have let her come into our conversation, our special night."

Anna shook her head furiously.

Massimo topped off her wine. He went on, his voice a caress, "She was always doing that, wasn't she?"

Anna's eyes widened and her face flushed. Cautiously, as if afraid of having a treat snatched away, she ventured, "Doing . . . doing what?"

Massimo straightened and caught the passing waiter. "Let's move to red, shall we? Can you bring us a bottle of Barolo? Whichever you recommend. Price is no object." He reached across the table and took his mother's hand. The waiter started at the request, but then nodded and hurried to the kitchen.

She stuttered, "Barolo! Really? But it's so strong!"

Massimo smiled easily. "You deserve a grand night, Mamma. After all you've put up with over the years, with how patient you've been. You have a good time. I want you to be happy."

"Oh! I am happy, Massimo. So happy." She drained the last of her white wine, as Massimo topped off his own glass, which had hardly been touched.

The waiter brought the new bottle and stemware, uncorking the bottle with a flourish. He paused when he noticed Massimo's full glass. Massimo shook his head and said, "I'll have some with *secondi*. I'm fine for now. Try it Mamma, dear. Is it wonderful?"

"It is, darling." Anna brushed her hair off of her face. "It's so wonderful."

Faint pinpricks of stars glittered across Santa Lucia's onyx sky.

Ava and Edo huddled deep in conversation, their heads low across the bar.

Edo insisted, "I still say you need to talk to them. If Elisa is in trouble, they need to know. She's close to them, they can protect her."

"But Elisa has just started trusting me! I can't blow that now. If I tell them and she finds out..."

Edo straightened, shrugging his shoulders. "But it's for the best, right? I mean, if Fabio goes to the police—"

The end of Edo's sentence was lost among Ava's swearing. He waited and then went on softly, "If Fabio talks to the captain when he's back tonight, and the police show up there tomorrow, and she's living alone..."

"I know. It's dangerous. They could take her. But how would telling Luciano and Isotta about it help? What could they do?"

Edo shook his head in frustration. "Take her in! I don't know! Something!"

Ava said, "She would still be in the crosshairs, and with her mother not around, they could *still* take her away." Ava sighed. "I wish *I* could take her in. This is one of the hidden downsides of living with your parents."

Edo grinned. "What, that you can't bring home preteens whose mothers may well have killed their fathers?"

Ava's face stilled. "Edo—"

"Too soon?"

"Too...something." Ava bit her lip. "Killed sounds so...cold. According to Elisa, it happened when her father was furious. We know he beat Concetta. From the sound of it, Concetta decided to fight back and something went wrong."

"But burying the body?"

Ava shivered. "I know. She must have been out of her mind. She'd sent the kids out to get help, knowing Carlo was about to start up. She must have not trusted what would happen. Who would believe her?"

Edo said, "Maybe I should be sorry that he's dead. But I'm not."

"Who is? What a rotten, rotten man."

Edo said, "And Elisa has been carrying this on her own."

Ava nodded. "Right. She didn't confide in Luciano. Or Fatima. In fact, I don't think she even admitted it to herself until Carosello dug up the body."

Edo began wiping down the bar. "What happened with Fatima? I used to see those two running all over town hand-in-hand, and now...I only ever see Elisa when she's on her way to Luciano's, and I only ever see the back of Fatima's coat. She's forever scurrying up and away."

Ava shook her head. "I asked Elisa about it, or not really. She's too skittish for that...but when I took her to Giovanni's to stock her refrigerator, I asked if she might want to pick out something for Fatima and she said no. That Fatima was too old to play with her. I couldn't get much more out of her, but it seems clear they've grown apart."

Edo said, "They were sweet together. Heartwarming, the way they held hands and skipped down the street together."

"I know. I can't help but think that maybe they've grown apart because Elisa has been carrying this big secret."

"I can't imagine what a weight that's been for her. So once it comes out—which could be anytime—then you think Elisa and Fatima might mend railings?"

Ava shrugged. "Maybe. Fatima has been through a lot herself. Maybe if she sees that Elisa isn't sitting pretty, that she understands darkness—" Ava stopped with an exhale of breath. She shook her head, staring at her hands clenched on the bar.

"Hey."

Ava shook her head again. She said, "Anyway, if the child welfare department takes Elisa away—"

Edo leaned forward to convince Ava to talk to Isotta and Luciano, but the door opened.

Both of them shot looks at the newcomer.

Edo blinked in surprise and said, "*Ciao*, Isotta."

"*Ciao*, Edo." Isotta approached the bar, belly first. When she stood alongside Ava, she said, "I'm Isotta, by the way. I don't think we've met."

Ava blushed, and tried to smile. "Ava." She pretended to take a sip from her empty cup.

Isotta looked to Edo, who shrugged with a bemused grin. He scratched his chin in thought momentarily before announcing, "So, Isotta. Ava and I were just talking about you."

Isotta leaned backward warily. "You were? Well, I can't imagine you're the only ones."

Edo chanced a look at Ava who was glaring at him. "No, we're not telling tales. I promise. It's about Elisa..."

Massimo looked at his mother's plate of untouched beef slices, sprinkled with rosemary and green olive oil. He pushed her glass of Barolo closer to her elbow. Taking a large bite from his own plate of *tagliata*, he chewed thoughtfully.

Anna's eyes were liquid as she gazed at her son over the top of her glass. Draining the last of her wine, she giggled, "It's so funny! I'm not at all hungry!"

Massimo smiled and took her hand across the table. "That's okay. I wanted to hear more about what you were saying earlier—"

"About how I think the mayor has a crush on...on Magda? It's not just me, you know—" Anna's words slurred to a stop.

"No, not that part. Though that is certainly fascinating." Massimo's smile showed all his teeth. "I mean earlier still, about Giulia."

Anna leaned back. "Her again. It's all you want to talk about. Giulia, Isotta...why do they matter?"

Massimo gazed levelly at his mother and cocked his head to the side. "They *don't* matter, do they? They never did."

"They...they never?"

Massimo ignored the dribble of wine on his mother's chin. "With their demands and their secretiveness and their awful possessiveness! They never respected that I was yours before I was theirs."

Anna's response was incomprehensible.

He scowled. "And their infernal whining!"

Anna leaned forward, rubbing her hand across her chin.

Massimo smiled. "Ah, it feels so good to get all this out in the open! I feel so much closer to you!"

Anna started to say something and then stopped herself.

"What is it, Mamma?"

"Nothing, I was just going to ... nothing."

"Mamma? Is there something you aren't telling me?"

Anna nodded, slowly.

"A secret?"

Anna nodded again.

"Ah, Marcè, your mother told me I might find you here."

Marcello grinned at his old schoolteacher. "*Buona sera*, Maestro Luciano." He lifted his glass of wine. "I'm off duty, so this is okay!"

Luciano chuckled. "I'm not going to reprimand you, Marcello."

Shaking his head, Marcello grinned and faced the bar again. "Well, you can hardly blame me. All those years with you making me re-write my homework."

Luciano said, "Good penmanship is never outmoded."

Marcello said, "Yes, I love the compliments I get as I write tickets."

Edo laughed as he buffed the glasses before placing them on the shelf in preparation for closing.

Marcello gestured to his wine glass. "Did you want one, *Maestro*?"

"No, I thank you."

Marcello turned back, and began humming with the radio. He turned and appraised his former teacher. "Wait, does Mamma need me home?"

Luciano said, "No, I stopped by your house hoping to see you." He glanced at Edo.

Seeing the expression on Luciano's face, Edo wiped his hands on his apron and announced, "I need to go upstairs to get, uh . . . bottled water. If anyone comes in, can you tell them I'll be back in a moment?"

Marcello raised his fingers to his forehead in mock salute. He took a sip of his wine and turned to Luciano. "So, what's up?"

Luciano ran his hands along his cheeks and then lightly placed them on the bar again. "I suppose you heard about the leg?"

Marcello nodded. "Sort of. Rumors, mostly. We can't figure out who to talk to for more information." He shrugged. "Bones turn up from time to time." He took another sip of wine.

Luciano gazed levelly at his former student and watched his reaction as he announced, "Not usually a bone with pants on, though."

Marcello sputtered. "Pants? You saw this?"

Luciano didn't blink. "No."

"But somebody did? I need to interview them—"

"I don't think that will be necessary. As far as I understand it, Fabio is speaking to your captain now. It wouldn't surprise me if he sent you out in the morning to investigate his claim's veracity."

"Fabio! He tried making a report already, but it was all third hand. If he had actual information, I'm surprised he didn't march in already, puffed like a peacock." He shook his head, musing, "He's not changed since high school."

Nodding, Luciano answered softly, "Yes, I'm afraid that's true."

Marcello rubbed his finger against the base of his wineglass. "What do you mean? Is this about the rumors back in high school? About those girls Fabio insisted he was dating?"

"No."

"What is it then?"

Luciano breathed for a moment and then replied, "It's a complicated situation that I believe Fabio wants to expose. Let me tell you a story about a little girl."

~

"Mamma? What is it?"

"I . . . I can't tell you."

Massimo poured the last of the wine into Anna's glass. He looked around, glad that this was Italy, where no waiter would disturb them, bring them the check, or even hint at their leaving. They had rented this space for the evening, no one would shatter this moment.

When Anna continued to sit in silence, Massimo began rubbing his thumb over her fingers, tentatively at first, but then with surer pressure.

"Mamma. This could be the thing we need. Since Giulia died, there has been a gulf between us. A darkness. I'm sure you have felt it."

"And Isotta?" Anna bit out the words.

"Isotta?" Massimo sat back, withdrawing his fingers from hers to clasp his hands behind his head. "What is she to me? A distraction." He sighed, thoughtfully. "No, in fact, if I could feel as close to you as I used to, I could get rid of Isotta altogether."

Anna's mouth hung open. She closed it and cut her eyes to the side. "You're serious." Her words slurred again.

"I am."

She ventured, "And Isotta's child?"

Massimo hesitated so briefly, it might not have happened at all. "If I must own the truth, I think you are right. As always. The child may not even be mine."

"I knew it!"Anna squealed so loudly the closest diners cast their table curious looks. She smiled before draining her wine. She dropped her voice and whispered conspiratorially. "I knew it! How did you . . . find out?"

Massimo shrugged. "I suppose some part of me has always suspected. What with the fact that she doesn't care to move back where I can be a proper father to the baby. But more than that, what kind of..." here he barely hesitated, his voice gaining strength, conviction, "whore, what kind of *whore*, has sex with a man the very afternoon they meet."

"And she said she was a virgin." Anna giggled. "A woman's oldest trick. And you, my son, fell for it."

He said, "When I think about how close Isotta came to tearing us apart. So manipulative. Just like Giulia."

"She had no—" the rest of her words were lost in a mumble of invectives and coughing.

Massimo averted his eyes and said, "But, Mamma... you are supposed to look out for me. And instead, you let me fall into the traps of not just one, but two vindictive women." Massimo pouted, a strange expression for a full-grown man, warped through the lens of adulthood. But Anna's response suggested it wasn't odd at all.

"Oh, darling. I, I didn't mean to... I tried to stop..."

"I should leave. Leave now. Since nobody really cares about me." Massimo threw down his napkin.

"No! Wait!" Anna reached across the table and grabbed her son's wrist. "Wait!"

"What? What can you possibly tell me to change the history? You let me go. You let me go to them."

"Oh, *tesoro mio*, I didn't. I never did. I did what I could, I tried to stop—"

"You didn't try hard enough. Two marriages now stand between us. Two other women, and you never cared enough to stop them—"

"I stopped Giulia! I did!"

"You didn't."

"I did! When she walked in, and she saw us—"

"Saw us? What do you mean, saw us?"

Anna floundered, unsure of her words.

"I can't . . ."

Massimo clasped her hand and drew it to his mouth, pressing his lips across her fingers. "Oh Mamma, you can. You can tell me *anything.*"

Anna's eyes roved around the restaurant, looking for a shred of safety, a sign of how to proceed. But Massimo's eyes intent, full of love, pulled her forward, toward him.

"She . . . she walked in while we were napping."

"Napping?" It was Massimo's turn to look confused.

"Yes, at the house. At the ocean."

"I remember. She wasn't going to come at all because of her mother's illness, they thought she took a turn for the worse. But it was something else . . . food poisoning? She got better. Giulia joined us in the afternoon."

Anna nodded, her eyes unfocused. "She came during *pausa,* and she saw us . . . sleeping . . . the same bed."

Massimo bit the side of his cheek and paused before saying, "Such a natural thing for mother and son, to sleep in the same bed."

"Yes! She saw . . . all of it."

"You mean us sleeping."

"Yes . . . and . . . yes."

Massimo shook his head fiercely as if to rid himself of a leash around his mind. He said softly, "It's so good you are telling me this."

Anna was lost now in the memory. "She grew hysterical. Giulia did. I needed her to be quiet."

"I remember. You gave her tea."

"I did."

"You were always giving her tea."

"She wasn't feeling well . . ."

"The pregnancy."

"Yes," Anna retorted bitterly. "The pregnancy."

"She was always complaining about it." Massimo guessed.

"She was! Such a whiner. I couldn't take it anymore."

"Of course you couldn't," Massimo soothed. "Who could? You wanted to stop her, we all did. But everyone was too cowardly, too stupid to figure out how to solve the problem. But not you."

"No, not me! I knew the woman to talk to."

"A woman to help you."

"Yes, she gave me the herbs, the oils, the tinctures."

"To . . . to end the pregnancy."

"Yes!"

"And you gave her some after she walked in on us . . . napping."

"Yes!"

"I remember she said the tea tasted funny. You must have given her more. More than usual? She'd never said anything before."

"I had to stop her. I had to get rid of her. Before she told you what she saw. Before she ruined everything."

"Of course you did, Mamma. But then she perked up and wanted to go for a walk on the beach."

"I was worried, so worried she would say something to take you away from me."

"Impossible, Mamma. Your apron strings have always been snug across my neck."

"Massimo?"

Massimo dropped his head in his hands. "It's late. Let's go home and get you to bed."

Massimo practically carried Anna from the parking lot to their house.

Fumbling one-handed with the lock, he escorted her into her room, where he tucked her into bed fully clothed. Massimo kissed his mother's forehead.

"Massimo? Massimo!" she cried out against the pressing blackness.

"Yes, Mamma. I'm here," Massimo sighed.

"Will you lie down with me?"

"No, Mamma."

"But I'm lonely."

"No, Mamma. Not tonight."

"But Isotta is gone. Giulia is gone. No one will be here to judge us, to get in the way. It can be you and me now. When you love someone," she yawned expansively, "it's always right."

An arrow of memory slid across the bow of his mind.

Massimo could hear the sheets sliding against each other as Anna shifted in the darkness.

Anna murmured something.

Massimo asked, "What?"

Anna kept muttering, unaware of his question. "It's why you took so long to wean."

Massimo turned away, gagging.

"Mmm-hmmm." Anna curled up on her side.

Massimo withdrew to the kitchen. He didn't bother turning on the light. Vision was irrelevant.

He waited, jaw set against the swirling snatches of loosened memories.

Impossible. It was impossible.

Looking back, yes, it was true that Anna had always shoved everyone out of his vision so that she'd be directly in front of him, to pour into him her frustrated love and devotion. But this!

Massimo's heart crumpled in disgust, and he fought the urge to vomit. How many times had his mother crossed a line, convincing him this was normal and good? How could she? How could he have allowed it? What was wrong with him?

And people, people must have seen, they must have wondered. They must have known.

He was no idiot. He knew people speculated that he had killed Giulia.

It was inevitable, given the circumstances of her death. But did they think he did it to be with his... his mother?

At some level, had he grown as warped as she was?

No. No.

It couldn't be.

Massimo stood. Like a trout on a line, reeled out into the streets, walking without thinking.

Left, then right, and before he knew it, he was before the Madonna.

He breathed deeply and drank in the beneficence of her smile, her hand raised gently to forestall his protestations. She stood, eternally ready to forgive, to welcome him back to her grace.

Closing his eyes, he focused on the beam of love that emanated from her presence.

Until suddenly his eyes flew open at the shuffle of a step coming down the street.

"Luciano?"

It was hard to tell, the man wore a pale poncho that shimmered in the darkness. He looked like a ghost.

"Massimo?"

The men were close enough to each other now to recognize each other, cloaked in night. They shifted their weight, one foot to another.

Massimo ventured, "Isotta? Is she okay?"

"Yes. Sleeping."

"Good. She complained of some aches yesterday. I think her time may be soon."

"Agreed."

"You have been very kind to let her stay with you while we... we worked on things. It can't have been easy."

Luciano startled at Massimo's words. His gaze shifted to the Madonna, glowing in her niche before he answered. "I enjoy having her here. She fits."

Massimo smiled. "She does, doesn't she? She is something."

Luciano smiled back. "She really is." He blinked a few times and then went on, "So what brings you into the night?"

A gentle voice approached. "Probably what brings all of us."

The men turned. "Chiara!" They started in surprise, and then laughed at their symmetry.

Chiara was pulling her arms through the sleeves of her sweater. "Looks like I'll have to take a number."

The early morning sun drifted onto the villagers, huddled together in the *piazza*. A serious Giovanni cast furtive glances across the square to the police station. "We don't have much time. It has to be now and it has to be fast. Before anybody wakes." Nods all around. Patrizia handed out old gloves and said, "We got it, Giovanni." She pulled her husband's arm and they led the group to Elisa's house. Quietly, so as not to wake anyone, the collection of villagers began digging. Paola and Patrizia held out burlap sacks, heads tilted to the side so as to avoid the contents. Giovanni hissed, "Hurry! Hurry! The police will be here any minute!"

Meanwhile, a trio of officers stepped out of the station. Marcello led them, saying, "So we're agreed. We'll keep the investigation light. Luciano says this girl is already terrified and confused." The officers nodded and crossed the *piazza*.

Right then a white flash dazzled Chiara's vision. Followed by a boom of heavy thunder. Chiara strode across the bar to peer at the Madonna. She shook her head. Thunder? But the clear sky—

She shrugged as heavy drops began to fall. It must be a sudden spring storm. About time, too. They needed the rain.

Back in the *piazza*, the officers threw their hands up over their heads and dashed back to the station to wait out the freak weather.

The villagers working at the grave breathed a sigh of relief. The rain would wash away their tracks. They heaved the bags and carted them to Giovanni's Ape, waiting on the street. Ava waved at the villagers to hurry. Dumping the bags into the bed of the three-wheeled truck, the villagers then scattered through the falling rain. Giovanni jumped into the passenger's seat. "There!" He pointed. "Down the road . . . those dumpsters. They get picked up in half an hour."

Ava followed his directions and the two leapt out of the truck and threw the bags and the gloves into the dumpster, covering them with newspapers. She jumped out of the driver's seat and fled like the rest of the villagers, home to shower, while Giovanni drove the Ape back to the alley beside his shop. He got out as the rain lightened. Under the cover of the arched alleyway, Giovanni watched the clouds part and dissipate, revealing a sky of brilliant blue.

The three officers strolled out of the station, and Giovanni greeted them, "Some storm, eh?"

They laughed and waved before continuing down Via Romana.

At their knock at the door, Elisa sighed. The benefit of everybody knowing everybody's business, at least the police couldn't take her unaware. She knew they were coming to her house today to investigate a murder. The best she could hope for was being taken away for living alone as a minor. The worst, they would assume, for lack of a better candidate, that she was the one who'd murdered her father. Not even her real father. She wondered if this made it better or worse.

She opened the door. "*Buongiorno, signori.*"

Marcello said gently, "*Buongiorno.* Elisa right? We've come to—"

"I know. This way." Elisa walked through the house, unaware of the knot of hair standing at attention on the back of her head. The officers gestured behind her but said nothing.

She opened the door to the outside and stepped back to allow the officers to pass. She pointed at the mound.

The officers walked across the grass to the lip of the exposed grave.

They stopped, staring. One officer crouched down to get a closer look.

Elisa bit her lip and then, finding some wellspring of courage, she called out, "I know you—"

Hearing a noise behind her, she paused and called into her house, "Hello? Who's there?"

Fabio strode out, hands swinging freely as he grinned. "Ah!" he said. "You finally got here. Saw you passing the hardware store. Figured I'd check on your progress for the captain."

He stopped at the sight of the officers glowering at him.

"Very funny," Marcello said.

Fabio asked, "What? What are you talking about?"

"Is this your idea of a joke?" Asked the shortest of the three officers, pointing into the hole at their feet.

"I don't—" Fabio stopped and then ran to the hole.

Where were the bones? There were no bones, only—

"Bunch of burned wood." Marcello observed. "By the look of it, I'd guess from the *castello*. The workers must have thought this was public space to dispose of debris."

Fabio whispered. "No. There were bones. They were right here. I saw them."

Marcello's voice carried backward and forward. "Maybe you didn't pay attention in police training—Oh, I apologize. I forgot you didn't get into police training." His fellow officers guffawed and nudged each other as Fabio grit his teeth. "If you had been accepted, maybe you would have learned the difference between bones and wood." Thumping Fabio on the back he added, "It's okay. That can be really tricky." The three officers hooted with laughter.

Fabio shouted, "You idiots! Don't you see what happened! This stupid girl moved the bones away. Dig in the hole, take samples, investigate!"

The officers grumbled, "There you go again . . . telling us how to do our jobs."

Fabio practically stomped his feet. "No! This isn't like that! A man was murdered—"

The officers laughed, "Yeah, yeah, just like the hardware shop was robbed."

Elisa watched the scene, her head bobbing between the actors like it was a soccer match. A scent like lavender wafted past and suddenly Ava was beside her saying, "Am I too late?"

Fabio pointed at Elisa. "That girl is living here by herself! Take her away, question her!"

Ava wrapped her hand around Elisa's. "She's not by herself. I live here."

Fabio hissed, "You live with our parents, you loser."

Ava sucked her teeth. "You seem as ever behind the curve, Fabio. I moved in here when Elisa's mother had to go on a trip. I agreed to stay here with Elisa, right Elisa?" Ava stared hard into Elisa's eyes.

Slowly Elisa nodded. "Yes. That's right."

Ava reached into her handbag. "And thank goodness I did. What a trying time! Here, I have the note from Elisa's mother asking me to help out for a few weeks. I know it's here somewhere."

Marcello said, "Oh, don't worry about it, Ava. I talked to Luciano. I already know all about that."

The officers voiced their agreement.

Marcello went on, "So let's leave these ladies to get on with their day, shall we?"

"Mamma!" Massimo shouted from the doorway. "You need to get up. It's almost noon."

"Noon! It can't be," Anna yawned. "I haven't slept past ten since I was in high school."

Massimo grumbled, "Well, you might not have drunk like last night since then either."

"What was that?"

"Nothing. Just ... come into the kitchen."

"My, my, Massimo! You need your mamma today, don't you?"

"When is Margherita coming home?"

"She's not, remember? I'm going to pick her up later this evening. My sister is taking her to the Perugina factory today for chocolate samples."

"Okay, good."

"What's going on?"

"I need to talk to you."

Anna tittered, "Well, that much is obvious, my darling. But first, Mamma needs an aspirin. Be a love and bring some to me?"

"No."

"Please?" Anna wheedled.

Massimo turned on his heel and called over his shoulder, "I'm waiting in here."

"Okay, okay," Anna rubbed her forehead with her hand as she shoved her feet into bedroom slippers. Pulling her robe over her head, she shuffled to the kitchen. "Oh, Massimo, it's too bright in here, can't you—"

"We need to talk."

Anna slumped into a chair, her head falling into her hands. "Yes, I think you mentioned that once or twice."

Massimo stared at his hands, gripping his knees. He took a shuddering breath and said, "I've been doing some thinking." He looked into his mother's wan face. "You need to leave."

A clattering quiet filled the kitchen.

"Leave?"

"Leave."

"Just ... Go?"

"Yes, that's right."

"For the afternoon? To get Margherita you mean."

Massimo raked his eyes upward to meet his mother's. "No. I'll get my daughter. I need you to leave and not come back."

A sharp intake of breath. "You aren't serious."

"I am."

"But why? What?" Anna stuttered, "Why would you say this? Why would you *do* this?"

"Last night—"

"We had such a good time!"

Massimo shook his head. "I know about Giulia. I know about the . . . things you did. That you *are* doing. I need you out of my life, or I won't have one anymore."

With labored breath, Anna said, "It's Isotta isn't it? You want to bring her back into this house, this house where I raised you, that I—"

"Stop."

"It is! It's that witch's fault! You want her to take my place!"

"I want her to move back in, yes, but that has nothing to do with—"

"A-*ha*! I see it all now! She's bewitched you! Poisoned you against me!"

"Actually, Mamma, you did that long ago. It took me too long to figure it out."

"That doesn't make sense. You realize that, right? You are talking like a crazy person. You're infected with a brain disease, like Luciano."

"Don't bring him into this."

"See? You've turned! Turned against everything important!"

Massimo shook his head and started to stand up. "Time for you to go. Let's get you packed."

Anna stumbled out of her chair, pleading, "You can't! This is my house!"

"Papa left it to me."

"You know I deserved it after the hell he put me through! All his mistresses! All his put downs! You remember—he was a bastard!"

"He was. Maybe that's what made me easy prey."

Anna's face worked. "You want the house—*you* should leave!"

"My house. My rules."

Anna crumpled onto the floor, sobbing. "You can't! You can't! You can't!"

Massimo turned. "I believe I just did. I'll go get some boxes. I heard Chiara say she had an overflow from people bringing them when she thought she was leaving."

A howling followed his footsteps out the door. "It's Isotta! She did this! She's the bitch that ruined everything!"

Massimo closed the door on the sounds of anguish echoing throughout his family home.

"Isotta! Where are you? Are you okay?"

Isotta had never heard Massimo sound so frantic. She turned away from Elisa so the sound carrying from the phone wouldn't alarm the child. Elisa was too apt to startle at loud noises.

"Of course, I'm fine. A little cramping, but you know the doctor said—"

"Oh, thank God. Where are you?"

Isotta looked around, half expecting Massimo to come flying around the corner. "I'm at the park."

"Get out of there."

"What? Massimo, what's going on? You're scaring me."

"I don't have time to explain, but my mother—I think she's out of her mind."

"Your mother? What are you talking about?"

She could picture his face, jaw tight in frustration as he strained to say, "My mother she's, she's not *right*. I told her to leave. She lost it, and when I came back from getting boxes, she was gone."

"Wait, I'm trying to keep up. You asked her to leave?"

"Yes!"

"And now she's after me?"

"Yes!"

"Massimo, you know I don't exactly love your mother, but she wouldn't hurt me." Isotta glanced over at Elisa and saw her eyes open wide. More to make the child smile than anything else, she added, "And if she tried, I could take her."

Success. Elisa grinned and got up to walk to the slide.

"Isotta, I'm serious. I can't explain now, but—"

"Don't worry, Massimo. I can handle myself."

"She killed Giulia."

Isotta's heart slipped icily to her toes. Her mouth gaped. Turning away from Elisa she breathed into the phone. "That's not funny, Massimo."

"I know it's not. Get out of there."

"It's too much." Her thoughts raced. "I can get to Luciano's in a few minutes—"

"No, I'm sure that's where she went. Find another place, call me when you're safe. I'm headed out now to find her."

"Okay."

The phone clicked off.

Isotta whirled around, eyes scanning the edge of the park for her mother-in-law hurtling toward her, knife raised. She caught sight of Elisa, sketching at the top of the slide ladder, her brow furrowed in that funny way she had.

Isotta hurried toward her. "Elisa, *cara?*"

Elisa looked up.

"Sweet, can you help me?" How could she tell the child without terrifying her? "There are some grown-ups playing hide and seek..."

"*Nascondino?*"

"Yes."

"That's a kid's game."

"I know. It's really silly. But I'd like to win. I need a place to hide. Maybe

I can hide in your house?"

"Fabio keeps barging in to yell at Ava. I'm sorry, I—"

"No, Elisa, it's okay. It wasn't fair of me to ask." Isotta rubbed her eyes thinking. This town was small, impossibly small. Where could she go where she couldn't be found? There were eyes everywhere, people would see her, people were everywhere. Massimo must be wrong. There was no way Anna would have killed Giulia. How could she?

But then Isotta flashed on Anna's stormy face at any of a number of times when Massimo and Isotta were together. Was it possible?

Elisa ventured, "I could help you find a different place."

"You can?"

"Yes, I know one."

"Would I . . . would I win the the game?"

Elisa's face lit up. "Oh, yes! Definitely!"

Isotta bit her lip trying to figure out the next step, all the while imagining the sound of running footfalls approaching. "The game has already started, so can you get me there without anyone seeing?"

Elisa nodded eagerly. "Easy! Come on!" Elisa clutched Isotta's hand and yanked her forward, toward the groves. As they disappeared into the trees, Isotta was sure she saw a dark shape barreling down Via Romana.

"Quietly now, Elisa! I don't want anyone to see us!"

Elisa held a finger over her lips and smiled before racing deeper into the trees.

Isotta pressed a hand to her belly. Then she scrambled after Elisa. When she caught up, she said, "And Elisa, once I'm hidden, you can't tell anyone where I've gone, okay? No one. No matter how much they ask."

Elisa shook her head with a smile. "Never. You can count on me."

Isotta put pressure against her stomach again and said, "I know I can."

～

Elisa crept back down Via Romana. If she moved slowly, maybe nobody would notice her.

Of course, she stood out like a beacon.

"Hey! You girl!"

Elisa startled.

Massimo's mother hurtled across the *piazza*, her blue cardigan flapping. "You know Isotta. I've seen you with her and Margherita." The older woman was practically spitting.

Elisa concentrated on making her face blank.

"Don't look stupid!"

Elisa's shoulders buckled and she tried to move away.

"Don't you move away from me!"

Elisa stopped mid-stride, shaking. On the edge of her vision, she saw Fatima walking up Via Romana. She hadn't seen her old best friend outside of school in weeks, and now this? Elisa's face flushed in shame.

Anna strode around to face Elisa. "Where is Isotta?"

Elisa stared at the ground and shrugged.

"Where is she!"

"I don't know," Elisa mumbled.

"You do! I can tell you're lying!" Anna's grip on Elisa's arm was a vise, squeezing. "Tell me or you have no idea what I'll do to you."

Elisa whimpered. "I'm not supposed to say!"

Anna started shaking Elisa until the girl began to cry. The words tumbled out. "She walked through the groves, out of town. To the stump down the hill."

Holding Elisa's face inches from her own, Anna's breath reeked like fermented paint fumes. "You better not be lying to me, girl."

"I'm not! I'm not! She's on the path right next to the road. I saw her! She's sitting on the stump."

Anna's eyes searched Elisa's. "The stump next to the Santa Lucia sign?"

"Yes! That one! Please! Leave me alone!"

Anna gripped Elisa more tightly. "If I find out you were lying to me—"

"I'm not!"

Fatima's voice carried toward them. "Hey! What are you doing to Elisa?"

Anna raked her eyes over Fatima. "I don't know who you are, but you aren't from around here. This isn't your concern." Anna looked back at Elisa. "She's on the stump."

"Yes! I didn't mean to tell you! Now I'll be in trouble!"

Anna smiled and let the girl go. "Okay then." She brushed imaginary dust off of Elisa's shirt as she gazed around innocently at the faces that had started poking out of the shops. "Go on and play, girls!" She ordered, before spinning around on her heel and heading up the hill to the parking lot.

As she raced away, Fatima turned to Elisa. "Are you okay? What was that about?"

"She wanted to know where Isotta was."

"Why?"

Elisa shrugged. "They're playing hide and seek."

"Then you gave Isotta away."

Elisa looked into Fatima's eyes, that were once so open but now seemed hard and hooded. She muttered, "It's only a game."

The breeze carried the scent of new flowers. Chiara stood outside the bar and inhaled, letting the fragrance fill her lungs. Clearing out the dark patches that had taken up residence in her ribcage, replacing them with balm-like air. After that sudden shower, the day had turned unexpectedly lovely.

The last week had been like all her previous Christmases rolled up into one. Customers walked in whooping and cheering. Coming to the precipice of all they had to lose had made the villagers less inclined to complain about their neighbor's cat defecating in their flower bed and more apt to revel in the joy of a simple *espresso*. Much hand-clasping. Hugs and kisses all around.

Running her hand through her hair, Chiara closed her eyes and faced the sun, letting it warm her. She turned back into the bar and switched on the radio.

Nothing.

She clicked back and forth, then checked the outlet. A small squeal, but then silence. Chiara frowned. A few weeks ago, she would have assumed this portended something evil. She wasn't normally superstitious, but she had been so tense and searching for a way to interpret the unknowable. Plus, she loved that radio. It had been with her for twenty years. Maybe more.

Now though, she patted the radio like a naughty toddler. It would be okay. Everything would be okay. Without the benefit of radio accompaniment, Chiara belted out the song that had been in her head all night. An overplayed pop song. She washed the few dishes, letting the warm water fall over the clattering saucers and cups as she sang, swinging her hips.

She didn't notice the door of the bar open.

Dishes stacked, she turned off the water, snapped the dishwasher closed, flung the towel over her shoulder and turned around, the tune still in her throat.

Until she caught sight of Fabrizio. Then she lost not only the song, but also her breath. She staggered backward, clutching the back counter for support.

Fabrizio rushed forward in concern. "Chiara? Are you all right?"

Chiara's eyes flit over her former lover. Had he lost weight? Was he sporting a thin beard, or had he forgotten to shave? His hair was longer, almost brushing the top of his collar. She shook her head. "Yes, yes. I'm fine."

Only then did she realize that Francy was standing behind his father, closing the door gently.

Her shoulders tightened. "Welcome back. Can I get you

boys something?"

Francy smiled. "Nothing for me, Chiara. Thank you. I realize I've never seen the falls in the morning . . . okay if I . . ." Chiara nodded her assent and Francy stepped out the back.

Fabrizio leaned forward across the bar. "I wanted to talk to you."

Chiara crossed her arms over her chest and leaned against the back counter. "What about?"

"I did it all wrong."

"It?"

"You. Me. Us."

Chiara snorted softly. "And here I was thinking there was no us."

Fabrizio ducked his head.

"In fact," Chiara ventured, "I thought there was a you and someone else."

"Someone else? Why would you think that? There's no one else."

Chiara ran her teeth over her lower lip and considered. "I got a paper in the mail. It showed you and another woman."

Fabrizio closed his eyes in thought. "I don't know—Oh! Wait. Yes, I do. That's my ex-wife, Francy's mother. She begged me to go to a function with her, told me there would be writers there who could help my career. It wouldn't surprise me if she sent you that paper. It's my fault, I apologize. I knew I shouldn't have spoken so highly of you, but I missed you so much."

"You did?" Chiara's eyes were suspicious.

Fabrizio said, "Such surprise. But I understand." He burrowed his right hand into the the inner pocket of his slightly threadbare suit coat. Drawing out an envelope, he said, "I sent you this right when I got to Bologna. It's a letter."

"I can see that."

Fabrizio smiled. "It's a letter where I explained my doubts."

"Doubts? About what?"

"Well, about you."

"Me?"

"Or more precisely, how you felt about me. I had started to wonder if you cared about me the way I cared about you."

"What? Why would you—"

"It doesn't matter now. Probably masculine immaturity. I'd never met someone like you before, Chiara. So full of life and so completely her own self. I started wondering what you could see in me."

"That is literally and spectacularly stupid."

"Maybe, but it's how I felt. So I sent you this letter. Again, not the most mature course of action. I suppose I wanted you to get it and write me full of protestations about how much you love me and how you'd move to Bologna for me and how your feelings for me were strong and true."

Chiara frowned at the letter now resting innocently on the bar. "Then why didn't you send it? I don't know if I could have offered all that, but—"

"I did send it. And you shouldn't have offered all that. I see that now. I spent years with an unreasonable woman, I think it rubbed off. I was too suspicious and needed reassurance that's really not your job to give me."

"Wait. Too much." Chiara held up her hand. "What do you mean you sent it? It's right there."

Fabrizio sighed. "A mail carrier brought it to me last night. Apparently in my emotional state, I had garbled both your address and my own. It's been all around Italy before the *posta* brought it round last night, wondering if it was mine."

"That's awfully responsible of the *posta*."

"I know. It surprised me, too. All I can say is that I send a lot of mail and they know me. Maybe they figured there would be a bottle of fine grappa for whoever could do me a favor. An accurate assumption, as it turns out."

"So you got this returned last night?"

"Yes. I called Francy. He came over and I told him about the letter. I told him how I had sent you some postcards from time to time, hoping to prompt you into responding to my letter."

"But I—"

Fabrizio held out a hand to forestall her. "I know. Without this letter, you couldn't have known what the postcards meant."

Chiara shook her head. "They were so coded and cold. I wondered if you were trying something out for one of your books."

Fabrizio said, "I'm afraid I'm not that clever. I only wanted you to respond with a long love letter of your own. But you never did."

"Of course I didn't."

"Of course you didn't." Fabrizio dropped his head into his hands and ran his fingers through his hair a few times. Looking up, he said, "So when I realized last night that you had never gotten the letter, I spoke with Francy and he insisted we come to Santa Lucia right away."

Chiara gazed out toward the doorway that Francy had left through. "He did? Francy?"

"Yes. He said the time for letter writing was over and I had to see you and tell you how I felt."

Rubbing the knuckle of one finger, Chiara hesitated. "And . . . how do you feel?"

"Chiara. Since the moment I met you, standing here in this bar making *espresso*, I have fallen further and further in love with you."

Anna shouted at Carosello. "Get away, you mongrel! Get away from my car!"

The one-eyed dog leapt with surprising grace, then jogged into the groves. Three vultures lining the railing shuffled at the dog's approach before slowly flapping their wings and taking flight. Their heavy bodies dragged low over the olive trees. Anna watched, her heart beating quickly as the black birds gained enough momentum to find drafts to carry them upward. She grumbled to herself as she flung open the car door and dropped in the driver's seat. A quick flick of her wrist and the car engine roared to life. Now Anna smiled.

Just ahead. That stump by the turn, it was just ahead, right past the town limits.

She felt pinpricks under her arms. Excitement? Fear? No, the car was stuffy. The car had been baking all morning in the spring sun. She opened the windows and breathed in the fresh air.

Anna flexed her foot on the accelerator and tugged at her seatbelt, making sure it was snug enough to protect her on impact. Isotta would barely dent the front bumper but the stump... that would be an obstacle. Playing out that juddering stop in her mind, Anna paused, her foot on the accelerator easing.

Anna flicked on the radio and started singing. She didn't know the words, the song was new, and she never listened to the radio. It didn't matter. Soon everything would be put to rights. She could sing whatever words she wanted. Soon, everything would be wonderful.

Massimo would be so proud of her. She wished she'd had time to burn an effigy. To make an offering so as to protect her errand.

But there'd been no time. She knew Massimo, in his bewitched state, would try to stop her. Thank the Madonna she'd run into that homely little girl.

A few minutes and it would all be over.

Once Isotta was dead, the veil over Massimo's heart would be lifted. He'd cherish her again, he'd make her feel like she made the sun shine and the birds dance. It would all be back to normal. No, better than normal. Now, she wouldn't allow any woman to enter her home. She had thought she'd be able to control his marriages, but she underestimated the power of a harlot's scent.

The olive groves blurred past, faster now. Anna pictured Isotta sitting, reading one of her stupid books. She did love reading in the groves, like some sort of professor.

Speeding as if chased, Anna noticed a blur out of the corner of her eye.

A black shape arcing toward the passenger side window, a comet whose path seemed magnetically sealed with her own. Anna turned her head in surprise at the very moment that a mass of ebony wings, claws, and a beak built for ripping dead tendons flew into the car.

Anna shrieked and her hands flew over her face. Too late, too late.

The vulture shrieked, the rasping call twining with Anna's gulps of horror, the two locked in an epic embrace of flesh and feathers and hair and blood.

The car skidded out of control past the empty stump, but Anna didn't notice. Her hands forced the giant bird away from her. But the beast, furious in its panic, beat both powerful wings all the harder, clamoring to get out the window, scrabbling over Anna's head.

Again and again, Anna shrieked, calling for help, as the car launched over the edge of the road and down into the ravine. Her face and chest torn to ribbons by the vulture's razored claws, all Anna could see was a haze of slapping black feathers tinged with trails of red.

Her voice faded out as the car somersaulted down the only part of the hill with power lines rather than olive trees. The impact of the nose of the car slamming against the ground before flipping head over tail jostled the bird loose from Anna, and with a mighty howl of protest it pushed off from Anna's sightless eyes through the window and up into the azure sky.

Fabrizio and Chiara looked up at the jangling sound in the distance. They gazed back at each other, shrugging. Haltingly, Chiara finally said, "I . . . I don't know what to say."

"I know, Chiara. I know my own insecurity has likely cost me the best thing in my life. But I had to come to tell you. I needed you to know. Whatever happens now, I needed you to know."

Chiara turned away and held back the tears that threatened to betray her. She alternately wanted to shake Fabrizio for being so daft and lean against him, sharing everything that happened since he left. But how could she trust him?

Behind her, Fabrizio murmured, "You need time, of course. I'll go."

Chiara whipped around, drying her tears with the back of her hand. "Go? You're leaving already?"

Fabrizio raised his hand, like he wanted to beckon Chiara toward him, but he stopped himself and clumsily drew his fingers together. "For now. I'll stay in Santa Lucia until you tell me my presence here is unwelcome."

"You're staying at the same place?"

"No, at Magda's. I thought that might buy me a bit of grace in Santa Lucia. I'm sure the town hates me."

Was this the time to tell him how since he left so much had happened that Santa Lucia probably had no more than an aftertaste of an opinion about him? No, not yet. Instead she nodded. "But it's for tourists . . . so expensive. You should stay at Benito's. I'll talk to Magda."

Fabrizio took a breath. "So, that's the other thing."

"Oh, no. More?"

With his sideways smile that landed like a thud in her ribcage, Fabrizio said, "Well, hopefully not that big of a deal. But I want all my cards on the table. That way, if you forgive me, I won't have to pretend any longer."

"Oh, Madonna."

"I hope it's not as bad as all that." He paused. "This is ridiculous! Okay, here goes . . . I have money."

"You have money."

"Yes."

"Congratulations?"

"What?"

"I don't get it. You have money, I have money, we all have money."

That sideways smile again. "No, I mean I have a lot of it. Heaps, in fact."

The light of recognition dawned over Chiara's expression. "*Oh.*"

A beat.

Chiara went on, "And you didn't tell me because you thought I'd just ... what? ... want you for your money?"

Fabrizio startled as if slapped. "No! Definitely not. Quite the opposite. I worried you'd think of me as arrogant or self-important. When people know I have money, it's like they read all my behaviors through that lens. I know I can be awkward sometimes. If people don't know I have money, they think it's a charming artifact of a writerly existence. If they know, they assume I'm narcissistic or worse."

Chiara thought for a moment. Would she have done that? She liked to think not, but it was possible. She nodded once and said, "Okay. Thanks. I'll bear it in mind."

Fabrizio grinned at Chiara.

A clatter from the stairwell alerted them both to Edo's entrance. "*Buongiorno*," Edo called, as he closed the door behind him.

"*Buongiorno*, Edo," Fabrizio smiled.

Edo whipped around, his mouth gaping open.

Chiara chuckled. "That's about where I am."

Fabrizio laughed. "It's okay, Edo. I'll let Chiara fill you in. Let me get Francy and we'll go to the bakery. Chiara, you know where to find me."

Chiara nodded, her eyes lingering on the face she'd imagined so constantly these last six months.

Edo said, "Francy knows you're here?" He coughed and corrected himself. "I mean, Francy is here?"

Fabrizio said, "Yes, he came with me for moral support. But then vacated out the back to give us some privacy. He'll likely stay a day or two."

As Fabrizio went to the back of the bar, Edo mouthed to Chiara, "What's going on?"

Chiara shook her head. "I'll tell you later. I hardly understand it myself."

Fabrizio and Francy's voices announced their return. Francy stopped in the doorway at the sight of Edo. The two men stayed a moment, Edo wondering if he should reference their meeting in Spello. Perhaps Francy was wondering the same thing because he said, "It's been an age, Edoardo. I hope you are well?"

"Yes, very well, thank you."

"And how about your friends in Santa Lucia? Ava? The retired school-teacher? How are they?"

Edo grinned. "That's a lot to answer as you're walking out the door."

Francy's gaze reverberated across the room."I suppose so. Perhaps you'd consider taking a walk with me tomorrow? I never did see those Roman ruins."

Edo gazed at Chiara through his half-lowered lids. She was regarding him curiously. He breathed and said, "Yes, I'd like that."

"Okay, then. *A presto?*"

"Yes, until later then . . ."

Fabrizio stared at his son, as Francy reached for the door.

Chiara recalled him. "Fabrizio! Did you want your letter?"

He turned slowly and saw it sitting on the bar. "It's yours. It's all yours. Do with it what you will."

With that, he turned and followed Francy out the bar.

Edo crossed his arms and glared at Chiara. "What was *that* all about?"

Chiara smiled. "I could ask you the same question."

"Fatima? *Fatima!*"

Fatima stared hard at the sign outside the *comune* that Luciano knew perfectly well she couldn't possibly be interested in. He quickened his gait, holding out his hand to get her attention.

She sighed. "What is it?"

"Fatima, I'm so glad I caught you." He stopped to catch his breath, his hand drifting to his chest. "It's Isotta. Have you seen her?"

"No. Why would I?"

Luciano winced at the bite in Fatima's voice. "No one has seen her since this morning."

"It's only the afternoon. Maybe she went on a walk."

"Fatima, this town is the size of a ball of rice, how far do you think she could go? With child?"

Fatima rolled her eyes. "I don't get the concern. It's not like she's in a coma."

Was she wearing eyeliner? Luciano shook his head and went on, "Massimo's mother, she was looking for her and she was . . . angry."

Fatima shot Luciano a look he couldn't interpret. "I know."

"You know? How—"

"I saw her threatening Elisa if Elisa didn't tell where Isotta went."

"What? Why didn't you say anything?"

Fatima shrugged. "It's not my business."

"Fatima, for the love of God, please just help me."

"What do you want me to say?" She fairly yelled.

Luciano pitched his voice low. "I apologize for that, Fatima. I know things aren't easy for you."

"Things are fine. I don't know what you are talking about." She lifted her chin. Yes, she was definitely wearing eyeliner. It glinted in the waning sunlight.

"Fatima, my dear. Things are most decidedly not fine. I thought it best to give you breathing room. Maybe that was wrong. But it doesn't seem like anyone else is telling you the truth—you're crumbling."

"Crumbling? I have no idea what you're talking about."

"Crumbling away. From us, it seems from yourself. I can see you are angry, but suspect even you don't know why."

"I'm not angry!" Fatima yelled.

As her furious voice echoed down the alley, both of their mouths twitched despite themselves. Luciano answered, "I stand corrected."

Fatima turned away, gathering her thoughts.

Luciano ventured, "I can guess why you're angry with me." He paused and then said, "You took care of me for so long and then I failed you when you needed me. I failed to save you from the fire."

Fatima shook her head, tears coming to her eyes. "That doesn't make sense. You couldn't have known I was there."

Luciano's gaze was full of affection. "Sometimes our feelings defy logic. Particularly when we don't take them out into the light of day."

Fatima considered. Was that why she felt angry? She hardly knew anymore. She said, "You were drinking. And you *promised*."

Luciano said, "I swear to you Fatima, I wasn't. Massimo was angry, he lunged at me, hit me, that's why I was unsteady." He hesitated. "You felt you couldn't count on me anymore."

Fatima bit her lip and shook her head.

"Oh, *cara*. I may make mistakes, but I'll always care for you." As Fatima fought back her tears, Luciano went on, "But Elisa... why push her away?"

Wringing her hands, Fatima said, "I don't know. I guess I was angry with her, too."

"Because she stole that coin from you?"

"She told you about that?"

Luciano nodded.

Fatima said, "She apologized. I shouldn't be mad, should I?"

Luciano considered his little friend and said, "I wonder, Fatima, if you are angry with Elisa because in making that mistake, in taking your coin, you felt she stole the one friend you have."

Fatima said nothing, but the tears spilled over her cheeks.

Luciano added, "Sometimes loneliness is less painful then confronting anger."

Fatima shrugged through her tears. "*Boh*."

Smiling, Luciano said, "So Italian now, Fatima." He added, "And so the distance between you and Elisa grew."

Fatima said, "It's too big now." She paused, her burnished cheeks shining. "I don't think she wants to be my friend anymore. After the way I treated her."

Luciano risked touching her shoulder, half expecting Fatima to pull back. But she leaned forward, resting her head against his woolly cardigan. He held her for a moment before saying, "Elisa loves you. We all do."

Fatima shook her head, blinking rapidly. "About Isotta. Elisa told Massimo's mother that Isotta went to sit somewhere."

Luciano look baffled. "Sit somewhere?"

Fatima nodded. "Right outside town. Oh! A stump."

"The stump? You mean on the main road? The one by the sign?"

"Yes." Fatima paused. "Do you think Anna would hurt Isotta?"

Luciano's lips tightened into a thin line. "According to Massimo, there's not much she wouldn't do."

Massimo burst into Bar Birbo. "Isotta! Who has seen her?"

Chiara shook her head. So did the assembled townspeople. Bea suggested, "I saw her at the playground with Elisa earlier, did you check there?"

Massimo ran his hands feverishly over his face. "Yes!"

Dante asked, "Did you try her mobile?"

Massimo almost yelled, "Yes! Of course!"

Chiara thought for a moment. "Maybe she's visiting somebody—she mentioned something about helping Ava with a project last night. Or maybe she went with Luciano somewhere?"

Massimo shouted, "No, no, no! I've talked to all those people! She's nowhere! She's been missing since noon!"

Chiara soothed, "It's okay, Massimo—"

"It's not! You don't understand. My mother, she's out of her mind. She threatened her."

This got everyone's attention. Magda barked, "You don't think she'd hurt Isotta?"

Massimo said, "I think...I think she killed Giulia."

Quiet fell like a blanket. Chiara broke the silence by slamming down her towel. With shaking fingers she began unknotting her apron. Massimo's voice quavered. "What...what are you doing?"

"I'm turning this town upside down until I find Isotta."

Edo announced, "I'm coming with you."

Bea heaved herself off her barstool, grumbling, "I always knew that Anna was trouble. A damn lunatic." She took Magda's arm to steady herself. One by one the townspeople gathered their hats and purses and canes and started pushing through the door.

Massimo hurried outside and fidgeted, waiting for his neighbors. His hands flapped ineffectually at his sides. Where could she *be*?

From up the street, footsteps reverberated. Figures appeared under the arch that framed Via Romana. Massimo watched, his heartbeat quickening as the silhouettes slowed. With a start, the figures began waving their arms above their heads and bellowing, "Massimo! Massimo! We found her!"

Massimo sagged in relief as the men—local farmers, he recognized them now—ran toward him.

"*Isotta!*' He yelped. "Everybody! They found Isotta!"

The men drew even with Massimo, shaking their heads. They regarded each other before the rotund farmer stepped forward, tugging his hat lower over his eyes. "No. Not Isotta. I'm sorry." His voice softened. "It's your mother."

The flashlight Elisa had pressed into her hands faded out with a crackle.

The darkness consumed everything. Isotta had never realized how even a moonless, cloudy night was still illuminated by a whisper of leaves or a murmur of grasses, releasing a faint glow. This darkness. It was absolute.

She reached out her hand to the wall and snatched it back, her fingertips moist with something that felt like blood.

Isotta tried to laugh at her overactive imagination, but she couldn't help noticing that her fingers were definitely sticky and smelled of iron.

She wondered if she should turn back, she'd only gone about fifty paces into the chamber. If she could find her way back in the dark. Wait! Her phone flashlight! Still no signal, given the fact that she was surrounded by stone, but there was a bit of battery. She could get back to the trapdoor with the help of the light. And then she would wait.

How much longer should she stay? An hour? More? Suddenly she felt like she couldn't get enough oxygen. Her breath rasped in and out of her lungs, and she felt lightheaded. Calm down! *Calm down*! She was fine! She wasn't some child afraid of the dark!

She would be fine, she just needed to focus her mind.

*Piano, piano.*

One step at a time. Isotta shuffled her steps to avoid tripping on the uneven ground.

She took a breath, and then let out a wail as the seam that knit her inside and her outside together ripped asunder. The pain!

Labor?

No, it couldn't be. It was panic. She was panicking. She needed to find her way back to where she started, and wait. After another hour, she'd creep out and make her way to Luciano's. Massimo must have found his mother and stopped her by now. And anyway, it would be dark, and she'd be careful. She needed to wait—

Another inhuman wail escaped her, taking all her breath with her until she crumpled onto the ground, her phone skittering out of her hand. A fine snapping sensation brought her back to the present. Her ankle. Her ankle had bent at a dangerous angle. Now she was in labor with a broken ankle where nobody could find her. Why did she have to make such a big deal to Elisa about not telling anyone where she was! She should have told her to tell Luciano! She had been so intent on not scaring the child, not alerting her to the danger, she hadn't thought . . . and now she was trapped.

No!

No.

This couldn't be happening. Maybe it was a dream, or maybe the dark had fomented some sort of hallucination. She would breathe and massage her ankle. It was probably only twisted. She would get up and breathe and the pain that was surely false labor would abate.

And if it wasn't false labor?

She couldn't think that way.

Her mind darted anyway.

Would anyone hear her?

Would anyone look for her?

She didn't belong to this village. If she disappeared, would anyone care?

Massimo said he wanted to make a life with her, but who knew? He'd lied before.

And Luciano . . . he *seemed* to love her, but maybe what he loved was having a daughter replica.

The only people she felt sure would notice her absence were Margherita and Elisa. One could barely speak, and the other she'd ordered not to disclose her location. How funny, she'd never thought much about children and here she was in a situation where the two people she knew loved her were—

The pain tore through her again, shaking her out of lucidity as she screamed and screamed and screamed.

Fatima's voice stopped Elisa as she was walking into her house.

Elisa turned slowly. "What do you want now?"

Fatima peered into the house. "I want to ask you something."

Elisa walked in and dropped her sketchbook on the table. "You want to *ask* me something? Or tell me something?"

"*Ask*! Look I'm sorry about what happened in the groves—"

Elisa shook her head angrily. "I don't want to talk about it. Say what you want to and leave." Elisa's chin quivered at the unfamiliar tone in her voice. She turned away so Fatima wouldn't notice.

Fatima gazed around. "Where's your mother?"

Elisa looked away and said nothing.

"Elisa!"

"What!"

"Where's your mother?"

"Out!" Eventually she spit out, "Oh, come on. You must have heard about the leg bone. And how my mother left. I know everyone's gossiping about it."

"My parents didn't say... I haven't talked to anyone."

"Of course not! You're so busy being smart and playing your stupid death games and your *castello*—" Elisa paled.

"Elisa?" Fatima said, "What about the *castello*?"

Elisa turned away again.

"Elisa! What do you know?"

Elisa shook her head, furiously.

Fatima tried to keep her voice calm but the volume pitched up to a squeak. "Is that where Isotta is? Under the *castello*?"

Elisa stared at her shoes. "You should go now."

"Elisa! You have to tell someone!"

Slumping into the chair, Elisa moaned, "I'll get in trouble! I promised Isotta! And they'll take me away! I heard that bad man, that Fabio talking. He blames me—"

"It'll be okay, I promise..."

Elisa's head dropped in her hands as she cried, "They'll take me away..."

"No! They won't! Come on, come with me! I'll tell them it was me, I'll lead them to the *castello*, but you have to come tell me where she is!" Fatima held her hand out to Elisa.

Through tear streaked eyes, Elisa regarded the hand with suspicion. "Why are you being nice? You were so mean."

Fatima bit her lip. "I was. I'm sorry. I didn't mean to be. I've been...messed up. Since the fire."

"The fire?"

"Yes. It's been weird and I don't always understand and I'm sorry."

Elisa looked at her feet. "I thought you got smoke in your head."

Fatima smiled. "That is very wise."

Elisa's gaze drifted up to Fatima's face. The old Fatima looked down at her. No, not quite the old Fatima. This one's eyes had darkness hidden in the corners, but the expression of openness and love, it was the same. Gently, she slid her hand in Fatima's.

Fatima squeezed her hand and pulled. "Come on!"

The girls flew out the door.

Together.

Elisa gasped, "Fatima! You're going too fast!"

Fatima shook her head and kept running, pulling Elisa beside her. They approached Bar Birbo. Peering in, Fatima noticed a clutch of people surrounding Massimo, their hands on his back. He must be really worried about Isotta. Fatima paused, should they tell him?

No, she didn't know him well enough. Maybe he'd react poorly and blame them.

Elisa stood, watching the action in the bar through the glass. Her mouth hung open a little as her eyes hopped from one person to another.

Scanning for a friendly face.

Fatima tugged Elisa on.

Their feet slapped against the cobblestones, hair flying behind them, streaks of waving black and lank brown.

Up ahead, a figure tottered, walking slowly, peering into doorways and alleys. Luciano!

Fatima yelled, Elisa echoing, "Luciano! *Luciano!*"

He turned, confusion turning to alarm as the two girls raced toward him. Before he could get words out, Fatima gasped, "Isotta! She's under the *castello*!"

Luciano stared at Fatima, eyes sliding to Elisa in his search for understanding. "*Under* the *castello?*"

"Yes!" shouted both girls.

Luciano gazed levelly at the girls. "You're sure?"

They nodded furiously, hands still gripped.

Slowly he said, "I suspect there's no need to ask how you know this. Perhaps you were at the *castello* and heard something?"

Fatima and Elisa exchanged glances. Fatima said, "Er. Yes, that's about right. We heard noises. We're very *very* sure that's where she is. There's a trapdoor..."

Luciano took the girls by the hands and strode down Via Romana. Briskly now, he said, "Did you notice if anyone was in Bar Birbo?"

Fatima nodded. "A lot of people."

Elisa said, "Massimo, too."

"I see."

They pushed Bar Birbo's door open with more force than anticipated. Chiara looked up. "Luciano?"

Luciano announced, "Isotta."

Massimo's back straightened and he spun around on his stool. His face haggard and white. "Did you find her? Is she...okay?"

Luciano looked down at the girls. "Fatima and Elisa heard noise at the *castello*. We believe she's there."

Magda snapped, "That's ridiculous. I asked the workers—"

Luciano spoke over Magda, "I'll be clearer. She's *under* the *castello*."

Muttering broke out among the townspeople. "Under? What do you mean *under*? In the groves beneath, maybe?"

Luciano shook his head angrily."We're wasting time! I need strong people, flashlights, ropes. Immediately!"

A quick shuffle as the crowd organized itself. Edo ran up the stairs and returned with an armful of flashlights, Fabrizio and Francy bolted to the *alimentari* to ask for use of the Ape in case Isotta required transport. Bea and Magda buffered Massimo as he moved hazily toward the door. "Isotta? Is she okay? She's pregnant. Have you seen her?"

The crowd pushed up the stairs, toward the *castello*, fingers skimming across the hem of the Madonna's gown. She watched, quiet and still, as the townspeople's voices faded to a gentle rustle. She remained silent, as Luciano's bellow broke through the murmur of the crowd. Calm, as Fatima and Elisa crept to the hidden hatch that led to the steps under the *castello*.

The Madonna's raised hand seemed to quiver with the sound of the secreted door slamming open, triggering a murmur of voices. A shout, as again Luciano called for quiet. Out of the darkness, a thin response, the wisp of an extinguishing candle. Voices and bodies crowded again, jockeying against each other. Then Massimo's growl as he shoved everyone out of the way, and flung himself into the dank opening.

Nobody dared breath.

An eternity later, or maybe it was merely a few minutes, the sound of a guttural yell emerging from the *castello* underground. Frantic footsteps as Massimo rushed across the castle yard, shouting orders as he reached the stairs. "Call the ambulance! She's hurt, she's in labor! The baby, it's coming fast!"

"The ambulance is on its way, remember? For Anna—"

"No! There's nothing they can do for my mother, tell them to come here. I don't think she has much time."

As if in agreement, Isotta's moan of anguish split the plum-colored evening air.

"Put me down!" moaned Isotta.

"Put her down, Massimo, put her down!" shouted the crowd.

"I can't! Can't you see? Her ankle's hurt, she's in labor. We need to get her to the hospital. Giovanni, can you take us to meet the ambulance?"

Giovanni bit his lip, staring at Isotta's writhing. "Massimo, I watched my wife birth three children. I think this baby is on its way out. Now."

"She can't have our baby in the street!"

Bea barreled through. "Who says she can't. All we need is some space."

Massimo demanded, "And who do you propose deliver my child?"

Bea nodded curtly. "I will. I practically delivered all my own, and my last grandchild was born so quickly I had to catch her. I'll do until someone fetches a doctor."

Isotta pushed against Massimo's chest, her head rolling from side to side. "Put me down," she growled.

Massimo whispered, "In the street, my sweet, with everyone here?"

Isotta nodded feebly. "The baby, I feel it—"

Chiara pushed her way from the back of the crowd and shouted, "Into the bar, take her into the bar! Up the stairs to the apartment!"

Massimo lofted Isotta a little higher and strode into the bar but before he could step toward the door that led to Chiara's apartment, Isotta wailed, "No! No steps." She twisted in Massimo's arms. "Put. Me. Down. Now!"

Massimo buried his nose in his wife's hair. "Okay, okay."

Bea pushed everyone out of the bar and closed the door. She lowered the blinds, clicking on the light. "Quick, put her down. Let me see where she is."

Massimo gently laid Isotta on the floor.

Bea washed her hands, calling over her shoulder, "Put those seat cushions under her body. The floor is rough."

Massimo obeyed, cradling Isotta's head in his lap as Bea hurried, wiping her hands on a clean dishtowel. Bea settled herself in front of Isotta and clucked, "Okay then, child. Let's see what we have here."

She folded back Isotta's skirt and gasped.

Massimo gasped without knowing why. "*What is it?*"

Bea smiled. "This little baby held on as long as he could."

"He?"

"Or she. You still don't know?"

Massimo shook his head. "Isotta didn't want to know."

Isotta panted, "The baby . . . it's okay?"

Bea soothed, "So far so good, my child. A lot of hair. Now wait and when you feel the pressure building, go ahead and push."

Isotta closed her eyes, feeling the clamping wave steadily increasing. As it reached its crescendo, she bore down with all her remaining energy, curling her body around the roundness of her belly. A moan seethed out of her, culminating in a yell of release.

"There we go, the baby's coming, there are the shoulders! A bit more Isotta . . ." Bea said, turning the baby to ease its passage. "Here it comes—"

Isotta felt the baby suddenly slip out of her body.

"A boy!" Bea shouted.

From beyond the door, a muffled cheering erupted.

Isotta and Massimo laughed through their tears. "A boy!"

Isotta held out her arms and Bea cleaned the baby in her no-nonsense way before placing him in his mother's arms. Massimo rocked back on his heels, sobbing openly.

The door flung open. In response Bea barked, "Nobody in here!"

A uniformed woman with a medical bag ignored her, standing still to appraise the situation. She kneeled beside Bea. "Baby okay?"

Bea gestured to the newborn rooting around Isotta's chest. She chuckled. "Right as rain. She hasn't passed the afterbirth yet. It's good you're here. I'm not so good with that part."

The doctor pulled a clamp out of her bag and nodded toward Massimo. "The father? What's his problem?"

Bea shrugged. "Who can say?"

The doctor grinned. "Okay, Mamma, let's turn that baby just a hair. I need to clamp the umbilical cord so we can get the afterbirth out and you can get off the floor of this god-forsaken bar."

Isotta couldn't take her eyes off her son. "It's the most beautiful bar in the world."

Bea whispered to the doctor, "Delirious."

The doctor worked for a moment before she asked softly, "Does she have anybody else for support? Her husband is on the useless side."

A cackle escaped Bea. She turned toward Isotta. "Do you want me to bring Luciano, child?"

Isotta looked up with shining eyes. "Oh, yes, please. I want him to meet my son." Her voice quivered in wonder at the word. Casting a look at Massimo hunched over his knees, Bea pushed herself to standing. She hobbled for a moment and then caught her balance, opening the door. "Is Luciano out here?"

Voices protested, "How is she, Bea? What's going on?"

Bea grinned. "That is one seriously beautiful baby boy."

Joy shook the crowd.

Luciano nudged his way forward. Bea caught sight of him and gestured. "She wants to see you." Lowering her voice, she added, "This is all a bit much for Massimo."

Luciano nodded and stepped through the door Bea held open.

He stood in the doorway, the light from outside turning his flyaway white hair into a halo. "Isotta, *cara*—" he began.

Before clutching at his heart and slumping to the ground.

The doctor looked up at the sound of Luciano's body hitting the floor like a falling rug. "I sure hope this little boy is made of sturdier stuff than the rest of the male population in Santa Lucia."

But Bea had seen his face, his gesture. *"Dottoressa!* I think it's his heart!"

Ale picked at his dinner.

Craning her neck, Madison checked that the daughter of the Spanish ambassador was still in the bathroom. A long visit to the bathroom, but Madison had learned that eating disorders ran rampant in embassy circles. She thanked her lucky stars that consistent dieting and exercise kept her lean. Her silver mini-dress hung on her curves exactly how she liked.

She hissed at her husband. "Ale! What are you doing?"

Ale glanced up from mashing his pomegranate-glazed snapper into his cumin-scented carrots. "What?"

"You've barely said a word all night! You *know* I want an invitation to Sofia's family yacht. Her brother is engaged to an *actual princess*."

"Okay."

"Okay? What do you mean, okay? What the hell is wrong with you?"

Ale dropped his fork. "Doesn't this all seem kind of . . . empty?"

"Are you insane? This is what we wanted! We're on our way, honey. Oh, I can picture it now. Me and my handsome Italian hubby, tanning on recliners as we sail past Croatian islands. That's where they filmed *Game of Thrones*, right?"

"I don't know."

"You do! We watched it together last month!"

"Did we?"

"God, Ale. What's happened to your memory?"

"I don't know. Was that before or after you rubbed your breasts all over that Russian oligarch?"

"Don't you dare throw that in my face. I was hurting. You hurt me." Madison cast her eyes down and pouted prettily. "With a boring, plain...she's not even beautiful, right, Ale? Not as beautiful as me?" When her eyes darted up to beseech him, she jumped. "Sofia's back! Now act normal!"

Madison plastered a dazzling smile across her face. Ale tried to rally. He asked Sofia questions about the ambassador's work in Kenya, but given the annoyed look on her face, he suspected he'd mixed up two dignitaries. Then he noticed his ultramarine water glass. He raised it to the light, murmuring to himself about Santa Lucia's sky. Madison rolled her eyes at Sofia before the two of them escaped to the bathroom together and came back giggling. Drugs? He thought Madison quit years ago. The three of them piled into the limousine, and Madison plunked a shaken bottle of champagne onto his lap to open. He obliged, sending the women into peals of laughter when bubbles frothed over the neck of the bottle. They wiped champagne off of each other's shoulder and chests with daring glances at Ale. He ignored them and stared out the window.

What was he doing?

How had this become his life?

But, he thought, as neon signs slipped past the window, who was he *without* all this? Without the wild parties and the fine liquors and the monied experiences?

Madison and Sofia had their heads ducked together now, a celebrity magazine spread open across their laps. As Madison pointed out a singer who had failed to lose her baby weight, Sofia rummaged around her purse and pulled out what looked like coke. Again?

Ale shook his head. He didn't want this. Any of it. But to walk away was to walk away from...everything. His entire existence.

If he had nothing, wouldn't he be...nothing?

∾

The doctor leapt up and leaned over Luciano. "He's breathing." She reached for her stethoscope and put it against the old man's chest.

Isotta turned white. "What's wrong with Luciano?"

Bea chided, "You just pay attention to that little baby now." Isotta didn't move. Bea went on, "The doctor is working, child. He'll be fine."

Isotta started to unbutton her top with shaking fingers. Bea swiped her hands away and undid the buttons with sure movements, asking Isotta, "Has Luciano been drinking again?"

Isotta shook her head. "No. Not for months. Longer. Since I've been back, at least. But he hasn't been well in so long. He kept making excuses—I should have known. I should have insisted he go to the doctor. It's my fault—"

The doctor looked up. "Drinking? He's a heavy drinker?"

"He was," answered Bea.

Luciano moaned and fluttered his eyelids. The doctor helped him sit up.

Bea asked, "Is he okay?"

The doctor nodded. "My guess is that he's experiencing the after-effects of heavy drinking. His heartbeat is irregular. Sometimes it causes lightheadedness and chest pain and fatigue."

Bea watched Isotta, who said, "Yes, that sounds right."

The doctor snapped the bag closed. "We'll have to do some tests to be sure. But that's what my money's on. I'll take him in to the hospital once we get you settled."

"Settled?"

The doctor chuckled. "I imagine the owner might want to clean up a bit. And beautiful as this bar is"—The doctor rose—"it's not where you want to cozy up with your newborn." The baby snuffled as his head roved against Isotta's chest.

Growing serious, the doctor gestured to Massimo. "What to do about that one?"

Massimo was quiet now, watching the action play out in front of him like a spectator at a slightly boring wrestling match.

Bea barked, "Massimo! Get up!"

Massimo shot to standing. The doctor looked at Bea curiously. Bea shrugged. "He's used to taking orders from older women." She turned back to him. "Okay, Massimo, let's get you home. You can visit Isotta when she's had a nap. And food and water, I expect."

For the doctor's benefit, Bea added, "She's been trapped under a *castello* for the better part of the day."

"Ah," nodded the doctor. Before cocking her head in puzzlement.

Bea opened the door. "Chiara! Do you have a bed we can put Isotta in?"

Chiara moved forward. "Of course! Let me put sheets on the spare bed upstairs. She can have that room."

"Good."

"I'm happy to have her here, it's certainly easiest, but if she'd rather go to Luciano's we have the Ape here to take her—"

"Luciano needs to go to the hospital."

A general gasp went up as the townspeople spread this news. Bea shouted to be heard, "He's fine, people! He's fine! Just needs a tune-up."

She sighed. "Okay! We need help getting Massimo home—"

Calls from volunteers.

"Help getting Luciano and the doctor back to the ambulance or car or whatever brought her—"

Calls from volunteers.

"And someone to help get Isotta upstairs once Chiara gives the all clear."

Calls from volunteers.

Bea nodded then turned and wrapped her arm around Chiara, pulling her back into her bar.

❧

Ava found Elisa in the crowd and rested a hand on her arm. "Hey. Are you okay?"

Elisa nodded, mutely.

Ava ran her lip between her teeth. "Let's get you home."

"*Un attimo*—" Elisa turned, scanning the crowd.

"I'm right here." Fatima slid her hand into Elisa's, before appraising Ava. "You're Ava?"

"Yes."

"And you're living with Elisa?"

"Yes."

Fatima's gaze raked over Ava, before she said with a slight smile. "Okay. I think she should miss school tomorrow. It's been a rough day."

Ava smiled. "Duly noted. Thank you . . . Fatima, right?"

Fatima nodded.

Ava went on, "You'll come by to visit Elisa tomorrow?"

Fatima thought for a moment. "Absolutely." She drifted deeper into the crowd until she disappeared.

Ava put her arm around Elisa's thin shoulders. "Ready to go home, Elisa?"

Elisa nodded, leaning against Ava.

Not knowing what else to say, Ava asked, "Are you hungry?"

Elisa shook her head.

The two began walking down Via Romana, neither of them speaking.

As Ava opened the door and shepherded Elisa inside, Elisa moaned. Alarmed, Ava asked, "What is it? Are you okay?"

Elisa nodded and slid onto the sofa. "The baby," she whimpered. "That baby was born to a mother and a father. He's so lucky and he doesn't even know how lucky he is."

Ava sat on the couch next to Elisa and pulled the girl's head to her shoulder. "Oh, Elisa—"

Elisa shook her head in frustration. "I know it's stupid. But I don't understand why some babies are lucky and some babies are me."

Tears tumbled from Elisa's eyes, dropping onto her clenched hands.

Ava hesitated. "Elisa, I'm so sorry." And she sounded sorry, too... her voice shook with emotion. "I know it's... it's not fair."

Elisa replied, "It's not!" She sniffed. "And I'm happy for Isotta. I am! Isotta is so nice and now she gets a baby and I'm happy for her. I am!"

"I know you are, *cara*."

"I want to be happy for me."

Ava drew in a shaky breath. "Well, Elisa. Maybe I should... I don't know how happy this will seem for you... But you do have a mother."

Elisa shook her head. "No, I don't. She's never coming back. My brothers said—"

Ava rested her hand on Elisa's. "That's not what I mean. I mean... your mother, the one that gave birth to you. That never stopped loving you..."

Elisa looked up into Ava's eyes and breathed, "Do you know who she is?"

Biting her lip, Ava nodded. "I do."

Elisa sat up straight. "I didn't know you knew that! Can you tell me? Please tell me!"

Ava whispered, "It's... It's me."

Elisa sat by Luciano's bed, swinging her feet. Luciano sipped a canned chocolate drink while Elisa prattled on. "And then she said, 'It's me.'"

Luciano looked up. "I apologize. I must have missed something. Your mother is—"

"Ava!"

Luciano's hands clenched his drink as it drifted down to his lap. "Ava? Ava is your... mother?"

"Yes!"

Luciano shook his head. "How can—I assumed the woman who birthed you left Santa Lucia years ago."

"Why? My other mother," Elisa giggled. "'Other mother'! She told me it was someone here. Remember?"

Luciano said, "I do remember that. I admit I suspected she was . . . mistaken."

Elisa swung her legs again. "Nope! I didn't think it was true, about Ava I mean. But we went to her house last night and she made her parents tell me everything."

Luciano wondered aloud, "*Ava's* parents? I cannot picture—"

Elisa nodded. "They didn't want to talk about it at first, but Ava made them. Said it was time to 'own the truth'."

Scratching a mosquito bite on her arm, Elisa mused, "Ava was young. Really young. And she didn't want to give me away, but her parents made her. They said so. They said they knew she'd never have a life if she had a baby at fourteen."

"Fourteen! That's barely older than you!"

"Yup. She said she wished she hadn't had to give me away, but she had no choice."

"But, *cara* . . . why now?"

"I asked her that, too. Or I asked her why she didn't tell me before. She said she didn't know I was her baby for the longest time. Her parents never told her who adopted me. So she watched all the girls who were the right age, but she didn't know if her baby had stayed in Santa Lucia. Once my dad disappeared, and everyone knew I was adopted, she thought I *could* be her baby. Then she asked her parents—did you know I have grandparents now? They said I can come over whenever I want to watch TV together! Anyway, she asked them if I was her baby and they said yes and then they all cried together. That's what they told me."

"Cried together?"

"Yes. They hadn't wanted to give me away either, but they were scared about what would happen. They said ... wait ... I think they said they thought the church would arrest them or something?" Elisa frowned in thought. "I don't get that part. Anyway, after that, Ava talked to my mamma. She broke some rule to talk to her, so she was nervous, but Ava had to know. Ava says Mamma was real nice about it. Ava thinks that's why Mamma left. Because she knew Ava would take care of me."

Elisa looked out the window, watching the swallows swoop and dive in the warm drafts. "But I don't know about that."

Luciano's gaze drifted to the same swallows, and the two sat quietly watching the dancing birds inscribe arcs and patterns against the blue sky.

Finally, Luciano spoke. "This is a lot to take in, Elisa."

Elisa laughed. "That is exactly what Fatima said."

Luciano probed gently, "Fatima ... you've spoken to Fatima about the situation?"

Nodding, Elisa answered, "Yes." She cocked her head. "She didn't seem very surprised."

Luciano chuckled.

Growing serious, Elisa asked, "But how about you, Maestro? You're feeling better?"

Smiling, Luciano answered, "I am at that." Elisa's happiness set her feet to swinging again.

Luciano said, "Elisa? Did Ava tell you who ... who your father is?"

Elisa shook her head. "No. I asked. She said that it was too soon to talk about it and let's get settled with 'the new normal'. Whatever that means."

Ava couldn't believe the branching in her life. Not even Fabio getting wind of the gossip and taunting her with what a fake Catholic schoolgirl she was could detract from this joy. She had her daughter back.

For the last eleven years, a piece of her had been missing. Like those stories she heard about soldiers who lost limbs and then could feel those phantom parts of themselves tingling from time to time. When she least expected it, she would experience the weight of her newborn in her arms, those moments before the nurse whisked the baby away, ordering Ava not to give in to sadness. There had been something afterwards about the importance of praying to God to forgive her sins, but at that point, Ava had been screaming, "My baby! My baby!"

Later the milk in her breasts would throb, but it was nothing to the pain of remembering the sudden lightening in her arms as her baby was taken away from her.

Ava shook her head. So much lost time. She couldn't go down the road of what would have happened if she'd never given Elisa up for adoption. For her own life, but more for Elisa's. Elisa was only beginning to talk about it, but Ava knew sorrow and pain marked her daughter's upbringing. Ava couldn't help but feel responsible.

Her parents felt the same. They realized that in their haste to remove this scandal from their lives, they neglected to consider the suitability of their granddaughter's home. While Elisa was a face in the street, it had been easy to push aside concerns. Her presence at the dinner table served as a full-throated reminder of what their hasty decision had meant for her. And for them.

Ava wondered if too much had happened for her and Elisa to ever have an easy mother-daughter relationship. Especially since Ava didn't know how to mother and Elisa didn't know how to be mothered. She was still skittish and sometimes sulky. Not having other children, Ava didn't know if that was normal or a side effect of the tumult of the child's last year.

At least Ava had the real delight of discovering that Elisa's rejection of Concetta's landscaping had nothing to do with hating gardening and everything to do with avoiding the body she suspected was buried in the yard. Ava was careful not to suggest gardening there, even though the bones were gone and the earth smoothed over. Instead they had started planting in the *piazza*. Impressed with her daughter's sense of hue and line, Ava asked questions about her artistic leanings. Which prompted Elisa to shyly bring out some of her artwork. It left Ava breathless. How had Elisa learned to do this? Elisa shrugged and smiled and said that she liked drawing and that Isotta had provided her with pens, first a black one and later colored ones.

Ava had nodded, mutely. She resolved to get Elisa the biggest damn art set money could buy. Or at least, her money could buy.

Without her work at the *castello*, her income had dried up again. The *castello*. Thoughts of the *castello* still triggered memories of Ale. Ava looked forward to the time when she stopped seeing him in every far-off figure.

Ava put down the basket of pansies that she and Elisa were going to plant after Elisa's visit with Luciano. She closed her eyes, trying to focus on the good thoughts—Elisa had agreed to move in with her family! Yes, her options were few once the landlord stopped by and said that not paying rent was grounds for eviction. Still, Elisa's joy at leaving her home behind was gratifying. Ava had already started thinking of how to fix up Fabio's old room to make it pleasing for her daughter. An art desk! Wouldn't that make Elisa happy?

Smiling, Ava leaned down to pick up her basket. Yes, her earth was turning over, ready to receive changes in her life. Things felt simpler, better. In most ways.

The peal of bells from San Nicola reminded Ava that she would be late for lunch with her parents. Bending to pick up her basket, she caught sight of Ale walking toward her.

She shook her head. When, oh, *when* would she stop seeing her lover in the shape of the rotund baker and the lean shopkeeper? Eventually, someday, he would drift from her mind enough that—

Her breath caught.

It *was* Ale.

Walking toward her, arms outstretched.

Ale, saying—"Ava?"

Edo checked his phone again. Did he get the time wrong? Opening Instagram Direct Messaging he nodded. No, Francy had suggested 16:00 to meet at the park. Edo put his phone down. Francy must be running late. Or maybe he changed his mind?

Edo flipped his phone back on the bench beside him and realized it was 15:50.

Oh. Francy wasn't late. Edo was early.

Frowning, Edo wondered how that happened. He always ran late. Not rude-late, but, as he liked to think of it, "Santa Lucia late." He stood, wondering if maybe he should leave. It wouldn't do to appear too eager. He'd already put on a new linen shirt, slightly daring for Santa Lucia with its pattern of embroidered blue flowers on a white background. This was stupid, he shouldn't have changed, he shouldn't have put more product in his hair, and he definitely should not be early.

What was he thinking? There was no way Francy could still be interested in him. Edo flushed, remembering the words he'd hurled. Anyway, maybe Francy had never actually been interested in him. Maybe he had been polite, asking him out. Edo couldn't help but remember that Francy hadn't thought he was particularly attractive.

He should go. Go and come back in twenty minutes. It wouldn't do to let Francy see his eagerness—*cavolo*. There was Francy. Approaching the park, raising his hand in greeting. A smile lighting his face.

Despite himself, Edo grinned and waved back.

Within a moment, Francy was beside him. "Oh, good. I thought I was early."

"Nah. All good. I'm sorry we couldn't meet yesterday—"

"With what happened in the bar the night before? I'm glad you could get away now." Francy smiled. "So the Roman blocks? They're over here, right?"

Edo ducked his head before responding. "Yes. But, before that . . . Francy there's something I have to say."

"Oh. Okay."

Edo gestured to the bench and they sat down, facing the sunlit valley.

Before he could lose his nerve, Edo blurted, "I know about you saving the bar. And I . . . I can't tell you how grateful I am. How grateful Chiara would be if she knew."

Francy's face recovered some of its old chill. "I didn't think Riccardo would be so indiscreet. Or Ava. I suppose that's how you got your information."

Edo blushed. "Ava didn't mean to say anything. She let one thing slip . . . she's had so much on her mind . . . and I wouldn't rest until I pulled it all out. She feels awful."

Francy squinted at the sky and said nothing.

Edo went on, "I wish there was something we could do to repay you. I haven't told Chiara, I won't tell her. But I know she would feel as I do."

Francy regarded Edo levelly. "If you will thank me, let it be for yourself alone. Your aunt owes me nothing. As much as I respect her, I believe I thought only of you."

Edo had a hard time drawing a breath. What did Francy mean? He couldn't . . . Edo decided to change the topic. "Respect her? From our last conversation, I thought you saw her as, what was it? Cold and distant? 'Gold-digger', I believe was mentioned."

It was Francy's turn to blush. "If you have any kindness at all, please don't remind me of my foolishness. I'm mortified enough as it is."

Edo smiled. "You don't feel the same?"

Francy shook his head.

Edo leaned a little toward him. "What changed your mind?"

Francy stared at Edo's hand, between them on the bench. "After you said the things you did."

Edo looked away. "My turn for humiliation."

Francy cocked his head quizzically before continuing. "What did you say that I didn't deserve? It made me realize that I had been seeing Chiara through the lens of my paranoia. And also, if I'm going to be honest—"

"Please do."

Francy sighed. "I suppose I always wanted my parents to get back together. Childish, I know. But I never understood their split and I guess I felt protective of my mother."

"And now?"

"After talking to you and realizing how expectations blinded me, I talked to my father and made him tell me why he left my mom. He told me some things . . . some things I didn't know. About my mom and being married to her." He shook his head. "I can't explain it, but when he told me, it was like a soap bubble burst. For years, my mom had made my dad out to be a serial philanderer, and when I realized he most certainly wasn't, everything else became clear. He wants to love and be loved. He should be. He's a good man. Much better than me."

"You got that Chiara loves him from me, or from your own observation?"

Francy frowned in thought. "Both, I suppose. You seem a grounded guy. And once I stopped needing to see Chiara as the problem, and thought about what I knew of her and how she was with other people and how my father seemed with her, I realized how wrong I was."

"Is that why you came back? To see?"

Francy shook his head. "No . . . Maybe a little. Mostly I wanted to see you."

"You did?"

Francy put his arm across the back of the bench and lightly touched Edo's hand before looking Edo directly in the eyes. "Edo, you are too good to trifle with me. If you still find my interest in you . . . unpleasant, please tell me and I'll not bother you again. But I had to see, to know. I had to try. One more time."

Edo stared at his lap, unable to catch his breath. Feeling Francy's eyes still on him, he dared meet his gaze. "I feel so differently, I don't have the words."

Francy startled. "You mean . . ."

Edo nodded, and with a slow grin assured him, "Yes."

Francy's smile became a chuckle and then a laugh. He took Edo's hand and pressed it between his own.

Edo's breath caught. He couldn't take his eyes off Francy. Francy's eyes searched Edo's as the two leaned toward each other. Their lips touched gently, and then slightly more firmly, their hands tangling in the space between them.

Ava stiffened and ordered her hands to stay at her sides. Formally, she said, "I didn't know you'd be coming to town, Alessandro."

Ale flushed. "Ava, please. Hear me out."

Ava turned and began walking up the hill toward the *piazza*.

Ale almost shouted, "I left my marriage."

Slowly, Ava turned around. "You left Madison?"

"You haven't been on Instagram?"

Ava shook her head. "I decided it was no good for me."

"Ah, then no wonder you're surprised. Madison is currently living it up in the Greek islands with her man of the hour."

Ava said, "But what about your job?"

Ale smiled tremulously. "I quit."

Ava said, "But . . . I told you. I can't decide this—"

"You didn't. I did. And I should have done it a long time ago."

Ava paused, running her tongue over her lip. "I think I'm missing something."

Nodding, Ale moved toward her, but avoided reaching for her again. "I know. I'll give you the Cliff Notes version now in the hopes that when I walk you through every detail, you'll not look at me so suspiciously."

"What does this mean—'Cliff Notes'? And I have every right to be suspicious."

"You do, Ava, you do. Okay," he said. "Cliff Notes aren't important. Here's what's important—I left everything."

Ava stood silent.

Ale said, "Oh, Ava. I walked away. I quit my career, I quit my high-flying social scene. I quit my marriage. And maybe it would be better, more romantic, if I said I did it *all* for you. Maybe that would be the best way to win you back. But I need to be honest with you. That life, it's not what I want anymore."

"What do you want?"

"If I'm wishing?" Ale moved closer. "I want a life here. I want a life with you. Planning gardens together, driving to the coast for an afternoon to eat seafood. Slow dancing in a moderately ruined castle courtyard at the end of the day. I want a life with you."

"But you need an income."

Ale waved away her concern. "I have enough in the bank for awhile. Anyway, I wasn't ever meant for finance. I want to *create* something. I've been talking to a friend of mine about app development." Ale shook his head with a smile. "It will work out. Not without some sacrifices on my part, but I'm not worried about that."

Ava's eyes searched his. "You're sure?"

Ale's voice dropped. "Very sure." He tentatively reached to tuck a tendril of hair behind her ear. "Ava..."

Tears sprang to Ava's eyes.

Ale went on, "My heart is yours. Always has been, since you appeared out of the *castello* smelling like rosemary." He bit his lip at the memory. "You were right, I was unfair to you. I was so confused, so scared, and I put that all on you. I promise if you take me back, you can be you and I can be me, with no pressure."

Ava took a breath. "Things have changed, though. Since I left Rome."

Ale bit his lip. "You found someone else." He slid his eyes away and whispered, "Damn. I should have known."

Ava smiled, shaking her head. "No. Well, yes, I suppose. But not in the way you think. All that time, Ale, you wanted me to give myself to you with no reservations. I couldn't. Not because I didn't want to, but because I needed to tell you something that was too scary to say out loud. Something about me, and what happened when I was a teenager."

Ale risked clasping Ava's hand. "What is it?"

Ava squeezed his hand. "It's hard to begin."

"I have all the time in the world."

"No way," Ava insisted.

"Yes way," Edo laughed.

"Edo, you are messing with me right now."

"I'm not!" Edo laughed again and then attempted to rearrange his features into a semblance of seriousness. "I'm really not. Francy asked me out again, and we went out to dinner in Girona and it was . . . oh, it was just wonderful."

"But you hate him!"

"I most certainly do not."

"Well, you did," Ava corrected with a knowing grin.

"Feelings change. As you well know."

Ava colored slightly. "*Touché*, my friend, *touché*."

Edo set Ava's *cappuccino* in front of her and pushed the cocoa nearer so she could sprinkle it on as she liked to do. He said, "I'm elated for you, by the way."

Ava grinned. "I'm happy for me, too. Ale is . . ." She sighed and shook her head, unable to complete the sentence.

"And dare I ask? Madison?"

Ava said, "Ale says she's jet-setting and drinking cocktails with a Spanish duke or something on a private island. I can't help but think it's a reaction though. She loved him. It's the part I feel awful about."

Edo shook his head as he took the broom out from the corner to sweep up the grounds on the floor. "She couldn't have loved him. She didn't know him."

"That's what Ale says. She's pushing for the divorce as fast as possible." Ava sighed. "At least she'll get almost all the money. Ale was right about that. Once he said he wanted a divorce, her dad fired him. And blackballed him. There's no way he'll get a job in New York again."

"Ouch."

Ava shrugged. "There are worse things."

"So he's staying here?"

"Yes. The *castello* is almost done enough for him to live in at least part of it. Thank goodness his parents kept his citizenship so he won't have any trouble staying. And he's got some startup idea that will take some time but could work eventually."

"How will he support himself in the meantime?"

Ava smiled shyly. "Well, we have this idea. It's probably a terrible, terrible idea. But the *castello* is nearing completion. Then it will just need some furniture, which my uncle—you know, the one who owns the antique market—can get us, no problem. So we thought . . . if it works between Ale and me . . . we might turn it into a B and B together. The *castello* is paid for, so if we live there, and rent part of it out, that's income free and clear. It's a terrible idea isn't it?"

Edo's mouth fell open. "No! It's a fantastic idea!" He laughed, "Magda won't like it much though."

Ava nodded. "I thought about that. But Ale and I agreed to turn the gardens into a public space. Her guests would be welcome to use it, so would the town, which makes Santa Lucia more of a destination. She'll still be enraged at first, but—"

"She'll come around."

"I hope so." Ava paused in thought. She checked the door behind her and when she saw no one on the street she leaned forward. "Edo, there's another thing."

Edo, caught by her tone, put the broom back and put his hands on the bar, giving Ava his full attention. "What's that?"

"About Elisa. Being my daughter."

Edo rushed on, "I wanted to ask, but wasn't sure if you wanted to talk about it."

Ava touched Edo's hand. "I know, it's been a crazy time and I haven't been able to catch you up. I'm okay. I mean, I was a child when she was born. I was a mess. I should never have consented to give her up, but the father—"

"The father?"

"I'm not ready for that part," Ava's eyes flashed. "Yet. I'm not ready yet."

Edo nodded.

"Anyway, I didn't have a choice. My parents wouldn't let me keep her because of the scandal, the father wouldn't support me if I kept her. Threatened to ruin us all. So I sent her to live with those people. Who never loved her like they should have." Ava bit back a furious sob.

Edo squeezed her hand again. She went on, "Anyway, Elisa is going to live with me."

Edo gave a whoop. Ava shushed him and pointed toward the ceiling. "Isn't Isotta napping with the baby?"

Edo nodded. "Yes, with Luciano recovering and Massimo being a little . . . odd . . . we all thought it best that she stay."

Ava said, "How lovely for all of you."

Edo gazed at his friend quizzically. "I thought you didn't like her."

Ava shrugged. "I didn't know her. I only knew what I heard. Anyway, it was her having the baby that forced the conversation with Elisa. It's hard not to feel that her having this baby gave me mine back."

"Plus, you're sort of in love with the world right now, aren't you?"

Ava grinned. "Takes one to know one."

Edo rocked back on his heels. "So, I'm guessing you told Ale about Elisa?"

"I did. He always knew there was something I was holding back. I think he's happy it's this and not something dire. He always wanted kids and Madison didn't, so he says he's excited that we get a head-start on a family."

"Sounds like Ale. What does Elisa think of him?"

Ava drummed her fingers on the bar. "Not a whole lot yet. I've introduced him as a friend of mine. She knows he's the castle owner, and that's about it. I figured we should take it slow. She and I will live with my parents until the *castello* is done, and if there aren't any emotional hiccups, the two of us can move into the *castello* then."

"No emotional hiccups?"

Ava grinned. "A girl can dream."

The setting sun hung orange as a persimmon, ripe and full. It hesitated over the silhouetted mountains for a breath before dipping behind the horizon. Bound for Santa Lucia's dawn.

But no one paid attention to this marvel, on this of all nights.

Instead, they filled the streets, alleys, and the *piazza*. Their eyes flicked at the sudden swish of darkness that grazed the sky as the sun sank away, but their conversations barely stalled. Bar Birbo, too, was filled.

Luciano leaned toward Chiara, trying to get her attention as she nodded with Bea and tried to extract her hand from Fabrizio's to turn and pour a glass of wine for Dante. Chiara caught Luciano's eye and stepped toward him. "What can I get you, *Maestro*?"

"When is she coming down?"

Chiara's lips quivered in her attempt to not smile at this, the second time Luciano asked the question. "Soon, I think. Last I checked, she was getting the baby dressed. But she's still recovering, so it's slow going."

Luciano smiled and stared into his empty cup of tea.

Chiara cocked her head at him. "You're looking much better."

He looked up. "I feel quite strong. Medication, of course. And simply having optimism that I will feel better—that helps."

"Sure. Makes it less scary."

Luciano nodded. "Yes. So many times I thought I was having a heart attack. The panic from that no doubt exacerbated my symptoms."

"No doubt." Chiara nodded seriously.

He said, "I'm so delighted I'm better now. In time for this. When is she coming?"

Chiara grinned. "Soon."

As she started to move away, Luciano leaned forward. "Wait! Those two..." He inclined his head toward Edo and Francy, their heads tucked together in whispered conference.

Chiara beamed and said, "Those two."

"Really?"

"Really."

Luciano sat back, a smile spreading across his face. He watched for a moment, as Francy slid his finger down Edo's cheek to cup his chin as they gazed at each other. Edo's face was lost in a dream.

Bea barked, "When are they coming down?"

"Soon!" Chiara laughed.

Bea grumbled, "I did deliver that baby. You'd think I'd get early rights."

"If it was up to Isotta, you would have, but the *dottore* was strict...no visitors beyond Edo and me. And that only because we come with the place."

Edo looked up at hearing his name. "She needed the recovery time. I can't believe she was able to push out a baby after being stuck under the *castello* for so long."

Magda shoved her way to Edo's side. "With a broken ankle!"

Chiara shook her head. "Not broken, thank goodness. She's able to walk on it. If she's careful."

Magda turned to look around the bar. "And Massimo?"

Chiara shrugged. "We've barely seen him. He's come by a couple of times, but when he sees his son he bursts into tears. It's upsetting to Isotta so we make him leave."

Luciano nodded. "He seems undone."

Magda cocked her head. "You've seen him?"

Luciano said, "Yes. He brought Margherita by to visit when I was recuperating, and I saw him yesterday when his cousins arrived. They're helping with Margherita. And I heard they may be interested in purchasing L'Ora Dorata."

Magda glared at some invisible foe. "About time somebody bought that decrepit restaurant...I hope they listen to my ideas about how to make it a profitable and fitting addition to Santa Lucia." A beat, and then Magda added, "Is Massimo coming tonight?"

Luciano said, "I believe so." Shrugging, he added, "He has the help now."

Fabrizio waved Chiara over. "Chiara! If you have a moment..."

Chiara flipped her towel over her shoulder and sashayed toward him. "What do you need?"

Fabrizio put his fingers in her apron string and pulled her toward him. When her face was against his, he whispered in her ear, "You, in point of fact."

Chiara pulled back, giggling. "Later. I'll come to Magda's after closing."

Fabrizio grinned, his eyes crinkling in delight, though he pretended impatience. "Well, if I have to wait—"

"You do."

"A glass of *prosecco* then. I'm feeling festive."

At that moment, the door leading to the upstairs apartment creaked opened. Isotta stood in the doorway, in her jeans and a white, flowing button-down shirt, holding the baby to her chest. All the bar could see above the aquamarine blanket was a swirl of black hair, such a contrast to Isotta's own blond hair drifting loose around her face.

Isotta said, "This is quite a crowd."

Chiara grinned. "Word got out."

Isotta smiled in return. "I should have known." She carefully turned her child so he faced the room. The baby blinked slowly, regarding the bar, his lips drawn together as if prepared for a kiss. "*Allora*, Santa Lucia. Meet Jacopo."

"Jacopo!"

"I didn't know that was his name!"

"Like President Kennedy! Or the ocean guy!"

"No, stupid, that would be Gianni!"

"I don't think that's right."

"*Jacopo!*"

Chiara offered her hand to Isotta to take the last, and steepest step, into the bar. "I didn't know you had decided."

Isotta concentrated on her balance and said, "I kept waiting for Massimo to help, but he couldn't. It's taking him some time—" she broke off. "Anyway, today I texted him Jacopo, and he texted back a thumbs up and I think that's the best I can hope for right now."

She stepped gingerly into the bar.

Luciano maneuvered around the crowd. "Isotta!" He kissed her cheeks and then drew the blanket back from Jacopo's face to more fully admire the baby whose gaze was trained on him. "Oh, Isotta. Look what you made." He beamed at her, eyes bright with tears. He laughed, "And you are radiant!"

She smiled. "You're looking good yourself. Much improved." She looked around as the burbling of the crowd began again. "Is Elisa here?"

Luciano answered, "Not yet. She and Fatima are coming with Ava soon."

"Ava! I could hardly believe it when Chiara told me."

Luciano nodded. "It was complicated for Elisa as well. She's growing used to the idea, though I suspect that road will not be perennially smooth."

The door flew open.

Elisa flung herself into the bar, followed by Fatima and then by Ava and Ale, walking side by side. Eyes flashing, their grins barely contained.

Elisa yelled, "Isotta! Come here! You have to see this!"

Isotta shook her head. "I don't know...walking with the baby. Can you tell me about it?"

Elisa shook her head impatiently. "No!"

Fatima added, "I think you should see this."

Luciano offered his arm to Isotta. She wound her hand through, carefully hugging the baby to her chest. "Okay, Jacopo, I guess this is as good a time as any for you to see Santa Lucia...not far though, right Elisa?"

"No, right outside." Elisa bounced up and down.

The crowd in the bar backed up, giving Isotta space to cross the room. She stepped outside, pulled now by the fragrance of honey and vanilla and orange blossom.

The bar filed out, following her. Massimo appeared at the edges of the darkness. He stood against the wall, quietly. Tears glittered in his eyes, and his jaw set as he watched the scene unfold.

Elisa and Fatima led Isotta to the castle steps. For a moment, Isotta's heart caught. Flames of light erupted from the wall. Yells flew all around. Not another fire! Just when the village was recovering—

But no, as they drew closer they saw that the Madonna's niche was filled with candles. What they thought were flames was a kind of glow they'd never witnessed from the blue niche. As the villagers crept closer, they realized that the statue of Mary wore a crown and a necklace of wildflowers. Poppies and snapdragons, the kind of tender flowers blooming around their olive trees. The statue's face was the still that comes before movement—a pause, a hesitation, threaded with an undercurrent of grace.

From the crowd came a murmuring. "It's another miracle."

Isotta dipped her head to breathe in her baby's soft scent. She swayed, and Luciano and Elisa moved to press against her, holding her steady. Fatima held tight to Elisa's other hand, and Elisa looked over at her friend, beaming. Her eyes skipped to Ava, and she found this woman who was her mother watching her, a smile of amazement flashing across her face. Ale watched Ava and Elisa grin at each other, his eyes shining. Edo stepped behind Ava, and rested his hand on her shoulder. She looked back at Edo and Francy, her expression suffused with wonder. Chiara grasped Edo's hand. He squeezed it, nodding at his aunt and Fabrizio. Magda murmured something in Chiara's ear, and she leaned to repeat it to Bea who put her arms around Patrizia without taking her eyes off of the Madonna.

Gathered faces flickered in the candlelight, creating a chorus of brilliance and shadow. Suddenly, they all fell quiet, hushed, as if a strand of music had drifted down the stairs. But there was no music. There was only this—gold leaf stars above their beloved statue trembling into existence. Perhaps the simple stars had always been there, faded into the celestial hue of Mary's niche. The villagers had no memory of ever seeing the stars before, or even hearing the stars spoken of. Yet, after a bare moment, the phenomenon seemed not surprising. Simply part of their story.

The people of Santa Lucia nodded in recognition as the golden stars shone, not just with the candles' flames but with their own inner resonance.

Illuminating the blue of the Madonna's sky.

# THANK YOU FOR COMING BACK TO SANTA LUCIA!

There's even more rumor and romance afoot in *The Stillness of Swallows* (*mybook.to/TheStillnessOfSwallows*), book three of the *Santa Lucia* series. So pick up your copy today!

Can't get enough of Italian village life? I'd love to welcome you *The Grapevine* (*michelledamiani.com/grapevine*), your source for extra stories as well as book releases and sweet giveaways.

Speaking of sweets, did you know that reviews are like gelato on a summer's day for independently published authors? I'd be so grateful it you took a few moments leave a review of *The Silent Madonna* on Amazon.com (*mybook.to/TheSilentMadonna*) and/or Goodreads to help new readers discover our little Umbrian village.

Now, there are no strangers in small towns! Visit *michelledamiani.com*, where you can reach me by email or by any of the usual social media channels. I'd love to hear from you.

Until then, keep dreaming,

— Michelle

# ITALIAN WORDS IN THIS TEXT

~

## CONVERSATIONS

| | | | |
|---|---|---|---|
| *a dopo/ a presto/alla prossima volta* | see you later | *buonasera* | good afternoon |
| | | *buongiorno* | good morning |
| *allora* | well now | *cara* | dear |
| *amore mio* | my love | *castello* | castle |
| *anch'io* | me too | *che succede ?* | what happened? |
| *andiamo* | let's go | *ciao* | hello and goodbye |
| *arrivo* | I'm coming | *come no?* | why not? |
| *aspetta* | wait | *comunque* | anyway |
| *(un) attimo* | just a moment | *davvero?* | isn't that right? |
| *auguri* | congratulations | *eccoci qua* | here we are |
| *basta* | that's enough | *fa un freddo cane* | literally "it makes a dog cold", used to express that it's freezing outside |
| *bella* | beautiful | | |
| *bentornato* | welcome back | *fidanzato/a* | fiance/e |
| *boh?* | no real translation, similar to "who can say?" and often given wth a shrug | *gita* | field trip |
| | | *grazie* | thank you |
| *bronzato* | tanned | *lo so* | I know |
| *buono/a* | good | *ma dai!* | Come on! |

| | | | |
|---|---|---|---|
| *maestro* | teacher, often used as an honorific | *ragazzi* | guys |
| *moda* | fashion | *salve* | greetings |
| *nascondino* | hide and seek | *senza peli sulla lingua* | without hair on the tongue (plain speaking) |
| *nonno/a* | grandfather/mother | *sono d'accordo* | I agree |
| *paesano* | country boy | *stronzo* | bastard, piece of crap |
| *per favore* | please | *tesoro mio* | my treasure |
| *piacere* | nice to meet you | *tutto bene/ tutto a posto* | everything's okay |
| *poverino/a* | poor | | |
| *prego* | you're welcome | *va bene* | it's okay |
| *pronto* | literally "ready" but used as "hello" when answering the phone | *zio/zia* | uncle/aunt |

~

## ABOUT TOWN

| | | | |
|---|---|---|---|
| *alimentari* | shop that sells cheese and cured meats, as well as some other basic foodstuff and household supplies | *palazzo* | palace |
| | | *palazzo comunale* | seat of civic authority, like a town hall |
| *Ape* | a three-wheeled truck with a small motor | *Perugino* | Umbrian Rennaisance painter; his paintings (or those of his students) adorn many Umbrian buildings |
| *comune* | where administrative aspects of the town happen | | |
| | | *piazza* | town square |
| *farmacia* | pharmacy | *polizia municipale* | police department |
| *festa* | celebration/party | | |
| *forno* | bakery | *rosticceria* | shop to buy pizza by the slice, and sometimes cooked items for takeaway like fried rice balls (arancini) |
| *fruttivendolo* | produce shop | | |
| *macelleria* | butcher shop, often with other fresh items | | |
| | | *trattoria* | informal restaurant |

# FOOD & DRINK

| | | | |
|---|---|---|---|
| *albicocca* | apricot | *frutti di bosco* | literally fruits of the forest, mixed berry |
| *aperitivo* | cocktail | *lampredotto* | tripe sandwiches |
| *Barolo* | a red wine from the north of Italy | *latte caldo* | hot milk |
| *biscotto/i* | cookie/s | *mandarino* | mandarin orange |
| *buono/a* | good | *panino* | sandwich |
| *cacio e pepe* | pasta with grated cheese and pepper | *pecorino* | sheep's milk cheese, sold at different levels of ripeness; Pecorino is also a kind of white wine from Le Marche |
| *caffè* | espresso specifically, or coffee more generally | | |
| *caffè lungo* | espresso pulled slowly so that there is more water and a fuller cup | *lumaca* | snail |
| | | *normale* | my usual |
| *cappuccino* | espresso with milk | *prosecco* | bubbly wine, Italy's version of champagne |
| *cenone* | a big, festive dinner (typically on New Year's Eve) | *salumi* | cured meats, like salami and prosciutto |
| *ciambella/e* | donut/s | *tagliata* | sliced, grilled beef, often scattered with rosemary and olive oil |
| *cornetto/i* | Italian croissant/s | | |
| *cornetto con marmellata* | Italian croissant filled with jam | *tagliatelle* | fresh pasta, cut similar to linguini |
| *cornetto con crema* | Italian croissant filled with cream | *tartufata* | black olive and truffle |
| | | *torta* | cake |
| *farro* | an ancient grain, similar to barley | *vino* | wine |
| *frizzante* | bubbly water | | |

## A WORD ON ITALIAN MEALS

Italian meals are divided into appetizers (*antipasti*), first course of pasta or soup (*primi*), second course of meat or fish (*secondi*), side dish of vegetables (*contorni*) and dessert (*dolci*).

ALSO BY MICHELLE DAMIANI

*Il Bel Centro: A Year in the Beautiful Center*

*Santa Lucia*

*The Stillness of Swallows*

*Into the Groves*

*The Road Taken: How to Dream, Plan, and
Live Your Family Adventure Abroad*

*More on these books and works in progress can be found at*
michelledamiani.com

# ACKNOWLEDGMENTS

This book would not exist if not for the care of a talented group of individuals. Kristine Bean, who is the master of eradicating adverbs and passive voice, Nancy Hampton who makes sure I reign it in, Dorita Joffroy de Piña who has exceptional vision for errors I miss even if I reread a sentence a hundred times, Katrina Ryan who encouraged me to wonder what lies beneath a medieval castle, and Stella Mattioli who keeps my Italian correct. And then there's Paul Austin Ardoin who not only helped me shape narrative arcs and thicken central characters, but acted like I granted him the most enormous of favors by allowing him yet another read through and yet another conversation about dialogue.

Also, huge thanks to my family who brought me back to reality over and over when I faded out to wonder how to solve a tricky Santa Lucia tangle and particular gratitude to my astonishingly patient husband, Keith, for making all my books look so pretty.

Especial thanks to my hero, Jane Austen. I am always, literally *always*, in the middle of rereading a Jane Austen novel. Her books have ground into my psyche so thoroughly that her words often manifest into my writing without my awareness. It was a real treat this go around to give that influence wing. It'll never measure up to even the least exceptional of her writing, I know, but the creation of a kind of homage to one of my favorite authors fills me with joy. Even though I'm not totally sure what she would make of a gay, Italian Mr. Darcy and transforming the role of Lydia Bennet into an Italian bar, I like to think she'd give it all a saucy wink.

Made in the USA
Columbia, SC
08 September 2020

19701480R00221